The Goddess's Gift

Book 1

The Goddess's Gift Series

Sarah Uzzle

Ebook ISBN 979-8-9930299-0-0

Paperback ISBN 979-8-9930299-1-7

Hardcover ISBN 979-8-9930299-4-8

 Formatted with Vellum

To my lovely ladies, Diana and Stroopwafel, the beautiful queen and the goblin menace, I love you so much.
To my brother, Isaac, who always encouraged me, this book wouldn't exist without you.
To my sister Ella, whose only companion is a Squishmallow chicken, I stole your curly hair and inability to suffer fools for Winna, I really hope you don't mind.
To Adriana, for being my bestie and dealing with my crazy.
To my mom, for always telling me I should do something with my writing.
And to Christian, because you're my other bestie. Thank you for working so hard on this with me.

Chapter 1

Snowfall

"Oh! A kitty!" I smiled at the little void cat. If not for the flash of his brilliant green eyes, I wouldn't have noticed him all huddled up beneath the pine branch.

The cat opened one gorgeous eye to glare at me.

"Let's get you somewhere warm," I told him, reaching out my hand so he could sniff my fingers, in case he was friendly. He hissed instead, so I backed off. "Goodness!" I chuckled. "I didn't even do anything!" It was true, but cats who were wary of people always had their reasons. "It's alright! I promise I'm not going to hurt you! But I also won't try to pet you, okay?"

The little feline watched me, body tensed and green eyes baleful.

"Oh, if looks could kill!" I giggled. "Relax! I just happened to notice you." I shook my head, frowning. "It is an awfully cold day." Would the poor thing be warm enough outside?

The temperature had been dropping dangerously low at night lately, even for animals. I could bring him in, just for the night. There was room in the cottage for another kitty, even if the two cats I already had wouldn't like having him there. Well...they could just get over it. But that was only *if* he'd come inside.

He might prefer to stay in the barn. Given how he'd hissed, I was pretty sure he wanted nothing to do with me. The magical heating stones that I'd bought from Dern, the local dwarvish merchant, kept my barn animals toasty, so this little newcomer would be perfectly comfortable there.

The clouds hung thick and low overhead, threatening snow. If the little cat would go into the barn, he'd avoid the snow and bitterly cold wind that was sure to come.

"Hm." We weren't far from my cottage, so I hatched a plan. "You wait here, and I'll be right back with a treat for you!" Standing, I turned, and hurried back towards home, breaking into a run for the last bit, and darting up the stairs two at a time.

Bursting through the door, I apologized to my two grey tabbies, Stroopwafel and Diana. Pausing, I stooped, and gave them both a swift kiss on their fluffy foreheads. "Sorry babies, I gotta help another little kitty. I'll be right back!"

Grabbing a big chunk of dried fish from the pantry, I hurried back outside. I quickly made my way back to where I'd left the black cat curled up beneath the large pine branch.

For a moment, I didn't see him. Disappointment filled me.

Keeping this little guy safe, at least for as long as he wanted to hang around, would have been nice. It was why I'd taken Stroopwafel in when I'd found her wandering around as well. I'd struggled through a briar patch to rescue my Stroopwafel, and I'd do it again for this little fella, as much as I didn't want to get all scratched up again. *If* I could find him again, anyway.

A flash of iridescent green caught my eye. "There you are." I smiled. He'd moved, actually having come out a little ways from his hiding place.

Movingly slowly, I approached, pausing before I got too close. He glowered at me with those piercing green eyes.

"You're such a handsome boy!" I giggled, breaking the fish into small pieces. "I brought you a snack. And I can give you a nice warm place to stay. You could stay in my cottage with me and the other kitties, if you wanted, but I don't think you'd do that. Instead, how about the barn with the other animals? It's nice and warm in there, I promise!"

There was no reply, of course, but his eyes blinked once. I pretended he understood.

"Alright, snackies first." I reached out slowly, holding a morsel of fish.

The stunningly green eyes watched my fingers get closer. He hissed once more, warning me, and for a moment I was afraid he'd scratch me. Instead, he leaned forward slightly and sniffed warily.

"It's fishy! I use it as food for my two girls, and I figured you'd like it as well," I murmured. "I hope you do, anyway. If you're anything like me, you like a good snack." Putting a few pieces down on the ground, I took a couple of steps back. "Go ahead! I won't bother you!"

The cat stared at the treats I'd left on the ground, craning his neck to sniff at the tasty little morsels. He glanced up at me, and took a step forward. As he did, I noticed the little guy didn't put any weight on his left paw.

"Oh, are you hurt?" I asked softly, growing extremely sad.

Of course, the cat didn't answer. He couldn't, given that he was a cat. But he had started to eat, at the very least.

Maybe if I could convince him to let me touch his paw, I could help him. My healing abilities were weak, but they were at least better than nothing. I'd be damned if I'd let an injured little kitty run off into the cold, no matter how much he didn't like me. Not when I could help said kitty with my magic. It might take some time, but it would be no problem, I had all the time in the world. Especially where cats were concerned.

Once the fish was gone, I caught his attention again, and held up more fish so he could see it. I made another pile, then stepped back further in the direction of my cottage, and thus the barn.

After repeating the process multiple times, which was pretty slow going, we eventually made it to the barn door.

"Well, that's half the battle." I sighed, opening the barn door as the cat ate the most recent pile of treats I'd made for him. "Now, let's win the war! If I can get you into the barn, anyway."

Warm air enveloped me, thanks to the magical heating stones nestled in their little holding box. They really were wonderful. Some day, I'd save up enough to buy a stove and oven powered by the same magic. If it worked as well as the dwarvish merchant said it did, I'd be able to cook things faster and more reliably, since my current stove was old, and both the burners and the oven often heated unevenly.

"Please come in, kitty. I can do the food trail again, if that's what it'll take." To my surprise, the cat stretched luxuriously, taking care not to put weight on his hurt paw, then waltzed right through the barn door.

"Well, that worked." I shook my head. "Probably felt how warm it was in here, didn't you?" I crouched, smiling at the cat as he prowled about the barn. Cats did love a nice warm place to snuggle down in, so it was really no surprise. I was a lot like a cat, in that way. Probably in more ways, if I was being honest. "You make yourself comfy, I'll get you a little nest made up for you to curl up in, and get you some food and water and a sawdust box," I told him.

Leaving the barn, I shut the doors so he wouldn't escape and hurried back into the cottage.

After managing to fit all the supplies into a large box, I carefully made my way back to the barn. Slipping in, I paused to flick the lamp on. The lanterns I used to light my house and barn were another genius piece of dwarvish innovation, as I only needed to flick a switch to light them since they held their own lighting mechanisms. I just had to keep them filled with oil as needed, and I was good to go! They had been my first purchase from Dern. I'd had them for several years now, and they'd never had a single problem.

The dwarf had first arrived in the nearby village, Greenwood, about ten years earlier. His coming had alarmed folks a little, given how few magical beings we had in these parts, other than me. In their minds, I really didn't count as a magical being, given that I was human, and had lived among them my entire life. But when the people had seen how Dern's wares had improved the quality of life of those who bought them, they'd gladly accepted him.

Dwarves were very competent in making useful things. Their wares were never pretty, but they worked well and reliably. Must be nice. All I could do was make healing salves and mend small scrapes, cuts, and burns, and even *that* sometimes required outside help.

Sure, the magic in my veins gave me an unnaturally long life, but it wasn't as useful as you might expect. The family lore said that the goddess's gift to my ancestor had grown weaker with each generation, and the faintness of the triangle-shaped mark on the back of my hand belied how feeble the gift had indeed become. My brothers didn't have the mark at all. They would live unnaturally long lives, probably a couple hundred years, but they wouldn't stay young forever, like I would. But I would almost certainly be the last of my kin to have proper magic.

"Alright, little fella, let's get you a nice warm bed made." I pushed my thoughts on the failing family gift from my mind, and sat the box full of supplies down on the work table.

Grabbing some extra hay that had spilled from the trough, I distributed it evenly into one of the two smaller boxes I'd brought before putting a soft blanket down on top. "There we are!" I smiled, satisfied with my quick work.

Looking around to see where my new little feline friend had gone, I saw him sitting upright on one of the short walls between Daisy and Poppy's enclosures. Daisy, my cow, sat there amicably, apparently without a concern in the world. Meanwhile, Poppy, my pony, snorted and tossed her head.

"He's not hurting anything! Besides, it's just until he wants to leave, anyway. It's very, very cold out," I told her. "We have to be nice to everyone, even strange kitties!" Not that it was strange for me to want to be nice to strange kitties, to be fair.

Poppy snorted again, but more softly this time.

"Thank you." I chuckled, and told the cat, "I'll leave the bed on the work table, since it's up off the ground." Cats preferred higher perches. Not only did it give them a vantage point, but in cat hierarchy, whoever sat up highest was in charge. Or felt like they were. That meant that, in my little cottage, Diana usually sat somewhere above Stroopwafel, who preferred to lounge on the floor.

After a few more moments of work, my little visitor had a food bowl, a water bowl, and a sawdust box.

"Okay, I think that's that!" I told him, dusting off my hands. "You're welcome to stay as long as you want. If you ever decide to come into the cottage, just let me know."

After bidding the rest of the animals goodbye, I switched off the lantern and left, returning to my ladies inside the cottage.

"Alright, babies!" I sang as I entered. "I'm finally back in!" Given how cold it was getting, I wouldn't be going back out unless I absolutely had to. With the quickly gathering clouds, I had to turn the lamps on indoors now as well.

Stroopwafel maowing pleadingly at me. "Oh fine, you can have treats too!" I laughed, going to get them some dried fish as well. At this announcement, Diana joined her silly sister in rubbing against my legs and purring loudly. "You two are so spoiled!"

I stroked my kitties' soft fur for a little while as they munched on their treats. Some movement out the window caught my eye, and I glanced up to see falling snow.

"Looks like I finished up inside just in time," I murmured, glad the black cat would be safe and warm in the barn that night.

Snow was pretty, but it would make my chores outside more of... well, a chore. I already worked hard enough, and something that only made my life more difficult wasn't particularly welcome, even as beautiful as it was. Although this would likely be one of the last snows of the season, thankfully.

Seeing that twilight was falling, I glanced at the clock. "Dinner time." I sighed, stretching my arms, then staggered to my tired feet and headed to the cottage's small kitchen area.

It had been a long day, and I didn't feel like cooking, so I raided the cupboard and the cold box for whatever nibbles I could find.

Soon, I sat down to a meal of toasted bread, cheese, slightly withered winter greens, and dried fruits from the fall harvest, which had been particularly good that year. The wild blueberry bushes nearby on the eaves of the forest had been particularly bountiful that year, and they were pretty good dried, still sweet despite their wrinkled state.

Looking around my little cottage, I thanked the goddess for my calm, cozy little life. Sure, it was a little lonely at times, but it was good. Peaceful and good.

After eating, I washed the few dishes I'd dirtied, and sat down with my sewing kit to patch the elbows that had worn through on a dress. Once the mending was done, I let myself give in to my sense of whimsy and added some pretty, embroidered flowers, simply because I could.

Some people thought embroidery was dull, but I loved it. It was a nice way to add a bit of brightness to an otherwise plain dress, or spruce up a room with floral flourishes on a throw pillow. Embroidering did take patience, though, and I suspected that's why most people found it boring. Or maybe I was just boring. If I were, that was alright. I was content with my life and myself, and whether other people thought I was interesting was irrelevant. I was at peace with myself and my life, and that's what really mattered.

Smiling at my handiwork, I glanced outside and saw that the snow was now coming down pretty fast. Indeed, it already covered the ground in a light blanket. We'd probably have a couple of inches at least, but if it kept falling at the same rate, we'd have more than just a couple.

Yawning, I stowed away my sewing things before going to my bedroom. After changing into my nightgown, I threw a robe over it, shoved my feet into my fluffy slippers, and then headed to the wash-room for a bath.

Usually, bathing in the winter was a miserable chore. Thankfully, when I was a child, my parents had saved up so that traveling dwarvish workmen could put in hot and cold running water, as well as a cold box in the kitchen. In doing so, they'd paved the way for other such amenities in the village, making it a little easier for the folks there to accept Dern and his wares so many years later.

My family wasn't particularly wary of magic, all things considered, though we did know the dangers it could cause if misused, as everyone did. That's why some folks were wary of it, understandably so. It could be frightening, but when used to heal, help, and protect, it was perfectly fine. Luckily, magic generally wasn't common in these parts, other than mine and Dern's, and we were both peaceful sorts, so no one really had to worry about us misusing it.

Soon, I was sinking into the warm bath, and thanking my lucky stars that I was fortunate enough to have such a luxury.

It was so nice and warm.

There was a scratching and insistent maowing at the door. I snorted. "Stroopwafel, I'm just taking a bath! I'll be right out! Go play with your sister!"

I'd have to be up early to wade through the snow, so I could take care of the animals, and that would be cold. Very cold. But I'd just have to bundle up as warmly as I could and deal with it.

That's just how life was when you lived alone; you had to do everything for yourself. But that was alright, it was the life I'd chosen for myself, and I was happy with it.

Chapter 2

A Little Progress

Unfortunately, a full night's sleep wasn't in the cards for me.

A terrifying howl woke me with a start. It was far too close for my liking. My startled awakening sent Stroopwafel and Diana scrambling from their spots beside me to hide beneath the bed.

"Wolves!" I gasped, clutching the blankets close to my chest.

Gathering my courage, I swung my feet out of the bed, forced myself to get up, and ran down the hallway. Throwing on my warmest coat, I shoved my feet into my boots and my hands into gloves, then grabbed the ax that I kept by the door.

As much as I didn't want to go outside, and potentially face wolves, I had to check on the animals in the barn. I needed to make sure that they hadn't managed to escape out of fear, or that the wolves hadn't managed to get in. It had happened once when I was a child and had been a tragedy. Though Dad had rebuilt the barn to be far stronger, we'd all still worried whenever we heard wolves in the middle of the night, and he would go outside to check, just as I was about to do now.

Steeling myself once more, I took a deep breath, then flung the door open, and charged outside, praying the goddess would protect me.

Snow still drifted down, but not nearly as thickly as it had when I'd gone to bed. It blanketed the ground, at least four inches deep in most places. Though it would make it more difficult to walk and run, it reflected the light of the moon and made it very easy to see.

Standing on the porch, I clutched my ax tightly, and scanned the area for anything out of place.

Something moved near the corner of my vision, and I froze, seeing a single, shaggy gray wolf slinking around by the barn.

"HEY!" I shouted, feeling another thrill of terror race through me. I stumbled down the front steps, and stooped, grabbing for the stones that I knew were hidden beneath the snow. "Get away from there!" I cried. Reeling back, I flung the stone with all of my strength in the general direction of the wolf.

I hadn't really aimed, as I didn't want to actually hit the animal. It was only hungry, after all, but I still didn't want it to get into my barn. All I wanted to do was scare it off.

The stone crashed against the barn with a loud thwack, which did as I'd hoped, prompting the wolf to bolt off into the eaves of the forest backing the property.

Giving a sigh of relief, I hurried down off the porch, knowing I should still check on the animals in the barn, to be safe.

Slipping inside the warm structure, I flicked on the light, and asked, "Everyone okay?"

The black cat lifted its head from the box and maowed sleepily.

"Sleepy!" I giggled. "Are you alright?" If the cat was still asleep, then there was no chance that anything dangerous had made it into the barn.

More relief flooded me as I looked around at the other animals, and walked a quick circuit around the animals' enclosures.

Daisy mooed softly, and Poppy gave a little whinny, as if they were both assuring me they were alright too. The silly sheep didn't move a muscle, but remained asleep.

All was well.

To my surprise, the cat hopped up from the bed I'd made for him, and came to perch at the end of the table near to where I stood, staring expectantly at me with practically glowing green eyes.

I smiled. "You're a handsome boy!"

He continued to stare at me.

"Would you like head scratchies? Both of my kitties like their nosies scratched." I set down the ax and held out my hand, leaning over so that he could sniff it easily by extending his neck a little.

He blinked, looking up at me, and maowing softly.

"No pets, then?" I asked, tilting my head to the side.

The cat blinked, and tossed his head, as if telling me I was being ridiculous. Then, much to my surprise, he lifted his injured paw.

"Oh! Well, I can probably help with that," I said. Could the little guy tell I was a healer? Sometimes animals could, and it wouldn't surprise me that a cat would be able to; they were always inclined to the supernatural, it seemed. "Can I touch that paw? I have to in order to help." I reached out my hand again, taking a step forward.

The little void studied me again, and bopped my hand with its nose in confirmation.

"You're very smart." I blinked, half wondering if the cat actually did understand me.

I took another few slow steps forward, and carefully reached for the cat's injured left front paw. He flinched as I touched it, but didn't run. "Good," I murmured. "This won't hurt."

Taking a deep breath, I pulled for my magic. The mark on my hand tingled and glowed with a weak golden light as I urged the energy into the cat's paw.

He closed his eyes, and maowed softly.

"Yeah, it feels nice, doesn't it?" I smiled. Mom's healing magic had always felt nice. Since it was too difficult to use healing magic on yourself, I didn't actually know what my own felt like. But I suspected my magic felt as nice, or almost as nice, as my mother's had.

As the magic finished its work, the cat opened its eyes, and growled, prompting me to let go of his paw. "Sorry! Yes, it's finished." I stepped back hurriedly, not wanting to get scratched.

The little kitty sniffed its paw, and licked it a few times before bobbing his head at me.

I giggled. "Well, good!" I went over to see if he still had food and water, and was pleased to see he did. "I'll bring more when I come back in the morning, okay? So eat up!" I told him, adding, "And if you want to come into the house at some point, just let me know, cutie patootie! My two inside girls probably wouldn't mind more company. Diana would probably baby you."

Diana, though a cat, was actually the family familiar, and was older than I was. She was regal, wise, and very sweet. Stroopwafel was a garden variety, white-socked gray tabby who I'd found wandering outside, all alone as a kitten,. Of course, I'd taken her in, though I'd had to chase her through brambles because she was scared and hissing at the time. Now that she'd settled in, she had a silly personality, though very little in the way of brains, and never failed to make me laugh.

Her name, Stroopwafel, even made me laugh. Stroopwafels were cookies from a far away land that some traveling merchants had brought through the area. They were two thin waffle crisps with a caramel-like syrup between. Eating them just like that was good, but the merchants had shown us how, when you set them over a warm beverage like a lid, the steam rose and warmed the syrup inside, making them gooey and heavenly. So I'd borrowed the name for my goofy cat, since it both sounded silly to me, and because, like her namesake, my little Stroopwafel had taken a little while to warm up to me.

The black cat maowed in answer, and I took it to mean he'd understood. Let's be honest, he probably hadn't understood a word I'd ever said to him, but it was the middle of the night, and we were pretending here, so it was okay.

"Well, goodnight, little fella." I sighed happily. "I should think of something to call you while you're here. Hm. It'll have to be a pretty name for a pretty boy!"

I swear the cat rolled his gorgeous green eyes at me.

"Alright, alright! Goodnight!" I snorted and left, remembering to grab the ax before I left.

Going back inside, I kicked off my boots, and struggled out of my gloves before sliding out of my coat.

Diana and Stroopwafel were waiting for me, the latter maowing in complaint that I'd left.

"I'm sorry, ladies," I murmured, smiling, and bending to pet my two girls.

Diana nuzzled my hand fondly, purring loudly. Stroopy flopped over, waiting for me to pet her tummy so she could bear-trap on it, which I enthusiastically let her do, laughing, "Ouch!" as she bit my hand none too gently. I extracted my hand from her paws and mouth, and told them both, "Back to bed now, girls!"

Diana led the way back down the hallway. Stroopwafel trailed behind me, maowing in annoyance at having her prey, my hand, taken so rudely from her little white paws.

I climbed into bed, and the two gray tabbies resumed their positions, curled up on either side of me.

Sleep slowly descended on us once more.

This time, my subconscious summoned a very strange dream for me

I was in the barn, but it was totally empty, and there was no light other than the light that pierced through the shadows from the high gable window.

A pair of glowing green eyes regarded me from just outside the circle of light.

For a moment, I thought it was the black cat, since the pupils were slits, much like a cat's. But as I observed them, I realized they belonged to a much larger figure, the silhouette of which I could only sort of make out from the single beam of light. There was a head and shoulders, and it seemed to be sitting on the work table, legs and arms crossed, but other than the eyes, I couldn't make out any specific features.

The barn was silent, and dust motes floated to and fro in light from the gable.

Finally, I broke the silence, unable to stand it any longer. I asked, "Are you just going to stare? Why are you in my barn?"

It was quiet for a moment longer.

Suddenly, a man's voice spoke, "You said I could stay here." It was a strange voice. Deep, yes, but also odd in a way I couldn't find a word for. Maybe the strangeness I thought it held was due to its slight accent.

"I mean, it's a dream. I've not said anything other than what I just did," I told him, frowning. "Although, I guess it doesn't matter, given that it's a dream."

"Don't sass your betters, child." The voice sounded vaguely bored.

"Excuse me? This is my barn! You're the one sassing me! You're not my better! And I know I'm not old, but I'm not a child! I'm thirty now!" I crossed my arms. "I've half a mind to just wake up if you're going to be unpleasant!"

Before the rude barn-intruder could reply, I felt something brush against my legs and looked down. Diana was there, in my dream.

No Stroopwafel, just Diana. And my little familiar was not happy.

Normally a peaceful creature who preferred sleeping all day to running around like Stroopwafel, Diana's tail was fluffed up and bushy. The hair along the ridge of her back was raised, and her body was stiff and arched as she gave a low growl and a hiss.

"What's this?" The voice took on a note of surprise. "A familiar?"

I knelt, and stroked Diana, hoping to calm her. Even though it was just a dream, I hated seeing even a dream version of Diana so distressed. "Hush, Miss Annie!" That was one of her many nicknames. "It's alright, it's just a dream!"

"It's certainly not just a dream. She's right to be worried. That's a powerful familiar to be able to intrude, and sense what I am. How did a weakling like you come by her?" the voice asked, sounding vaguely interested. I heard its owner shifting, and looked up to see the stranger had slipped off the table. I still couldn't make out any facial features, but could sort of make out its hands now, which seemed to have more fingers than they should.

Diana hissed again, growling and taking a couple of steps forward.

"Diana! It's okay!" I cried, frowning and worrying about my little dream kitty. "She's my family's familiar and guardian."

"Damn, an inherited familiar?" the voice murmured in a mild tone. "That's interesting."

"I guess." After a pause, I asked, "Who are you?" Doubt had begun to pluck at my mind. Maybe this was actually a bad dream instead of just a weird one.

"Are you scared?" The voice sneered, as if sensing my concern.

I frowned. "I'm trying to decide if I should be."

"You should be." This time, the words were a quiet hiss, and something about them rang true, which sent me shivering in distaste.

But I still had to ask, "Then why hang out in a barn?" I arched an eyebrow at him.

"The setting was your choice." The green eyes glanced around us. "It's your subconscious, after all."

"So you finally admit this is a dream!" I snorted, feeling triumphant, the sense of concern that had been growing in me faltering. "That means I really don't have to be scared!"

"Of course it's a dream," the man said slowly. A frightening smile flashed across his face, revealing a pair of fangs. "But that doesn't mean you shouldn't be scared. Not all dreams are harmless."

"Well, you've not hurt me." I shrugged.

"Yet." The word hung in the air.

"Do you intend to?" I stood from trying to calm Diana, and planted my feet apart, hands on my hips.

"I haven't decided," was the cool reply, "You amuse me."

My anger flared. "I'm not here for your amusement!" I jabbed my index finger in his direction. "You know what? I'm tired of this dream, I'm just gonna ignore you until I wake up. For some reason, my subconscious mind has decided to give me a weird, scary dream with some jerk who hides in the shadows and speaks in riddles. I'm not a fan!"

"Well, if that's the case..." Without any warning, the stranger leapt at me, passing through the beam of light in the blink of an eye. In that brief moment, I saw a flash of dark feathers, something sparkly, and claws.

A shriek of surprise escaped me, and suddenly, a burst of pain across my face woke me with a start.

Something tumbled off my chest as I sat bolt upright in bed. Clutching my cheek, I blinked in confusion, gasping, "What the hell?!"

I realized Diana must have been what I threw off my chest, as she was busily picking herself up from the bed. Once settled, she began to lick her paw daintily.

"Sorry about that, miss," I muttered, reaching out to pet her.

She nipped my hand, seeming a bit annoyed with me, probably at being thrown around when I'd sat up so quickly.

"I said I was sorry!" I sighed. Pulling my other hand away from my stinging face, I saw blood. "Did you scratch me while I was asleep?!" I demanded, surprised. There was no other explanation.

My very prim familiar finished licking her paw, and fixed her iridescent, sea-green gaze on me. It was a stern look.

"That was kinda shitty, you know?! What did I do to deserve it?! I didn't even wake up until after you scratched me!" I protested, throwing my hands up into the air.

Stroopwafel maowed sleepily, rolling over onto her back. I plunged one of my hands into the soft fur on her tummy. "At least Stroopy-loopy doesn't scratch me when I'm sleeping," I mumbled.

No, Stroopwafel would just bite my head if she decided I wasn't paying her enough attention while I was asleep.

Diana rolled her eyes at me before shifting and curling up into a ball.

"Alright, well, we'll discuss this more in the morning," I told my oldest friend, wanting to get back to sleep, given that my rest had been interrupted twice that night already.

Chapter 3

A Patient

"Good morning, all!" I said, slipping into the barn, and holding my lamp up to see everyone.

The black kitty was up already, sitting upright on the table, watching me expectantly with his luminous green eyes. Unfortunately, they reminded me too much of the odd dream I'd had the night before, and I repressed a shudder.

Then, realizing how silly I was being, I shook my head and smiled at him, chirping, "Hello, Mr. Kitty!"

The lovely eyes blinked once.

"I gotta think of something to call you," I told him as I went forward, and set the lamp on the table a few feet away from him, then went about refilling his food and water bowls, and dealing with the sawdust box.

Once the cat was taken care of, I set about the usual chores of feeding the rest of the animals, and making sure that their enclosures were clean. When my parents were still alive, there had always been at least one milk cow to milk every morning and evening, but Daisy wasn't a milk cow. She helped pull my cart and plow the field.

There was a dairy farm nearby now, which made it easy and relatively inexpensive to buy whatever milk I needed and keep it in my cold box. The dairy farm had opened within the last ten years; that was four years after my parents had died, and I'd sold our milk cows. It hadn't been a bother to just go without milk, I didn't use it for much, but if I did ever need it, there was always someone who'd been willing to sell me a little.

Before long, everything was nice and neat. Or as neat as a barn could be.

"There we go!" I dusted my hands off, and surveyed my work.

The cat was licking his formerly injured paw languidly.

"Is that paw okay, buddy?" I asked, smiling at him.

He paused, glancing at me before resuming his licking.

"Good." I nodded as I headed to the door, holding it open. "Well, I won't make you stay here. Do you want to go out? I can't leave this door open, all the hot air would get out, but I can let you back in when I come back for the evening feeding, if you want."

The cat put his paw down, and stared at me, unmoving.

I stood there a moment longer, just to be sure, then said. "Alright, then! I'll ask you again tomorrow morning, but I'm not letting you out tonight. It's going to be cold again, and I have a feeling we'll be getting more snow!"

The green eyes blinked once, very swiftly, as if in acknowledgement.

"Alright, handsome boy. See you later!" I laughed, shutting the door behind me as I left, and went back into the cottage.

With the outside chores done, I had to get to work inside. Since winter was there, and I didn't have gardens and trees to tend, I was able to make the bulk of the products I would take into town the next year to sell.

Whenever I wasn't otherwise busy with the plants and such at my cottage, I would load up my cart early in the morning and drive into town with Daisy. We'd spend the day selling the wares on the town green, and I'd drop off some of the salves and such to a nearby business that sold them for me. They took a small percentage of the profits as my thanks for selling them when I was too busy to be there myself. It worked pretty well, because it meant I could collect the profits from the store whenever I went in, which was usually once every two weeks or so.

It was always enough money for what I needed, and enough that I could save up for anything special I might want as well, like the lovely heating stones.

Soon, I was busy toiling away in the kitchen, and worked for many long hours. Finally, rows of glass jars covered the countertops and table, ready to have the burn salve I was making poured into them.

Just as I'd finished pouring the last jar, I heard a commotion outside. Frowning, I hurried to one of the windows looking out over my porch to see some people slogging their way through the snow towards my house.

I wiped frost off the window, and realized I recognized at least one of the faces, so I went and threw the door open. "Jedda, what's wrong?" I could see Jedda and his son were carrying his son-in-law between them, while Jedda's daughter danced around them, fretting.

Jedda's family were good people, and were indeed the same folks who'd bought the cows from me after my parents had passed.

"We had a fire in one of the barns! We got all the animals out, but Biren got trapped under some burning wood that fell from the roof!" Jedda cried.

"Oh no!" I gasped. "Hurry up and get inside!" I stepped aside and let them stumble in. "I'll do what I can!" Any medical emergency in the surrounding area was always brought to me. At one point, my mother and aunt had taken on all the medical things. They had taught me everything I needed to know about healing, but now, I was the only one left with the healing power, and I had to go it alone.

Well, not entirely alone.

Diana, sensing she was needed, appeared beside me while I gave directions to Jedda and his family.

"Put him on the floor here." I really needed to make some kind of pallet, or to get a cot for such times.

They did as I said, laying the poor man out on the warm stone floor.

"It's good and warm in here," Jedda said softly, sounding grateful.

"The heating stones are to thank. Dern does excellent work. They're well worth the investment," I told them as I inspected the wounds closely. "These are pretty severe and will need treatment over time." I paused, glancing over at them, and murmuring apologetically, "I'm not nearly as strong as my mother and aunt were, even with Diana's help."

"Oh lass, we're just grateful you can help at all," Jedda assured me, smiling sadly. "It's not your fault that blessings wane."

"Well, I'll certainly do my best to help him," I said. "First, I need to get this cleaned, but I need to sit here and keep the pain down, so I'm going to need your help." Diana was a great help when it came to healing, but in addition to being cat-sized, she suffered the large disadvantage of a distinct lack of thumbs. "There's hot water on the stove from where I was working, please get it, Jedda. Bring it and some clean cloths from the drawer to the right of the sink." Giving a specific person tasks was better; that way there was no hesitation regarding who I was talking to, and no assumptions that someone else would do a given task. "Ena," I addressed Jedda's daughter. "Please get the bandages from the closet over there." I nodded in the direction of the medical supply closet. "There are some already torn, but you and Marden," Jedda's son, "might need to make some more. There will be plenty of fabric in there ready to be torn up, so get one of the extra sheets out and get to work on it."

As they all hurried to do as I asked, I took a deep breath, and reached out to take Biren's uninjured hand. Pulling for my power, I pushed a gentle magic that would ease the pain, and I heard his breathing deepen and slow.

"Diana, I'll need your help with this," I murmured, though I knew she was already aware.

The sweet cat maowed softly, and brushed reassuringly against me.

I smiled. "You're right! It might just take longer than it would have for Mom." Taking another deep breath, I reached out and put my free hand on Diana's back. "Are you ready?"

She confirmed with another soft maow, and I closed my eyes, pulling for my magic.

I felt Diana's magic as well, pushing through me. She had far more magic than I ever would, but as she was a familiar, she couldn't focus or direct it. That's what I was there for, as the conduit. Yes, I had my own magic, but I could also tap into her powerful well of magical energy and direct it as needed.

"It's wonderful," Marden breathed.

I smiled, opening my eyes. "Diana is always pretty, but she's spectacular when she uses magic." My only tell was the mark glowing weakly on the back of my hand and the spark of my magic traveling across whatever I was doing, but Diana's fur glowed with a heavenly light whenever she lent her magic, showing her status as a goddess-given familiar.

"She's a lovely cat," Ena murmured.

"She really is!" I giggled, then told them, "He's going to be okay. There might be some scars, but beyond that, there'll be no lasting effect, once I'm done here. It'll be best if he stays here tonight, just in case, but you should be able to take him home tomorrow morning. That said, he should come back in a couple of weeks so I can make sure it's doing alright."

"Thank you, Winna. I don't know what we'd do without you. Your family has done so much good for the people of this area," Ena told me earnestly.

"I'm glad to help. That's why we have the gift, to help others." I smiled, shrugging, and letting the magic slowly ebb away. A sense of melancholy filled me, and I murmured, "You...you know I'll probably be the last, right? My own gift is so weak that I can't see any child I have carrying it on." And that was if I ever got married and had children, which I wasn't even sure was something that I wanted.

"Aye, lass. I've often wondered. No offense to you, but when your brothers didn't have it, and yours being less than your mother's...I did wonder." Jedda sighed, then smiled, adding, "But that'll be a long time from now."

"Yes. Maybe we'll be able to get some other magical folk in the area who can help out by then." I smiled, nodding.

"Perhaps we will!" Jedda managed a quick bark of laughter.

After a break, Diana and I used more healing magic before I started to bandage Biren up, with a little help from Ena.

I glanced at the clock. "It's about time for me to get outside and feed the animals again. Can you continue here while I do that?"

"Can you put up our horse in your barn for the night?"

"Of course. I'll take care of it, you stay here."

After shrugging into my coat, slipping into my boots and gloves, and grabbing my lantern, I went outside.

Going over to the small cart that they'd brought Biren to the cottage in, I quickly freed their horse and walked her to the barn.

As I entered, I greeted the occupants, "Hello all! You have a guest that's going to spend the night, so be nice, okay? I also can't stay and talk today, I have a patient I need to get back to. But remember, I love each and every one of you!"

The black cat opened a green eye and watched me as I got the horse into a spare stall, and made sure she had plenty of food and water before seeing to the rest of the animals.

"Alright." I picked up the lamp, and went to the door. "I'll see you all tomorrow!"

As I was shutting the door behind me, a fluffy shadow darted out, startling me.

"Oh!" I gasped, seeing the black cat scamper a few steps away before sitting. He paused and looked back at me. "Do you want to leave?" I'd be very sad to see the little fella go, but I'd also promised that I wouldn't keep him.

He continued to stare, but didn't leave.

"It's going to be cold out tonight!" I told him, frowning, and holding the barn door open. "I can't leave the door open for you, you really should go back in!"

The cat looked away, then started off.

"Alright, I did say I wouldn't make you stay." I sighed, blinking as I realized he was making a beeline straight towards the cottage.

Indeed, he was soon sitting on the porch, watching me expectantly as I picked my way back through the snow.

"Well!" I smiled. "Would you like me to make you a house out here? Or would you like to go in?"

His gorgeous eyes blinked once, but of course he didn't reply.

"Let's see if you'll come inside," I said, going up the steps, and slipping past him. I went to the door and stepped in, holding it open for him.

The cat walked right up to the threshold, but paused and looked up at me, as if waiting.

"Well, come in if you're going to come in!" I laughed.

As if that's what he'd been waiting for, the black cat slunk inside, and I shut the door.

Chapter 4

Three Cats In a Cottage

"Sorry that it took so long," I told Jedda and his family members as I slipped out of my coat, boots, and gloves. "That kitty has been hanging around for a little while, and I wanted to see if he'd come in."

"He's very pretty!" Ena smiled.

"He is!" I agreed, then laughed. "Almost as pretty as Annie!" Going outside to tend to my animals had helped me relax a little after the tenseness of the situation with Biren. There hadn't been an emergency patient for me to treat in quite a while, and it had startled me from my cozy little existence.

Speaking of cats, Stroopwafel had wandered into the room, and immediately went up to sniff the black cat. She flopped onto her back to show him her tummy, and started wiggling around, wanting to play with our little guest.

Diana approached more slowly, sniffing the air warily. Suddenly, she arched her back and hissed, growling angrily.

Well, that was odd! Reality was mimicking my dream from the night before! Although it was a little black cat Annie was reacting to, not some strange, shadowy being with wings and too many fingers.

"Diana!" I blinked, startled at her reaction. "Calm down, my love! He's just visiting! I mean, he can stay if he wants, but I'm not going to make him! He doesn't have a home, like Stroopwafel didn't!" I hastened to her side, and stroked her fur. She turned and bounded away down the hallway. "Rude!" I snorted, shaking my head. Cats could be so persnickety!

"That's unusual for her, isn't it?" Marden asked. "She's usually very friendly." He'd broken his arm a couple of summers before, which had meant he'd visited my cottage often. During those visits, Marden had fallen a little in love with my Annie, though he'd liked Stroopwafel a good deal as well. She was such a silly creature that it was hard not to like her.

"Yes, yes, she is, even with the farm animals." I frowned, then sighed and shook my head. "Ah well. It's alright. They'll settle in. I'll keep him in his own room at night so she can sleep in peace."

"Good idea." Ena nodded.

I sat back down, and inspected their bandaging work. "Looks good! Thank you for finishing that for me," I told them. "When I send him home tomorrow, remind me to send a jar or two of the burn salve with you."

"Yes ma'am." Jedda nodded.

"Well, I have three empty rooms here, do all three of you fancy staying here with Biren tonight?

"No, I'll head home," Marden said. "My Jeani will want me there."

"I'll stay," Jedda replied.

"I'll stay as well," Ena said, turning to her older brother to ask, "Will you and Jeani keep the children tonight?"

"Of course!" He smiled, getting up, and putting his boots and coat back on before bidding us farewell, and slipping outside.

"I'll start on dinner."

"Let me help you," Ena said, joining me in the kitchen.

After clearing away my work from earlier, Ena and Jedda both pitched in, and we soon had a hearty soup bubbling away on the stove and rolls baking in the oven.

"I want to get one of those fancy ovens that Dern makes," I told my companion as I stirred the pot of soup.

"I got one a few months back, and I love it so much!" Ena exclaimed.

"I'm so jealous!" I laughed. "Does it work well?"

"So well! It has four burners instead of two, and it cooks very evenly. *Definitely* get one if you can!"

"It'll take me a little while to save up a bit more, but I think I can manage it by summertime, if I play my cards right," I told her.

"Excellent! I'll come over, and we can break it in together with a baking party and a lovely tea!" She beamed at me.

"Oh, I do love a good tea party." I grinned back. "Do you like baking a lot?"

"Yes!"

"She's good at it, too," Jedda interjected.

"You'll have to teach me some good recipes. I can do some basic stuff, but I don't know anything particularly good."

"I'll write down my favorites and bring them to you as thanks for helping my Biren." She smiled warmly.

"No thanks necessary! But I do appreciate it."

"Of course we owe you our thanks," Jedda said, coming into the kitchen area to help me set the table. "Your family has done so much for everyone in this area. So many folks would have severe disabilities, or have simply died, without your family and now you."

"It's our job." I shook my head. "The gift is for helping others."

"It's alright to accept thanks, lass."

"Well, you're very welcome." I smiled at him.

"Now, as to payment."

"You know I don't ask for a fee." I shook my head again.

"And I know that you should. We don't have hospitals or infirmaries in these parts, and those places charge money. You work hard for everyone in the area and deserve to be fairly compensated. I know you don't ask so that people who can't pay aren't too ashamed to come for help, but we can afford it, I promise. You don't charge enough for those salves you sell either. You should be making a lot more than you do, except for your kindness in keeping the prices low."

"My parents did as well," I mumbled.

"I know. They were good people." He patted my shoulder. "And we miss them almost as much as you do." Jedda had been my father's good friend. He pulled out his coin purse, and pushed some money into my hands, saying, "Now take, this, lass."

"That's far too much!" I protested, trying to push it away.

"Take some and buy yourself a new dress, Winna. That one is falling apart. Save the rest for your oven," he said gently.

I frowned, but let my fingers curl around the gold coins. "Th-thank you," I whispered, quite aware that both of the elbows in the dress I was wearing needed patching. Again.

"No, thank you! You saved my son-in-law's life!"

"He'd have lived. He'd have just been in a lot of pain, and have a lot of scars," I mumbled, wiping my eyes to make sure no tears spilled out.

"That's no kind of life to live." Ena shook her head. "Thank you for helping us."

"Th-thank you for always being so kind to me. Your family has helped me so much since my parents passed."

"They'd have wanted us to. Besides, I've always thought of you as a niece." Jedda beamed at me. "Now go put that somewhere safe." He motioned at the money in my hand.

I nodded and scampered down the hallway. Diana was sitting in the middle of my bed, and opened a sea-blue eye to observe me. She maowed softly, then shut it again. Well, at least she wasn't still in a bad mood.

Kneeling, I stashed the money in the box I kept beneath my bed. It wasn't the most creative place, but crime was extremely rare in our neck of the woods, thankfully. If all went to plan, I'd soon have enough to buy that new stove from Dern, as I'd discussed with Ena.

Once I had it, the baking possibilities were endless, and I'd be able to try some recipes that required a less finicky cooker.

Returning to the living area, I washed my hands, and we sat down to a cheerful meal together. It was nice to have company while I was eating again. Well, human company. I loved my cats dearly, but they weren't very good conversationalists.

"So, it was a fire in one of the barns, you said?" I asked, spooning soup into my mouth.

"Yes, in the one with the cows. We were lucky to get them all out." Jedda shook his head.

"I'm glad you did. How are my old girls?"

"Just fine," Ena assured me.

"It was strange, we can't figure out how the fire started. All I can think is that a lamp got kicked over, but all the farm hands swore they hadn't left one burning in there." The old farmer sighed. "In the end, no great harm was done. We can rebuild a barn, but lives can't be replaced."

"We're lucky it didn't spread," Ena murmured.

"Very lucky." Jedda agreed.

"I'm always scared of a fire here," I told them, shaking my head. "That's partly why I got the heating stones. Dern said there's no chance of them causing a fire, that they'll just stop working before anything like that happens."

"Magic is wonderful, isn't it?" Ena sighed happily.

"It is," I agreed wholeheartedly.

Once the meal and the washing up were done, I settled down by Biren once more for another healing session. Diana didn't come out, evidently still upset at the presence of the black cat. Normally, Stroopwafel was my prickly cat, not Diana, and I was vaguely amused by the fact that she was sulking in my bedroom.

The black cat in question had settled himself on the corner of the now disused fireplace. The lack of my familiar was alright, for the moment, because I could handle one session by myself. This session was just meant to speed up the healing process, which my own magic was sufficient to do. But hopefully Diana would come out later that evening to help again, once I'd put the new kitty into his own room for the night.

"Please go settle into whichever of the empty rooms you'd like," I told my two uninjured guests. "I'll stay out here to keep an eye on Biren, and do healing sessions throughout the night just to make sure he's doing as well as possible before I send him home."

"Are you sure? Should I sit out here with you? Your couch is very comfortable," Ena said, motioning at my sitting area.

"No, no, go ahead. I'll sleep there between healing sessions. I'm used to it, and it's no trouble. Please go make yourselves at home."

They disappeared down the hallway, and I heard doors open and shut.

I finished my healing session and stood, dusting my hands on my dress. Approaching the fireplace, I addressed my new little friend. "Well, handsome boy, will you come with me to your own room? Diana is a bit uneasy about you being here, so I'd like to let her have the space to roam tonight. I don't want to pick you up, but I'll do it if I have to."

The cat blinked once, then I swear he sighed before stretching luxuriously, then leaping gracefully down from the fireplace. He padded over and looked expectantly up at me.

"Well, alright then! Thank you!" I smiled at him. I led him down the hallway, pausing and listening to see which of the usually empty rooms were occupied before taking him to the remaining empty one. He followed me inside, and immediately hopped up onto the bed.

"Excellent! I'll bring you food and water and a sawdust box," I told him, then went and did just that, arranging them in separate corners of the room. "There we are!" I looked around. "This used to be my parents' room," I told him, although I'm not sure why. He was just a cat, after all. Shaking myself, I sighed, and said, "Well, good-night, little guy! I hope you sleep well!" Then I left the room.

As I was shutting the door behind me, Diana slipped down the hallway, and paused beside me, looking warily at the door. She sniffed the air cautiously, gave another low growl, and backed away.

"Hey Miss." I knelt and stroked her fur.

She turned her large, beautiful sea-green eyes to me and blinked slowly. It never failed to amaze me how her lovely iridescent eyes seemed to shift from green to blue and back, like the actual sea.

"I love you too, gorgeous," I told her. "It's so unlike you to be unwelcoming. What's wrong?"

Another slow blink from my oldest friend.

"You're usually so sweet." I smiled, bending to kiss her little forehead.

Diana maowed softly in response, then finally started to purr.

"Oh my good girl." I scratched the bridge of her nose.

Sensing that I was giving out nose scratchies, Stroopwafel be-bopped her way down the hallway, demanding the same attention.

"It's a good thing I have two hands!" I laughed as I scratched both of my cats' noses the way they loved. "You two are my silly girls! Just because we have another kitty around doesn't mean I love either of you any less. I have infinite amounts of room in my heart for kitties!"

Ena poked her head out of the hallway and smiled. "Aww!"

"They're spoiled rotten!" I laughed, then told her, "The wash-room is at the end of the hall, and I have hot running water if you'd like a nice bath!"

"Oh, that would be lovely! We don't have hot water yet at our house! Father says sometime next year."

"Did you say something about a bath?" Jedda poked his head out as well.

"You're welcome to all the hot water you want!" I laughed.

"I think I'll take you up on that, lass!" The old man chuckled.

I stood. "Well, I'll leave you two to sort out who gets a bath first. I'll take one when you're done. Diana can sit with Biren while I'm busy, so you two can just go right ahead and rest."

Ena caught my hand and squeezed it gently. "Thank you, Winna."

"You're very welcome! I hope you sleep well!" I smiled, heading back into the living area to check on my patient. He was still sleeping peacefully.

Given the amount of magic that had been used on him, I didn't expect him to wake up for several more hours at least.

Settling down at my loom, I started to weave. If I could keep working regularly like I had been lately, I'd have a handful of shawls finished by springtime, and could enchant them with simple heating and soothing magic to sell in the Greenwood. I'd done it before, and they were always snapped up.

I was so glad to have added them to my repertoire of goods to take to the village, and it was nice to be able to lean into my artistic inclinations a little. Most of my chores were just that, chores, but at least weaving was creative and productive.

Chapter 5

An Introduction

L ear stretched luxuriously on the bed. That was one of the nice things about being in cat form: any person-sized bed was absolutely enormous. The downside was that his magical abilities were limited.

His powers were limited even more than usual, at the moment, thanks to the damned poison still coursing through his veins. But between the rest he'd gotten as well as the healing magic, food, and water the young woman had provided, it was likely he'd be able to take on his proper form again.

Weak as the human girl was, she hadn't been able to sense the poison he was struggling with. But she likely wasn't used to dealing with fey folk, making it even more unlikely that she'd have taken note of it. Though, in all honesty, it was very lucky he'd run into any kind of healer at all, this far into the human countryside.

The familiar, though...she was an unexpectedly potent being.

Unlike the filth that had gotten lucky in poisoning him, if it came down to who had the most powerful magic between him and Diana, he wasn't sure he'd be the winner. That said, if what he thought he felt was correct, there was something of the divine about the feline familiar, which might mean that the cat couldn't actually use the magic she possessed. That's why the young woman...what had they called her? Winna, yes, that was it. That's why Winna existed. She had her own magic, of course, but the cat, Diana, provided a large sea of magic for her person to pull from. Other familiars could use their own magic, of course, but familiars connected to deities had restrictions on what they could do, typically being limited to acting as magical batteries for their mage. They were also the only familiars that were ever inherited, really.

Despite her immense power, Diana was still just a cat, and that meant she couldn't get through the door separating them. Since that was the case, he was going to risk a transformation attempt.

Lear pulled for his magic, grimacing through the pain the poison still polluting his veins caused. Despite the pain, its power was weakened just enough that he could slip some magic through and...

The fey man's magic finally surged, as wild and restive as ever, and in the next moment, he was standing in his proper body once more, veins throbbing from the effort. He immediately sat on the bed and examined his left arm, which had taken the poisoned dart. Lear had been in cat form, technically, so the dart had hit his paw, but that's still where his original form bore the injury.

He'd been too careless. Careless and overconfident. It had almost cost him his life. That wasn't a mistake he'd make again.

The fey soldier was lucky he'd transformed when he did. It had been an instinct to make himself as small a target as possible in the split second after he realized he'd walked into Veris' trap. If Lear hadn't taken his cat form, the damage from the poison would have been much worse; since his magic was lessened in his feline form there was less overall damage it could do. Indeed, the poison's presence inside him had already started to ebb away, albeit very, very slowly. He'd even been able to creep into the young woman's dreams the night before to tease her, though that really didn't take much magical effort to do, given how close dreaming was to magic anyway.

Lear turned over the brief, nearly fatal attack. He *would* face

Veris again, once he was healed. Leaving a mission unfinished wasn't his style. What would Asher say if Lear came back with his tail between his legs after having failed his mission, not to mention spending precious time recuperating out in the sticks?

He could well imagine the fey king's arched eyebrow and sarcastic remark, probably something about him not being able to commit to anything, least of all a mission.

Lear's long fingers strayed to where he'd been hit. The wound had healed, thanks to Winna's efforts. It hadn't been a deep or serious injury, after all, no more than a thorn, really. But the poison that thorn had carried was another story. It would have been deadly to a weaker fey, and even he had gotten lucky in that he wasn't worse off right now. It would have left him totally incapacitated, and his opponent would have had no trouble killing him.

Lear studied his reflection in the full-length mirror. The brilliant green cat eyes, which he was famous for, glowed, though their usual mischievousness was somewhat tempered by the pain from the poison. It wasn't debilitating or particularly bad unless he used magic, but it was enough to remind him that it was there.

The opalescent scales on his neck reflected the moonlight that streamed in the window with a satin luster. The patches of those scales on his back and arms were hidden by his clothing, but he could feel that they'd properly appeared as well. Normally, his pitch black wings would have reflected some of the light as well, rendering it into a faint rainbow, much like oil. He had the wings hidden for the moment, though, given that the room was relatively small, and the enormous mass of feathers would have knocked everything over any time he moved much. Lear smiled, baring his venomous fangs, sensing that he'd transformed properly despite the poison in him.

A sudden noise caught his ears, and he spun, flicking his second set of eyes open and peering out the window. The heat presence of all living beings in his immediate vicinity was instantly visible. Noting nothing suspicious outside, the fey man turned again, this time more slowly as he searched out all the occupants of the house.

The four humans were all asleep. Two in the rooms nearby, the father and daughter, and Winna out in the living area where the son-in-law, Biren, slept on the floor. The normal cat, Stroopwafel, was asleep on the couch with her mistress. The familiar, however, was sitting outside the door of the room he was in, facing it and staring. What he'd heard must have been a floorboard creaking as Diana had come down the hallway to investigate, likely having felt his magic when he'd transformed.

Having found the source of the noise, he closed his second set of eyes. Though he'd had it his entire life, that second layer of sight could be very overwhelming, especially when he already wasn't feeling particularly well.

"Relax," he muttered, knowing Diana's ears would pick up his words. "Believe it or not, I'm not here to hurt anyone." Lear idly flicked the claws in and out of his fingertips as he spoke. He wasn't perfect, but even he wouldn't repay the kindness he'd been shown with evil.

Walking into the girl's dream hadn't been cruelty. Or he hadn't meant it to be cruelty, anyway. It was just so easy to jump into someone's dream. So his curiosity had gotten the better of him, and he'd taken the chance to see how she reacted to his poking.

Given that the young woman only displayed a sweet, gentle disposition up until that point, he'd expected her to be frightened and wary of him. He'd presented himself as a somewhat threatening, shadowy figure, even if it was just a dream, so of course he would expect her to be scared. Instead, she'd confronted him with a fair measure of confidence and indigence at his prodding.

Then the familiar had appeared and tried to warn him off. But it would take more than that to scare him away. Besides, he still needed to heal. As to leaping at the young woman, well, Winna had wanted to wake up anyway. He'd known that the moment he touched her in the dream, she would wake. He *had* intended to scare her a little, though, just for the fun of it. But Diana had intervened before he could reach her and scratched her mistress awake, likely uncertain as to his motives and not sure whether he could actually hurt Winna. Even if he had been able to hurt her in the dream, he wouldn't have, of course. Still, the panic that had flashed across her face the moment he'd leapt at her had been dreadfully amusing.

There was a soft maow from the other side of the door.

"I'm injured. It's poison." He paused, then continued. "I just want some time to heal. Then I can be on my way."

Another low maow.

"If I open the door, please don't scratch me. I'm in no mind to kill innocents right now."

An annoyed hiss.

"Alright, alright." He sighed, crossing to the door and opening it. He looked down at the little diluted tabby, who was loafing right in the doorway. "For such a powerful familiar, you have a very unimpressive shape." Even he had to admit that she loafed magnificently, though.

Diana blinked her gorgeous, blue-green eyes at him. She really was a beautiful cat.

"Those eyes give mine a run for their money, though," Lear admitted, slightly annoyed. He knelt to get closer to the familiar's height. "I guess you and your mistress are really only healers, so there's no cause for you to look intimidating."

The cat's ears twitched, and her eyes flickered.

"Yes, this is me. I do have my wings hidden, they're kind of big."

Her nose twitched.

"What do you mean skinny?" The fey captain arched an eyebrow coolly at her in protest. "I'm a soldier, I promise I'm not just skinny." Indeed, he was considered the most available bachelor in the feylands, much to his own annoyance. Having a pretty face and a fair form, along with incredible power, would do that.

A bemused twinkle flickered through the familiar's eyes, and she seemed to soften towards him.

There was a pause.

"So, can I stay?" he asked, tiredness washing over him. He

wanted to get back to sleep, but needed to ascertain his standing with the powerful creature before he did that. "I'm not here to hurt anyone. I'd have remained in cat form, but I needed to see if I'd recovered enough to transform."

She blinked once.

"Thank you." He nodded. "Is it okay if I take my proper form, whenever your mistress is asleep? Just every now and again, most likely."

Another blink.

"Thank you. Do you want me to swear aloud to my intentions?"

A soft maow.

It was Lear's turn to blink. "Take my word for it?" He couldn't keep the surprise he felt from creeping slightly into his voice. "That's not very wise, I *am* fey. Although I guess we can't lie. But we are still very tricky."

The cat snorted and rolled her eyes.

"Whatever you say," he muttered, wondering what her game was. "You're a formidable foe."

Diana stood, flicking her tail.

"Goodnight." He nodded, standing and shutting the door as she turned and made her way back down the hallway.

-

"Thank you again, Winna." Ena hugged me tightly.

"I'm happy to help! But it's just as much Diana as me. She's the one with the most power around here these days. I'm just the silly human who directs what she has. Gods know I can't handle much without her!" I snorted, shaking my head.

"Thank you too, Diana." Ena laughed, waving at the sweet, diluted grey tabby.

Diana blinked her iridescent, blue-green eyes at them slowly, and bobbed her head in reply.

"She says you're welcome!" I giggled.

"She's a pretty cat." Biren smiled tiredly.

"She really is!" Jedda agreed.

Stroopwafel maowed loudly, wanting attention as well, and the black cat watched with vague disinterest from the spot he'd claimed for himself on the corner of the fireplace.

"Oh Stroopwafel!" I laughed.

"This one is a very silly cat!" Biren laughed, bending and petting Stroopwafel with his un-bandaged hand. "She was running around before you'd woken up this morning like a crazy thing, trying to get the black cat to play with her."

"Yeah, she's goofy and playful!" I grinned, leaning over and scooping my Stroopwafel up. "Keeps life interesting! Everyone needs a silly cat like Stroopwafel and a sweet cat like Diana in their lives."

"I want a kitty, Biren." Ena pouted, linking her arm through her husband's unhurt one.

"Oh fine." He rolled his eyes, but smiled

"Two kitties. You owe me for scaring me half to death!"

"I'm not sure that's how it works, but okay. Two kitties," he agreed.

"Thank you!" She giggled, bobbing up to kiss her husband's cheek, and he smiled fondly at her.

"We'd best be off now, kids," Jedda said, ushering them towards the door.

"Come back a couple of weeks from now, and we'll make sure it's still doing well," I told Biren as I followed them outside, stopping at the top of the porch stairs.

"Yes ma'am." He nodded.

"Thanks again, Winna!" Ena waved once she was in the cart.

"You're welcome! Come see me soon! I look forward to trying out those recipes!"

"Sure thing!" She grinned at me.

Jedda flicked the reins, and the horses started off.

I waved until they were out of sight, then sighed.

It was nice to be able to help people.

Turning, I went back inside, and looked around my little cottage, hands on my hips. "Back to normal life, now, I guess! Although I hope we can all get acclimated to having a new friend around." I smiled at the cats, who were sitting in various places throughout the living area.

The black cat was still on his fireplace perch, Diana was sitting primly near the entrance to the back hallway, and Stroopwafel was sprawled out in the middle of the floor by the heating rocks.

A giggle of joy bubbled up from me. Their personalities were evident even in how and where they sat. Diana was queenly, but kind and down to earth, and Stroopwafel was goofy with no dignity at all. The black cat was still wary, preferring to watch from up high until he was used to the place; he also likely wanted to stay out of Diana's way, given her reaction to him the day before. My little familiar probably wouldn't let him sit repeatedly higher than she did, as she *was* the kitty in charge in this house. But hopefully, they'd start to get along soon, cat hierarchy aside.

Stretching, I went to put away the now-clean breakfast dishes, as Ena had insisted on staying long enough to help with the washing up. It had been very nice to be in a family atmosphere again, and it made my heart ache a little for the years before my parents had passed.

I smiled sadly and pushed the melancholy away. That was just the way of the world. Death was just another part of life, even though my mother should have had the same immortally young life as I did. But being immortally young didn't protect from injury or illness, and, though we were healers, there were some things that even magic couldn't fix. Certain diseases were resistant to magic, and if an injury was bad enough, sometimes magic just wasn't enough.

Fourteen years ago, there had been an earthquake, and many people had been trapped in the rubble, so my mother, father, Diana, and I had gone into town to try to help. Diana and I had been tending to a hurt child while my parents had been helping lift rubble from a partially collapsed house, which was trapping the child's mother. A small aftershock hit, and the rest of the house collapsed without warning, crushing my parents and killing them immediately. I was sixteen.

In a strange twist of fate, the falling rubble that had killed my parents hadn't struck the woman they were trying to save. Other helpers had been able to rescue her, and Diana had helped me heal her leg, despite the fact that I'd been bawling my eyes out at the time. The poor lady they'd died trying to save had been horrified, apologetic, and grateful all at once.

I shook my head, thinking of how awful she must have felt. What a complicated mass of emotions to feel, though it hadn't been her fault.

I'd been heartbroken at the time, of course, but knew that I couldn't stop helping the other victims from the earthquake, since I was literally the only person around anymore who could heal. If I stopped to grieve, people would die; people I could save.

So I'd continued on. Only when I'd managed to get healing magic into every single person who'd been injured did I stop and finally break down completely. I'd stayed with a close friend's family for a while after that, just so I didn't have to be alone.

It was at that time that Jedda had come and asked if I'd needed help with anything. I'd been having to go back to the cottage every morning and every evening to take care of the animals. It was a burden, going back and forth like that, so I'd asked if he could maybe help me by taking the milk cows off my hands. He had refused to simply take them, but had bought them from me instead. Jedda had also helped me plan the funeral, which I had used the money from the cows to pay for. He'd offered to pay for the funerals himself, as he and my parents had always been close friends, but in the same way Jedda had refused to take the cows as a gift, I'd refused to let him pay for the funerals, so we were kind of even.

Normally, my brothers would have come immediately, but given the destruction they themselves were facing from the earthquake, not to mention the appalling state that the roads were in at the time because of said earthquake, they hadn't been able to make it until just before the funeral took place.

After the funeral both brothers had insisted I move in with either of their families, but I didn't have the heart to leave the family home.

So they'd checked in on me frequently to make sure I had everything I needed. Once I'd turned eighteen, and they were satisfied I could take care of myself, they visited less often, and now I only saw them once or twice a year. It was alright, though, because I knew that they were both busy with their own families and careers.

Chapter 6

New Friends

Shaking myself from my sad thoughts, I began to gather the things I'd need to make more burn salve, only to realize that I was running low on whistlebell, one of the herbs I used.

Luckily, whistlebell was a very hearty plant and grew even in the winter. Unfortunately, it wasn't an herb I'd ever managed to grow on my own, so I'd have to go and forage for it in the forest. Since it was still pretty early in the day, I'd have enough time to find some and get back before it got dark.

I packed a quick lunch, then bade the cats farewell as I slipped outside, throwing the satchel with my lunch and other supplies over my shoulder, and resting my herb basket in the crook of my arm. Taking a deep breath, I headed towards the forest that my property backed up against.

Hopefully, the wolves weren't out prowling around during the day. It wasn't likely that they would be, but it certainly wasn't unheard of, especially when they were starving in the winter months.

I walked slowly for a long while in the direction I knew I'd gone before when I'd found the herb in question, scanning the ground for any sign of it.

"Whistlebell. Whistlebell," I repeated to myself every so often, carrying the image of the leaves in my mind.

It was a pretty plant, with bell-shaped flowers in a pale, icy blue, but it was the leaves that I was after. The leaves were glossy and spiky, almost like holly, and had some property that caused a cooling effect, which went very nicely with the healing magic I always infused into the burn salve.

Finally, I spotted the pale, telltale blossom. It was one of the only flowers to live this late into the winter months.

"There we are!" I smiled and knelt, setting my basket down before rummaging in my pack to find the knife I used for taking herb cuttings. Soon, I was busily trimming leaves and putting them into the basket.

It was a large patch of the plant, and would provide me with plenty of the leaves, but I never took more leaves than a particular plant could handle losing. After all, I wanted the patch to keep growing, so I could come back in the future to get more leaves for my salves.

After working for what seemed like a short while, I stood, stretching my back and craning my neck up. To my surprise, I saw that the sun had climbed high into the sky and that it was now midday.

"Oh! Time for lunch then!" I'd gather a few more leaves after I'd eaten, then head home.

I found a large tree to lean against, and settled down, rummaging in my pack once more and pulling out the paper parcel containing my food.

There was an apple, cheese, bread, pickles, a bit of bacon leftover from breakfast, and some dried apricots. Altogether not a bad little lunch, really. I sipped water from my water-skin as I munched away happily.

The sun came out from behind a cloud and streamed through the barren limbs of the tree I was using as a chair. I closed my eyes, leaning back and turning my face up to soak up the rays.

Despite the nip in the air, the sun was warm enough that, with my belly full, I slipped into a blissful sleep. This wasn't surprising, given how I'd had to wake often the night before to check on Biren.

Suddenly, I woke up with a start. "Oh!" I gasped, blinking and shaking my head. Then I froze as I saw an altogether strange being sitting by my feet, looking just as startled as I was.

It had a fairly cute, human-esque face, with large brown eyes much like my own, a button nose, a mouth, and curly brown hair. But it also was crouched down on a pair of spotted, deer-like hind legs with hoofed feet, though its hands were much like my own. I noted it was wearing a faded red shirt and matching pants.

The little creature stumbled away, squeaking in dismay, and my surprise faded. Realizing that it hadn't meant me any harm, I managed to push away my confusion and smile. "H-hello there! I didn't mean to scare you! Then again, I didn't mean to fall asleep here, either."

The strange being watched me warily, but I saw its eyes flicker down for a moment to the food that lay beside me, the paper wrappings acting as a plate.

"Ah, you're hungry!" It was mid-winter, and all forest dwellers would be struggling to find enough to eat. Did that mean the fey folk who lived there were hungry as well? "Well, I packed far more than I needed. I can share." I smiled, moving slowly, and pushed the remnants of my lunch forward as far as I could reach, then sat back, curling up against the tree.

Its dark brown eyes stayed trained on me, but after a few moments, it took a few hesitant steps forward. It reached out and snatched up the food, then retreated once more, sitting down a few paces away to nibble on the food. I'd eaten all the bacon and the apple, but there was a good bit of bread, cheese, and apricots left, and the little creature chowed down on it.

Unexpectedly, it spoke in a quiet voice, "You're not fey." Something about its speech told me it was young, if not a child.

I blinked. "That's right, I'm human."

"You smell kind of like one of us."

"Oh? Well, I can use magic. Maybe that's it."

"No." It shook its head. "You've been around a fey person, though. Someone strong."

"Uh...not that I know of? You're the first fey person I've ever met." I blinked again.

"Maybe you were around one and didn't know it," the small fey person suggested. "We can usually hide from humans."

"I mean, that's definitely possible. Are there a lot of fey in the woods here?"

"I don't know how many is a lot," it told me.

"Well, I live on the border of the woods, so they might pass by my house or something." I shrugged, then paused before saying, "You're not hurt or anything, are you? I'm a healer, if you need that kind of help."

"No. Just hungry. It's close to my snack time." It shook its head, pausing before adding, "Thank you for sharing."

I smiled at the little thing. "You're welcome!" I tilted my head to the side. "What kind of fey are you?"

"I'm a faun."

"Oh, that makes sense, in hindsight." I laughed, then sighed. "What's your name?"

"I'm Mira."

"That's a pretty name." I smiled.

"Mama says it's a pretty name for a pretty girl." She smiled shyly now.

"Of course it is!" I assured her. "I'm Winna."

"I like that name."

"Thank you!" I chuckled.

"What are you doing in the forest?" Mira asked.

"Picking whistlebell leaves." I motioned at my basket. "I make a burn salve with them. Do you live in this area?"

"Not far from here."

"I see. Well, if you ever see me out and about in the forest, feel free to say hi." I stood, knowing I needed to get back to picking so that I could make it home at a reasonable hour. "And you can come visit me at the cottage sometime, if you like. As long as your parents are okay with it, anyway. I'm not sure they'd want you to visit a stranger." I didn't know enough about fey folk to know whether they were as protective of their children as humans were, but I suspected they were.

Just about the only things I really knew about fey folk were that many of them were beautiful and that they couldn't lie. They could obfuscate in other ways, I'd heard, but they couldn't lie outright.

"My mama would like you." Mira tilted her head to the side. "You said you're a healer, right?"

"Yes." I nodded. "You and your family can come to me if you need healing, and I'll do my best to help. I'm not very strong, but my familiar is. Just promise no trouble will come of it, and everything will be fine."

"We don't cause humans trouble," Mira murmured. "We're peaceful for high fey."

I didn't know quite what she meant by being 'high fey', but I nodded. "Then you're most welcome."

"Be careful of saying that to other fey folk, not all of us are nice," Mira warned me.

"I know that much. But I'm a pretty good judge of character, and can see you're very sweet," I assured her, then picked up my basket and knelt in the patch of whistlebell once more. "Want to keep me company while I finish picking?"

"Sure!" the little faun chirped happily.

"When you're done with that paper, put it in my pack right there, okay? I'll take it home so I don't leave garbage in the forest."

"Okay." Mira nodded, taking the seat I'd vacated against the tree.

I set to work picking some more leaves. "I never knew there were fey folk in the forest here."

"We live everywhere. Since we can hide ourselves, humans often don't know we're around. It's mostly low fey folk in these parts, but there are some high fey folk around."

"I'll admit, I don't know what you mean by low and high fey folk." I laughed, sitting back on my feet to wipe my face off.

"Oh!" She blinked. "My family are high fey. We're kind of shaped more like humans. Low fey usually aren't. Normally they're not as strong as us, either, it depends. But they can still use magic, too."

"Ah, I see." I nodded, leaning over again. "What kind of magic can you use?"

"My family can use all kinds! We're not particularly tough or strong in our bodies, but we can use a lot of different kinds!"

"I'm only a healer, so that must be incredible!"

"Yes, we were blessed." She giggled.

"I have a blessing too, which is why I can heal, but it's very old and getting weak, so I'm not very strong."

"I'm sorry." Mira sounded sad.

"Oh, it's alright." I looked up to smile at her. To my surprise, I saw another faun approaching. This one was larger and taller than Mira. "Oh! Hello!" I sat back, wiping my face, having a feeling this was one of Mira's family members.

Mira looked over. "Mama!"

"Mira, haven't I told you not to talk to strangers?!" the fey woman scolded, then looked warily at me. "Who are you?" she demanded.

"I'm Winna. I'm a healer who lives on the edge of the forest."

"Oh, I've heard of you from some of the animals." The mother faun relaxed a little. "I'm sorry if my daughter bothered you. She shouldn't be showing herself to humans, she knows that." She cast a stern look at her daughter, who quailed a little.

"Well, she wasn't bothering me. I've never met one of the fey folk before, but she mistook me for another one, at first, somehow, so please don't be too upset with her."

The mother tilted her head to the side, "I can see how a little one like her would have." She tousled her daughter's hair lovingly. "You do have the lingering scent of one of the fey on you, a strong one, too. I'm shocked to hear you say you haven't met one of us before."

"Well, from what I understand, you're all able to hide yourselves from humans very well, so maybe they're hiding themselves from me? There's an owl I see pretty frequently around my barn, maybe that's actually a fey person." I shrugged.

The mother smiled. "It's possible."

Standing, I stretched. "Well, I have enough whistlebell for my salves now. I hope I wasn't trespassing or anything by being here."

"No, not at all. We don't begrudge humans use of the woods. At least not in these parts. We're a peaceful bunch, and everyone can benefit from the forest."

"Thank you." I bowed to her.

"Here's your pack!" Mira scampered forward and handed me my pack, and her mother came forward as well.

"Thank you!" I took the bag from her, then told her mother, "If you or your family, or any fey person that promises not to cause me any trouble needs healing, they can come to my cottage, and I'll do my best to help."

Mira's mother blinked, looking momentarily surprised, then smiled. "You're very kind. Thank you. Hopefully we won't ever have to take you up on that, but it's much appreciated."

"I didn't really know I had neighbors here in the forest, or I'd have extended the invitation sooner!" I laughed.

"I'm Pima."

"It's nice to meet you, Pima. And your daughter."

"You as well, Winna." She nodded.

"Well, I'll be going, I need to get home to my kitties, and start on some more salves."

"Safe travels," Pima said.

"Bye!" Mira giggled.

"Goodbye!" I waved as I turned and left, going the way I'd come.

Chapter 7

A Revelation

What a strange thing! Apparently, I smelled like a fey person. That was definitely news to me. I'd only half-jokingly suggested it was Mr. Owl who was fey, but it just as likely could be a fey being I'd never actually seen anything of, given how good they were at hiding from humans.

I arrived back at my cottage after a while of walking. Pausing at the barn, I went ahead and took care of the animals a little earlier than normal, so I wouldn't have to go back outside again, then headed back into the house.

"Hello, babies!" I called as I entered. Stroopwafel immediately be-bopped up to me. Diana looked up from her place on the couch, and then stretched luxuriously before coming to greet me as well. The black cat was perched on the table, and watched me with half-closed eyes, but didn't approach for pets as the other two had.

"I had a very strange day," I told them as I knelt to love on my two gray tabby girls.

Diana sniffed me curiously, and looked up at me, as if questioning the strange smell she'd undoubtedly noticed.

"I met fey folk in the woods!" I told them, smiling. "I was lucky, they're a peaceful sort called fauns. One of their children mistook me for another fey person because apparently I smell like one. Both the mom and the kid said there might be one hanging around that I wasn't aware of." I knew Diana could understand every word I said, though she couldn't herself speak, and as she was my familiar, I liked to keep her abreast of everything that happened when I was out and about on my own.

It had been an altogether strange occurrence. I'd had no idea there were any fey at all in the area until I'd met Mira and her mother, Pima. Although I guess it only made sense that I didn't know about their existence if they preferred to stay hidden from humans.

Standing, I put my pack on the table and set about getting the whistlebell leaves prepped to be dried.

I was busy washing and rinsing the leaves when a knock at the door startled me. Another visitor?

Worried it would be another patient in need of care, I hurried to the door and flung it open, crying, "Welcome! How can I-" I cut off, frowning when I saw no one there. "Well...that's...I don't even know. Whatever." I sighed, then shivered as a sudden, strong gust whipped through the door, tossing my skirts and drawing an annoyed, "Goodness!" from me. I quickly shut the door, then went to stand by the heating stones, having been thoroughly chilled by the cold wind. "I... guess it's just supposed to be a weird day. Maybe I imagined it." I shook my head.

Diana appeared down the hallway, maowing softly, and turned her iridescent, ocean colored eyes to stare at a corner of the room. Powerful familiar though she was, my Annie was still a cat, and prone to sitting in boxes, chasing bugs, and staring out into nothing.

Soon, Stroopwafel was sitting beside her, staring at the same spot.

"Y'all are silly!" I laughed.

The black cat stayed where he was, now perched on the fireplace once more.

"I really need to think of a name for you, little fella," I told him.

He merely yawned in response.

"You're so cute!" I laughed, then went back to working on the whistlebell leaves.

A short while later, I felt something tugging at my skirt. "Just a minute, Stroopy, my hands are wet." Stroopwafel often tugged on my skirts or bit my feet when she wanted attention or if she thought I was cooking something and wanted a sniff or a bite.

More tugging.

"Just a second, silly goose!" I laughed, turning to look at her, but the smile on my face faded, inverting into a frown when I saw she wasn't standing there. Indeed, none of the cats were there. "Maybe I'm finally losing it." I sighed, shaking my head as I turned back to the sink.

One of the cats, I think the black one, maowed as if in agreement with that statement. "Oh hush!" I rolled my eyes.

After a little while, I felt the tugging once more, and immediately whirled to find nothing there yet again.

"This is getting ridiculous!" I threw my hands up, determined that if it happened again, I would ignore it. Resuming work, I finished washing and rinsing the leaves, and began to lay them out to dry.

Suddenly, I felt another tug on my dress. Biting my lip, I ignored it. The tugging came again, a little more urgently this time, and I ignored it again.

Then there was sharp pain in my ankle as Stroopy bit it, maowing in complaint.

"Oh Stroopwafel!" I gasped, spinning to see her standing there this time, looking irritated. I burst into laughter. "I'm sorry, pumpkin!" I bent and scooped her up, letting her look at the whistlebell leaves, and holding one up for her to sniff. "At least it was you this time, and not just my imagination!"

She started to purr, and rubbed her face against mine.

"Oh my love." I smiled, peppering her little forehead with kisses. "You're my baby!"

Then suddenly, something tugged on my dress again. Taking a deep breath, I ignored it, and decided to walk away from the kitchen.

Going over to the living room area, I sat down on the couch and curled up with Stroopwafel, who was content to sit on my lap, purring loudly. After a few moments, I felt sleepiness washing over me for the second time that day. I pulled the blanket off the back of the couch and shifted, curling up with my kitty under the blanket.

The whistlebell leaves could wait, it was no pressing chore. I'd get them dried and could make the burn salve when they were done. Tomorrow, I'd make a general healing salve instead, since it didn't require the dried whistlebell leaves.

My mind strayed drowsily, and I was soon fast asleep.

-

A hiss and a yowl of fear jerked me awake, and I felt pain in my arm as Stroopwafel scrambled, claws out, off the couch, apparently scared by something.

"What?!" I gasped, then froze, seeing something truly terrifying.

A knife hovered in the air not a yard above me. The blade wavered, then began to fall, its tip plunging down towards me.

I screamed, trying to scramble off the couch. Diana hissed and growled, and I felt a surge of magic in the room. A figure materialized beside the couch, reaching out to catch the knife before it stabbed me with one hand while the other grasped the air a few inches away from the knife.

Only, instead of a handful of air, there was suddenly a creature standing there, its neck clutched by the six-fingered hand.

"You thought I'd let you get away with something like that?" The taller of the two figures standing there asked in a mild tone. The voice was strangely familiar, I realized.

"You didn't care that I was teasing her earlier!" the smaller creature gasped in a strangled voice. It was maybe two feet tall, with strange, mottled green and brown skin, bulging red eyes (although that might have just been because it was being held by its throat), and large, flapping ears.

I scrambled away, off the couch, and away from the strange sight.

My heart was pounding in terror and confusion as I gasped, "Wh-what's going on?!"

The taller of the two intruders cast a swift glance at me with a pair of practically glowing green eyes, sighing annoyedly. "Be patient."

More confusion filled me as I realized the being's eyes were familiar. Luminescent green with slit-like pupils, as they'd been in the dream, and in the face of the little black cat I'd let into the cottage the day before.

"Y-you're the cat!" I cried, the puzzle pieces finally clicking into place.

"No shit," he muttered, then shook the creature that had been about to stab me somewhat violently, making it sputter as it tried to breathe. "Tell him to get out."

"Wh-what?!"

"You need to rescind your welcome. Tell this filth to get out of your house and to never return. He'll be forced to leave," the strange man snapped. "He took you saying welcome as you opened the door when he knocked for permission to enter, whether you intended it or not. Tell him to get out and to never come back."

"G-get out and don't ever come back!" I stammered.

The smaller creature gave a loud, irritated howl, then was jerked from the taller one's many-fingered hand, and flew towards the entryway.

In the blink of an eye, the green-eyed being was over at the door, flinging it open, so the smaller one could soar through before he shut it neatly.

It was quiet for a few moments.

"Y-you're...I-I...I thought you were a cat," I whispered.

"I know." The tall one shrugged.

Fey. He was fey. Just like Pima and her daughter. One of the high fey, too, by Mira's definition. I suspected the one that I'd just banished had been one of the low fey by that same definition.

I stood slowly. Diana and Stroopwafel appeared, both rubbing against my legs.

"That's why Diana didn't like you," I muttered, finally putting two and two together.

"She sensed what you could not." He shrugged, then reached out and turned on a lamp, allowing me to see him properly for the first time.

His ears were long and gracefully pointed, and he had raven hair styled in a short undercut with longer bangs, which framed his practically glowing green eyes. His features were sharp and dangerously attractive, but still somewhat inhuman. Indeed, now that the lights were on, I saw that the darkness had hidden what seemed to be a second set of eyes. They didn't have eyelashes, and were set back and down from his green ones, located near his high cheekbones. They were also currently closed.

The fey man also had opalescent scales wrapping around the back of his neck, with a gap in the front over his throat. They disappeared down beneath the simple white shirt he wore, though I couldn't see more on his arms. As I'd noticed earlier, his hands had one extra finger apiece, and I noticed that both of his bare feet had one less toe than mine did. He was tall, at least a good four inches taller than both of my brothers, who weren't small men. He had broad shoulders and a well-built frame that wasn't too bulky.

Though strange and inhuman, he was altogether ridiculously good-looking, which made my face heat.

"What, something on my face?" He arched an eyebrow at me, reaching up to brush his long fingers against his sharp jawline.

"S-sorry." I looked down, embarrassed to have been staring. "I-I haven't seen many fey folk."

"So I gather," he replied dryly, crossing his arms.

"How did you get into my dream like that?!" I blurted.

The fey man's strange eyes blinked in surprise. "Dreams are a lot like magic to begin with. It doesn't take much to just hop into one." he paused, "Not that it's a common gift. But if you can sense them, you can enter them."

"I...see..." I didn't see, but something told me it wouldn't make sense unless I could do it myself.

It was quiet for a few moments.

I finally broke the silence to ask, "What...what are you doing here?"

"You told me I could come in." He shrugged. When he spoke, I noticed he had a set of gleaming white fangs.

"I-I mean...I get that, but...why?"

He sighed, then went to sit on the couch opposite where I was standing, crossing his legs, and stretching his long arms out along the back. "I was injured when you found me. I needed time to recuperate."

"I-I healed you, though! Wh-why not be on your way?"

"You healed the wound, not the poison I'm still fighting," he muttered.

"Poison?" I blinked, surprised.

"Yes." He sighed, sounding annoyed and crossing his arms. "It's a stubborn kind. I'm still not up to one hundred percent."

"Oh." I frowned, not sure what else to say.

It was quiet again for a few moments.

"I...I guess you already know my name?" I asked.

He nodded.

"What should I call you?"

"Lear."

"Well, I guess it's nice to meet you, Lear." I bowed slightly, and sighed, "You're welcome to stay as long as you promise not to cause trouble, and I'll do what I can to help you. Or rather, I'll ask Diana to help me help you."

"Indeed." He rolled his eyes. "I'll tell you what I told Diana. I'm not here to cause trouble."

"Fey can't lie, right?"

"That is correct."

"Then promise you won't hurt me or any of my animals or friends or my familiar," I told him.

"Diana didn't make me." He snorted.

"What?"

"We talked last night, while you slept out here." He motioned at the living room area around us. "She took my word for it."

"I guess I'm not so trusting. Promise," I insisted.

"Very well. I promise."

"Say the whole thing."

He gave a long-suffering sigh. "I promise not to hurt you, your animals, your friends, or your familiar."

"Thank you," I said softly. How odd that Diana, in all her wisdom, hadn't made him promise such a thing. Although to be fair, she was still just a cat.

"And, just so you know, you can banish me from the house just like you did the small fry earlier, just by rescinding your welcome at any moment," he told me, lifting his hand and picking idly at a set of claws that had seemingly appeared out of nowhere.

"Claws?!" I gasped. "Where'd those come from?"

Lear's iridescent green eyes blinked once, and he held up his hand, fingers spread. "They're retractable." The claws slid slowly back into his fingertips, then leapt back out.

"O-oh."

"I have wings as well, but they're big, and I'd wind up knocking everything over if I kept them out all the time, so I keep them hidden."

"Wings?!"

He sighed annoyedly. "Yes. Try to keep up, Winna."

My face heated and I looked down. "I-I just...this is new to me."

It was quiet for a few moments.

"I know." He broke the silence. "Forgive me." He paused, then continued, "It's because of me that you saw fauns in the forest today, and that the goblin attacked you."

Chapter 8

First impressions

"That was a goblin?" Winna asked in surprise.

"Yes."

"Why was it your fault? Did you do something?"

"We can sense one another's presence," Lear replied evenly.

The young woman seemed to have trouble meeting his gaze, and dropped her wide brown eyes to where her cats were sitting. She knelt and petted them, murmuring, "Mira said she could smell another fey person on me. She thought I was one, initially. Her mother said I smelled like one as well."

"Whether we can smell it or sense it another way, we can usually tell when someone has been around us." The fey man nodded. "Normally, I'm strong enough to be able to shield my presence, but the poison affects my magic, so I've been unable to."

"Can you still sense the presence of other fey folk?"

"Yes. Although I don't smell it like the fauns do."

"I see." Her voice was quiet. "So, your presence somehow drew the goblin here?"

"I believe so. It probably passed by, sensed my presence and thought it'd be easy to get in, given I had." He doubted the goblin had realized he was strong enough to hide his presence, or it wouldn't have tried to intrude.

"So I need to be careful about opening the door, right? And definitely not say 'welcome' as I do, if that goblin was able to construe me opening it as giving permission to enter, I mean."

"Yes." He paused, then offered, "I can tell if it's a human or one of my folk at the door, so I can warn you before you open it."

She looked up at him, blinking. "Would you?

"Yes."

Winna lowered her eyes again. "Thank you."

It was quiet for a few moments, and he let himself study her more closely than he had previously.

The young woman was pretty enough, for a human. She had long, curly, honey-blonde hair that sprang up wildly, framing her dark brown eyes. Her face was sweet, with freckles sprinkled across her nose and upper cheeks, and she had a faded raspberry cupid's bow for a mouth.

She was on the taller side for a human woman, but had a slim figure, and always moved like she was in some kind of hurry. Her hands seemed perpetually restless; whether they were petting her cats or busily weaving at the loom, or occupied with making one of her salves, she was always doing something. Though, to be fair, there was a lot for her to do in a day, from what he could tell, and she worked hard to complete all of her tasks.

"Why didn't you stop the goblin sooner? It was bothering me earlier," Winna asked quietly.

"I wasn't sure if I should show myself," he replied. "I'd told Diana I'd stay in cat form while you were awake, and I didn't want to incur her wrath by taking my proper shape. Besides, it was relatively harmless, at first."

Winna smiled slightly, leaning down to kiss Diana. "I love you, miss."

Diana maowed contentedly, and purred loudly. Stroopwafel maowed in complaint, wanting more attention as well. Winna giggled, leaning over to kiss the rather silly, white-pawed tabby. "I love you too, my little menace!"

Lear shifted a little uncomfortably as the poison throbbed in his veins.

"Are you okay?" she asked softly.

He blinked, surprised she could read his discomfort so easily. But she was a healer, so perhaps it wasn't all that unusual. "This poison is uncomfortable," he muttered.

"Oh. How can I help?" Winna asked, standing and dusting off the skirt of her threadbare dress. To his surprise she sat next to him on the sofa, though she took care to leave an entire cushion between them. "Or...is it even something I can help with."

"I expect you and Diana can help at least ease the pain."

"Alright, then." She nodded, and Diana walked over, knowing she was needed. "I need touch to work." The young woman held a small hand out.

Just like that, she was willing to help him. He'd done nothing but deceive her, and had only acted to rid her home of the other intruder when he'd absolutely had to, but she was still willing to help him without any real prompting. She didn't owe him a damn thing, but was going to help him anyway.

Lear reached out, taking her small, five-fingered hand in his. Her ears were rounded as well, and he knew her body bore no scales or fur or feathers.

Humans were strange creatures. Five fingers and toes, with no particularly good means to protect themselves. It was why they were often very standoffish around fey folk, he knew. They couldn't even use magic. Or most of them couldn't, anyway. The young woman before him was an exception, of course. Her magic would even keep her young, and he expected she'd already stopped aging, though thirty wasn't very old at all by fey standards.

Winna looked away, her face heating slightly at the contact of their hands. "Diana," she murmured, and the cat hopped up between them. The human mage reached out and placed her other hand gently on the cat's back, then took a deep breath.

Magic surged, and Diana glowed with a golden light, her iridescent blue-green eyes sparkling like gemstones. The pink triangle on Winna's hand glowed weakly, and Lear felt the magic ease into him as golden sparks skittered across his entire form.

"F*cking hell..." he groaned, leaning his head back against the couch.

The magic felt wonderful, like slipping into a bath after a long day. Any and all pain melted away.

"Are you alright?" Winna asked softly.

"Yes." He sighed. "It just feels good."

"Good," she murmured, sounding pleased.

After what felt like far too short a time, the magic faded, and she pulled her hand from his. For a split second, he fancied keeping her hand in his, just to see how she'd react, but instead he let her pull it away. There was no point in poking fun at her, really, and she'd just helped him, so teasing her would be poor repayment of that.

"Thank you."

"You're welcome!" Her sweet smile appeared. "Let me know if it starts to hurt again, and we'll be happy to help again." The smile faltered. "How long does the poison linger?"

"A while," he admitted, then added, "But with you and Diana's help, it'll go faster, I expect."

"Right."

"May I stay until it's gone?"

"I already said you could."

"It doesn't hurt to ask again."

"Fair point." She shrugged, standing. "Are you hungry?"

"Yes."

Winna walked to the kitchen. "I'll make dinner. I'm sorry it's so late."

He followed her, leaning his back against the countertop.

"Don't apologize. You were resting, and I can handle waiting. In theory, I could have gotten food for myself if I were particularly hungry."

She paused, turning to grimace at him. "You've been eating cat food this whole time! I'm sorry."

"If I cared, I'd have done something about it," he told her. "It was dried fish, anyway. It was a perfectly acceptable thing for me to eat."

"Still," Winna mumbled.

It was quiet for a few moments.

"I'm terrible at cooking," Lear admitted, "but if you'll give me a task and show me exactly how to do it, I'm usually a quick study."

Her dark eyes blinked. "Oh, um...Sure." She thought for a moment, "Think you could peel potatoes."

"I'm decent with a knife." He shrugged, pleased she'd picked an easy task. Though given that he'd already told her he was bad at cooking, she'd have hardly picked anything difficult.

"Alright then." Winna showed him how to peel a potato, though he probably could have figured that much out for himself, then had him sit at the table and set him to work.

"Put the peels in a separate bowl. I'll make vegetable stock with them."

"Yes ma'am." He nodded.

Her dark eyes blinked, and she turned back to the carrots she was peeling. "You're surprisingly polite."

"Did you expect otherwise?"

"Well...in that dream, which I realize was more than just a dream now, you weren't very polite," she muttered.

Lear shrugged. "I was trying to see how you'd react."

"Why?"

"To see if you were really as you seemed."

"As I seemed."

"Naive, flighty, easy to intimidate." He waved his hand idly.

"Geez, thanks," the young woman grumbled.

"Don't be upset. I was wrong. You weren't quite as naive as I expected, and not nearly as easy to intimidate," he replied, then added, "Though maybe a little flighty."

Winna paused, then sighed and murmured, "I am all three of those things, though. I thought it was a dream, so I didn't take it as seriously as I should. I...know I'm naive. I've stayed in the same little area for my entire life. I know very little of the world, and am scared of so many things."

"You're not scared of me," he pointed out. "Or, not as much as you should be."

Winna turned to him, clearly confused. "You saved me from getting stabbed, why should I be afraid?"

"I could have done it with the expectation of a favor in return," Lear replied evenly.

She cocked her head to the side, dark eyes appraising. "You didn't, though, I can tell."

He nodded. "See? You're not as naive as you think, either. You have good instincts."

I frowned. "I...I don't know."

"Trust those instincts. They're good," Lear told me, then asked, "Do you want me to chop the potatoes too."

"Uh, yes. Try two-inch pieces."

"What are you making?"

"Oh, um, roast chicken with potatoes and carrots, and rolls. Is that alright? You're not vegetarian or anything."

"No."

"Any allergies I should know about? I'd hate to kill you with my cooking." I grimaced.

"No. I'm not picky either, given I can't cook."

"It's a good skill to have," I told him.

"I'm sure. I may be skilled in many things, but I've burned enough food to know that it's one area I'm not inherently gifted in. Cutting vegetables is easy enough, but actually cooking is more difficult."

"Well, I guess not everyone can be good at it. How'd you survive so long if you can't cook? I guess your spouse does the cooking."

His green cat eyes blinked. "I'm not married. I have kitchen staff."

"Oh."

It was quiet for a few moments. I finished chopping up the carrots, and began kneading flour for rolls.

After a short while, Lear brought the potatoes to me. "Here."

"Thank you!"

"You're welcome." He nodded, drifting back to the table and sitting again.

"Kitchen staff. Must be nice," I mused. So he was wealthy, then, wealthy enough to have at least kitchen staff. That meant more than one; had it been just one, he'd have said he had a cook. Something told me that, if he had kitchen staff, he likely had even more servants. Goodness, what must he think of my simple little life here at my cottage?

"Yes."

"This must be quite a change of pace then," I murmured.

"You're not wrong," Lear replied. "But it's peaceful here."

"Well, normally it is. It's been a bit lively here the last couple of days." I sighed.

"That's my fault. Again, I'm sorry."

"Jedda's barn burning down was hardly your fault." I scoffed, shaking my head slightly.

"I wonder about that though," he said thoughtfully, getting up to stand beside me, leaning against the counter once more, arms crossed.

"What do you mean?"

"He said his farm hands insisted that no lamps had been left on. So how did it catch fire? It wasn't as if there was a thunderstorm where lightning could have struck the structure."

"True." I shrugged.

"And I got the sense of a fey about them."

"Oh, that's what you were getting at. Why not just lead with that?"

"Well, it could just be coincidence. Fey folk do live everywhere, whether anyone else realizes it." Lear shrugged.

"Do you think a fey person caused the fire?"

"It's possible. Jedda and his son-in-law smelled like smoke, given they'd been helping fight the fire, and the smoke's presence had a slightly magical feel to it." The fey man let his voice trail off.

It was quiet for a few moments.

"If...if there's a chance that fey folk caused the fire, whether maliciously or otherwise, we need to warn Jedda and his family, so they can keep an eye out and hopefully keep it from happening again."

"That would be wise." He nodded.

"But without proof, I'm not sure they'll believe me. I know we're close, but given that we've always thought there weren't many fey folk around here, without proof I'm not sure they'll really buy it."

"Having a fey person on your arm would go far to convince them, I think. I'll go with you."

"Are you sure?" I looked over at him.

"Yes."

"Then we'll go tomorrow. I don't want anyone else getting hurt in any more fires," I told him, putting the pan of rolls into the oven.

"Of course." Lear nodded.

I pulled off my apron. "Dinner will be ready soon."

"Thank you."

"You're welcome. I don't always feel like cooking, and sometimes just kind of eat whatever. Will you be okay on those days? You'll be welcome to raid the cold box and the pantry, of course."

"I'm not always at home with staff to cater to me." He snorted, "And when I'm away, I still manage."

"If you say so." I shrugged.

It was quiet for a few moments.

"Where are you from?"

"I live in the forest of the feylands."

I frowned, going to sit at my loom and starting to work. "You're pretty far from home. What took you this far north."

"Orders," he replied.

"Orders?" I blinked, realizing what that meant. "You're a soldier."

"Yes."

"What orders were they?" As far as I knew, no humans had really had military dealings with any fey for a very long time, and there had been peace between the human and fey crowns for centuries now.

Lear was quiet for a few moments. "I was sent to deal with an errant member of my kin."

I could read between the lines. "An assassin mission?"

"More or less." He shrugged, coming and standing behind me. The fey man reached out and touched the top of the shawl I was working on, which was still attached to the loom. The six long fingers on his right hand danced lightly over the rich blue fibers. "You have clever hands."

My face heated. "Thanks."

"What's it going to be?"

"A shawl. I'll infuse it with some magic, warming or healing, with Diana's help, and take it to town to sell. I'm going to do that with more than just this one. I have several more already made and ready to be enchanted."

"I can see how they'd be popular." He nodded.

"I'm trying to save up for a new stove. Dern, he's a dwarf who lives in town, has some that are magical, like the heating stones, and I'd really like one."

"Is there something wrong with the one you currently have?"

"The legs are starting to rust, the front of the oven has already fallen off several times, and I've had to rig it up in order to keep using it, and it doesn't heat evenly."

"I see." He nodded.

It was quiet for a few moments.

"I might keep one of the shawls for myself. I'll leave it unenchanted, but I could use a new one," I muttered. I could use an entirely new wardrobe, really. Jedda had noted that the dress I'd worn had been in bad shape, but it definitely wasn't the only one.

"How many have you made so far?"

"Oh...about five. This'll be six, I think," I told him.

"Can I see them?"

I blinked, surprised at the request, but wasn't displeased. In fact, it was kind of nice to have someone want to see something I'd been working so hard on. I was pretty proud of them, too, since I'd used several patterns. "Sure!"

Chapter 9

Food

Winna brightened visibly at his request. Her sweet features lit up, and her eyes sparkled. She had too few people to share her art with, after all, she lived a fairly isolated life out in her little cottage. Because her weaving was art. He idly wondered if she realized exactly how much skill she had in it.

The young human woman stood, crossing the room to a closet from which she retrieved a box. Walking over to the table, she set the box down almost reverently, and pulled out its contents, laying them carefully out for him to see.

A rainbow of rich hues soon splashed across the table.

"You're a very skilled weaver, Winna," he told her, reaching out and carefully lifting one of the shawls to inspect it. "Did you do the embroidery as well?"

"Um, yes," she murmured, her face flushing in pleasure at the compliment.

"It's very nice as well." He placed the piece back down, then reached out to brush his fingers against the rest of them. He noticed her dark eyes were drawn repeatedly to one that was a spring like green, dotted with pink petals and golden flowers. "Is that one your favorite?"

"Yeah." Winna smiled, reaching out to brush her small fingers lovingly against it. "It'll fetch a good price though. I'll keep one without the embellishments. It'll suit my simple wardrobe better."

Lear reached out and picked up the green shawl, stepping forward and slipping it around her small shoulders. "It suits you. You should keep it, if it's your favorite."

"But-"

"Why keep a plain one?" he asked. "It serves no purpose. You worked hard, you should keep the one you like the most. The others will sell, so it doesn't matter."

Her face flushed more deeply. "I-I..."

The fey man studied her for a few moments. What he'd initially thought of as just a passing interest struck him suddenly as a deep-seated sense of attraction to the lonely, young, human woman who stood before him. A strange development indeed, especially over the course of just a couple of hours. And given her reactions to him, blushing and trying not to stare, it wasn't entirely one-sided. That wasn't so strange. Fey were known to draw humans in, even those of his folk who were less conventionally attractive by fey standards than he was.

To his surprise, she stepped away, looking down. "I-I shouldn't."

"Why not?"

"I know it'll sell," she mumbled.

"That's no reason not to keep it, especially if you like it." He tilted his head to the side. "There's no reason for you to not have things you like. Especially if it's something you yourself made. Keep it."

Winna's dark eyes flickered up to him. "I-I...guess you're right."

He stepped towards the human mage again, reaching out to tie the shawl loosely, holding her gaze. Lear knew full well that his eyes were somewhat hypnotizing in nature, and his flirtatious nature desperately wanted to draw her in, to see how she'd react. To lean down and pull her close, to have his lips so close to her skin that-

But the young woman broke that train of thought and desire by shaking herself suddenly, blinking, and pulling away once more as she glanced at the clock.

"The food will be ready soon," she announced, as if sparks hadn't just been flying between them. Or maybe it had just been on his part? Had he misread her so badly?

Winna hurried back into the kitchen area, still wearing the shawl, her small fingers curled into the loose knot he'd tied.

Lear felt his hand drift out, wanting her to return. He pulled it back with an effort. Normally, it was fey folk who easily wove (pun not intended, but very appropriate) a spell of enchantment over humans, yet it was he who found himself oddly entranced. How strange.

The flush that lingered on her face told him that he hadn't misread her reactions. There was a mutual sense of attraction. But she was human, and that meant she was probably different from anyone he'd ever found himself interested in before. As much as he preferred to be physical very quickly in regard to his attraction, he recognized that she might not. Whether that was because she was human, or it was just her personality, he didn't know. What he did know was that he could slow his pace to something more comfortable for her. There was no point in upsetting her, after all.

Seeing she was busy getting the food into serving dishes, he darted to the cupboard and put out the place settings.

"Oh. Thank you," she said, upon turning and seeing the table ready.

"Just because I can't cook doesn't mean I can't set a table." He shrugged.

"Fair point." Winna bobbed her head as she put the basket of rolls on the table, and then the dish that held the main course. "Normally I'd have a salad with this, but given it's winter..."

"This is plenty," he told her. After a pause, he added, "And it smells amazing." Compliments never hurt anyone.

Her face warmed again. "Thank you." She motioned at the table. "Have a seat. What do you want to drink?"

"Any chance you have wine?"

"No, sorry. Just milk and water, really. I should have led with that, given the lack of options." She frowned.

"Water is fine." He shrugged, sitting.

Winna got them both a glass of water, then sat across from him. "Please help yourself."

Lear's luminous green eyes had dominated my vision for a few moments. I could see myself sinking into them and never coming up again.

But my common sense had slapped the daydream of what it must be like to kiss him right outta my thoughts, and I'd immediately torn myself away.

Fey folk were strange, I knew, and I shouldn't have stared so shamelessly up at him. He was only staying until he was healed, and then he'd be gone. There was no sense in getting a crush on him. Besides, I was just a weak, little, country-bumpkin, human mage. Nothing to write back to his fey home about.

I chided myself for dwelling on how attractive he was. The fey man had four eyes, scales, claws, wings, fangs, and the wrong number of fingers and toes, for crying out loud! There was also every chance he was just toying with me until he had to leave.

Dinner had been pleasant enough, with small talk about the weather lately, how it had been a dreadfully cold winter, though we'd had altogether less snow than usual. It had all been very respectable, no gazing longingly into one another's eyes. Or me gazing into his eyes like an idiot, flattering myself to think that he earnestly returned the attraction.

Stretching out my legs in the warm water, I sighed. Soaking in the bath was perfect for easing away worries. And embarrassments, in this case.

Finally, I hauled myself out and dried off, slipped into my night-gown, then left the bathroom. "Lear, do you want the room you slept in as a cat?" I asked, walking into the living room area.

"I don't care where I sleep. That room was fine."

"Alright." I nodded.

"Everything okay? You were in there for a while," he commented.

"I just needed a good soak. It's been a long couple of days." I sighed. Not that he'd actually been there long enough to know how long I usually spent in the bath. That said, I couldn't help but appre-ciate his concern.

"Fair enough. Diana was sitting at attention. I worried something had snuck in without me noticing, but there weren't any unexpected heat presences."

I blinked, frowning at that. "What now?"

Lear's second set of eyes flicked open. Instead of having white parts and irises, they were completely blue. No whites, no irises, just a somewhat luminous, deep blue. "These see heat."

Feeling confused at being confronted with his inhuman nature, I looked away. "O-oh."

"Something about that...bothers you."

"No, not exactly. It's just different."

"I'm not human." He took a step forward.

"I know." I fell back half a pace. "This is just still new to me." I forced a smile and looked up. "Sorry, I hope I didn't offend."

"Very little you could do or say would offend me," was his quiet reply. "I know you're not used to fey folk yet."

"Maybe don't use those second eyes to look at me while I'm in the bath, though? That's an invasion of privacy." I arched an eyebrow at him.

"You're right. Please forgive me." He nodded, "I'm not typically a peeping Tom."

"I hope not!" I frowned. "Otherwise, I won't be letting you stay!"

72

"Understandably so." Lear shrugged.

There was a pause.

My curiosity led me to break the silence, "Do you usually keep your second set of eyes open all the time? If so, please don't keep them shut just because I'm still getting used to all this. Just...don't watch me in the bath." I snorted.

"I don't, actually. Two layers of sight at all times is a little overwhelming. I do appreciate the thought, though."

"Fair enough." I shrugged. "Well, I'm getting ready to head to bed, but don't feel like you have to."

"I probably will as well."

"I want to head to Jedda's farm pretty early. I'll take care of my chores, we'll eat breakfast, and then go around eight, is that alright."

"Of course." He bowed slightly. "Goodnight, Winna."

"Goodnight, Lear."

-

Early the next morning, I was sitting on the floor, re-lacing my boots when, much to my surprise, the door opened, admitting Lear.

"The chores are done," he announced.

"Oh." I blinked, having not realized he was even awake.

"I'd have made breakfast, but given my inability regarding cooking..." he let his voice trail off, then shook his head. "I'd like to at least partially pull some weight around here."

"Well, thank you." I kicked off my boots. "I'm glad to not have to go out into the cold so soon after waking up, for once. Were the animals alright?" He would know all the chores I did from watching me do them for the couple of days he'd lived in the barn as a cat.

"Yes." He held out a six-fingered hand to me.

I took it, and let him pull me up. This took him seemingly no effort at all, and put me fairly close to him. Remembering my mistake of standing too close to him, and staring into his eyes the night before, I averted my gaze and immediately stepped away. Heading towards the kitchen, I told him, "I'll start on breakfast."

Lear didn't say anything, but I heard his light footfalls following behind me.

Finally, he asked, "Is there anything easy I can help with?"

"No, just relax." I smiled, shaking my head. "But I appreciate it."

"Would you teach me?"

"What?" I turned, surprised at the request.

"To cook. I said I've burned enough things to know I'm not good at it, but..." his iridescent eyes drifted to the stove, "I've never actually tried very hard to learn."

Another smile found its way across my face. "Of course! Mind you, I only make simple things, but I'm happy to share what I do know!"

"Thank you."

"Come on, I'll show you how to fry eggs. That's pretty easy. And instead of biscuits, we'll make toast."

Soon, I was narrating every movement that I made.

"So, it's really not very hard," I explained, sliding a couple of eggs onto a serving plate. "But having a stove that's better at keeping a steady heat would help solve most of the problems I had."

"I see." He nodded.

"Do you want to try?"

The luminescent eyes blinked once. "I..."

"Come on, you can do it," I told him, smiling. Stepping aside so he could take my place at the stove, I pushed the spatula into his hand. "I'll stay here and walk you through it."

"I'll probably burn it," Lear muttered, unconvinced.

"Have some faith in yourself!" I laughed. "And me! I'll keep an eye on the heat too. I'm not going to not help."

"Alright then." He eyed the spatula warily.

It was kind of funny, really. He was a fey soldier, and had likely seen and done terrifying things, but here he was, wary of cooking.

Lear cracked an egg into a bowl, and had to pick out a couple of bits of shell with his long, lithe fingers.

"That's alright. It still happens to me, too, and I've been cooking for more than twenty years now," I told him.

Soon, the egg was crackling away in the pan.

"It's cooking a little fast, turn the heat on the burner down," I suggested.

"Alright." He reached down and cranked the burner down.

"Not that far! Sorry, I wasn't specific enough!" I reached out and adjusted the heat.

"Sorry." He grimaced slightly.

"No, that was my fault!" I laughed, shaking my head. "I'm probably not a very good teacher, which doesn't help. But you're doing well despite that!"

"A slight miscommunication hardly makes you an inept teacher," he replied in an even tone, reaching out with the spatula and prodding the egg in the skillet.

Something about that made my face heat, and I looked away, stammering, "Y-you can probably try flipping it."

"Sure." He shrugged. Sliding the spatula under the egg, he flipped it easily with a slight jerk of his wrist.

"Good job! That's better than I manage most of the time!" I laughed. "Are you sure you're not just pretending to not know how to cook?"

"I'm a spoiled rich brat, I have no clue how this works. It's more like black magic than anything I've ever encountered." Lear snorted, shaking his head.

That drew another snort of laughter from me. "Well, you're doing fine. Keep up the good work!" I told him. "Do you drink coffee?"

"Yes."

"Alright, then." I set about making the fragrant drink.

Soon, he had a pile of fried eggs on the plate.

"That's probably enough! Unless you think you'll want more? I'll only eat two," I said as I pulled the coffee pot off the stove, and poured the coffee over a strainer into mugs for us.

The fey man nodded. "It'll be enough."

Next, I showed him how to make toast, which we did by cranking up the heat in the oven and putting slices of bread onto a wire rack until they achieved the desired color.

"That's even easier than the eggs," he observed. His tone was mild, but not displeased.

"Yes, the oven behaved this time," I told him. "Sometimes it doesn't and burns everything. We lucked out."

"I'm glad."

Soon the table was set, and I brought him a cup of coffee. "Do you want anything in that?"

"No, I take it black."

"Alright." I nodded, getting the milk jug out of the cold cabinet and splashing some into my own coffee. "Oh, the fruit." I hurried and tossed some dried fruit, leftover from that year's harvest, onto a plate. "It's dry, but it's still pretty good."

Lear took some dried apple slices, and added them to his plate. "Thank you for teaching me."

"You're welcome!" I smiled, "You were right, you're a quick learner."

The fey man only shrugged.

It was quiet as we ate for a few moments. "I'd like to learn more, if you don't mind to keep teaching me."

"Of course!" I nodded. "Like I said, it's a good skill. And when you're out on orders, you can translate it to cooking over a fire, if there's not an inn to be had."

"True."

Chapter 10

A Visitor

They lapsed into silence again, but he could feel Winna's curious eyes on him. Looking up, he caught her gaze and smiled. "Ask your question."

Her face flushed, and she looked away. "I...just worry it's rude."

"Like I said before, very little you could say or do would offend me. Please ask."

"Why were you a cat?"

"That's not rude," he assured her. "I'd shifted shape to escape from a bad situation, and got hit by the poison. It kept me too weak to change out of cat form until your magic broke through it."

"Oh. Why a cat, though?"

Lear shrugged. "Why not? I like cats, they're small and agile and able to protect themselves." He paused, then added, "I don't actually have a choice in it. That's the only other shape I can take. But it suits me just fine." He reached over and back a little, to where Diana was sitting, listening to their conversation.

The little familiar stared at his hand, unimpressed.

"Still not a fan, eh?" he asked, smiling

Diana sniffed, shaking her head back and forth rapidly, like she did whenever something got in her ear.

Stroopwafel, on the other hand, maowed and be-bopped forward, happy to have the attention if her sister didn't want it. The ridiculous little feline purred loudly, pushing her head into his hand.

"What silly gooses!" Winna giggled, getting up from the couch to sit on the ground beside the two cats. She reached out to pet them both, petting Stroopwafel on the back, which allowed Lear to continue scratching the cat's ears. Diana allowed her mistress's touch and began to purr as well.

Lear let himself watch the young woman, taking in every inch of her small face and form with his excellent vision. Wanting to see her even more clearly, he opened his second eyes. Her heat signature was a warm, rosy pink.

As he watched her, somewhat enamored, he heard movement outside the cottage. The fey man turned, frowning and alerting her, "We have company. Human company."

"What? This early?" She frowned, seeming startled.

There was a knock at the door. Lear's heat vision told him it was a man.

Winna hurried to the door, and opened it. "Yes."

The fey man shut his second set of eyes, and watched the scene unfold.

"I'm sorry to bother you so early Winna, but I knew you'd be up already," the man said. He appeared to be in his thirties with brown hair, blue eyes, and a handsome enough face.

"Is something wrong, Paz? You're not hurt, are you?"

"No, no." He shook his head. "I just didn't know who else to go to about it, it's...kind of strange, and you're the strangest person I know, magic and everything."

"Geez, thanks," Winna muttered.

The man, Paz, flushed. "No, sorry. I didn't mean it like that. It's just...something odd has been going on with my sheep. I didn't know who else to go to, since it is very weird. I wanted to ask what you thought before we did anything. You're pretty smart about stuff." An admiring note had crept into the man's voice as he'd spoken the last sentence.

Lear didn't like the man's admiring tone, nor the way he gazed down at Winna. The fey man had known her for a mere handful of days, and she'd really only known him for one, at most, but the situation irked him. He knew he had no right to her or any sort of claim on her, but the potential for competition in regard to her affection riled him.

"I don't know about that, but come in out of the cold." Winna sighed, stepping aside. Lear stood and walked over to join them.

"Thank you." Paz stepped in, then froze upon catching sight of Lear. "What the-?!"

"Oh, I should have warned you, I have a guest. This is Lear, he's staying here until he's healed," Winna told the man matter-of-factly.

"A fey patient? You've never taken fey before." Paz's gaze was mistrustful.

"There's a first time for everything." Winna shrugged. "I'd have taken them sooner if the opportunity arose. I don't turn anyone away, provided they don't cause me trouble."

"Fey often cause trouble though," Paz muttered.

"You're not wrong." Lear replied mildly. "But I'm not here to cause any problems, just to heal. She's already helped me more than I can repay."

"I-I don't know about that." The young woman's face flushed pink. Pink looked nice on her, in his not-so-humble opinion.

Paz blinked, then said, "You're too kind, Winna, I'm always worried someone will take advantage of that kindness." His eyes flickered to Lear as he spoke.

"I won't allow it," Lear said quietly, opening his second set of eyes, wanting to unnerve the man.

It worked, and Paz looked away.

"Are you two done with whatever is going on here?" Winna crossed her arms, looking back and forth between them, apparently not blind to the tension that hung thick in the air.

"What are you talking about?" Paz asked, trying to save face.

"Not nearly as naive as you think. Give yourself more credit." Lear smirked, sitting down. In his mind, it was better if she knew that he found her attractive, lest she worry the attraction was only one-sided.

Winna narrowed her eyes at them, then scoffed. "Men. And people wonder why I'm not married!"

Paz's face flushed at that comment, and he opened his mouth to speak, but Lear bore into him with his gaze. The other man took the hint and remained silent.

"Now, have you had breakfast yet, Paz?" Winna asked.

"Uh, yes, but I could eat again." The human man glanced hopefully at the table.

"Have a seat," she said, going and pouring another cup of coffee, and setting it down on the table in front of him before resuming her seat. She waited until Paz had a mouthful of food before saying, "I'm teaching Lear to cook, how'd he do."

The man choked, then coughed, taking a drink of coffee before sputtering, "It's fine!"

"Good. Now what's going on with your sheep? It must be something really weird, if you came here this early."

"We've had several sheep killed lately."

"Wolves."

"No, that's just it. Not a scratch on them, just stone-cold dead."

"Are there any signs of illness or anything? I can treat animals, you know."

He shook his head. "That's what we thought at first, but then one night, I swear I saw..." his voice trailed off.

"I can't help you if you don't tell me what you saw, Paz." Winna rolled her eyes.

"I swear I saw a shadow moving on its own. It...it disappeared

80

into a sheep's shadow, and the animal collapsed a few moments later. I ran forward to check on it, and as I approached, I saw the weird shadow slip away. There was nothing to cast it or anything. And the sheep was dead."

"Ah shit." Lear sighed, rubbing his face.

Paz looked up at him. "That's not appropriate language!"

"Paz, I've heard you say far worse. Don't act like we didn't go to school together." Winna crossed her arms, looking annoyed.

"I wouldn't say stuff like that around you now!" Paz protested.

"The point is, I don't care." She turned her dark eyes to Lear. "Why the reaction?"

"Sounds like shadow demons."

"Demons?!" Paz's voice was a shocked sort of squeak.

"It's a misnomer. They're not actual demons, they're a type of fey. Dangerous enough, but not too difficult to deal with if you know how."

"What should I do?" Winna asked softly. "I'm just a healer, I don't know if I could do anything even if I knew what to do."

"You're right, I don't think you could do anything, no offense."

"None taken." She shrugged. "But we can't just let the sheep keep getting attacked. What if they move on from sheep to humans?"

"They will, given time. But I'll deal with them. Are you still wanting to go to Jedda's farm?"

"Yes."

"We'll go speak with Jedda, then we'll deal with this."

"Alright then." Winna turned to the human man. "Paz, we'll be along after we go to Jedda's."

"Alright." He nodded, drinking the last of his coffee and standing. "Thank you for coming." He directed his comment to Winna, but his gaze flickered to Lear, still clearly mistrustful.

"He's not going to cause any trouble. Now scoot." The young woman rolled her eyes at him again, and he made for the door, then paused.

Turning, he said, "Thank you, I really appreciate it." Paz gave what he probably thought was his most winning, lady-killing smile.

It only got him another eye roll from the mage. "Get." She shooed him from the cottage.

"He did not like me being here." Lear snorted after the door swung shut.

"You didn't do yourself any favors." She arched an eyebrow at him. "He thinks any male being that looks at me is some kind of competition, though I've no mind to ever be with him."

"Why not?"

"Thinks women should stay in the kitchen."

"Ah, one of those sorts. And here I was thinking he'd reacted so poorly at me having made the food because I was fey."

"It was a little bit of both. That's why I waited until he'd eaten it to tell him!" She giggled mischievously.

Lear grinned, pleased to see she had a rebellious streak. Then his smile faltered. "So he thinks women should stick to the house, but was perfectly willing to come get you to help with this."

Winna's dark eyes rolled yet again. "Only because he wants me to hop-to for him, and try to convince me to let him court me. Unfortunately, it's a little hard to say no to helping when I am willing to help everyone to the best of my ability."

A thrill of anger coursed through him. "And he had the audacity to say that he worried someone would take advantage of your kindness?!"

"Yeah, he was projecting." She shrugged, and resumed eating.

"Tch." Lear shot an annoyed look at the door. "Piece of shit."

Winna snorted. "He's not really a bad man. He just thinks he can change my mind, but in the end, I'm not interested, and he can't get that through his thick skull."

"I'm sorry."

"It's alright. I should probably feel flattered. I'm something of an old maid now that I'm thirty."

"That's not old." It was Lear's turn to roll his eyes.

She shrugged. "Most women are married by twenty-one around here, and usually they get hitched younger than that. I'm sort of an odd one out. But it's alright, I'm not worried about it." Winna looked around fondly at her cottage. "I'm happy with the life I have here. I have everything I need."

"Good for you," Lear murmured.

It was quiet for a few moments.

"On that note, why aren't you married? You're handsome enough and have a pleasant personality." She looked at him curiously.

"I guess it does beg the question." He sighed. "I've never felt inclined. It's different for my people, though. Humans pair off for life, or that's typically their intention. It's less frequently the intention with my kin. So much so that a fey marriage, in its oldest and truest sense, is incredibly rare, given it's magically binding, and doesn't allow the married couple to feel anything but love for one another, and leaves us unable to feel desire for anyone else. Very few of us are interested in such a binding situation.

"That sounds like a good thing though. Love forever, and no wandering eyes. How is that a bad thing?"

"We in the high fey courts often wear our promiscuity like a badge of honor, of sorts. So to bind ourselves in such a way to one person is seen as giving up what's considered a very intrinsically fey aspect of our beings." Lear shrugged. "And it kind of takes away an aspect of our free will, which we don't like the thought of. That said, the one couple I knew that went so far are very happy and in love."

"Huh. I wish humans had something like that," she muttered.

"Well, it also really is something to be cautious with. Just because you love someone doesn't mean you'll be happy with them. Imagine being stuck in a marriage where you're compelled to love the other person, and they you, but you're ultimately not happy or fulfilled in life, and a different, more wisely-chosen partner might have not led to that."

Winna was quiet for a little while. "I...I see your point. I shouldn't equate love with happiness. That's a fallacy, really. Just because you love someone doesn't mean you'll be happy."

"Exactly."

There was another pause.

"Well, I've learned a lot more about fey folk than I ever thought I would in the last few days."

"I hope that's not a bad thing." Lear smiled slightly.

"It's not. I like learning," she assured him, then stood. "We should get going."

"Of course." He stood and helped her clear off the table, and they quickly did the dishes.

"Thank you for helping," the young woman murmured.

"I want to pull my own weight as much as possible." He shrugged.

"I still appreciate it." She sat down and started struggling into her boots, then frowned and looked up at him. "You don't have any boots or a coat or anything."

"No, I don't."

"I think I have some of my dad's old clothes stashed away somewhere." She stood again, went to a closet, then started to dig through it.

"I don't actually need them. We don't feel temperature extremes the same way humans do."

"Oh?" She pulled out of the closet to look at him for a moment, then sighed and shook her head. "Well, I think folks around here will find you a little less...unusual if you dress like they do, based on the weather."

"Fair enough." He shrugged. It was in his best interest for the locals to not dislike him.

"I hope it'll fit though, you're taller than dad was, and both of my brothers." The young woman frowned.

"I can adjust clothing to fit with magic."

"Oh? Well that's handy." She finally pulled out a coat and a pair of socks and boots. "Here."

Lear took them. "Thanks."

"You're welcome." Winna nodded.

He slipped his feet into the thick socks, then into the boots. "The boots fit well."

"Good." Winna looked over from lacing up her own shoes. "And the coat."

"Too tight in the shoulders. I'll just make it a bit bigger," he muttered, then pulled for his magic to adjust it. Intense pain shot through him as his magic surged, thanks to the poison. He grimaced, reining his power back in and shrugging out of the coat with a wince. "Uh...it's fine. I don't need one."

"The poison?" she asked softly, looking up from tying her boots.

"Yes." He hung the coat on the coat rack. "I'll be alright."

"Are you sure you won't be cold?" Her face was full of concern.

Gentle warmth spread through him at her worry for him. It was entirely misplaced, but very sweet. "I'll be fine, I promise."

"I keep forgetting you can't lie." Winna chewed her lip in a way that was surprisingly endearing. "Tell me you won't be cold or uncomfortable."

"I won't be cold or uncomfortable," he told her readily, then reached out and helped her up.

Instead of immediately stepping away, she frowned, eyeing his shirt. It was long-sleeved, but likely not as thick as a human would want in the winter.

"Hm. Well, I at least have a scarf you can wear." She went to the coat rack, pulled a scarf off, then paused and brightened. "Oh, wait! I have a cloak! That'll work!" She hurried back to the closet, dug around again for a moment, then triumphantly held out a long black cloak.

"Yes, that'll work." He took the cloak, and shrugged it on. "It does fit well."

"Good." Winna smiled, clearly pleased with the end effect.

"Well, let's go. I'll need to hook Poppy up to the cart if we're both going to get there."

"No need. You can ride, I'll fly."

Her large, dark eyes blinked. "I forgot you have wings."

"It's not surprising, you haven't even seen them yet."

"I guess."

"Come on. I'll help you get her saddled, and then we'll go."

Chapter 11

A Trip

L ear could move very swiftly, when he wanted, and Poppy was saddled up in record time.

"Do you want help getting into the saddle?" he asked.

I blinked as I stroked my sweet pony's mane. "Are you calling me short?"

"A little."

"Well, I'm not that short. Not really. I'm just shorter than you." I swung up onto Poppy. "See?"

"Point taken." He flashed a wickedly attractive, fanged smile at me.

"So..." I toyed a little shyly with the reins, peeking over at him. "You're going to fly?" I had to admit, I'd been looking forward to seeing that, given that I'd never seen anyone fly before. It wouldn't be a big deal for him, since he was fey, but it *would* be interesting for me.

"Yes, but you'll need to take this." He shrugged out of the cloak. "I'll put it back on when I land. It doesn't have slits for my wings."

"Oh, right." I took the cloak.

There was a surge of magic, and Lear grimaced briefly, then suddenly, a pair of enormous, jet black wings materialized from thin air. "There we are. This is all of me." He bowed slightly, as if meeting me for the first time.

"I see why you keep them hidden! They're huge! How does that work, though? Do they just disappear from sight, or are they really not there?"

"They're really not there. I can explain later, but we should get to Jedda's, right? That way, we can go deal with the shadow demons for Paz in a timely manner."

"Yes, yes of course." I shook myself, tearing my eyes away from his lovely feathers.

"Alright." He took a few steps back, flashed another grin at me, then leapt with seemingly little effort some ten feet up into the air. The enormous wings opened with a snap, and he shot higher into the air with a couple of powerful down-strokes.

I stared in awe. Honestly, it was ridiculously attractive, somehow. How was I supposed to not be attracted to the ridiculous fey man?! Gods, this really wasn't fair.

"Don't drool," he called down, smirking. Knowing that he was really just toying with me was the worst. Hopefully he wouldn't comment on how red my face had flushed as his comment.

I shook myself. He was very well aware of how attractive he was, and wasn't afraid to tease me with it and about it. "That's really not fair," I muttered, then nudged Poppy with my heels, setting out on the path that would take me to Jedda's house.

"I'll take you up sometime, when it's not so cold," he called down.

I blinked, looking up and asking in a normal voice, "Can you hear me?"

"Yes!" he called, as he flew almost lazily above me and Poppy, easily keeping pace.

"Oh."

"I have good hearing. My folk often do."

"Clearly! So I can't whisper secrets to anyone with you around."

"Who would you be whispering to? You're only really around me."

"I might want to tell Diana something!" I replied, sticking my tongue out at him.

His laugh was carried down to me on the wind. I'd have stopped to appreciate the view of that laugh, since his smile really was ridiculously attractive, but the wind was bitterly cold, rendering me too busy to do anything but shiver. I huddled down into my coat, wishing I'd worn more layers.

"Put the cloak on if you're cold." His voice was now concerned.

"Oh, good idea." I tossed the cloak I was carrying for him around my shoulders, and buttoned it. "That's much better."

"Good."

"It's kind of nice having company," I mused aloud.

"It is," he agreed.

"Are you usually alone?"

"Yes."

"I know you were sent on a specific sort of mission this time, but do you not usually travel with other soldiers?"

"Very infrequently, these days. Though, when I am back home, I typically coordinate with other soldiers and train new recruits."

Given what I knew about how the military worked, that meant he wasn't just some enlisted man. "You're an officer."

"Yes."

"What rank?"

"A captain."

"Interesting. My dad was in the military when he was younger."

"Oh."

"He wasn't an officer, though, but he was proud to have served."

"He should be. I've heard it's an honor for humans."

"Is it not for fey."

"Not particularly. We're a lot harder to kill, so it's less of a noble gesture and more because we want to be violent."

"I see."

"Not that we don't take our military service seriously." He paused. "Or rather, I take it seriously."

"Did you join because you wanted to be violent?"

My fey companion swooped low and hovered close to me, keeping pace with Poppy. "Would you think less of me if that was the case?" He cocked his head to the side, emerald green eyes trained on me.

"I don't know," I admitted.

Lear was quiet for a moment, then sighed, shrugging slightly. "I joined when I was a young hothead and wanted to fight. So yes."

"Well, when you put it like that it doesn't sound quite as bad." I smiled at him. "You can't lie, but that doesn't mean you can't sugar-coat, does it?"

"You're not wrong," he muttered. He looked away, down the path, for a few moments before asking, "Do you think worse of me?"

It was my turn to think for a moment. "No, I don't think I do."

"Then it worked, I guess." Lear's beautiful green cat eyes flickered back up to mine, and it was now my turn to look away. His gaze was hard to meet, and that he wanted me to think well of him made my face heat.

"I've not made you uncomfortable, have I?" His voice was quiet.

I shook my head, not wanting him to feel bad for any reason. "No, no. It's just hard to look you in the eye sometimes."

"Sorry. I know my eyes are...different." Lear grimaced slightly.

I was surprised, but also glad, that he hadn't taken the opportunity to tease me, because it had been pretty obvious that it was his gaze that had made me blush. "No. I mean, they are, they're just intense. That's all. Pretty, but intense." He had to know that I thought his eyes were pretty already. After all, I'd probably told him as much while he was still a cat.

"Still," he murmured.

We rounded a bend, and Jedda's farm came into view. "That's Jedda's house."

There was a pile of ash, fragments of blackened wood, and scorched earth where one of the barns had once been, though nothing else seemed to have been damaged.

"And the remnants of the fire." Lear frowned, pumping his wings and shooting up and away, towards the burned-down building. He circled above it a couple of times, then swooped low over it.

As I approached on Poppy, I saw Jedda and a few of his farmhands appear. They ran out to the remnants of the barn, shouting and waving their hands like he was some crow they could easily frighten away.

Oops, probably shouldn't have let Lear go on ahead by himself. I was kind of used to his presence already, but no one else would be.

Lear stopped darting around in the air, and hovered, looking down at the group on the ground.

"He's with me, Jedda!" I shouted.

Jedda's head jerked in my direction, and he calmed his employees with a few words. He jogged to meet me as I rode up. "The fey person up there is with you?!"

"Yes, it's a long story." I sighed. "He's just trying to get a look at the burned down barn. He's promised not to cause any trouble."

"And you believe him."

"They can't lie, Jedda," I reminded him, smiling a little. "Besides, I'm helping him heal. His injury isn't an obvious one, so he can be out and about."

"I didn't know you took fey folk." My old friend tilted his head curiously to the side.

"I'll take anyone who needs help who won't cause me trouble." I nodded.

Jedda smiled. "You've a kind heart, lass."

"I don't know about that. My gift is meant to help others." I shrugged, then swung down off Poppy.

We walked closer to the burnt barn, where the farmworkers were watching Lear suspiciously.

The fey man flew over, and landed easily beside me. "I'm sorry for alarming you." Lear bowed politely to Jedda.

"I'm sorry we shouted. It's...unusual for us to have fey folk around these parts." The farmer waved away his assistants, dismissing them back to their work.

"Jedda, this is Lear. Lear, Jedda."

Lear nodded in way of greeting, saying, "Fey folk aren't nearly as uncommon in these parts as you all think." He turned his iridescent eyes to the charred remains of the barn. "I suspect this was caused by one of us."

"Oh?" Jedda looked taken aback.

"That's why we came here," I murmured. "Paz dropped by early this morning and said that some shadow thing had been bothering his sheep, he thought, and coupled with this...well, Lear thought they might both be caused by fey folk."

"The sheep issue definitely is, just going by the description he gave," Lear said, still studying the ashes. "But I'm pretty sure this is too."

"That's...that's not good." Jedda seemed deeply troubled.

"The sheep, yes. I suspect this could have been an accident, though. The kind of fey who live in the area seem to be mostly pretty peaceful beings, with few exceptions. They're of the lower courts, and are what you'd usually think of as nature spirits and such. The higher courts consist of fey who are more like me, and are more dangerous. We're also more likely to cause trouble for humans." He smirked slightly. "Not that I'm here to cause issues."

"So Winna tells me," Jedda replied coolly.

"I am a fey of my word." Lear bowed slightly again. "I don't want to lose access to Winna's magical assistance, so I will do as she asks."

"You make me sound like I have some great power." I snorted.

"It's more than you give yourself credit for," Lear replied mildly.

"You yourself have said I'm weak!" I rolled my eyes at him. I wasn't offended; it was true.

"A human with magic, weak or otherwise, is pretty rare. I was lucky to stumble upon you, and even more lucky that you have skill as a healer, or I'd still be unable to change out of cat form."

"Hang on a minute, you were the black cat!" Jedda exclaimed, then chuckled amusedly. "I see what happened! Winna, lass, you can't go on taking in every stray that crosses your path!"

"Well, Stroopwafel didn't turn out to be some powerful fey soldier." I pouted, kicking the ground.

Lear snorted in amusement, and Jedda threw his head back and roared with laughter.

"I'm fifty-fifty regarding my track record for cats I've taken in, that's not all that bad! And most will probably turn out to just be normal kitties!" I protested.

"Jedda isn't wrong, though. You should be more wary about who you let into your home. Most of us can use illusion magic to disappear entirely, and some of us can make ourselves look less dangerous. Some of us can even look human, if we want," Lear told me.

"Can you?"

"Normally, yes." He nodded. The more I learned about what he could do, the more I realized just how much a hindrance the poison was to him, as far as his magic usage went.

I sighed. "Point taken."

It was quiet for a few moments, and Lear turned his gaze back out to the burned building. "Will it bother anyone if I use my second set of eyes?"

"Do you need to see a heat presence?" I asked, confused. "The fire was put out days ago, now, and I doubt any critters are really rummaging around in it."

"Magic has a unique heat signature, and it lingers for quite a while," he told me. "If it was used specifically to start the fire, I may be able to see remnants. I do sense the presence of fey folk here, but I'll be able to better determine if it was purposeful or not, that way."

"Oh. I mean, I don't care. You could leave them open all the time, if you wanted, but I know you don't." I mean, it was a little disconcerting, because his heat-sensing eyes did remind me of just how inhuman he was. I wouldn't hold that against him, of course, nor tell him he couldn't open them when he wished, as long as he didn't watch me in the bath, as we'd discussed the night before.

"Second set of eyes?" Jedda sounded confused.

Lear opened his other eyes. "These."

"Oh! I didn't notice them!" Jedda shook his head. "That's useful, though."

"They definitely can be," Lear muttered, scanning the area. "Mm. No specific spells. I'd say this was an accident of some kind."

"U-um...e-excuse me!" a small voice squeaked, making us jump.

Or rather, Jedda and I jumped. Lear merely smiled slightly, and turned, closing his heat-sensing eyes. "I wondered if you'd come out."

A small creature, not more than a foot tall, stood there. It was very clearly some kind of bug-type fey. It was a fiery orange color, and had totally black, bug-like eyes on a defined head that sat above a body covered with a bulky shell. The fey person, because it undoubtedly was one, had one set of legs, and two sets of arms, each with three clawed fingers on the end.

"You can tell it was an accident?" The creature's little voice sounded slightly relieved.

"There was no definite spell used. That would indicate intent." Lear knelt. "What happened?"

"My child was exploring the barn. He knows not to bother the humans, but I think he got excited, feeling your presence in the area, sir," he nodded at Lear, "and got a bit adventurous. He was playing around and fell from the hayloft and sparked because he was scared, then he ran because he was still scared. It was quite a fall, and he's not a strong flier just yet."

"I see. What are you called?"

"Tark."

Lear looked up at Jedda and me. "Tark is a firebug. Peaceful creatures, but they do accidentally start fires from time to time. Not usually on purpose, though." Lear addressed the firebug again, "Normally, you all live in deserts or volcanic areas, I thought."

"My wife likes forests. We're normally very careful with our sparks. We don't want to burn down our home here." Tark looked over his armored shoulder, and said, "Pip, come here."

A smaller bug flew up, his wings buzzing nervously even after he'd landed. "I-I didn't mean to!"

"They know. We wanted to come and tell you, and to apologize, but...well, you're not used to seeing us around here. We didn't want to frighten anyone by appearing suddenly. It can be dangerous for us if we do stuff like that." Tark sounded upset, but then smiled. "But when you showed up with Miss Winna, we knew we'd be able to."

I blinked. "You know my name."

"We live near your cottage, and are familiar with Pima and her family." Tark replied, bobbing his bug-like head at me.

"Oh. Well, that explains it." I nodded.

Tark turned to Jedda. "I am very sorry for the trouble and danger Pip caused."

"I-I'm so sorry! I-I didn't mean to burn anyfing down!" Tears came to the little firebug's black bug eyes.

I looked at Jedda, hoping his reaction would be good. He was a good man at heart, I knew, but it might be a bit much, even for him.

Chapter 12

Welcomed In

The man who might as well have been my uncle didn't disappoint me.

Jedda sighed. "Don't cry, little one. No one was purposely harmed. We're lucky Winna could help Biren. Gave us a very good scare, though."

"We're happy to do whatever we can to help rebuild it. We're stronger than we look, and can fly as good as he can." Tark nodded at Lear.

"That's very kind of you." The farmer smiled. "I'd be pleased to have as much help as I can get, once we're ready to rebuild it."

"There are quite a few of us, so the work will go fast," Tark buzzed, sounding optimistic.

"Well, that'll work out just fine." Jedda smiled. "Why don't we get into the house and out of the cold?"

"We're happy to enter your home, but please know you can rescind the offer as well at any time," Tark said in an informational sort of tone.

"Aye, I know that much about fey folk!" Jedda laughed. "It's an important thing to know, for us humans! Just as it's important for fey folk to know which humans will accept them, I'm sure. You and your family are welcome here. Please try not to burn down any other buildings, though, if possible."

"We really would rather not burn anything down!" Tark said, shaking his head. "Pip, run home to your mother and tell her all is well."

"Yes, papa!" Pip buzzed off.

"We should go look into the sheep," Lear told me quietly.

Jedda overheard and interjected, shaking his head a little, "Don't go just yet, Ena has those recipes for you, Winna."

"Alright, but then we have to go." I nodded, and we followed Jedda to the farmhouse.

Jedda and I paused to tie Poppy's reins to the post before entering, but Tark and Lear lingered at the door. "We do still actually need permission. I prefer direct invitations or welcome when it comes to entering a dwelling," Lear said.

"I do too." Tark nodded, then explained, "Fey who aren't trouble-makers typically do."

"Then come in, both of you." Jedda motioned for them to enter, then went to look for Ena.

"Thank you!" Tark buzzed, hopping over the threshold.

"I think I said, 'come in if you're going to come in' to you, as a cat. That counts?" I asked Lear as he stepped inside, the door swinging shut behind him.

"Yes." The tall fey man nodded. "You'd made your invitation to enter clear enough for my purpose." He lowered his voice to tell me, "I wanted Jedda to know I'm following the general spirit of the law."

"But when you came into my cottage, you knew I didn't know you were fey! I thought you were a kitty!" I rolled my eyes at him. "You're just pretending not to be a troublemaker!"

The fey soldier smirked, then leaned down to murmur in my ear, "I never once said I wasn't one. Usually, I make the worst kind of trouble."

His words made my face burn scarlet. "U-usually?!" I squeaked.

"But you made me promise to be on my best behavior." Lear plucked one of my curls, making it spring up into my face before leaning back as he said in a more serious voice, "Besides, you'd have let me in even if you knew I was fey."

"Y-you're not wrong," I mumbled, looking away. A troublemaker indeed, teasing the way he did!

"Winna!" Ena followed her father into the room, then stopped short at seeing Lear and Tark. "Oh!"

"We have some other guests," her father said, smiling knowingly.

"Ena, this is Lear, and Tark." I motioned at them respectively.

"It's a pleasure to meet you!" Tark buzzed.

Lear only bowed his head in acknowledgement of the introduction.

"Well! This is a new experience!" Ena laughed off her surprise, though her face had heated when she'd seen Lear. Something told me a lot of women would have that reaction to him.

"It is!" Jedda agreed. "Tark is going to stay and chat, but Winna and Lear have to go help Paz."

"Oh yes, I've heard he's been having some strange trouble with the sheep."

"So he told me." I nodded.

"The ladies in the market were talking about it yesterday afternoon. Sounds a little scary!"

"Yes, it does! I'm hoping Lear will be able to help him solve the problem."

"Well, good! Anyway, here are the recipes!" She handed me a stack of cards.

"Thank you so much, Ena! I'll have a lot of fun trying them out! I'm teaching Lear to cook, so maybe he'll help me."

"As you wish," Lear murmured, nodding.

"Only if you want to, you don't have to."

"If you want me to, I will," he told me. Though he wasn't purposely doing so, his words made my face flush again, though not as deeply.

"I mean, I want you to do what you want to do," I muttered.

"Then I want to help." He shrugged.

"Just say that next time?" I tilted my head to the side. He was truly confusing sometimes. Must be because he was fey.

"Fine, fine." He waved a languid hand, then reminded me, "We should go."

"Right." I shook myself. "Thank you so much, Ena! I appreciate it! Tell Biren I said hi, and remind him to come by sometime next week or the week after for me to check and make sure he's still healing well. Once I've practiced these recipes a little, we'll have a tea party!"

"You're very welcome! I will! And I look forward to it!" she said, waving.

"Bye, Jedda. I'll see you all later. It was nice to meet you, Tark!" I waved my farewells, and Lear and I left the farmhouse.

I untied Poppy, and swung back into the saddle as Lear launched himself up into the air once more, then asked, "How far is our next destination?"

"Not far. Paz's farm is just over the next hill." I motioned in the general direction.

"Alright."

We traveled along in silence for a little while.

Instead of swooping around high above me as he had initially before, Lear stayed relatively close to me.

"The poison really hinders your magic, doesn't it?" I asked him softly.

"Yes," he murmured.

"Will you be able to deal with the shadow things?"

"There's more than one way to get rid of them. They don't all require magic."

"Oh."

"Yes. We're allergic to rowan berries."

"Should you be telling me that?"

"I should have told you sooner, actually. You should start keeping some on hand at the cottage, just in case, given my presence has already drawn one unruly fey to your home."

"That's not a bad idea." I sighed, then asked, "I've heard iron can cause damage too. Specifically, cold iron, is that true?"

"Nope." He shook his head. "I don't even know where that came from. Humans have iron in their blood, and if we had a weakness to iron, we wouldn't be able to enchant you, but we can. So, no iron weakness, no."

"I guess that makes sense."

"That said, we're not indestructible. If someone were to stab us with a sword, provided they could get a hit on one of us, it'd do damage. Maybe that's where it came from, but why assume iron is the problem instead of the actual weapon and the force behind it?" he mused.

"I see. Any other things I should know in order to keep myself safe?"

"Hm. You can rescind welcome, we're allergic to rowan berries... Mm...those are the general ones I can think of. The different races of fey might have other specific ones. Like water on the firebugs. That's why they like deserts, less rain. Not that it kills them, it just takes away a good deal of their fire magic for a bit."

"I see." I tilted my head to the side. "I've seen fauns, a goblin, firebugs, and I've heard of others, of course. Ogres, redcaps, dryads, elves, sprites...even dwarves, though that's only a technicality. But what are you considered?" He didn't seem to fit what I pictured for any of those.

"I don't fit neatly into one category," he replied, shaking his head slightly. "The higher courts are more blended than the lower courts. Sure, plenty of us are pure redcap, or whatnot, and the selkies tend to stick with other selkies, but plenty of us have all sorts of different blood in us. My height and build come from an elvish ancestor, my wings are from sylph blood, ogre blood gives me the ability to shapeshift into my cat form, I've some merfolk somewhere too, thus my scales...and that's not even everything."

"Well. I learned something new today." I paused. "Ogre blood, huh."

"They present themselves as scary because they can, and they do really enjoy terrifying you lot. Humans forget that ogres are really just shape-shifters, and can take on a very fair appearance too, if they so choose. Between them and the elves, who are just naturally pretty, I suspect it's how we got to be so ridiculously good-looking in the high courts, ogres making themselves attractive and passing on those attractive genetics. And I'm not going to complain about that. Nor would anyone else, we like being called the Fair Folk."

"I'm sure!" I snorted, shaking my head. "Why are the lower courts not so diverse? Do they like one another less? Or do they just prefer to keep to themselves."

"It's less a problem of not liking one another, and more that they're too distantly related. Firebugs lay eggs, like bugs typically do, but hamadryads are the spirit of an ancient tree. They literally couldn't have kids together."

"Ohh, I see." That made sense. I thought for a minute, then frowned as a thought occurred to me. "How does it work for mermaids, then?!"

"Do you really want me to get into details about fey reproductive processes?" He snorted.

I grimaced. "No. No. Absolutely not. That was a stupid thing to ask."

Lear grinned wickedly at me, saying, "I'll hint, then. Despite how it looks, a merperson's tail isn't just one piece. They keep it twisted up like one tail, but it's actually two leg-like appendages."

"Ohhhhh," I muttered, feeling my face heat. "And you know this how?"

"What about us wearing our promiscuity like a badge didn't you understand?" He arched an eyebrow at me. "I get around."

"I shouldn't have asked," I muttered, covering my eyes with my hand, my face positively on fire.

"I've some mer-blood anyway, like I said." He shrugged, waving a hand languidly, as if it explained everything.

"Your legs don't curl up into a tail, though, do they?" I'd never seen his legs beneath the simple black pants he wore. They could be totally strange for all I knew.

"No, don't be ridiculous....but it is likely why I only have four toes on each foot."

"What's the normal number of toes for high fey folk?"

"Depends on what they are, really, but six fingers and toes tend to be about right. That said, it's not odd to have a different amount, especially if you're not all one thing, like me."

"I see," I muttered. I really had learned a lot about fey in the last few days.

"You're very curious." His tone was mild, but I could tell that he himself was curious.

I shook myself. "Well, I don't know much about your people. Given that they're starting to show themselves a little more around here, it might help me to know some stuff. Reproductive practices aside."

"We're both adults, you can say sex." Lear snorted in amusement.

My face heated. "I mean...you're the one who phrased it that way first."

"I thought you'd burst into flames from embarrassment if I said sex." He laughed.

"We can stop this conversation now," I mumbled. Paz's house was in sight, anyway, and this was not a topic I particularly wanted to be discussing within hearing distance of him, lest the idiot get any ideas.

"If you're uncomfortable, absolutely. If you're only ending it because you think it's not something that should be discussed, I'd disagree, it's just another part of life."

"I-I'm uncomfortable," I admitted, staring hard at the path ahead of Poppy and me. "I-I was curious at first, but now it's a bit much."

"That's fine, then," he said lightly, pausing, then adding, "If you have any other questions, feel free to ask. I'm an open book to you."

"Thank you," I said softly.

We fell quiet for a few moments.

"I didn't offend you or anything, did I?" he asked gently.

I blinked. "What? Oh, no. You were only answering my questions. I should have thought about how the topic might make me uncomfortable. Thank you for dropping it when I asked."

Lear shrugged, muttering, "I just want you to like me."

My face heated, but I didn't say anything. Coming from him, who couldn't lie, that meant something. Or it did to me, anyway. But maybe I was reading too much into it.

As we approached the house, he dropped to the ground, walking beside me.

Taking his cue, I stopped Poppy, and slid off, only for my foot to hit the ground oddly. I stumbled, gasping, "Oop!"

Immediately, Lear's hands and arms shot out, steadying me. "Careful."

"Sorry!" I whimpered. "I landed weird!"

"You're a hazard to yourself, woman. I should have just flown you," he muttered. "Did you tweak your ankle?"

"I think so." I frowned, leaning away from him to put a little bit of weight on my foot, which sent a sharp, shooting pain through it. "Yeah, a tweak. I don't think it's really bad, though."

"You can't heal yourself, can you?"

"No, how silly is that?" I shook my head.

"It's not. It's very common for people with healing magic. Your body doesn't recognize the healing magic as being different from the magic already in you, so it doesn't react."

"Oh. Well, that makes sense." I frowned.

It was quiet for a few moments, and I realized I'd probably stayed too close to him for too long. "Here, I'll just sit on the ground for a few minutes, or something."

"No, it's alright, you're not hard to hold up."

"No, it's fine." I hopped away from him, balancing on one foot without his help. He was as strong as I'd have expected, and warmer than I'd have guessed, though that might just have been because it was cold.

"You'll only hurt it worse. Let me hold you up. It's fine," he protested, frowning.

"You just want to tease me or something!" I shook my head.

"Stubborn," he muttered, then flashed his brilliant, fanged smile at me, taking a step forward. His hands came up to my arms as he gently steadied me again. "And of course I want to tease you, I'm good at it, and it's fun."

I blinked, having caught the full force of his smile. But instead of being flustered, which, let's be honest, was pretty par for the course, I'd noticed something else about him as he'd spoken. "Your tongue is forked?"

His large green eyes blinked once. "Yes."

"Huh."

"Problem?" He tilted his head slightly to the side, curious.

"No, of course not. I just happened to notice it right then." I shrugged.

"Don't look, but your boyfriend is watching us through the window," Lear said conversationally, then added, "He's not happy about it, either."

"He's not my boyfriend!" I snapped, but didn't look. "And that's why you're being so flirtatious right now, isn't it?! You don't like him, so you're teasing me to bother him!"

"It does make it more fun. But you did hurt yourself, and I'd help you regardless of if he was watching or not."

"And I guess you can't lie." I sighed.

Chapter 13

Paz's Problem

"No, no I can't," he agreed with her. "I can suggest the truth is other than it is, or obfuscate in other ways. If you want to pin me down, demand a direct answer. Do it with any fey. It'll make us squirm."

"Why do you like teasing me?" She narrowed her eyes at him, putting what he'd just told her to use.

"It's fun." He shrugged. This was true, yes.

But she clearly suspected there was more to it, demanding, "Is that the full truth."

He didn't answer, but arched an eyebrow at her. Gods, she was fun to mess with.

"So it isn't."

Lear shrugged. For all she knew, he could just be messing with her still. And he sort of was. She was right, of course. He hadn't told her that he found her ridiculously attractive, but he also hadn't done anything to hide that fact, either.

That was part of the fun of being fey, using his wits to outsmart the rules he had to live by. His mind had served him well, especially back in the fey palace, where a ballroom was often little more than a battlefield, with words as arrows, and glances as swords, despite Asher's attempts to try to make things less cut-throat.

"Come on, spit it out," Winna demanded.

He leaned down, his lips brushing her ear as he whispered, "Wouldn't you like to know?"

"Lear!" she squeaked, jerking away.

Unable to help himself, he burst into laughter as the door to Paz's house flew open, and Paz stormed outside, demanding, "What's going on here?"

"He's being a menace!" Winna shook her head, then sighed and added a somewhat exculpatory explanation, "No, not really, I tweaked my ankle getting out of the saddle, and he's helping me stay upright, that's all."

"Oh, well come inside out of the cold!" Paz told them, motioning back at the house.

"No, as cold as it is, I'd rather get this shadow demon problem taken care of," Winna replied.

Lear was glad the young woman hadn't agreed to go in; he wasn't sure Paz would have given him permission to enter, not that he could really blame him if he hadn't.

"Um, okay."

"I'll just hop back up on Poppy and let her do the walking." Winna made to hop over to her pony, and Lear felt a thrill of mischief course through him.

With a burst of his fey speed, he scooped her up and gently deposited her into the saddle.

"Oop!" Winna squeaked in surprise.

"There," he said mildly, adjusting the cloak around her. "You're taller than me up there."

"Well, that's the only way I'd be taller than you," she muttered, face bright red, then shook herself, and asked, "Where are the sheep at, Paz?"

Paz glared annoyedly at Lear. "This way," he muttered, and led

106

them towards a barn that stood a little ways away from the small farmhouse. "They're outside right now." They rounded the barn to reveal a large, fenced-in area with a good-sized flock of sheep grazing in what little grass was left.

Lear flicked open his second set of eyes and scanned the area. "It looks like we're in luck. There's only one hanging around right now," he told them, then asked Paz, "How many times have you seen it."

"Uh...several times from the corner of my eye, I think, but only once or twice in all honesty. And I only saw it actually kill a sheep the one time."

"It's getting bolder," Lear muttered. "Is there a rowan tree around?"

"What?"

"Humor me."

"Um, yes. There's one over there." Paz motioned at a tree growing a few yards away.

"We'll need some berries from it," Lear said. "Can I borrow that cloak, Winna?"

"You were supposed to be wearing it anyway." She grimaced and shrugged out of it, handing it to him.

"Thanks, I'll be right back." Lear darted off, slowing as he approached the tree. The very smell of it made his head ache. The poison in his veins had a rowan berry base, so he needed to be extra careful, lest he get more of the dangerous substance inside his body.

Using the cloak as a barrier for one of his hands, the fey soldier picked the vile berries, cradling the poisonous bounty in a sort of pocket he made with the cloak between his other arm and his chest. When he'd gotten a sufficient number, Lear shifted the cloak, dumping the berries carefully to the center of the fabric, and wrapping it up around his deadly prize, making sure not to squish anything.

He went back to them, and handed the makeshift bag to Paz. "Is the barn really dark? Like, even in the day."

"Uh, yeah. Why?"

"We need to separate one of the sheep from the others, and have it in a dark place."

"Okay. Why these?" Paz held up the berries.

"You'll see," Lear said, looking out over the flock. "Can I just grab one of the sheep? It won't get hurt."

"Um, sure."

Lear once more shot forward, and easily caught a sheep up. "Alright. Into the barn," he directed. The barn was indeed very dark, not having the gable window like Winna's did, which meant that Paz had to hold up a light so they could see. Or rather, so Paz and Winna could see, given Lear's cat-like eyes had excellent night vision. "Yes, this will work."

Putting down the sheep, he tied it to a post close to the middle of the barn, giving it a very short lead. He motioned for Paz to come forward. "Put the berries all around the sheep in a wide, full circle."

"Okay." Paz looked dubious. "If you're just messing with me, and the sheep dies, I'll be-"

Lear cut him off, rolling his eyes, "Shadow demons work by draining a being's life force, its essence, through its shadow. We'll leave a lamp in the barn so it'll cast a shadow in a relatively controlled environment. The shadow demon will go to suck out the sheep's life force, but since it can't really smell or see, it won't know the berries are there. So instead of sheep, it'll get the essence of the rowan berries. The berries are poisonous to it and will kill it." He left out the part about rowan berries being poisonous to all fey; he didn't want Paz knowing that.

"Oh." Paz sounded surprised. "That's simple."

"Not everything is difficult," Lear muttered.

Altogether, the countryside was a much simpler place, not like the feylands, where everyone demanded decorum from him, as the grandson of a duke, not to mention the son of a very old fey family. Sure, he was good at politics, but it was nice to get a break from it from time to time.

Once the berries were spread sufficiently out around the sheep, Paz handed Winna the cloak, and Lear leaned across to hang the lamp on the post, being careful not to step on the berries as he did.

"Now we leave, and wait for it to take the bait," Lear said, and they left the barn. Winna had stayed in the doorway, watching.

"That's clever, Lear," she told him.

"Yes, it is, isn't it?" He grinned at her, then told Paz, "If you ever have trouble with them again, you can do the same thing."

"Right." Paz nodded.

"How long do you think it'll take?" the pretty healer wanted to know.

"Not too long, I expect," Lear said. "Shadow demons aren't particularly bright, and are opportunistic killers, only thinking of where they'll get their next meal."

"They sound scary," Winna murmured.

"They can be, if you don't know how to deal with them. But they're really pretty uncommon."

"Good."

"How'd we end up with them out here?" Paz wanted to know.

"Who knows?" Lear shrugged a little. "They do tend to prefer dark forests, but sometimes they stray."

Suddenly, there was a hoarse, keening screech from the barn, as well as the alarmed bleating of a sheep.

Winna jumped in surprise, and Paz charged forward.

"Relax, that was just the shadow demon dying," Lear said, going after him, but not in any hurry.

Winna followed behind on Poppy, a little more wary.

Paz threw open the barn door, and saw the sheep still standing where they'd left it in the flickering light of the lamp. Only now, the berries on the floor were all squished, and their juice covered the area surrounding the sheep.

"Done and done," Lear said, nodding approvingly.

"Are you sure?" Winna asked, tone uncertain.

Lear opened his second set of eyes, and looked around briefly before shutting them and confirming, "Yes. No more shadow demons here."

"Well, good." Paz paused, then bowed a little stiffly to them. "Thank you."

"Of course." Lear nodded, then looked up at Winna. "Ready to go home."

"Yeah." She nodded.

They left Paz to untie the sheep, and reunite it with the herd, and headed out. This time Lear walked alongside Poppy, easily keeping pace.

"Can you leave the cloak outside when we get back? It stinks to high heaven of rowan berries," he asked, though he knew she probably couldn't smell it like he could.

"Of course! I'll do laundry soon and wash it." She nodded, then frowned. "You don't have any real laundry other than what you're wearing, though, do you."

"No."

"Sorry!" She grimaced. "That's gotta feel gross! I'll find more of dad's old clothes for you to make do with when we get back to the house, and then we'll get some that actually fit you the next time I go into town."

"Thank you." He nodded. "I should add, I don't particularly know how to do laundry, but if you'll show me how, I'm happy to help. Surely it can't be any harder than cooking."

"I think it is, but that's only because the clothes are kinda heavy when they're wet. Wringing the water out of them isn't an easy task either, and then it can take a while to hang them to dry, but they dry a lot faster in the winter now, with the steady heat the heating stones provide."

"I imagine with magic it'd go faster. Most things do," he mused aloud. "Not that I can help in that way just yet, but once I can, I will."

"I'll appreciate any help, manual or magical." She smiled at him.

"I'm glad to help."

"Although once you can do everything you normally can, I guess you'll go, so I shouldn't let myself get too used to it," she muttered.

Lear wanted to say he could stay. If he sent word home that he'd found a previously undiscovered human mage, and that it would be best if he stayed to ensure her safety, they'd give him permission to stay. But if he did say so, he suspected she'd only think he was teasing her again.

Though the fey man did enjoy making her blush and getting her flustered, he wasn't just teasing her. He'd taken to Winna very quickly, and wanted to spend a good deal more time with her. Exploring the quickly deepening attachment he had to her was his biggest motivation to stay put, for the meantime.

All that said, even with Winna and Diana's help, the poison would take its time leaving, so he'd be there without having to make excuses for a while longer yet. After that, he'd be able to make excuses for a while as well. He fully planned to make as many excuses as he could.

They ambled back to the cottage in relative silence.

"You okay?" he asked.

"I'm surprisingly tired," she murmured.

"Take a nap when we get back. I'll make sure no goblins try to stab you again."

"If there are any goblins left in the cottage that you haven't gotten rid of, I'm banishing you back to the barn," Winna grumbled.

He snorted. "There aren't any, I promise."

"And I can't nap, I need to work on making more salves, and then the shawls when I'm done with those."

"No rest for the wicked, huh."

"Well, if that's the case, how well do you sleep at night?" she asked.

Lear blinked, then laughed. "Fair enough! I sleep just fine, despite my wicked ways." He shot her a flirtatious glance, which made her flush, as he'd expected. Then, he paused, and told her seriously, "When we get home, you'll show me what needs to be done and give me very specific instructions, and then you can take a nap. Anything I mess up while you're asleep, I'll re-do later and make it right."

"No, it's alright."

"Winna, there's no sense in running yourself ragged. If you're tired, you should rest," he told her gently. "Is it all so pressing that it can't wait a couple of hours for you to rest."

"I mean...probably not, but I've not been able to work on it all as much lately because life has gotten so crazy," she mumbled.

"That's more than partially my fault, too." He sighed. "Let me help you. Even if just to make up for the time you've lost because I've made your life kind of hectic."

"It's not a big deal. I don't mind the work."

"If I can help, I want to," he said firmly. "It's only fair. We'll make enough so that you can get your new oven, and whatever else you need, like new clothes. Alright?"

Winna chewed her lip for a few moments, then smiled and capitulated. "Alright."

He nodded approvingly.

They arrived at the cottage a short while later.

"I'll have to get down off Poppy, but I'm afraid I'll hurt my ankle even worse," she muttered, eyeing the ground. It wasn't very high, but he understood her concern.

"Here." He reached out, putting his hands on her waist and lifting her easily from the saddle.

"Oop!" the young woman squeaked in surprise, and fell back a half-step once she was on the ground.

"There." He smirked, then took Poppy's reins and told her, "Go into the house. I'll get her put away. Unless you need help inside too."

"No, no, I can manage it," she muttered, hobbling away as swiftly as she could.

Lear let himself watch her for a few moments, then shook himself and took Poppy into the barn. He soon had her unsaddled, brushed, and rubbed down, resting in her roomy enclosure, and munching on oats.

"Now to go do the same with your mistress," he muttered, wondering how Winna would react if he dared try to rub her down. The thought made him grin. No, she wouldn't appreciate that, which almost made him want to do it even more, but he knew better. Instead, he'd settle with making sure she put her feet up, and had a snack and something warm to drink.

Lear darted back inside, but didn't immediately see Winna. Frowning, he flicked his second set of eyes open, and glanced around again, but didn't see her.

Finally, he thought to look up, and realized she must have climbed the ladder that led to the loft area, which he hadn't explored yet.

"What are you doing up there?" he asked loudly.

"I couldn't find any more of dad's clothes down there, but I knew there was some up here!" She called.

"And you climbed the ladder on that ankle?" he asked, tone stern as he darted up said ladder.

"It's mostly stopped hurting now," she mumbled.

To Lear's surprise, he saw that a majority of the loft area was full of rows and rows of bookcases. "I didn't know there was a library up here! I'd have come up sooner, if I had. I like reading."

"Um, well, you can try to read the books, but they're not in any language I recognize." Winna was looking through some boxes at the far end of the loft.

"What are they for? Are they magical texts?" He reached out and pulled a tome off a shelf at random. It was covered in a thick layer of dust, which he brushed away. It felt fragile in his hand, likely from age.

"I really don't know. Mom says some have family history in them, or that's what she was always told, she couldn't read them either."

"They're ancient," he muttered, carefully opening the book and leafing gently through the brittle pages.

"Yeah? That doesn't surprise me." The young mage straightened, now triumphant. "There we go! This is the box." She turned her dark eyes to him. "Would you bring it downstairs? It's a little stuffy up here."

"Of course." Lear went to her side and easily lifted the box.

"You make it look so light," she murmured.

"It is light to me." He shrugged, going to the ladder and scaling down, using one hand to hold the large box and the other to climb. After setting the box down, he darted up the ladder again, arriving at the top in time to stop Winna from starting to climb down. "Come on. No more ladders for you today, you'll just slip and fall or something."

"No I won't!" she protested as he scooped her up.

Soon, he had her back on the ground floor. "There," he muttered.

"I could have done it just fine!" she huffed.

"Maybe." Lear smirked a little, then ushered her over to the couch. "Sit."

"We need to go through the box though."

"I'll do it. I'll pick out what I like, and if you don't want me to use something, just say the word."

"Alright," Winna mumbled, sitting as directed.

The fey man settled down to sort through the clothes, and soon had a small pile selected. It wasn't anything fancy, but that didn't surprise him.

"Try some of them on and see if they fit at all, or if I need to let them out as much as I can, or whatnot."

"Sure." Lear took the clothes down to the bedroom he'd been occupying, and changed into them. "They're a better fit than the coat, that's for sure. A little short, but not all that bad, given they have a little stretch," he told her as he returned, wearing a simple white shirt and dark navy pants.

"Oh no, that's not bad at all," she murmured, brow creased as she scanned him with an analytic gaze. "The pants are short on you, but other than that, it's not bad. I wonder why the coat didn't fit as well?

114

Maybe that was one of my brothers' coats, and I just thought it was dad's."

"Whatever the reason, these are fine, for now."

"I'll work on letting out what I can after dinner tonight."

"Alright. I'll help. I know a little bit about that kind of stuff; sometimes we had to make do on our own in the military, and that included altering or repairing clothing from time to time."

Chapter 14

The Dwarf

Several more days passed, and I sort of settled into life with Lear around. Although, to be fair, I'd adjusted to having him around after just one day, really. The way we'd been introduced, him saving me from being stabbed by a goblin, had endeared me to him pretty quickly, despite the way he'd basically tricked his way into the cottage, which I'd more than forgiven him for.

Each day, he helped with what he could, learning what he couldn't already do as we went along. He really was a quick study.

"It's surprisingly warm out today," the tall fey man told me, coming in from outside.

"Oh?" That was heartening news. "Well, good. It's about time it starts to warm up. I'm ready for winter to be over!"

Lear shook his head. "Winter isn't over yet, there's still a month more at least. We're just having a warm snap."

"Pity." I sighed.

"Do you have a moment to use some magic on me?"

"Sure!" I stood up from the sewing machine, glad to give my foot a break from the pedal. "Annie!" I called.

My ever loyal cat familiar appeared and padded over to us.

"Hello, my love!" I giggled, bending to kiss her forehead. "Let's help Lear."

She maowed agreeably, and hopped up onto the couch, watching me and the fey man expectantly.

Sensing that attention was being shared, Stroopwafel be-bopped out from wherever she'd been hiding and demanded kisses.

"Oh, just a minute, Diana. You have a demanding little sister!" I giggled, bending to smother Stroopwafel with kisses, as she'd wanted.

Lear went ahead and sat on the couch. "Both of your sisters are ridiculous, Diana," he commented, reaching out to stroke her head.

My familiar had warmed up to him pretty well now, and allowed the gentle touch. She even started to purr.

"Aw, you're so sweet." I smiled, finally going to sit with them.

Reaching out, I put one hand on Diana's back, and Lear took my other hand in his. It never failed to make me flush slightly. I turned my focus to Diana. Pulling for my magic, I felt for hers, and directed it into Lear.

He groaned, as he usually did, and leaned back. "Gods, it's nice."

"Good." I smiled. "You're a little different, so I can't really tell how well I'm doing, but do you think it's helping at all."

"Yes. I should try a little more magic today."

That'd be interesting to see. "Just don't push yourself too hard, I know it hurts."

"I won't," he murmured, smiling at me, then standing and stretching. "I'll think of something fun to show you."

"Well, while you're thinking about that, I'll get started on salves again." It was a never-ending process for me, really. I stood, meaning to go to the kitchen.

Lear's head snapped suddenly towards the door. "Someone's coming." His second eyes flicked open. "Fey?" He frowned. "Or... no?" He darted to the window, then sighed. "A dwarf. No wonder."

"Oh?" I blinked, then hurried to the door just as there was a knock. I opened it. "Dern! How can I help you?"

The dwarf stood at about four feet tall, and had a long brown beard. He had thoughtful grey eyes, and wore a long, plain cloak over his simple clothing.

Dern bowed in the fashion of his people. "I was told you'a been helping some folk 'round here wif' some strange problems."

"As much as I can, yes." I stepped aside to admit him.

Dwarves were technically considered fey, but they were a branch all on their own. They were great smiths, crafts-folk, and inventors. I'd always been told they were capable warriors, and they were the one kind of fey who could enter dwellings without invitation, since they weren't particularly tricky or dangerous. They used magic predominantly in the form of runes, but I knew Dern also had a fire manipulation ability.

Dern turned to Lear. "I was also told you had a fey fella here." He bowed in greeting. "I'm Dern."

"Lear," the fey man replied, bowing in response.

"Don't usually care much 'fer high fey folk, but you seem like a polite chap."

I smiled. Dern was always somewhat blunt, but was also incredibly honest. I'd been told that was pretty common, amongst dwarves. They were trusty folk, which was why they weren't beholden to the same rules regarding dwellings as the rest of the fey.

"I'm behaving myself while under Winna's care," Lear replied slowly. He watched the dwarf with interest, and I wondered if he'd not had many dealings with them before.

"I see, I see. Might not wanna stick around here if you plan to misbehave once yer healed. Folk won't thank you if you do."

"I'll keep that in mind." Lear smiled amusedly.

"So, something is causing you enough of a problem that you walked all the way here from town?" I asked.

"Yes'm. Something has been eatin' my metal." The dwarf nodded.

"Eating...metal?" I blinked, taken aback.

"I've gone out to me forge a couple of days in a row now, and there have been bite marks in the ingots I keep out there. Contrary to what some folks think, we dwarves don't eat metal," he laughed at his own joke, "we just shape it! So I know it's not me sleepwalkin' or anythin' of that nature!"

"Of course!" I laughed. "Well, I'd be happy to try to help. I've never heard of anything that eats metal before though, but maybe Lear has."

"There are all sorts of fey, high and low." He shrugged. "I'll need to see more before I could say."

"Well, if yer not busy, I'd be obliged for you to come now," Dern told us. "That metal is part o' me livelihood, I can' afford to have it get eaten!"

"You caught us between tasks, so yes, we can go now." I nodded.

Lear was already slipping his feet into boots and said, "I'll hook Poppy up to the cart so we don't have to walk. Given we're going into town, you might want to change into something less dirty." He eyed my dress, which had dirt from the barn on it.

"Good point." I grimaced. "I'll go change and then be right out."

"I'll wait outside, 'tis a fine day!" Dern said, then went outside.

Lear followed the dwarf out, shooting me an amused look.

Hurrying back to my bedroom, I put on the one dress I had that could still be considered somewhat nice. Leaving again, I threw on my coat and nicer pair of winter shoes, grabbed my purse, and finally headed outside as well.

Dern was sitting on the top step of the porch, and Lear was leading Poppy, and the cart, from the barn as I stepped out.

An almost spring-like breeze tossed my curls. "Oh, what a lovely day." I sighed, tilting my head back to enjoy the sun on my face. "I can't wait for spring!"

"It's still winter, but jus' be patient! Spring will be here before you know it. Don't be so eager for time to pass, Miss Winna; it moves swiftly enough without our wishes," Dern told me.

I smiled. "I know, I know. I just prefer warm weather. I can open the windows and be outside."

"Ready?" Lear asked, stepping easily onto the cart's bench.

"Yep!" I nodded, and hopped down the stairs.

Dern followed at a more sedate pace, saying, "I'll ride in the back."

"Sure." I nodded. "Can I sit on the bench with you, Lear."

The tall fey man slid over, patting the spot next to him, and winking one of his gorgeous green cat eyes. "Any time."

"Oh, don't you start!" I rolled my eyes at him as he flicked the reins. Poppy started down the path. "Go that way," I directed. "It's a straight shot into Greenwood from here."

"Right." He nodded.

We rode in silence for a little while.

A thought occurred to me. The women would completely mob Lear, as wickedly attractive, interesting, and new as he was, and I didn't look forward to having to deal with that.

"Oh, also, I don't want you causing trouble by flirting with the women in town, alright?"

He shot a sidelong glance at me and murmured, "Jealous."

"What? No, of course not!" My face heated. "You'll give them heart attacks, or make them jealous! You're planning on leaving here once you're healed, anyway. Meaningful connections are something of a moot point when you're just going to leave!" Something about this filled me with immense sadness.

-

Pain crept into Winna's voice, and he saw tears in her dark eyes. She'd said similar things before, of course, and he'd suspected that, deep down, she didn't want him to go, even when he'd been healed, but he'd not seen any true evidence of it until that moment.

It struck him that it hurt to hear her upset, and to know she was hurting because of him.

"Winna-" he started.

But she cut him off, closing her eyes, and shaking her head. "I just don't want any drama or attention. I-I'm sure that if Dern knows that you're staying at my cottage, then the entire town probably knows, too! Goodness knows what they're saying about me, having you there, even if you are only staying until you're healed."

So, the young woman was upset that he'd be leaving; she hadn't really been able to hide that from him, but she was also upset about the idea that people were gossiping about her as well. How irksome. "Well, if you don't want as much attention, I could make myself stick out a lot less. You wanted to see more magic, right?"

"Uh-huh," she mumbled, nodding and rubbing her eyes with her fists.

"Alright then, I think I can manage simple illusion magic to look less interesting."

"Knowing you, you'll still be stupidly handsome," Winna muttered, still a little dejected.

Making himself look like a very plain, unassuming human would be perfectly simple, but he still wanted her to be attracted to him, so he didn't mention that fact. "Well, of course!" He snorted. "But they're more used to a good-looking human man than a high fey fellow just riding into town like he owns the place."

The young mage gave a watery sort of smile.

"Here." He passed her the reins, and pulled carefully for his magic, taking it slowly. The poison in his blood throbbed in protest, but then relented, and he smiled triumphantly, letting the illusion flow across him.

"Well, that's interesting," Winna said.

Lear opened his eyes, and took the reins from her small, five-fingered hands. "Better."

"Still handsome." She shrugged.

"Yep." Lear nodded. "Do you have a mirror? I have a general idea of what I look like, but I'd like to actually see it."

"Hmm, let's see. I should." The young woman rummaged in her purse, and held out a small hand mirror.

"Thanks." He took it and held it up with one hand, keeping Poppy on track with the other pretty easily.

Normal green eyes instead of a cat's, and certainly not a second set of eyes, no fangs, no forked tongue, no scales, no wings, and no claws. Not that he kept the wings and claws out all the time, anyway. And no pointed ears. Still good-looking though. Ridiculously so, she was right.

"You're recognizable," she told him thoughtfully. "I wasn't sure you would be."

"I wanted to look human, not trade my face for another's." He shrugged. "Besides, you like my face as it is; I didn't want to lose that."

Winna rolled her eyes at him. "Oh hush."

Lear reached out casually and let himself take one of her hands. "How do you want to play it if someone asks about me?"

Instead of protesting or rolling her eyes, as he half expected her to, she sighed and shook her head. "I mean, there's no harm in telling the truth, I guess. Or rather, maybe if they mention having heard there was a fey person with me, or something. I just don't want all eyes on us from the moment we go into town." Her small fingers tightened around his.

"Alright." He nodded.

"Nor do I want to be mobbed by every woman who sets eyes on you. I don't like being around people enough for that...though they might set on us anyway, with that face." Winna sounded pensive.

Lear laughed. "Just relax, it's going to be fine! We'll go straight to Dern's home and his forge, then leave."

"No, we should get you some clothes while we're here. That's why I brought my purse."

"I have money." Lear blinked.

The young woman looked startled. "But you didn't have any bags or anything with you, how could you?"

"Give me a little more credit than that! I had pockets." He laughed. That she'd left the cottage fully prepared to buy him new clothes with her own hard-earned money really was very touching, and he wanted her to know it. Lear pulled her hand to his lips. "You are one of the kindest people I've met. I'm very grateful to consider you a friend," he murmured, now serious. "But you don't have to spend money on me."

"B-but...how could a wallet that fits into a pocket in a way that I couldn't see it hold any great amount of money? Clothes aren't cheap!" she squeaked. Her face was bright red, but she still didn't pull her hand away from his.

Lear kissed her fingers again, then said, "It's enchanted, love. Much like the way I can hide my wings."

"Oh. How does that work? You said it would take some explaining, and we have time now."

"Hmm." He thought for a moment, trying to condense the explanation into something easy to understand. "The magic makes an expanded pocket of sorts within that we're able to access. For the wallet, you only have to open it up and stick your hand in, like you normally do. For the wings," he pulled out the necklace he kept beneath his shirt, revealing the rune carved onto the surface of the simple, black stone pendant, "we use a very small bit of magic to activate and deactivate a rune like this to pull them in and out."

"Tha's dwarf-made," Dern observed. The dwarf had mostly stayed out of the conversation until that point, which had been very tactful of him.

Lear nodded. "Yes. I've had one since I was young, so I don't always have to deal with my wings running into everything. Always of dwarvish make, they're the most reliable option because the magic is rune-based."

"Never falters, rarely fails!" Dern sounded proud.

"Very true." Lear nodded.

"That's very interesting...a pocket in space," Winna mused.

"It's very useful," Dern commented. "We dwarves use it mostly for storage purposes, but the fey folk have come up with some very clever uses, as is their wont."

"We are a clever bunch. Not as reliable as your kin though."

"Tha's true." The dwarf nodded readily.

Chapter 15

In Town

Soon, Lear saw the village of Greenwood ahead of them. He squeezed Winna's hand gently, then wove his fingers through hers. It was a little odd, given the difference in the number of their fingers, but he made it work.

It was larger than he'd expected, and sprawled out just beneath the shoulder of a fairly tall hill. Or was it a hill? It wasn't tall enough to be a mountain, but it seemed too big to call it a hill. That said, there didn't seem to be a better word for it, so hill would have to do. A big hill. Whatever.

As they rode past the first couple of buildings, he asked, "Did you go to school here?"

"Yes."

"So everyone here knows you pretty well."

"Yeah." The young woman smiled. "Turn left up there."

Lear steered the cart as she directed.

Most of the buildings didn't look all that different from Winna's cottage, though some were made of stone. Many had white walls, and most had thatched roofs. There were taller buildings on the town square, with second floors that were likely the proprietors' living quarters. The shops were painted eye-catching colors, one a pastel blue, another a creamy pink, and one a somewhat alarming shade of bright green. They were all built in a somewhat more upscale style than the village houses, with tile roofs, perfectly straight walls, and some cute little architectural frills on their facades. A few even had large, glass windows in the front.

They skirted the center of town only briefly, though, and soon turned down a quiet lane full of homes.

"Tha's my home right there," Dern spoke up, standing in the back of the cart, and pointing over Lear's shoulder at a modest home with a large building in the back.

"Right."

They pulled into the yard, and climbed down. Lear secured Poppy to a hitching post, and Dern motioned for them to follow him.

He took them past the house, and to the large building which housed his forge. There was a large table, several anvils, a wall of hammers, drawers undoubtedly full of other tools, piles of metal ingots, and several in-progress projects as well.

"Here's the most recent victim." Dern showed them an iron ingot.

Lear snorted, almost amused. "Yeah, I'd say that's a bite-mark!" He looked around, then flicked open his second set of eyes. There was residue from fey magic all over the place, as if something had prowled around, exploring. "Oh yeah. Definitely one of us. Hm." his eyes turned towards the forge, which blazed brightly, its heat so intense it was hard to look at. "Is the forge always on?"

"Yes, usually. It's rune-powered as well."

"That's where your culprit is hiding right now, I believe." He could just barely make out the outline of a creature in the belly of the forge.

"Oh?" Dern sounded surprised.

"Yes. How to get it out, though?" The fey man thought for a moment. "Well, it likes metal. Take some metal you don't care as much about, and let's see if we can tempt it out."

"Alright then." Dern shrugged. The dwarf caught up a metal rod, then took a chunk of what was clearly scrap metal, and sat them down on a granite-topped work table. He pushed the two pieces together, then, with a surge of magic, drew his finger across the joint.

The glow of heat was so intense that Lear snapped his heat-sensitive eyes shut immediately, and looked away. "Goodness."

"Oh, your eyes," Winna murmured.

"I'm fine." He waved her concern away. "It just surprised me."

Dern put on a pair of thick gloves, approached the forge, and opened the door. He stuck the metal into the forge a little, wiggling it around, and then drawing it back.

Suddenly, a little scaly snout popped into view.

"Oh!" Winna gasped.

"Ah, I wondered." Lear grinned.

"What is it?" the young woman asked.

Dern continued to try to tempt the little creature from his forge.

"It's a dragon," the tall fey soldier informed her.

"A dragon?!" she gasped in delight.

Lear smiled. Her joy was infectious. "Yes. It's still young though. But it won't get much bigger, these kinds are miniature, really."

"Can it talk? I know some dragons can."

"No, it's probably more like Diana, able to understand speech, and quite smart for an animal, but still an animal."

"I see!" She nodded, watching as Dern finally coaxed the rather large lizard from the mouth of the forge. "And it eats metal."

"Yes. It's an ore dragon. It can smell metal, even through the ground." Lear addressed the dwarf now, "I suggest offering to let it live in your forge, and feeding it, but in return, it should help you find ore. And I believe its droppings are likely an incredibly pure version of whatever metal it eats. Probably more pure than what you can make. Its body runs using a little of the metal itself, as well as what would be considered the impurities in the stuff. The ingots you have here would be like candy to it, tastes good, but not much substance to it, which was why it was eating enough that you'd notice."

"That makes sense." Dern nodded. He was letting the little creature sniff his hand.

The little dragon's silver scales were rapidly cooling, and it stared up at the dwarf with large, sapphire eyes. Given it was a ground-based dragon, it didn't have wings, and instead had curved claws well-suited to moving earth so it could dig for ore to eat, and a long tail that flopped around contentedly.

"Hello little one." Dern's beard shifted as he smiled. "Is the forge nice and warm?"

The dragon nodded, shivering a little.

"I won't keep you out of it very long. You can live here, but please don't just eat the metal in here. I need it to run my business!"

The little dragon gave a little chirp.

"I make things for people in the area. You can stay here, but in return, can you help me find ore veins?"

Winna giggled in delight as the small dragon nodded again. "What will you call it?" she wanted to know.

"Can I give you a name?" Dern asked.

Another yip from the ore-eating reptile.

"Are you a girl?" Dern asked.

The dragon shook its head.

"Then a boy."

A nod.

"Let's see. I'm not very creative, but I do think Silver is a nice name." The dwarf stroked his beard thoughtfully.

The dragon wiggled happily.

"Alright then, Silver it is!" Dern nodded approvingly. "Now go get warm again."

Silver chirped sweetly, then hopped back into the forge.

Dern turned and walked over to us. "That was a far easier problem to solve than I expected."

"I'm glad it wasn't anything more serious either. The last one we dealt with was far less pleasant, though Lear dealt with it easily enough," Winna told him.

"So I heard!" Dern nodded. "A shadow demon, right?"

"Yes. Definitely not nearly as cute or endearing as a hungry little dragon. At least a dragon can usually be reasoned with." The fey soldier grinned.

"Indeed!"

"Well, we should probably go. We still have to get Lear some new clothes," Winna told Dern.

"Of course." The dwarf nodded. "Thank you very much for stopping by. I know you've been wanting one of the stoves; I'd be happy to give you a discount on one when you're ready."

Winna blinked, then smiled a little sadly. "Dern, I didn't even do anything but stand here and think the dragon was very cute."

"Fair point." The dwarf nodded. "But I appreciate your willingness to come immediately, and you are a very loyal, repeat customer. So I'm happy to give you a discount. Twenty percent is good, I think."

Tears came to the young woman's eyes. "Th-thank you, Dern! I-I've been saving really hard to get it! I-I think I already have enough with that!"

"Even better!" The dwarf's beard and mustache twitched, and his eyes crinkled up as he smiled. "I guess I'll see you soon, then?"

"Y-yes!" she sniffed, wiping her face.

They bid the dwarf and his new dragon friend farewell, then left the forge building.

"We can walk to the shops from here, they're not far," Winna murmured. "Dern won't mind if we leave the cart and Poppy here."

Seeing there were still tears on her face, Lear caught her gently, and pulled her to face him, sliding his sleeve down onto his hand and wiping her face gently with it. "There. Let's go."

"Thanks," she muttered, starting off again.

Lear took a few quick steps to catch up, and caught her hand, then slipped it into the crook of his arm. "We've not been out and about together before."

Winna frowned. "Yes we have."

"Not in town like this, I mean."

"Oh. You're right. We've not had to go into town, though, until now."

"I know. We should have tea at the tea shop when we're done. My treat."

"Are you sure?"

"Absolutely."

"Okay, thank you." Winna leaned her head into his arm for a moment. "I like the fancy little tea cakes they have there. It's been a while since I've had any though."

"How come."

"I've been saving up for other things." She shrugged.

"You have incredible willpower to be saving up like you have," he commented.

"I don't know about that. I've just had to be responsible for my own finances since I was sixteen."

Lear patted her hand, murmuring, "Fair point." He left his fingers over hers.

"Winna!" A voice cried, making his small companion nearly jump out of her skin.

"Oh goodness!" Winna gasped, looking across the street, her other hand to her heart. "Bekka! You scared the life out of me!"

A cart trundled by as the young woman who'd addressed Winna waved, giving Lear a moment to ask, "Who's this?"

"Her name is Bekka, we went to school together," the young healer murmured.

"A friend?" He watched as the girl waited. This Bekka had dark skin, and dark, fluffy curls, which were currently held back by a floral crocheted headband.

"Yes, not super close, but a friend nonetheless." She nodded, smiling politely and waving as the other woman hurried across the road once the cart had passed, her fluffy curls bouncing around her head in an almost cheerful manner.

"It's a little odd to see you in town this time of year, isn't it?" Bekka addressed Winna, but her eyes flickered all over Lear.

Being ogled didn't usually bother him, but on this occasion he did find it a little annoying. The girl was a friend, but was barely paying attention to Winna in order to stare at him.

"Dern wanted my opinion on something, so I made the trip in." The human mage shrugged a little.

"And not alone! Who is your friend?" Bekka couldn't wait any longer, it seemed.

"This is Lear, Lear, this is Bekka." Winna motioned between them.

"It's a pleasure to meet you!" Bekka curtsied.

Lear bowed his head slightly, but didn't speak.

"Now Winna," Bekka put her hands on her hips, mock-sternly, "I'd heard that the fellow you had around was fey, but, no offense, sir, I don't think you look particularly inhuman."

"Magic is a wonderful thing, and illusion spells aren't difficult for me," he said, keeping his tone mild, to come across as bored as he could.

"Oh!" she gasped. "Well, I'll be! Oh, wait until I tell-"

"I'd rather not be mobbed, if it's all the same to you," Lear cut her off, letting his annoyance show. "And I'm sure Winna doesn't either. Neither of us are particularly in the mood to fight through a crowd, I think."

Bekka blinked. "Oh. No, I don't expect anyone would be. That's fair enough. Sorry, I didn't even think about that."

"A-and I'm sure people have been saying all sorts of things," Winna murmured, dropping her gaze. "Lear is only staying until he's healed. He's my patient. He's been helping with some other issues being caused by fey folk in the area, but he's not staying long-term. If you tell anyone, please tell them that. It's the truth."

"Even better, I'll tell her, since I can't lie," Lear said. "Winna has done nothing inappropriate, despite my best efforts to convince her otherwise. I'm her patient. I do think of her as a good friend though."

Bekka's mouth popped open, and she was speechless for a moment. Finally, she burst into giggles. "Well, I never thought anything improper was going on! I'd have thought 'good for her' even if it had! But don't worry, Winna, I'll set them straight. Once you've left so you don't get mobbed, anyway." She pretended to zip and lock her lips, then threw away the imaginary key as she winked cheekily.

"Thank you, Bekka." Winna's smile went from slightly forced to genuine.

"Of course, hon." Bekka nodded. "What shop were you heading to?"

"Ama's. It's a long story, but Lear could use some more clothes."

"Well, you two have fun!" She flashed a bright grin at them. It was startlingly white against her rich brown skin.

"Are you still working at the tea shop?"

"Yes!" Bekka's nod sent her curls bobbing around her face, despite her headband.

"We're going to stop by later, I think. Are you working today at all?"

"I was headed there just now!" She smiled, then glanced at her pocket watch and grimaced. "And on that note, I should get going. It was nice to meet you, Lear, and really good to see you, Winna, you should come into town more often. See you both later!" Bekka waved and hurried off.

"Well, that went better than you were worried it would," Lear commented. He'd been irritated, but Bekka's earnest nature had shown through as the interaction continued, and he'd found his annoyance with her fading. It seemed like she was just very friendly.

Had they been in the feylands, that would have gone very differently. Whoever had taken interest, and approached them, would have taken every opportunity to slight his lovely companion, but couched the cuts in terms that didn't make it obvious. Such was the sly way of the fey upper-crust. Many things, including politics, were communicated by suggestion and innuendo. In many ways, human society was much more straightforward, despite the fact that they could lie, and the fair folk couldn't.

Winna nodded slightly. "Luckily. Bekka is decent, and does know me fairly well because we grew up together. Other folks aren't so decent."

"Fair enough. I'll break some kneecaps if someone so much as looks at you sideways." He cracked his knuckles menacingly.

"Lear." She rolled her eyes at him, but smiled, which was what he'd wanted.

"I'm joking." He flashed a grin at her.

"I know." Winna shook her head, then frowned and asked, "Technically, that wasn't true...how is it possible for you to say it?"

"Because it was a joke. Intent matters, to some extent. It's a spirit of the law vs letter of the law thing, but we can usually get away with a joke."

"I see."

"We have lots of wiggle room, unfortunately, and use that wiggle room to great effect."

"Humans wouldn't be so wary of you lot if that weren't the case. We know the fey folk can be tricky."

"Fair enough." Lear nodded.

They walked in silence for a little while.

"That's the shop up there." Winna pointed just ahead.

The fey captain glanced around. "Well, we've done pretty well so far! You've only been recognized once."

"It's early yet, not everyone is up and about. We'll see what happens when we leave, and once we're having tea," Winna told him. "Here we are," she murmured, pushing into the shop.

A bell on the door jangled, and a woman's voice called, "I'll be right with you!"

Lear's clothing was all custom-made, given that he was the grandson of a duke, but this shop was full of ready-made clothing, which hung on various racks, hooks, or were folded neatly on shelves and tables. There was a counter along one wall that held various accessories, and a sewing machine on a low table, probably for adjustments that could be done quickly.

"It's just me, Ama," Winna replied.

"Oh, Winna!" An elderly woman with flyaway grey hair appeared. Her kind brown eyes flickered over Lear, but she didn't comment. "How are you, dear? It's been a while!" The shopkeeper's eyes took in Winna's dress. "It looks like it's high time for some new clothes, too."

"Well, I didn't come for me today, actually, although you're not wrong." The young woman grimaced a little, scratching the back of her head in embarrassment. "This is Lear, he's a patient staying at the cottage for a time. Lear, this is Ama. This is her shop, but she makes the clothes here as well."

"It's a pleasure to meet you." Lear bowed. Sure, he could just alter borrowed clothing with magic, as he'd initially done, but he was unfamiliar with sewing, so the fit would never be quite right.

"The pleasure is mine." Ama bowed politely in return. "So if you're not here for clothes today, Winna, I take it Mr. Lear here is?"

"Just Lear is fine. But yes." The fey man nodded.

"Well, I have a fine selection of men's clothes over here, if you want to look through." She guided them to one side of the store, then turned to Winna, "Why don't you come look at new clothes while you're here as well? That way you can go ahead and plan for what you want when you come to buy new things for yourself."

Winna chewed her lip. "Well, I think I'll have a little extra money after I buy the stove I've been saving for." That'd be thanks to the discount Dern was going to give her. "Oh, alright. I could probably buy something today. Just so I'll have one actually nice dress for when I'm in town again. Then come spring and summer, when I can actually make more steady money again, I'll be able to invest in more."

"Are your salves not selling well in the shop you keep them in?"

"They don't typically sell as well in winter." The young woman shrugged.

"What salves do you sell? I've never asked for specifics." Lear asked as he perused the men's clothing.

"I only really have two. A general healing salve, and then a burn salve that has cooling properties from different herbs."

"You could expand on that, I think. You could do anti-nausea, a salve for bug bites, one that specifically targets arthritis." He shrugged. "Stuff like that."

"I don't know how I'd do that." Winna frowned. "I'm not only pretty weak, but I also only know what I was taught. Books of magic are kind of hard to come by around here."

"I have no aptitude for healing, but I do have a good deal of experience in using magic, just generally, so I bet if we put our heads together, we could come up with some new things."

Ama's expression was extremely confused, "Are you also a mage, Lear?"

"You've not heard the rumors, then?" Winna asked, surprised.

"Well, I've heard there was a fey person keeping you company, but Lear hardly fits that description."

"No, I'm fey! Humans often seem to forget we can disguise ourselves pretty easily." Lear laughed.

"Oh...but you came inside the shop." Ama still seemed befuddled.

"I don't need permission to enter a shop. The welcome is implied because the purpose of the shop is to sell those wares, which requires customers to enter, so I'm able to come in because I'm a customer." He pointed at the ceiling. "Do you live above the shop?"

"Yes."

"I couldn't enter your dwelling above the shop without permission, but the shop itself is fine." He motioned at the store around them.

"Well, that's interesting." The elderly seamstress smiled. "I learned something new today."

"I've learned a lot of new things lately." Winna laughed.

Chapter 16

New Dresses

L ear arched an eyebrow. "They've been interesting things at least, though, right?"

"Yes, all very interesting." I nodded, then motioned at the clothes he'd been looking at. "Have you found anything you like?"

"Yes."

"Good."

"If you want to pick out some things and see how they fit, there are rooms in the back that you can use to try them on, and I can make adjustments as needed pretty quickly, depending on the issue," Ama told him, then said thoughtfully, "You're quite tall though, I expect I might need to let most things out."

"Oh, thank you. Yes, that's likely the case. I'll try some of these on." Lear selected several articles of clothing from the racks, and went to the fitting room that Ama had indicated.

Ama drifted closer, "He's not what I would have expected. Very polite."

"Well, he's on his best behavior, so I'll heal him, but we're also pretty good friends now." I smiled, shrugging a little.

"I'm glad. He sounds very willing to help you with your salves.

It'd be nice to have a more experienced magic user around again," the seamstress murmured, then added hastily, "Not that we don't appreciate what you do, dear!"

I laughed. "No, I agree! I'm pretty much limited to healing, which is helpful, but a fey person who can do more than just heal is definitely helpful in other ways!" I sighed. "I'll take his help for as long as he stays, but he'll go back to his home in the feylands once he's healed."

"What's wrong with him? He seems alright." Ama's tone was curious, but concerned.

"It's a very long story." I waved my hand at her, shaking my head. I didn't want it to get out that he couldn't use much magic at this point, it didn't seem wise. Though his magic hadn't been particularly helpful up until that point, his knowledge certainly had. I also knew that, were he to stay once he did have his full strength, his magic would be incredibly useful.

Not that I wanted him to stay because he'd be useful. Using people wasn't my thing. I did want him to stay, though. I hadn't known him very long, but I had to admit it to myself that I did, in fact, wish he'd stay. After getting emotional over the fact that he would eventually leave earlier that day, I couldn't deny it to myself any longer.

I was attached to Lear, and I wanted him to stay. It was hardly fair of me, and very selfish, but that's what I wanted. But he couldn't. He had a home to get back to, and a job that was probably wondering what had happened to him. Hell, he might even have a significant other that he hadn't mentioned! The fey soldier had said he wasn't married, but that didn't mean he didn't have some other kind of committed relationship. Or...maybe a not so committed one, given how outrageously he flirted.

What if he did have someone back home? The thought made me more than a little upset, for some reason.

If he did have someone back home, and he was still so teasing and flirtatious with me, then...I liked him a lot less. Yes, I knew he'd spoken of the overall promiscuity of the fey, though I think that really only applied to the high courts, or maybe he was even just projecting, but that didn't make it better. I didn't want to...to be very fond of someone who would cheat so easily. That's just not who I was.

Well damn it! I hated the thought, but it was looking like I'd just have to ask him about it. Lear had been relatively open about most things, so I'd have to gather what little courage I had and just do.

A pretty, pale green dress caught my eye, and I pulled it out. It was dotted with little yellow flowers. "This one is cute," I murmured.

"It does make me think of you!" Ama gave a girlish giggle. "You do look cute in green! Well, you look cute in most colors."

I grinned at her. "Thanks, Ama! I do like green a lot though." I always thought it looked nice with my honey blonde curls, especially sage green, like this was.

Lear stepped out. "Here's the fit," he said, turning so we could see his back as well. "This size shirt is long enough, and fits my shoulders, but I'd like it taken in a little through the chest just so it's not quite so loose. And the trousers do need letting out."

"Of course!" Ama smiled, going to the sewing table and picking up her measuring tape, pins, and chalk. She had him raise his arms, and put some pins here and there. "Would that be better?"

"Yes."

"Alright, go change, but mind the pins, and I'll do the same for the rest of what you pick out. It should go pretty quickly, and letting the pants out will take no time at all!"

"Alright." He went and changed. They repeated the process with several outfits. "That should be enough," he said, coming back out in the clothes he'd worn into the store.

"I'll get started on it. It shouldn't take me too long," the seamstress assured him.

Lear drifted over to me. "You were saying you liked a dress?" He'd probably been able to hear our conversation pretty easily, even from the dressing room, given his excellent hearing.

"Yeah, this one." I showed it to him.

"It's cute," he agreed. "Do you like green?"

"Yeah, it's my favorite color. Especially this sage color." I smiled, reaching out and touching the fabric again. It was very soft, and the little yellow flowers did make for a cute little pattern.

"It's a nice color." Lear nodded.

"You have very particular thoughts about your clothing," I commented.

"Yes. Clothes are important in the feylands, especially for anyone remotely important in the government. The importance of good quality, well-fitting, and fashionable clothing was drilled into me from a fairly young age. In some ways, it can be like armor. Good quality, fashionable clothing can protect you by winning admiration, which leads to power. Low-quality clothing can leave you vulnerable, since it leaves you open to accusations of incompetence, lack or misuse of wealth, or other frowned-upon traits." He shrugged.

"That's very odd to me." I blinked. To me, a dress was just a dress. Although I did feel nicer if it fit well, and looked good.

We were quiet for a few moments.

The thought that he might be cheating on a girlfriend or boyfriend or someone drifted through my head again. I couldn't distract myself totally from it, which made me a bit uneasy as I stood there beside him.

"Are you going to get it?" he asked.

"Yeah, I think so." I nodded.

We were quiet again.

Lear frowned. "Everything alri-" The bell jingled as other customers entered, and he cut off, looking to the door, and swearing in annoyance under his breath as he saw who'd entered.

It was a couple of girls who I didn't really know, but I was pretty sure had been several years below me in school.

"Welcome in! I'm working on an order right now, dears, but have a look around, and I'll be happy to help when I can!" Ama called cheerfully from her sewing machine.

"We're just looking today, Ama! Wanted to see if you had

anything new." One of the girls chirped. She had straight, flaxen blonde hair, sparkling blue eyes, and a willowy figure.

"I probably do, I've been a busy little bee lately!" Ama laughed as she worked.

"Excellent!" the other girl giggled. She was shorter and on the curvier side, with dark curly hair, and large, doe-like brown eyes.

Judging by the direction of their gazes, it hadn't been the clothes they'd come to look at. Or maybe they had, but now that they were there and had caught sight of Lear, they'd stay there to gawk to their hearts' content.

Great.

Despite my sudden misgivings about Lear's relationship status, I felt a pang of jealousy rise nonetheless. I had felt the same way when Bekka had ogled him, though it hadn't been quite as sharp a feeling, given that I at least knew that Bekka was ultimately a good person.

"I don't think I've seen you around before; are you new?" the blonde-haired young woman asked.

"We'd definitely remember if you'd gone to school with us!" The dark-haired one giggled.

Lear cast a glance at me, but I turned back to look at the dresses before he could catch my eye.

I couldn't let what I was feeling show, of course. The last thing I wanted was for him to know I felt jealous over him, because not only would he tease me, but it was also hardly fair. I had no claim on him whatsoever. Sure, I didn't want to be trapped in a crowd if he was bombarded by people, nor did I want the scrutiny that would fall on me if something like that did happen, and that was fair enough, but I had no right to get upset if other women flung themselves at him, really.

"I'm just passing through. I'm Winna's patient," Lear replied mildly.

"Wait, *you're* the one staying with Winna?!" the dark-haired girl gasped.

Here we go. I rolled my eyes, glad they couldn't see my expression.

"You were supposed to be some kind of fey person, I thought!" The blonde one sounded like she was pouting.

I felt a surge of magic, and turned in time to see Lear reveal his scales, claws, and second set of eyes, which he had wide open. "Who said I wasn't?"

They gave a squeak of surprised dismay, and fell back a few steps.

There was another surge of magic, and the fey features disappeared again.

I snorted, smiling a little and telling them, "Don't worry, he won't hurt you."

"Oh, I won't, will I?" he grumbled.

"Lear," I murmured, unable to keep from being amused with him. "It's fine."

He turned his green eyes to me. "No, it's not. You don't want the attention or the gossip. And that's okay. You shouldn't have to deal with it if you don't want to."

I managed to hold his gaze for a few moments before looking away, my face heating. "I-I know."

"I don't particularly want the attention either, believe it or not."

"No?" I tilted my head to the side. "And I guess you can't lie."

"No, I can't."

"So...are you two dating?" the blonde asked, brow slightly wrinkled as she tried to figure out our interactions.

"Not for my lack of trying." Lear shrugged. "But it seems like she won't have me."

"Stop being ridiculous." I rolled my eyes, and turned to the girls. "Like he said, Lear is my patient." Saying that was really starting to get old. "He's just passing through."

"Oh, would he take me with him when he goes?" The brunette giggled, apparently over the moment of fear that seeing Lear's true appearance had induced.

"No." Lear said flatly. "Now, if you'll excuse us, I was busy telling

Winna how much I'd like to see her try on these dresses." He reached out and grabbed the green dress I'd been admiring, as well as several others from various surrounding racks, seemingly at random. Then he gripped me firmly on the elbow with the hand not holding the clothes, and steered me towards the dressing room.

"Lear!" I protested.

"Go put them on. I want a fashion show," the fey man told me sternly, handing me the dresses, taking my purse, and pushing me into the changing room all at once, then shutting the door behind me.

"Lear!" I objected again, blinking.

"You're lucky I didn't come in there with you. Now change," he told me through the door.

"Lear!" I squeaked.

"As much as I like hearing you say my name," he said, tapping his fingers lightly on the door as he did, "go ahead and try them on." Oh gods...that man.

"They won't suit me! Other than the green one, you picked them at random," I muttered, knowing his fey ears would pick up my words.

"I didn't, actually. We were standing there for a bit after you showed me the green one. I saw them all then." Lear paused, lowering his voice. "Is...everything okay? You've kind of suddenly seemed off."

"It's nothing," I muttered, starting to change. I did want to see what the green dress looked like on me.

"Winna."

"Lear, please," I whispered.

"Alright," he murmured. There was a pause, then he asked, "Are you done changing?"

"Give me a minute."

"One minute, and then I'm coming in regardless."

"Lear!" I squeaked again, really not sure if he was joking or not.

His low chuckle carried through the door, and I realized he had been joking. I...I think.

I smoothed out the skirt, then opened the door so he could see. "There. Less than a minute."

Lear grinned, but cast an analytic gaze. "It fits well. Ama won't have to alter it at all."

"Are those girls still here?" I asked quietly.

"No, they left when I mentioned I liked hearing you say my name," he replied mildly, reaching out to put his hands on my shoulders and turning me around so he could see the back of the dress.

"Lear," I mumbled, now able to see us both in the mirror on the back of the fitting room wall.

Suddenly, he'd leaned down, and his lips brushed my ear as he murmured, "By all means, please keep saying my name."

"Le- mmm!!" I caught myself before I said his name again, and stamped my foot, flustered and upset all at once. "Please, I'm really not in the mood!"

It was quiet for a few moments.

"Winna, please tell me what's wrong." His voice was now serious and quiet.

I sighed, resigning myself to my fate. He read me too well, despite the fact that we really hadn't known one another very long. "If...if I do, will you promise you won't make fun of me?"

"Cross my heart and hope to die."

"Say it, Lear."

"I promise I won't make fun of you because of what you tell me regarding what's bothering you right now," he told me.

"Well, you're leaving yourself ample wiggle room for later, I see." I rolled my eyes at him.

Lear smiled wickedly, but he put his arms around my shoulders, and pulled me back into his chest. "Of course! That's what makes life interesting for fey folk! At least, back home, anyway. Now, what's wrong?"

I stared at him through the mirror, able to meet his gaze a little easier that way. "I...I realized I really don't know all that much about you."

"That's fair. What would you know of me? I'll tell you whatever you want to know."

"You flirt and tease and make me flustered all on purpose, but I don't..." I paused, then closed my eyes and made myself finish, "Well, you could have some dedicated significant other back home, and the idea that you flirt and tease so easily and freely while having one is upsetting to me. I wouldn't want anyone I was dating in any serious way to act the way you do, promiscuity of the fey be damned! And I don't really want to be friends with anyone who would treat a significant other in such a way, even when they're far away." Tears came to my eyes.

Lear set his chin down on top of my head. "So you imagined a significant other for me, and got upset on their behalf."

"Do you have one?" I pressed him, remembering what he'd said about pressing for the truth.

"No, I don't. I told you I'm not married." His tone was even.

"You could still be in some kind of relationship, Lear, that's what I'm thinking of."

"I don't have any kind of committed relationship beyond friendships," he told me slowly and seriously. "I am not cheating on or disrespecting anyone by flirting with you. I told you that I get around, and that's true, but I'm not in any serious relationships." The disguised fey man flashed a bright, mischievous grin at me. "So you can just let me get on with my flirting, and rest assured that it's totally innocent!"

I huffed, rolling my eyes and wiping at them. "There's nothing innocent about it!"

"Hmmm." Lear leaned down, and I felt his lips trail down my neck, which made me freeze. But when he spoke again, his tone was gentle and relatively serious, "I like that you don't want to associate with someone who disrespects their significant other or spouse by even just flirting." He squeezed me gently. "High fey folk get very desensitized to stuff like that, since it's pretty prevalent in our society. It's a nice change of pace."

"Well, I'm hardly the only human that feels that way," I mumbled.

"I know. But thank you for reminding me of it. Low fey folk tend to be a bit more like you lot, far more committed to significant others," Lear replied. He kissed my neck gently, but very briefly, then let go and pushed me back into the dressing room, pulling the door shut behind me.

I shivered. The idiot had kissed me. I stood there for a few moments, turning over what had just happened in my mind.

"Are you changing into the next dress?" he asked mildly through the door. "You have three minutes before I'm coming in."

"Hold up!" I protested, frantically struggling out of the dress, doing my best to get out of it quickly without busting any seams.

There was a very slight pause before he told me, "We didn't discuss the dress much, but it did look very nice, and I think you should get it."

"Y-yeah?"

"Yes. Which one are you trying on next?"

"Uh, it's red."

"Oh, good." He sounded pleased, and something about that worried me.

I slipped into the dress, then realized why he'd been happy about it. It was a relatively fancy dress, covered with sparkles, and was pretty tight and low-cut. I chewed my lip as I stared in the mirror, not sure whether I wanted to leave the fitting room in it.

"Ten, nine, eight-" he started to count down.

"Wait, wait, no, just let me try on another one!" I protested.

But he continued, "Seven, six, five-"

"Oh fine." I threw my hands up.

"Three, two, one." He opened the door, grinning wickedly, and I looked away, covering my cleavage with my hands, my face as red as the dress. His expression shifted, and his tone was very earnest when he said, "I think it looks nice."

"I-it's so tight. A-and too low-cut."

144

"Winna, it's a formal dress, of course it is." He took my hands and gently pulled them away, but kept his gaze on my face. "I misjudged the size though, so it's probably a bit more tight than it would be otherwise. I thought you were skinnier."

"Hey!" I protested. I wasn't a stick, but I wasn't exactly fat, either.

The fey man's iridescent green eyes blinked, then he laughed. "No, not like that! Sorry, my phrasing was rude. I meant that you're curvier than I thought. That's all. I'll go get a larger size."

"I'd really rather not," I muttered, staring hard at the floor. "I just want to put on my own clothes again."

Lear studied me for a few moments, then took some of the dresses that were in the fitting room, saying, "Wait here." He disappeared, then returned with different ones. "Try these instead."

"Why?"

"You'll like these better than the others. I'd grabbed those because I knew I'd like them on you. These are ones you'll like on you."

"Promise."

"I promise," he told me.

Chapter 17

Tea and Friends

Lear had been right; Winna had liked the second set of dresses he'd grabbed a lot more. He'd also stopped threatening to come in if she didn't try the next one on, since he'd realized that flustering her wasn't really helping the situation any.

That said, it was fun to fluster her. He'd quickly found it was one of his favorite things to do.

Part of him was also disappointed that she hadn't wanted to get the red dress. It showed off her curves in precisely the way he'd imagined it would. Most of the fey women back in the feylands were practically all stick thin, hard as steel, and cold as ice. At least, the ones he'd known from the upper-class, anyway. There were always exceptions, but still. On the other hand, Winna was soft and warm, thanks to her generous figure. Coupled with her sweet, gentle disposition, it was no wonder he was drawn to her like no one he'd ever known before.

Soon, Ama finished her quick alterations, so they paid, then were on their way to the tea shop.

The fey soldier took Winna's small hand and put it back into the crook of his elbow as they left the clothing store. "Are we good, now?"

Her dark eyes blinked. "Y-yeah."

"Good." The disguised fey man patted her hand. "I'm really looking forward to those tea cakes you mentioned."

"Me too!" She giggled, brightening at the mention of the treats. "They're so good!"

Lear smiled at her. He hesitated for a moment, then told her, "Just so you know, we have a meaningful connection, Winna. A very meaningful one. One I don't intend to abandon by leaving when I'm healed."

Her face heated, but she didn't say anything, keeping her eyes fixed ahead, though they looked a little glazed over.

He continued, "I'll have to go back home eventually, yes, but I'll stay as long as I can with you. And then when I have to go, I will come back, provided you're okay with that. I'd say you could come with me, but it's an awfully long trip, and the feylands aren't always pleasant for humans." Maybe, with some finagling, he'd get permission to set up a mushroom ring portal so he could travel back and forth more easily. It would take a lot of convincing, though. "I don't think you want to leave your home here, either. The cats wouldn't enjoy a trip like that, either, and I know there's no way you could ever leave them behind. Nor would I want you to."

Winna was quiet for a few more moments, but then set her head against his arm. "I-I...I'll probably leave here someday. But not...not now. I'm not ready for that. Maybe when everyone I know is gone, as sad as that sounds, but that'll make it easier."

"That's understandable," he told her. "We can travel in style, then, and you can take the ladies with you."

Unless, of course, he could get that portal set up. The various generals and ministers would be against it; they never liked his ideas. But in the end, his only real boss was the king, and Asher and Lear had known one another for their entire lives. Lear had always been Asher's right-hand man, perfectly willing to do the dirty work, even when that eventually wound up meaning becoming an assassin on his best friend's behalf for the sake of the kingdom. So no, it wouldn't be too difficult to convince Asher to let him set up a mush-room ring.

"Stroopwafel won't be around then," the young woman murmured.

Lear grimaced. "No, but I expect there will be another cat to keep Diana company on that long journey, though. One you love just as much."

She was quiet again, then took a deep breath and managed a smile. "You're right. I love them both very much, but I'll also love other kitties just as much, too. They won't replace my Stroopwafel, but I can love whatever kitty I have then too. I...I have infinite love for infinite kitties."

Lear snorted. "Good. And sorry, I didn't think before I spoke."

"Oh, it's fine. I shouldn't get emotional."

"No, it's okay. When the people we love die, it's sad. That includes pets. It's almost worse with pets, isn't it?"

"Yeah, cause they're innocent. I'm glad I have Diana. She's incredibly old, and basically immortal." Winna smiled a little.

"You know, I'm actually kind of curious about that."

"Yeah."

"Yes." They arrived outside the tea shop, and pushed inside.

"There you are!" Bekka sang, beaming at them. "Welcome in!"

"It smells good," Lear commented.

"It always does!" Winna sighed happily as Bekka showed them to a table.

The entire tea shop was decorated in pale pinks and creamy whites. Even the tablecloths were light petal pink with white polka dots. It was an altogether cheerful little place, and the large window at the front of the shop let in a lot of light.

After perusing the menu for a little while, they ordered, and Bekka traipsed happily away, sending her curls bouncing.

"So, you're curious about Diana?" his lovely companion asked, steering the conversation back to her beloved familiar.

"Yes. Divine-sent familiars are uncommon. Even more

uncommon than humans who can use magic. I think Diana is only like the..." he wrinkled his nose as he searched his memory, "fifth I've heard of. Ever."

"Oh?" Winna tilted her head to the side, curious.

He nodded. "Do you know which goddess blessed your family?"

The young woman shook her head, sighing. "No, I don't. That's one of those things that I think has just been lost over time. You'd think we'd remember something like that, though!" She gave a wry smile, then paused before adding, "I wonder if that's added to the lessening of the magic throughout the generations, that we don't even remember her name anymore."

"It's possible." He shrugged.

It was quiet for a little while.

Lear broke the silence, musing, "I would be very interested to know which goddess it was, though."

"Me too, honestly."

"If we could figure it out, you might be able to go to a temple and ask for reaffirmation of it."

"Reaffirmation of the gift?" She blinked, surprised at the suggestion.

"Yes. It'd restore the power that has been lost over the generations. If the goddess in question is willing, anyway. There's no guarantee."

"Interesting. I never would have thought something like that was possible, honestly, so I've definitely never considered it before."

"I'm not surprised, divine-given gifts like yours aren't exactly common. Normally, it's more like...you'll be wealthy, or gifted in archery, or an amazing musician, or something more like that. It's rarely the ability to use magic, even if it is only healing magic."

Winna shrugged, gesturing vaguely with her hands. "I know I should probably know this kind of stuff, but I don't, so...if you say so."

Lear smiled a little, shaking his head. "I know. Sorry, I'm not really expecting an answer. I know you don't know, by no fault of your own. I'm just musing aloud."

Bekka returned to the table with their order, which consisted of a towering, two-tiered tea-tray and two pots of tea. "There you go!" She smiled at them. "Now, if you need anything else, just give a shout, my liege." She bowed jokingly.

"We will!" Winna laughed a little. "Thank you, Bekka."

"No problem!" Bekka grinned, waving as she walked off to tend to other customers.

Lear poured them both tea, and added some sugar to his. He noticed that Winna took both sugar and milk in hers, which he filed away for future reference before turning his attention to the treats on the tea tray. "Now, I'm going to taste one of these famous tea cakes!"

"Well, I don't know about famous, but I think they're pretty fantastic!" His young human companion grinned.

They both took one of the treats. It was a small square piece of cake covered entirely in chocolate icing, piped in delicate swirls and hearts on top, broken only by the occasional, well-placed dot of pink icing, or a fresh raspberry. They bit into the delights in unison.

"Yeah, that's pretty good." Lear nodded approvingly. The cake itself was a moist, chocolate confection, with a tangy raspberry filling to cut the sweetness.

"I love them!" She giggled. "I'd say I should learn to make them, but then nothing could stop me, and I'd just have them all the time!"

Gods, he loved her smile.

They ate their treats and drank their tea, and were soon on their way back to Dern's house. The dwarf waved at them from his porch as they retrieved the cart and very patient Poppy.

"You're a very good girl, I'll give you oats again when we're back home," Lear told the beast, reaching out to rub the pony's neck.

"You spoil her." Winna grinned.

"Yes. There's no harm in spoiling animals," he told her as they climbed into the driving seat of the cart.

"You're right, there's really not." She sighed, tone happy.

"You spoil them just as much," he replied.

"I do my best." Winna nodded agreeably.

Once they were a little ways out of town, Lear removed the illusion magic.

"There you are." She smiled at him.

"I was never not here." He rolled his eyes.

"No, I know. This is just actually you, I mean."

"I know." Lear smiled back at her, then reached out and slipped his arm around her to pull her close. "Just so you know, whatever this turns out to be, between us, it'll be good, alright? Even if we part ways, it'll still be okay." He paused. "Do you trust me on that?"

"I...I think so," she murmured, leaning into him.

"Good." He nodded.

They rode for a long while in a comfortable silence, until the enormous hill that the village sat beneath seemed a lot smaller, and the cottage was visible in the distance.

Winna finally spoke, "What should we do for the rest of today."

"I mean, I have thoughts and suggestions, but I don't think you'd like them at this point." Lear snorted. There were quite a few things he'd like to do with her, but she probably wasn't ready for them yet.

Winna blinked. "I mean, I'm open to suggestions."

Realizing she'd missed his innuendo, he arched an eyebrow and shot her his most wicked smile, "Are you sure?"

The young woman immediately turned bright red. "Oh! No! No...no."

"I thought so. You missed my tone."

"You're the worst." She rolled her eyes at him.

"Yes, yes I am." He grinned, then thought for a moment and told her, "But in all seriousness, I'd like to get into some of those old books, see if I can decipher any of them."

"Sure." Winna shrugged. "I think I'll weave. I'm almost done with the last shawl."

"Alright. Let me know if you want help."

"I will."

They drove up to the cottage, and Lear dropped Winna off at the porch, then went to turn the cart around, meaning to take it back to the barn.

A sudden, strange feeling that he couldn't place caught him off guard, and he paused.

"Hm." The fey man frowned, flicking his second set of eyes open.

"What's wrong?" Winna was standing in the doorway, and looked back.

"I don't know if anything is wrong, per se," he told her. "Something just feels...off. I can't-" he cut off as a large heat signature hurtled itself at him from the sky.

Lear reacted, flinging himself sideways off the cart.

Poppy neighed in fear, rearing back as something she couldn't see blasted by her.

The fey man rolled, landing in a crouching position. He saw Winna start to leave the house. Terror that she'd be hurt coursed through him, so he shouted, "Stay inside!" He darted to his feet, claws extended, and attempted to make it to the cover of the cottage.

But the unseen attacker swooped back in and slammed into him, throwing him to the ground and then landing on top of him so hard that he worried several ribs might have broken. A pair of unseen hands grabbed his shirt, and Lear grabbed at the area, catching hold of whoever was there, and pulling for his magic. A hiss of pain escaped him as the poison hindered him, but he was able to direct the magic into his attacker and break the illusion spell that kept it invisible to normal eyes.

An unfortunately familiar face grinned and peered down at him, its skeletal face in a permanent, evil smile due to its lack of skin.

"Not so strong without your magic, huh?!" Veris hissed. "I should have killed you last time! That's what I get for assuming you'd just die on your own! But I'll finish the job now!"

"Lear!" Winna sobbed, starting to take a halting step out once more.

His eyes flickered to her. "Stay inside!" he screamed again, filled with horror at the idea of her getting hurt or killed. "He can't touch you if you're inside!"

The young woman froze, then withdrew entirely into the cottage. But she left the door open, clutching the frame, visibly trembling in terror as she watched.

"Oh, that's no fun!" Veris cackled. "I could stay amused for a long time with her!"

"Over my dead body!" Lear spat into the other high fey man's face.

"That's the general idea!" Veris sneered.

Lear had a few more tricks up his sleeves, and pulled for his magic to release his wings, kicking forward as he did and blasting the attacker off of him.

In a test of strength, Veris would usually be no match for Lear, but with the poison weakening his system, he was much easier prey. The only reason Veris had been able to hit him with the poisoned barb to begin with was due to the powerful illusion spell the crazed fey man excelled in. It was the same illusion magic that had masked his presence at the cottage just now, so that Lear hadn't noticed him until it was too late.

Terror seized me as I watched Lear and the horrible-looking fey attacker blasting around as they fought.

The...thing was a strange-looking creature, and looked like some kind of walking skeleton. Or rather, it was more than just a skeleton; I could see muscles and tendons, but there was no skin at all. It was altogether a grotesque sight.

My heart pounded in my chest. The fight wasn't going well for Lear, from what I could tell. For the first time, I desperately wished my magic had fighting applications instead of just healing, if only so I could help save my fey patient and companion.

The grappling pair slammed into the ground before the cottage, just by the front steps to the porch. Dirt, dust, and rocks filled the air for a moment. When it cleared, I saw the attacker had Lear on the ground, and was clutching him by the throat.

The strange bone-fey gave a terrifying, rasping laugh, and bore down, putting pressure on Lear's neck, which sent him gasping and scrabbling at the skinless fingers on his throat. His face turned an alarming shade of red as he struggled to breathe.

"Lear!" I sobbed, wanting to run outside, to push the dreadful, bony, muscly...thing away and drag Lear into the house where he'd be safe. But I knew good and well that if I set foot outside the protection of my home, I'd be as good as dead.

The thing slowly turned its horrible, skeletal face towards me. Its dark eyes burned with a terrible, evil delight. "Okay now, little girl. Let me in."

"N-no!" I cried.

"I'll rephrase. Let me in," he leaned down more heavily on Lear's neck, "or I'll make you watch as I kill him right now."

"No!" I sobbed, clutching the door frame so desperately in my terror that it hurt my fingers, though I barely noticed.

"It'll be slow and painful," the evil fey hissed, clearly delighting in the situation. "I'll strip his flesh, and then-"

"Stop!" I gasped, unable to take it anymore. "W-will you promise not to hurt us i-if I do."

"Would you accept the promise of a fey?" He snorted.

"I-I would. You can't lie."

"If that's what you want." It cocked its head back, hissing again, "Let me in!"

"D-don't!" Lear gasped, his voice literally strangled.

"I-I can't watch you d-die!" I squeaked miserably.

"H-he'll-" Lear started to protest, but the other fey bore down even harder on his throat, and Lear gargled awkwardly.

"You're running out of time, little girl. Let me in!"

"I-I-I...." I took a deep breath, then started to step aside. But before I could tell the evil thing to come in, a small grey shadow slipped by my feet. "Diana!" I gasped, terrified as the little familiar left the safety of the cottage.

"What's this?" The attacker was caught off-guard at the appearance of the little diluted grey tabby.

Totally unafraid, Diana walked forward, her tail raised in interest.

Much to my surprise, the skeletal fey man scrambled off of Lear, suddenly desperate to get away from my oldest, littlest friend. "Don't come closer!" he screeched.

"Diana, please!" I screamed. Gods forbid if anything should happen to her! I could lose both my Annie and Lear in one go, at this rate!

Lear gasped for breath for a few moments, clutching at his throat, then his eyes rolled back as he fell unconscious.

The fey attacker finally managed to haul himself to his feet, and had half-turned, I assume to run, before Diana was upon him, her incredible power welling suddenly and swiftly.

There was a sudden, blinding burst of magic, and I threw my hands up to cover my face, screaming, "ANNIE!"

Chapter 18

Diana's Gift

Lear woke to his throat on fire, and the rest of his body throbbing miserably.

The sounds of whimpering sobs met his ears.

Winna!

He forced both sets of his eyes open, and gasped for breath, which hurt immensely, but he couldn't just not breathe.

"Winna!" he croaked, looking around wildly.

The area had been exposed to an insanely strong amount of magic. Its presence lingered around them, a blanket of pale lilac to his heat-sensitive eyes.

What the hell had happened?!

Finally, he saw the young woman sitting a few feet away, clutching something to her chest. Weak golden magic skittered across her form, trailing into the little grey bundle cradled in her arms as tears poured down her face.

Horror filled him as he realized what the young human mage was holding. The still slightly disoriented fey man shifted, shutting his second set of eyes as he dragged his aching body inch by inch over to her.

"Wh-what happened?!" he groaned in alarm.

"D-Diana! Sh-she....sh-she-" Winna was crying so hard she could barely speak.

"Is she...gone?!" he gasped, seized with terror on Winna's behalf.

"N-no! No...not...not yet! I-I'm...trying to k-keep her f-from going! I-I c-can't...c-can't lose her too!" Her voice rose in volume and desperation as she spoke, ending in a hysterical scream.

"Breathe, Winna, breathe," he whispered, reaching out and putting a gentle hand on her back while he wracked his brain, trying to come up with some clever solution to the problem. But nothing came.

The little mage managed to take a deep breath. "Sh-she a-and Stroopwafel a-are a-all I have! I-I can't l-lose her t-too!"

"I know, Winna, I know." he coughed, grimacing as he pushed himself into a sitting position.

He took a brief moment to take stock of himself. Though covered in bruises and scratches, not to mention a nearly crushed windpipe, he'd ultimately escaped with relatively minor injuries. He'd gotten lucky.

Veris had gotten distracted by Winna, and had let his own desire to manipulate and kill the young human get in the way of killing Lear, which had allowed time for Diana to realize things were amiss, and interfere.

"Y-you're h-hurt too," she sniffled, "b-but i-if I stop..."

"Don't stop. I'll be alright. I'm not that badly hurt," he told her, reaching up to rub his throat.

"I-I...I-I wish I was stronger!" she sobbed.

"I know, honey, I know," Lear murmured, drawing himself closer. He reached out and circled his arms around them, pulling Winna, and, by proxy, Diana, onto his lap. There was really only one thing he could think to do. Closing his eyes, he pulled for his magic, ignoring the pain the poison caused in his veins, and directed the raw power into Winna. "Here. Use it. I'm no healer, but maybe it'll help a little."

Without another word, Winna began to direct his magic,

reshaping it to be more like healing magic, her brow creased with concentration.

The magic flowed down her arms and into Diana.

"Sh-she feels a little better now. M-more stable," the young woman whispered.

"Good." Lear groaned, setting his forehead against her shoulder. He didn't stop the flow of his magic.

The poison didn't lessen his magic reserves or magical endurance, but it did seriously strain how much he could use at one time. At the moment, he was capable of a weak stream, when normally, well, how do you compare an ocean to a stream? They were both water, but the difference was immense.

"I-I...I know if...if she did go, she's not...not really gone, she'd j-just go back to her goddess, but...I-I doubt I'd e-ever see her again," Winna whispered, leaning over to press her face gently into Diana's silken fur. "I-I love her very much!"

"I know. And she loves you," he assured her in his very hoarse voice.

There was a pause as Winna continued to push magic into her kitty.

Lear finally broke the silence, "What exactly happened? I assume there was a blast of magic."

"Pure magic. I-I've never...never felt a-anything like it before! And she's never done anything like it before, e-either," Winna mumbled.

"It's a divinely given familiar's last resort. They can't direct their own magic, due to severe restrictions put on them, since they're technically the servant of a deity, but, in a pinch, they can release all, or most, of it." He paused. "She used it to get rid of Veris. I imagine it literally evaporated him, as pure as her energy is, given how evil he is." He sighed, then told her, "It means she was willing to give up her life to save you, Winna."

Winna choked, and sniffed, and hiccuped, and sobbed, but didn't reply. Lear continued to hold her.

He reached out and stroked Diana's fur, murmuring hoarsely, "Sweet little queen."

"Sh-she is!" the mage wailed, bursting into tears anew.

There was a soft maow, and Stroopwafel padded carefully down the porch stairs, coming forward to sniff them. She had likely seen that the front door had been left open, and had finally come to investigate, now that the danger had passed.

"O-oh Stroopwafel!" The young woman sobbed, wiping her face, and reached out to pet her other cat, keeping a secure, but gentle, hold on Diana's small form in the crook of her other arm.

Stroopwafel brushed her head against Winna's fingers, then climbed onto Lear's legs and into Winna's lap, settling beneath where she was holding Diana. The usually silly tabby seemed to understand how upset her mistress was, and began to purr loudly.

As if sensing the other cat's purr, Diana's iridescent sea-green eyes flickered open, and she gave a weak maow.

"A-Annie!" Winna gasped, holding the kitty up and pressing her face gently into her grey fur. "Oh, my Annie!" she sobbed. "P-please don't go! I-I don't want you to go! I-I love you so much!"

Diana maowed again, her little voice slightly stronger, and shifted in Winna's arms, prompting the young woman to lower her for a moment as she showed her mistress her very fluffy tummy, and began to purr loudly.

"She said she's not going anywhere just yet," Lear translated.

"Y-yeah."

"Yes," he said firmly with a nod for emphasis.

"Oh, thank the gods," Winna whispered, and pressed her face gently into Diana's tummy. "Y-you saved us, miss! Th-thank you so, so much! B-but please don't...don't go...I-I still need you. I-I'll always need you!"

They sat like that for a minute before Stroopwafel maowed in complaint, also wanting attention, and Diana maowed again as well.

"She said she's okay now, that the worst of the danger has passed, and you can put her down," Lear informed the traumatized mage sitting in his lap.

"A-are you sure."

Another maow from Diana, and Winna shifted, dislodging Stroopwafel, who maowed in annoyance. The young woman gingerly put her oldest friend on the ground, then bent and kissed the little grey diluted tabby on the forehead.

Diana stretched luxuriously, licked her right front paw, and used it to swipe at her face and ears. She then headed slowly back towards the cottage with Stroopwafel trailing behind.

"Her...magic is very low," Winna murmured, watching her cats as they made their way to the porch, then turning her attention to Lear.

"It's a last-ditch thing. I'm...not sure how much of it will return. It's an uncommon occurrence." He sighed, rubbing his aching throat.

"Well, even if she can't help me anymore, I'm just glad she's alive." The young woman shook her head.

"I know." Lear coughed.

"Are you okay? I-I'm sorry I-"

"Don't apologize for a thing." He stopped her, putting his hand loosely over her mouth. "You were in an untenable situation. I understand." He let his hand fall.

"I-I...I-I almost let h-him in," she whispered, rubbing her eyes and shuddering slightly.

"I know. That's why Diana acted. She could sense his evil." He paused. "Veris is the one who poisoned me. He...he's as evil as a fey gets."

"You were sent to take him out."

"Yes, and he got lucky," Lear muttered, then sighed, shaking his head. "Had he gotten in, he would have killed you, then worn your skin and used your position as the healer of the village to slowly pick off people one by one."

Horror filled her expression. "Oh gods!"

"He wasn't always like that," Lear told her. He'd actually met Veris before he'd gone mad, and he'd been an alright sort of guy. No one really knew what had happened. "Somehow he lost his own skin and...well, that drove him mad, I think."

"Th-that's disgusting and terrifying!" She shivered again in distaste.

"It is." He nodded. "He caused enough trouble that I was finally dispatched to end him. He caught me unawares as I was tracking him, thanks to that wicked illusion magic of his, but I managed to change into my cat shape just before he hit me with a poisoned dart. It was lucky."

Winna leaned forward, setting her head against his chest. "I'll say." They sat there for a moment longer, and she pulled away. "Let's go in." She stood, then helped him up, and they made their way slowly back to the house.

The young woman helped him to the couch, then settled down beside him. "I know I can't do much, but I can still at least ease the pain."

"Anything you can do is enough, Winna," he told her, managing a smile. "I'm just glad we're all alive and safe. It could have easily ended very differently."

"I-I know," she murmured. Diana and Stroopwafel hopped up onto the cushion between them, purring loudly. They both automatically reached out to pet both cats at the same time.

"You saved all of us, Diana," Lear told the little cat in his hoarse voice. "I'm so, so grateful."

Annie maowed softly, and closed her eyes, slowly drifting off to sleep.

"I imagine she's very tired," Winna said softly.

"She's exhausted, but playing it off so you don't worry. She'll be okay, but..." Lear frowned, "It won't ever be the same again."

"You said you weren't sure how much would return, right?" Her voice was full of concern.

"Yes." He chewed his lip, then shook his head. "Unfortunately, it kind of takes magic to make more magic, which is why total magical exhaustion can be so dangerous, and difficult to bounce back from, especially for divinely-given familiars. They're magical beings, despite the fact that they're animals. Right now, she has enough magic to keep her alive, but not enough for her body to create more magic."

"I see," Winna murmured, then frowned. "I guess I won't really be able to do much for anyone around here anymore, without her help."

"I'm afraid not." Lear sighed.

They sat quietly for a few moments.

"Well, I'll still do what I can." She shook herself, managing a weak, watery smile. "There's no sense in falling into self-pity." Winna held out her hand. The fey man could tell that the fact that she wouldn't be able to help people nearly as well troubled her deeply. But the brave young woman was setting aside that worry and fear and deciding to move on all the same.

He took it. "You're right. There's no sense in that. You're very sensible and brave."

"I'm hardly that!" She sighed, shaking her head, and pushing her magic into him.

Lear sighed, setting his head back. It wasn't nearly as strong as when Diana helped, but it still felt very nice. "That's not true."

"Yes, it is. I get all flustered over you, which is hardly sensible, and was about to let Veris in to save you because I-I couldn't handle watching him torture you to death! A-and yet I-I couldn't leave the house b-because I-I didn't really want to die, either. I'm not sensible or brave!"

"Neither of those things makes you not sensible or not brave. To care for other people so much that you can't stand to see them hurt is brave, and to face continuing on with life as usual, even though you're scared because Diana can't help you anymore, is brave." He paused, then added as mischievously as his still slightly croaky voice could manage, "And I'm glad I fluster you. I really do try. I'm glad it works."

"Lear!" She rolled her eyes at him.

He grinned a little, and set his head back against the couch. "I'm grateful you weren't going to let him torture me to death, and grateful Diana intervened so he didn't kill us both. Or he might have left me alive, and forced me to watch him make you suffer. That would have been a fate worse than death, for me."

"We won't know, now. Thank goodness." Winna sighed softly.

It was quiet for a few moments, and she eventually wound her magic down. "I think that's the most I'll be able to do. We can do more healing later, and then again tomorrow," she told him. "The worst of the cuts are mostly healed."

"Thank you." He smiled at her.

"You're welcome."

Since Winna hadn't let go of his hand yet, he pulled her fingers to his lips and kissed them very gently. "I'm glad you're not hurt."

"I wish you hadn't been."

"I'll be alright."

"Your poor hoarse voice!" She frowned. "How about some tea? It might help."

"That would be amazing. And then let's be lazy for the rest of the day, we've more than earned it."

"You and Diana can be lazy. You two are the only ones who did anything. Stroopwafel and I will take care of you as you rest. And I still have to go out to take care of the barn animals."

"You don't have to earn the right to be lazy. And anyway, resting isn't laziness. Besides, I..." he hesitated, then continued, "I want you to stay close." The thought that she would be hurt had terrified him more than he'd let on. "I was terrified I'd lose you. Humor me."

"Oh...alright." The young woman sighed.

"And I'll go with you when you go out to take care of the animals, just in case. I'm certain that Diana killed Veris pretty effectively, but...I'll feel better if I'm with you, all the same."

Winna managed a weak smile. "Alright."

Chapter 19

Sick Day

My head throbbed as I woke. "Oh goodness." I groaned. Gods, I felt awful.

I tried to take a deep breath, only to find my nose was super stuffy. My mouth felt about as dry as parchment, so I reached out and took a sip of water from the cup on my bedside table. I grimaced as I swallowed, realizing my throat was very sore.

Great. It wasn't just a stuffy nose. I was sick. Just what I needed. Truly the icing on the cake after a day like yesterday.

Diana got up from her spot by my side, and came to stand near my head, purring loudly. "Hello, sweet miss," I murmured, reaching out to stroke her silken fur. "I feel like poopy this morning. It's not fun."

Thank the goddess that I hadn't lost her. Hell, thank the goddess that I hadn't lost any of them! Diana, Lear, or my Stroop-wafel! If Veris had had his evil way, I'm sure we'd have all wound up dead in one unpleasant way or another. I shuddered, pushing the thought from my mind. It was hard to believe that the attack had only happened the day before. Or maybe I was just struggling to wrap my mind around the fact that we'd been attacked, and that

Diana had lost most of her power. Normally, this area was so peaceful.

Not that bad things didn't happen; they did, but attacks, theft, and murder were all incredibly rare.

Hearing me awake, Stroopwafel got up from where she'd been lying between my ankles, and demanded pets by flopping down on my stomach.

"Oof!" I snorted, but smiled a little. "You silly cat! That's my bladder!"

Stroopwafel maowed loudly, indicating that she didn't care if she was on my bladder or not; she wanted pets! Or that's what I imagined she meant. After all, it was Lear who spoke cat, I still had to guess.

I indulged my silly cat, glad I had two hands, so I could pet the two kitties at the same time.

I let my gaze linger on Diana as I loved on my feline friends. She seemed pretty much herself ever since she'd woken up after exhausting so much of her magic the day before, but had slept even more than usual, which was saying something for a cat. Although that seemed totally understandable, given what had happened. That said, I would be keeping a pretty close eye on her for a little while, at least until I was sure she really was okay.

Shifting slowly, I gently pushed an annoyed Stroopwafel off my stomach, and glanced at the clock. It was a little later than when I usually woke up. It was okay, especially since I wasn't feeling well, but I did still need to get up to take care of the barn animals.

"Gooooods this isn't fun," I muttered as I hauled myself from the bed.

Since I wasn't feeling very well, I gave myself permission to stay in my nightdress, for now. Throwing on a robe over my pajamas, I shoved my feet into a pair of fluffy slippers I kept for when I had a little chill, as I currently did.

Shuffling a little dazedly from my bedroom, I was surprised to hear the sounds of breakfast already being made, and smiled.

Sometimes Lear could be an angel. Sometimes he was a little

devilish...I wasn't sure which side of him I liked more. Cause the twinkle in that handsome devil's eye was...shew, it was something else!

After taking care of the issue of my bladder that Stroopwafel had so helpfully exacerbated with a quick trip to the bathroom, I slowly made my way to the main living area of the cottage. The cats had already done so, and were lounging around. Stroopwafel was stretched out by the heating stones, clearly having not a care in the world, much less a thought in her head, and Diana was curled up cutely in the armchair, looking very cozy indeed.

"You didn't have to make breakfast," I told Lear, going over to the door, kicking off my fluffy slippers, then sitting on the floor to put my boots on, so that I could take care of the animals.

"I wanted to." He smiled at me, then frowned. "You okay?" His voice was still rough from being choked the day before.

"I feel like crap," I replied honestly. "Head hurts, sinuses pounding, sore throat, stuffy nose...ugh."

The gorgeous fey man was at my side in an instant, stopping me from shoving my feet into my shoes. "Oh no, you don't! You're sick. You're staying inside."

"But the animals-"

"I'll do it."

"You're making breakfast!" I protested, flicking my hand to gesture around the kitchen.

"And I can take care of the animals, too. The biscuits need some time in the oven. If you want to help, sit and keep an eye on them," he croaked, shaking his head. "Alright? I'll take care of the outside chores. All the chores, really. You just rest and get better."

"You're supposed to be my patient," I muttered.

"Oh, how the tables have turned! I bet I have a great bedside manner." He grinned at me, then scooped me up and deposited me in a chair in the kitchen, so I could watch the oven. "Stay here."

"I will," I mumbled.

"I'll be back," he said, then darted out the door in the blink of an eye.

Feeling kind of useless, I waited for a little while, then got up and put the tea kettle on. Then I sat back down and stared at the oven.

Lear was soon back, thanks to his fey speed, and joined me in the kitchen.

"I put on the kettle for tea."

"Oh. You didn't have to."

"I wanted to. Gave me something to do," I mumbled.

"Well, you should take it easy from here on out," he told me, lifting me easily again and taking me to the couch this time. Once I was settled, he pulled the blanket off the back and draped it over me, taking a few moments to tuck the blanket around my feet. "There! Now you'll be all cozy!"

"Thank you." I smiled at him.

He stooped and kissed my forehead, then frowned and flicked open his second set of eyes. He studied for a moment before shutting them again. "You have a fever."

"Doesn't surprise me. I feel pretty bad." I grimaced.

"But you were still going to go out into the cold and take care of your animals?" He smiled. "I admire your work ethic."

"Lear, before you came, I didn't have another option. No matter how much I felt like death warmed over, going out to take care of them is what I had to do." I shrugged. "They depend on me for food and water, especially in the winter."

"I know. I just...you work hard."

"I guess," I muttered.

The kettle whistled, and Lear went back to the kitchen to assemble the tea things. He carried it over to the coffee table, telling me, "Some tea will do you some good. I wish we had some lemons, lemon tea would really be nice for you, I think."

"It'd probably be good for your poor throat, too, if we had lemons. But unfortunately, we don't often get them here."

"I imagine not." He shook his head. "Probably not too much citrus in these parts at all, huh?"

"Mm, not really, unfortunately. We get enough so we don't get sick, but there's definitely not an abundance. They just take warmer climes. Otherwise, I'd grow them myself. Have a nice lemon tree and a little orange grove."

Lear smiled. "That would suit you. And then you could have as much lemon as you wanted in your tea."

"Yeah."

We were quiet for a few moments.

When the tea had steeped long enough, he poured me a cup, putting sugar and a splash of cream in it, which was exactly how I liked it, then handed it to me. "Here."

"Thank you, Lear," I murmured.

"Anytime," he said, pouring his own cup.

Soon the biscuits were done, and he'd brought all the breakfast things over. "Just biscuits and bacon, nothing fancy."

"I don't need fancy." I smiled a little. "Thank you for making it."

"I...wish I could give you fancy," he muttered. "But you're welcome."

"Other than the tea shop in town, we don't really do fancy around here. Although that probably isn't actually truly fancy. It's just our version of it."

"It's fancy if you want it to be fancy."

"I guess." I smiled. "But I bet you've been to some fancy places, huh."

"You could say that." He snorted, then coughed a little, throat probably hurting at least some still.

"What's so funny about that?" I rubbed his back absentmindedly, trailing my weak healing magic through him as I did, just to ease any residual pain in his throat.

"Well, you know I'm a soldier."

"Yes, we've discussed that many times." I rolled my eyes at him.

"Well, my squad is...kind of important."

"I'd assumed you were, given you were carrying out an assassination. I don't think normal soldiers do that."

"They don't."

"So...how important is your squad?"

"We answer directly to Asher, the king." He shrugged, like it was no big deal.

I blinked. "Oh. So when you say you've been to fancy places..."

Lear nodded. "Yeah. My apartment is in the fey palace. And my work office."

"Wow." I blinked again, a little surprised. "Did you grow up in the palace? I know you said you grew up with servants."

"I didn't, but I was raised in a manor. Grandfather is a duke."

"Oh goodness!" I laughed. "Do you have a title?"

"No." He shook his head. "But I do have money and connections."

"I see." I nodded. "Is the fey palace the fanciest place you've been to."

"Yes, probably. Not the most interesting though."

"Where's the most interesting place you've been?"

We'd both finished breakfast, and were now just passing the time, working our way through the rest of the large pot of tea Lear had made, which was being kept warm by a little tea light.

"Mm...I think a merfolk village."

"Like an underwater one?!"

"Yep."

"That's cool!" I grinned. "What was it like?"

"A lot like any other village, but with very sea-themed architecture. The buildings are built to resemble seashells."

"Oh! I bet that's pretty!"

He nodded. "It was. Lots of spikes and spires, as such."

"Yes, I imagine!"

"There was a tower in the middle of the town that looked like a tower shell. It had multiple stories and was honestly some of the most interesting architecture I've ever seen!" He grinned.

I grimaced and had to ask, "What's a tower shell?"

"Oh, one of the ones that looks kind of like a unicorn horn."

"Lear, honey, I've never seen a unicorn, and I've never been to the ocean. I only know what a couple of seashells look like because the people who have been to the sea have brought them back with them, and I've only seen artist's depictions of unicorns." I rolled my eyes at him.

He blinked, then laughed sheepishly. "Oh right! My bad. I didn't think." He got up, went over to my writing desk, and got a piece of paper and a pencil. He resumed his seat and drew a long, horn-like shell that had a spiral to it with a few skillful strokes. "It looks like that."

"Oh, ok! That's cool! And you're good at drawing."

"Fey folk tend to be good at artistic stuff." He shrugged. "We hold music and all artistic endeavors in high regard. There are entire schools dedicated to teaching new poets, painters, or pianists."

"It sounds wonderful," I mused. "I can't even imagine it."

"I'll take you someday," Lear grinned.

"Is that a promise?"

"Yes."

"Thanks," I murmured.

We fell silent for a few moments.

"So the building was like a big one of those?" I tapped the page, eager to hear more.

"Massive." He nodded.

"I can't imagine that either!" I laughed a little, shaking my head.

"It was an awesome sight."

"So...if it was all underwater, how did you breathe? I assume you didn't manage to hold your breath, unless that's a fey talent, too."

"No. It was magic." He shrugged. "Some dwarfs at our workshop in the fey palace worked with some merfolk to create a device that acted like gills for us."

"Oh, that's amazing!"

"It was." He nodded. "They were these helmets with enhanced glass visors to hold up at a decent depth."

"What did you have to go to a mer-village for?"

"Intelligence gathering. It was a while ago, now."

"What intelligence were you gathering?"

Lear shrugged. "We were trying to figure out if the rebellion we were trying to snuff out had any sway in that village. If it did, it might be a symptom of a larger issue amongst the merfolk."

"What did you find? Were the merfolk there revolting."

"No. There was just one mer-person who was only tangentially involved. They didn't realize what they'd gotten into, and were just helping a friend from the surface. They couldn't tell us much, and had never intended to help a rebellion. They didn't get in any trouble as such. I don't think the friend in question was directly operating for the rebels, so they didn't get in trouble, either."

"I take it you were able to stop the rebellion?"

"Yep! Although I let one of my squad members take the lead on it, since it was an issue that struck close to home with him." He gave a slightly wry smile. "Actually, he had to take down his own father."

"Oh?"

"Yeah. It's a long story, but...his father had it coming. He was a very bad man. Another duke, like my grandfather. But rotten to the core instead of just mildly mischievous like good ol' granddad."

I arched an eyebrow at him, amused. "Must run in the family, huh?"

"Oh, definitely." He grinned wickedly at me. "Although I like to think I'm more roguish than just mischievous."

"You're definitely something." I rolled my eyes at him, but smiled.

"Well, I do try!" Lear laughed.

We fell quiet for a bit.

"How are you feeling?"

"Pretty shitty still, honestly." I sighed, shaking my head.

"Is there any medicine you can take, or anything?"

"Yeah, I guess we could try some meds. What will help the most will be in the medicine cabinet over there." I motioned to the area where I usually tended to patients.

"Alright. I'll get it for you." He stood, going over to the area I'd indicated.

"It's in a blue bottle with a pink label." Lear rummaged through the cabinets, muttering, "You have a lot of stuff in here."

"Yep, it's accumulated over the years. And some of it is probably older than me. I should go through it and throw everything that's too old away."

"Not today, though. Today you're going to rest." He gave me the bottle of medicine, then went and got me a glass of water. "Here."

"Thanks," I muttered, accepting the water, and then swallowing two pills.

"Why didn't you take it sooner?"

"Eh, wanted to see if I felt any better without it." I shrugged.

"Next time just take the medicine." He shook his head a little. "I'm happy to take care of you, but I'd hate for you to feel miserable just because you didn't take the medicine you had available because you wanted to try to wait it out."

"Alright," I murmured, smiling at him.

"Now, you gotta rest today, okay?"

"I will. I don't think I could get up to much, even if I wanted to." I sighed. "I don't get sick very often; I wonder what brought this on?"

"If I had to hazard a guess, I'd say stress. Between everything that's happened since I got here, and then what happened to Diana yesterday...well, I wouldn't be surprised if you worried yourself sick."

"Ah...no, that does make sense." I sighed.

"So you just focus on getting better." He reached out and gently brushed some stray curls out of my face.

Diana, having heard me say her name a few moments before, got up from her spot on the armchair, stretched luxuriously, and then came to snuggle on my legs, purring loudly.

"Hello, gorgeous," I murmured, reaching out and stroking her silky fur.

"What a good girl." Lear smiled.

"She really is." I sighed, grateful that we were all happy and safe again, even if I was a little under the weather.

Chapter 20

A Problem

I chewed my lip, staring at the salves lined up on the table in front of me.

Lear had insisted that I take it slow and let myself recover before diving back into all the work I usually did. I was only just starting to feel like my usual self now, thanks to the miserable bout of sore throat and stuffy sinuses I'd woken up with the day after Veris' attack. Since I'd been taking it easy, I'd not had a chance to work on any salves. Instead, I'd spent the days reading my favorite books, doing a little embroidery, and loving on my kitties, not to mention thanking the goddess that I hadn't lost anyone to Veris.

But now I needed to get back into the swing of things, and that meant starting to make salves again, but I'd just run headlong into a massive problem.

"You look concerned. What's up?" Lear asked, coming to stand beside me.

"Well, Diana typically helps me enchant the salves I make," I muttered. This was a repercussion of Diana losing most of her power that I hadn't thought of until just now. "All the ones I've made so far have already been enchanted, including these here, but...I can't make any more that'll have any worthwhile healing effects in them without her help."

Lear's gorgeous green eyes blinked, and he frowned. "I see." He paused before asking, "Your livelihood, aren't they?" His throat was much better now, and was now all but healed, though every now and again a note of hoarseness still crept in, especially when he was concerned.

"Mostly, yes. I-I hadn't had the chance to get the shawls enchanted yet, either." I motioned vaguely in the direction of the loom. "I only just thought about it. It's...kind of a problem."

"More than kind of a problem," the fey man muttered. "I'd offer to let you use my magic in place of Diana's, but I don't think it'd work as well."

"No. It was one thing to direct it into her when she just needed magic in her, this is far more delicate, specific work." I shook my head, and stared down at the rows of jars.

It was quiet for a few moments.

A deep sense of sadness and panic filled me. "What...what am I going to do?" My voice broke, and tears rolled down my face. Embarrassed that I was crying over losing my main source of income, instead of just being grateful that Diana and Lear were both even alive, I covered my face.

Lear's strong arms came up around my shoulders, and he pulled me back into him. "Shh...it's alright," he murmured. "I think you'll find that the shawls will sell regardless of if they're enchanted or not. You're very gifted at weaving and embroidery." He paused. "So you're not going to worry about anything, you have a very relevant, marketable skill to fall back on."

"Th-they take me too long to make, though!"

"In the meantime," the fey man continued, "I'm going to start doing some research."

"Research?"

"We're going to figure out a little family history, and track down which goddess gave your family both your gift and Diana." His voice was firm. "And then, we'll take a trip to the closest temple, and we'll ask the goddess to replenish Diana's magic, and to hopefully reaffirm your own gift. Although asking for two things might be a bit much, you might have to choose."

"I would ask for Diana's magic to be returned," I told him immediately. Between having my own magic made stronger, or giving Diana her full power back, and getting to keep her with me, it was no contest, and never would be. Besides, if Diana's magic was restored, there was no need for mine to be any stronger than it already was.

Lear smiled. "I know." He bent, hesitated, then kissed my temple very lightly. "Everything is going to be fine, alright?"

"But wh-what if she ignores the request to return Annie's magic?!" I whimpered. It was entirely possible.

"It's less likely that it'll be her ignoring it, and more likely that the answer is just no, if nothing happens," Lear told me. "But if the answer is no, we'll go back to the drawing board and think of something else."

"I-I don't want to have to s-sell the cottage because I-I can't support myself a-anymore! I-I could maybe go live with one of my brothers, but...I-I...I belong here!" Panic began to rise in me, making my heart pound, and quickening my breathing like I'd just been sprinting. I struggled, trying to pull away, feeling the desperate need to pace.

But Lear didn't let go, and instead squeezed me gently, keeping me close. "Winna, it's alright. I'm not going to let you have to leave your home. We'll figure it out, okay?" His tone was warm, firm, and reassuring.

"B-but-" I started to protest.

He cut me off, "Shh. It's alright." The fey man rubbed my back gently in a circular pattern. "Just breathe. We're going to figure this out. Things are going to work out. We'll put our heads together and figure it out. Just breathe."

I did as he said, and took a deep breath, leaning into him entirely.

176

After a few moments, I regained some semblance of calm, and whispered, "Th-thank you.'

"Of course."

"What...what will I do, Lear?" I was no longer in a hysterical panic, but I was still very concerned. "I might be okay at weaving and embroidery, but I just don't think I can sustain myself with it. Not long-term, anyway. Especially if I can't enchant the shawls or anything anymore."

"Like I said, we'll think of something. Worst comes worse, we'll just, you know, get married, and then it won't matter anyway."

"Don't...don't be silly," I mumbled, rubbing my tear-stained eyes.

"I'm not." He snorted. "You could stay here, and I'd send money."

"Lear, that's not-"

He cut me off gently, smiling, "I know. You don't want that. It's alright, just an option. I wouldn't be opposed to it in the slightest, just so you know, which is why I brought it up, but, well, it can be a last resort, if both of our heads together can't come up with anything else that's reasonable, and nothing else works. And I wouldn't just treat you like some kept woman, or anything. I'd do the thing properly." He paused before continuing, "And that means getting married."

"You would marry me?!" I wondered if my voice could possibly convey the sheer amount of surprise I felt at that moment.

"Of course." I felt him kiss my neck. "I love you very much." He couldn't lie.

Surprise washed over me.

It had been there, fairly plain for me to see, though he hadn't said exactly how he felt up until that moment. It was in his gentle touches, his concern for me, his willingness to help with anything, the sheer terror I'd seen on his face when he'd been shouting at me to stay in the cottage when Veris had attacked. And though it was...maybe silly, I did love him. He was funny, kind, and surprisingly gentle for a fey soldier who readily admitted to going on assassination missions.

Lately, he had really only used his outrageous flirting to make me laugh when I needed a reminder that the world wasn't so bad. He probably wouldn't admit to it if I asked him though. And it was definitely a ridiculous way to go about making me laugh, but he was a ridiculous kind of person. Ridiculous, and I loved him for it.

But I did have one fairly large protest.

"B-but...I-I...you...we haven't really known each other all that long," I muttered, a little taken aback by his somewhat sudden admission.

He shrugged. "That's not necessarily a requirement. Although it is more usual, especially for humans. It's a bit different for fey." He paused. "I do understand you probably aren't on the same page, and that's alright."

"Oh." I tried to turn over his words in my mind.

He wanted to marry me, someday. That was...quite a thought. I loved him, and had known, in my heart, that he felt the same, but I hadn't considered, for whatever reason, that he might want to marry me. He hadn't really seemed like the marrying type to me, I guess, but...well, obviously I was wrong.

It was all just so...so fast. We hadn't known each other for more than a few weeks.

Neither of us spoke for a little while.

"Are you okay?" Lear's tone was concerned.

"I-I...I think so," I mumbled.

"I'm sorry if I upset you."

"No, no, not...not upset. I-I'm just...a little caught off-guard."

"That's okay." He shrugged again. "I know I'm not human, and that's different for you. But sometimes humans meet and fall for someone in a very short time as well."

I knew that, in my head, but it was still just a little jarring, somehow. Another reminder that he wasn't human. But why would that be jarring when humans did meet and marry very quickly sometimes too? Maybe it was just my own slight apprehension over him not being human causing problems more than anything.

"True," I mumbled.

"It's...it's okay that I'm not human, yeah?" he murmured,

suddenly sounding a little worried. Apparently, our thoughts had been running along the same tracks.

"Yeah. Just...sometimes it catches me off guard," I admitted, "but I'll always adjust."

"If you're ever having trouble adjusting to something, just tell me. I want to be able to talk things through with you," he said firmly.

"It...it won't upset you?" I whispered. The last thing I wanted was to upset him because of my own preconceived notions about him, or because I assumed he was different than he was, since that would really be a me problem, not something that was his fault.

Lear snorted. "No, of course not. You're still fairly unused to fey folk, whereas I'm used to humans. We're technically different species, I get it if there are things that might unsettle or confuse or upset you about me."

"So far it's not necessarily been a very negative feeling I've had when you're...feyishness hits me, it's more just...something I know I need to adjust to," I told him truthfully. "It catches me off-guard, and I remind myself that you're not human, and it's okay."

"Well, good. Hopefully it's mostly like that. If it's ever not, like I said, just tell me. I want to work things through with you," he reiterated.

"O-okay...what...what about when you have to go?"

"Let's cross that bridge when we get there, alright? It won't be any time soon, and you have enough stress right now, so it's not worth worrying over at the moment."

"That's a fair point."

Lear kissed my neck gently. "Can I kiss you more often?"

"Y-yeah," I mumbled.

"Excellent." I could hear his grin. He pulled away, finally turning me to face him. But instead of the cocky grin I expected to see, his expression was earnest. "We don't have to rush anything, either. We don't have to get married anytime soon, or ever, if you don't want it. I want you to take as much time as you need and figure things out. Alright?"

"Alright," I whispered.

"Good." He bent and pulled my lips very briefly to his. "There. Now we've kissed properly." He flashed a bright smile at me, then grimaced slightly. "And on that note...uh. I don't expect I'd ever accidentally let it happen, but my fangs are venomous, very venomous, so...just...know that. As much as I would really, really love a good make-out session, especially with you, the last thing I want is to cut your lip or your tongue or something on them. That'd be a pretty shitty way for you to go, and I'd hate myself forever."

I blinked once, then burst into giggles, and leaned into him, setting my head on his chest. "I-I...I love you, Lear!"

"Oh?"

"Yeah."

"Well, good." He stroked my hair gently, then asked a little uncertainly, "Why...why was that so funny just now?"

"You were just so matter-of-fact about it!" I couldn't keep from giggling again.

"I wasn't trying to be funny, but I'm glad you thought it was amusing instead of alarming. That might have been one of those things that would put you off."

"No." I sighed.

There was an annoyed sort of maow, and Stroopwafel tugged at my skirt. "Oh, fine, fine!" Lear snorted, pulling away to bend down and scoop the goofy, demanding cat up.

He trapped her between us as he pulled me against him again, and I bent to smother her little forehead with kisses. She purred loudly.

I'd have gone and gotten Diana as well, but my sweet queen of a cat was slumbering peacefully on the couch. She'd been sleeping even more than usual lately, trying to bounce back from saving all of our lives, I knew, so I wanted to let her rest.

"So..." Winna looked up at him.

"Yes?"

"You're going to look in the old books upstairs for information?" she asked, pulling the conversation back to the previous topic.

"Yes. There's got to be a reason they've been around as long as they have." He nodded. "I'll also get out and about a little and talk to the older fey folk in the area."

"Oh, that's a good idea!" The young woman brightened visibly, and planted another kiss on Stroopwafel's little face. The silly grey tabby was still purring loudly away, apparently in heaven.

"Would you like to come with me?"

"Yes, I would."

"How about we do that today, then? Having something to keep you busy might keep your mind off things." He motioned at the salves on the table.

Winna took a deep breath. "Yes. Then, when we get back, let's start looking through the books upstairs together too. I know I can't read them, but it'll help me to feel like I'm at least able to help do something about it instead of just leaving it all to you."

"I'd much rather have your help with something." He leaned down and kissed her briefly and gently again. She leaned into the kiss a little this time, and he cupped her face with one of his hands, but pulled away before he let himself get carried away. Again, venomous fangs and kissing didn't always mix very well. "I like being with you, believe it or not."

"Noooo." She rolled her eyes, tone sarcastic despite the flush he'd incited on her face.

He grinned. "You're cute, Freckles."

"Freckles?!" She was momentarily indignant.

"I like your freckles." He grinned, reaching up to tap the freckles sprinkled across her face lightly, then leaned down and gently kissed that area, then moved over, continuing to kiss the places dotted with her freckles. "There."

Winna was deeply red, and looked away, muttering, "...'s not fair!"

"Sorry." He snorted.

The clock chimed, and the young woman glanced over at it. "We should get going."

"Yes, probably."

They broke apart, which made Stroopwafel maow in protest, and Winna spent a few moments assuring the silly cat that she was still very loved, even if they couldn't hold her every moment of the day. Then she went to gather some things to take with them on their outing.

"You're bringing a lot," Lear observed.

"You'll thank me later, when you're hungry or thirsty," she replied mildly, filling up the second of two water-skins at the sink.

"I wasn't criticizing. Just observing. I'm glad you think ahead, it's a good skill." Winna seemed to think that she wasn't particularly smart or talented, but he knew otherwise, and wanted to make sure she knew how wonderful she really was.

"I try to. I can't foresee or plan for all the issues we might run into, though." She sighed, shutting off the sink. "And it's less thinking ahead, and more like common sense, I think. I have a good deal of common sense."

"Yes, yes, you do," he agreed. "Although it's really not that common."

"But for all my common sense, I went and fell for you, though," she mumbled. "That's the least sensible thing I could have gone and done."

Lear grinned. "Well, being sensible is rarely fun. Even you have to live a little, Freckles."

"Oh hush, you!" She rolled her pretty eyes at him, but smiled.

"And really, I'm not such an unsensible person to have fallen for," he said earnestly. "We get on well, and that's half the battle. That I find you absurdly attractive is only icing on the cake. Fey folk are supposed to be the enchanting ones, but here I am, caught up in you." He paused, then added in a murmur, "Your soul is a siren song."

Winna turned, her dark eyes now wide. "Siren song is dangerous..."

"I'm happy to drown, if it's you." He flashed his grin at her, letting her know he wasn't trying to be dark.

She flushed a deep red, murmuring, "You're silly."

It was quiet for a few moments.

Her brow was creased, and she kept glancing back over at where Diana lay on the couch, clearly preoccupied with something.

"It's...not your fault, you know. What happened, I mean. If anything, it's mine. I never considered that Veris would follow me here. Nor am I really sure why he did. I thought that he assumed I'd gone off and died, but...well, apparently I was wrong. He may have caught word of me being in this area through the grapevine. Fey folk are the worst sort of gossips. I thought I'd gotten far enough away to be safe, but I guess not."

Word of anything always spread super quickly throughout the feylands, and keeping anything secret could be difficult. That's partly why Asher had needed Lear to be his right-hand man. He could trust him implicitly, given they'd grown up together and were all but brothers. Then Lear himself had selected each member of his team, carefully curating the group to be nothing but discreet, loyal, and trustworthy. Those weren't always traits easy to find amongst the population of the feylands.

Winna took a deep breath, then managed a smile as she turned to pick up the bag she'd packed with snacks and a few other supplies. "I-I know. It's also not your fault. It's Veris' fault."

"You're right, it is," he agreed, reaching out to take the bag and water skins.

"Oh, I can carry them." She blinked.

"I'm a lot stronger. It's only practical," he told her, shaking his head.

"Fair point," the young woman muttered as she went to slip into her shoes and coat.

Lear put the shoes he'd been using on, and took the cloak as well, suspecting Winna might want it before the day was up, as the temperature had turned properly cold again since the day before.

They would be out for quite a while, and he didn't want her to freeze. That said, he could just hold her to keep her warm. Yes...that was a good thought. Lear filed it away for future use. Maybe even near-future use, if he had it his way. Having wings would help even more, since he could wrap her up in them while he held her close. Yes, that was an impressively good thought.

"Ready?" he asked.

"I think so." She nodded then looked up. "Oh wait, I gotta kiss the girls goodbye!"

"Of course."

Winna hurried to where both cats were now snoozing on the couch. "I love you so much!" she said, peppering them with a ridiculous amount of kisses, and hugging them gently.

Stroopwafel maowed and rolled onto her back for tummy pets, her white-socked feet sticking up cutely in the air. Diana purred loudly, opening her lovely eyes and slow-blinking at her mistress as she loafed magnificently.

"They both said they love you too," Lear translated.

Winna smiled, and stood. "Alright, now I'm ready."

The young woman walked over to him, and he caught her hand, weaving their fingers together as best as he could. "That's as good as it's gonna get." He sighed as they stepped from the house.

Chapter 21

In the Forest

"This is where I met them," I told Lear, motioning at the clearing where the whistlebell plants grew in abundance.

"Right." Lear nodded, flicking open his second set of eyes, and looking around the area. "Ah, good. That was easy," he muttered, then raised his voice and said, "We're not here to cause problems, but I have some questions that you might be able to answer!"

It was quiet for a few moments, and then a head popped out from behind a tree.

"Winna?" little Mira asked.

"Mira!" I smiled, glad it was a familiar face. "Do you play here a lot?" I really had hoped to talk with her or her mother again. They lived fairly close, and I wanted to know them better, since we were neighbors, of a kind.

"Yes. It's close to our home."

"I see."

"He's the one who we smelled on you last time, wasn't he?!" The little faun scampered fully out from behind the tree, coming to stand beside me.

"Yes, he was! He was pretending to be a kitty!" I giggled, kneeling to be face to face with her. "How are you and your family?"

"We're doing well!" she chirped.

"Good. I'm glad to hear it!" I smiled, then told her, "Mira, this is Lear."

"Hello," the little faun said shyly, barely peeping up at Lear.

My tall fey friend, er...boyfriend? Fiancé? I should ask him what exactly I should call him. Anyway, Lear crouched beside me, smiling in a friendly manner and saying, "It's nice to meet you."

"You too, sir!"

"You can just call me Lear."

"Okay!" Mira smiled cutely.

"Are your parents around? Winna and I have a question or two they might be able to help us with."

"They're at home. I can get them, if you want!"

"If they're not busy, and are willing to talk to us."

"Okay! I'll go tell them!" Mira smiled, then skipped off.

"She's very cute."

"She's older than you." Lear snorted.

"I didn't think about that. But yeah, I guess she would be."

"I'd say fifty or so, pretty young."

"Goodness!" I frowned. "It...doesn't bother you that I'm so young, doesn't it."

"The different fey species all grow and mature at different paces. That said, we honor the traditions regarding coming of age for other races, including humans. That said, I wouldn't want to date an eighteen or twenty-year-old. It's too young. Not that thirty is old, for a human, but...it'd be like you dating an eighteen or twenty-year-old, you just wouldn't have much in common."

"Yes, I wouldn't date someone that young either."

After a few moments, Mira skipped back. "Mama and papa said they're coming!"

True to her word, her mother soon appeared, with another fawn following just behind. I assumed it was her father. He was taller and broader in the shoulder than his wife, not quite as cute or pretty in the face, of course, and had a short, neat brown beard.

"I'm so sorry to bother you again!" I stood, grimacing apologetically. "We, uh...well...Something happened recently and-"

"Did it have to do with the enormous burst of magic that happened a day ago?" Pima asked, putting me out of my misery. Her tone was concerned, and her brow was creased.

"Yes." I sighed, rubbing my forehead.

"Who is your friend?" Pima asked, looking a little cautiously at Lear.

"This is Lear. He's the fey you smelled last time." Lear stood as I motioned at him.

"We guessed as much." Pima smiled, seeming to relax a little. "This is my husband, Tip."

"It's good to meet you." I bowed a little, and Lear followed suit. "I'm Winna. I live not far away, in the cottage on the edge of the woods."

"Pleased to meet you! My girls were right, you are courteous!" He chuckled in a deep voice, stroking his short beard. "How can we help you?"

"Well...my familiar, Diana, she had to release her magic to protect us all a day ago, and...I..." I faltered, feeling tears come to my eyes.

"Ah, that's what it was, then," Pima murmured, expression full of understanding. "What kind of familiar is Diana?"

"A-a cat. Sh-she's...been with my family for a long, long time," I replied.

"I see. That is very sad, then, she'd be very much like a pet, I assume."

"Yes. Well, my best friend, really." I nodded, taking a deep breath, and managing to banish the tears before they slid down my face.

"Winna has brothers, but beyond them, Diana is the final, most true connection she has to her parents," Lear said quietly, reaching out to put a hand on my shoulder and squeezing it gently.

"Oh lass." Tip sighed. "It's awfully cold out, I think, why don't you both come to the burrow? We can put some tea on and have a nice talk without Winna freezing!"

"We don't want to impose." I shook my head.

"They wouldn't ask us to come if they didn't mean it," Lear told me, smiling a little.

"He's right." Pima grinned, coming forward and linking her arm through mine. "Come along, dear."

The family of fawns led us a short way through the woods to a large hill with a door in the side.

Tip ducked inside, saying, "Please come in."

"Thank you," Lear murmured, and I echoed him as we ducked inside behind the little family.

The burrow was lit with warm lanterns. It had a hard-packed, earthen floor, but was neat, and full of well-crafted furniture of a rich brown wood. There was a kitchen, dining room, and a living room area, with a hallway in the back that I imagined led to the bedrooms. A lovely fire crackled on the hearth, and it was altogether very cozy.

"Please have a seat," Pima told us, and we did so.

"Your home reminds me of mine!" I smiled, looking around the little place.

"Why, thank you, dear!" Pima beamed at me as she bustled around, putting a kettle on the hook over the fire. "I work very hard to keep it clean, but as you might imagine, these dirt floors make that a little difficult, and sometimes little critters do get in, too!"

"You need a cat." I smiled.

"Yes, yes we do." Pima looked pointedly at her husband.

"Oh fine!" He threw his hands up. "We'll find a cat. And I'm working on a wooden floor, but plugging all the holes in the walls took a lot of time, dear."

"I do appreciate your efforts, dear. I know it's been a lot of work." Pima smiled fondly at her husband.

"If you need help, I'm crafty enough. I'd be willing to trade my assistance for any help you can give us."

"Well, I'll take that trade, you're very strong, I can see, but only if we're actually able to help you at all."

"Sure." Lear nodded. "I appreciate that."

"We're honorable folk," Tip said firmly.

My fey...well, I'd just call him my companion, for now...My fey companion smiled. "I know. Winna is lucky to have such peaceful, honorable, kind neighbors."

"Oh, stop it, you! What a flirt, Winna!" Pima laughed, but I could tell she was joking.

"You're not wrong." I snorted, rolling my eyes. I knew his flirting, and that hadn't been it. His flirting was outrageous and obvious. "But he's right, I know this is only the second time we've met, but I'm pleased you're my neighbors here."

"You're a good neighbor too, hon, never any trouble, and very respectful of the forest and us, now that you know we're here," Pima told me warmly. She turned to her daughter, who'd been sitting quietly at the table, listening to us. "Go play in your room, baby. You can come and say goodbye before they go, alright?"

"Yes mama." Mira pouted, but obediently left the table, and scampered down the back hallway.

We chatted pleasantly for a little while until we had lovely, hot cups of tea sitting before us.

"Now, how can we help you?" Pima asked, taking a seat.

"It's mostly information we're after," Lear told them. "Winna's family was blessed by a goddess with their healing abilities a long time ago, but we don't know which goddess that was. That same goddess gave them Diana as a familiar."

"I would like to try to figure out which goddess it was," I murmured. "My own magic is fairly weak, and I'm only able to do as much as I have been for everyone because Diana herself is so strong, but when she had to step in to save us, she used up most of her magic, and is now just surviving, really. She's okay, but we can't help people like we once did, and the village sort of counts on us." I paused. "I haven't really treated any fey folk other than Lear, but it means I won't be able to help any fey folk much in the future, either. I'd like to be able to ask the goddess to heal Diana, so I can continue to help people."

"Hm." Tip frowned. "Well, I can't say I know all that much about your family, but I've been aware of them since I moved here as a lad. They've long been healers, though, I know that much."

"I came to these parts later, so I know even less," Pima murmured.

"How long ago was it that you came here?" Lear asked Tip.

"Oh, about...three hundred years," Tip said thoughtfully. "Your family still inhabited the big house back then; they didn't move to the groundskeepers' cottage until at least twenty years later, I think."

"Big house?" I blinked.

"Oh yes, I came right after they moved to the cottage, if I remember correctly," Pima chimed in, sounding thoughtful.

"We lived in a big house? Like...a manor? Or just a bigger house?"

"A manor, yes." Tip nodded, stroking his beard.

"Oh my...I never knew that." I blinked. What in the world?!

Lear's hand found mine, and he squeezed it gently. "Where was the manor?"

"It wasn't too far from the cottage. It burned down, though. That's why the family moved to the cottage to begin with. They never did rebuild the big house, of course. I expect they'd come to the end of their money, and couldn't afford it."

"That tracks." Lear nodded.

"I believe they sold off land over the years whenever they were strapped for cash," Pima told us. "And I heard eventually they started selling healing potions and salves in the village."

"I still sell salves. Or...I hope to still do so, if we can ask the goddess to return or replace the bulk of Diana's magic."

"Of course." Pima nodded.

"So, how do you know all of this?" I asked them, bemused but not displeased.

"We fey folk are terrible gossips!" Pima giggled, then sighed, "It helps us to know what the local humans are up to, in case it somehow spills over and affects us."

"Oh, that's fair." I couldn't fault them for that. "We're pretty finicky and temperamental, so that really doesn't surprise me."

"You said the family was once wealthy. Did they have the power to go with it?" Lear wanted to know.

Tip nodded. "Yes, but it had begun to wane by the time I got here, from what I understand. There was also a large bout of illness that killed many humans in the area, including Winna's ancestors. It was a nasty one that I believe was difficult to heal even with magic."

"Those are very frightening." I shivered, glad I'd not ever seen or experienced such an illness.

"Yes, they are," Pima murmured.

"That epidemic really hurt the area as a whole, and it took a long time for it to begin to heal properly." Tip sighed, shaking his head. "We felt sorry for the humans then."

"I see," Lear said, seeming thoughtful.

It was quiet for a few moments as we sipped our tea.

"That's really all I know," Tip told us.

"Me as well." Pima smiled sadly, shrugging a little.

"What you were able to tell us is helpful. We knew nothing of that up until now," Lear assured them. "If we can find some fey folk who know more details, like maybe someone who's lived in the area longer, that'd be very helpful."

"Hmm..." Tip frowned. "I think there's a pretty old willow tree growing next to a stream that's not far from where the old manor used to be, before it burned."

"Oh yes! She's very sweet! We don't get out to see her very often, but she'd help you," Pima told us excitedly.

"A hamadryad?" Lear asked.

"Yes." Tip nodded.

"Can you show me where? I'm not super familiar with the area yet."

"I have a map somewhere." Tip nodded, going over to a writing desk and rifling through papers. He returned momentarily, and we moved our now mostly empty teacups so he could spread it out on the table. "This is the stream." Tip pointed at a wiggling line. "And she'd be about there." He tapped a spot.

"Oh, I know that area. Dad took me fishing there some as a kid. I think I even know the tree. A willow, right?"

"Yes." Tip nodded.

"There was a willow we'd play under. I bet that's the one you're talking about," I told them thoughtfully.

"She's the only willow I know of on that stream, so I imagine that's her." Pima smiled.

"Well, thank you. You've more than earned my help with the floor," Lear told them, grinning. "Let me know when you want to put it in, and I'll set aside my day for it."

"It's much appreciated!" Tip nodded approvingly. "We'll probably wait until it's warmer."

"Of course. Just send word and I'll come." Lear stood. "We should get going, I'd like to see if we can talk to the willow before it gets too late."

"Right." I nodded, standing as well.

"Mira, come say goodbye!" Pima called down the hallway.

Mira scampered out and over to me. "Can I hug you?"

"Of course!" I smiled, kneeling and holding my arms out for her.

The little faun giggled, and threw her arms around my neck, hugging me tightly. "Can we be friends?"

"Absolutely!" I couldn't keep from smiling. "Someday you all should come for tea at the house. That'd be fun! We'll have a tea party!"

"Oh yes!" Mira giggled, pulling away.

"That would be lovely! Just let us know," Pima told me warmly.

"Yes ma'am!" I nodded, standing. "Maybe while Lear and Tip are doing the floor, we'll have a tea party! And leave some for them when they're done, of course."

"Sounds like a plan!" Pima laughed.

Lear reached out and took my hand. "We'll get out of your hair now."

"It was really nice having you. I don't think we've ever had a human here before," Pima said as she walked with us to the door, Tip following closely behind her.

"I doubt many of us even knew you all lived here. Up until recently, I didn't realize that any fey even really lived in the area."

"We do like to keep to ourselves, when we can. Or those of us that prefer a quiet life do, anyway," Tip told us. "But you two are welcome here anytime, and let us know if you need any more help. We'll do what we can."

"Thank you all very much!" I smiled, waving as we shrugged into our coats, and took our leave.

We stepped out into the cold once more, and I shivered slightly. Lear removed the cloak he'd just put back on, and draped it around me. "There. Better?"

"Yeah...promise you're not cold?"

"I promise." He nodded

"Tell me if that changes, and you can have it back."

"I'll just pull you close. You know, body warmth and all that." Lear grinned, taking my hand again.

"Oh, hush." I rolled my eyes at him as we started walking. "Um...
"

"Yes?'

"I was wondering...what should I call you? I mean, like, boyfriend, or...what?"

"You can call me whatever you want. Boyfriend is fine. Fiancé is better, but I get it if you don't want to yet. Maybe someday."

"Are you sure?" I asked softly.

"I promise I'm sure. Boyfriend always seemed infantilizing to me, anyway. I know it was fast, and that alarmed you a little, but there's nothing stopping us from having as long of an engagement as we want before any wedding."

"Okay." I smiled. Despite the sad, somewhat scary situation that I was in, my livelihood tenuous, unable to help people, and my oldest friend left considerably weakened after saving our lives, I still had these quiet moments of happiness that made life good.

Truly, the goddess had blessed me. My life wasn't perfect, but it was good.

Chapter 22

The Willow

"How far do you think the stream is from here?" Lear asked her as they made their way through the forest again.

"Mm, maybe an hour's walk."

"How about we fly instead? It'll be faster." He flashed a grin at her.

"Can you fly while holding another person?"

"Have faith in me!" He snorted. "Of course I can! Besides, you're not heavy."

Winna studied him. "That wasn't a yes."

Lear rolled his eyes. "Yes, I can fly and carry you with me. But why would I offer it if I couldn't actually do it?"

"Fair point." She shrugged.

"Let's fly, then."

Winna chewed her lip apprehensively. "I...I don't know."

He took her hands and pulled them to his lips, kissing them gently. "I promise I won't drop you, Winna. And it'll be much faster. Besides, we'll be able to get home a lot sooner if I do."

"Oh, alright. But...don't make fun of me if I scream. I've never done anything like it before."

"No worries." The fey man chuckled, pausing to scoop her up like a bride, her arms around his neck. Using his magic, he pulled his wings out, and extended them, "Ahh. That's nice." He stretched a little.

"They're pretty," Winna murmured softly, her dark eyes studying them over his shoulder.

"Do you want to touch them?" Lear asked, smiling at her.

"I...can I?" Her face heated.

"Of course. It's just like my arm," he snorted, shifting his hold on her to one arm, and pulling one of her hands out to touch his feathers.

The young woman giggled in delight. "They're soft!"

"Well, they are feathers." The fey man snorted again.

"I mean, yeah," she muttered, embarrassed. "But what do I know? They might have been sharp, or something."

"I understand." He smiled again. "Alright, ready?"

"As ready as I'll ever be, I guess," Winna told him, letting her hand fall back into place, and setting her head against his chest.

"This is nice though," he muttered, then shook himself. "But we should go." Lear knelt, then launched them both up into the air with an easy leap.

A shriek tore itself from Winna's lips as they soared up into the air, and she buried her face in his shirt. His wings caught the air, and he flapped them gently, hovering upright for a few moments.

"You can look, love. We're not all that high, and I won't drop you," he told her gently, not wanting her to think he was making fun of her in any way, because he wasn't. It was understandable that she'd be scared.

The young woman slowly inched her face away from his shirt, her eyes were squeezed shut. Bit by bit, she opened them until she was squinting, then her brown eyes opened wide, and she gasped as she stared out at the world stretched out beneath them. "Whoa!"

"Not so bad, huh?" He smiled, turning slowly in the air so that she could get a good view of the entire area.

"No," she murmured. "It's pretty."

"It is," he agreed, then bent and kissed her briefly. "I'm glad I could share it with you."

Winna sighed softly. "Me too. Thank you, Lear."

"I love you." He grinned. "So much. I'll share whatever I can with you. Especially the beautiful things."

"I love you too," she told him. "But...don't hesitate about the bad things, either. I'm stronger than I look."

Lear blinked, then smiled. "I know." He hovered there for a little while longer, then asked, "Shall we go?"

"Yes. As beautiful as this is, I know we need to get to the willow tree for a chat."

Without another word, Lear launched them forward with an almost lazy flap of the wings. Winna clung to him more tightly, but didn't shut her eyes this time.

"It's so pretty up here," she murmured.

"Yeah. We could fly more often, if you want."

"I'd be okay with that." Winna smiled.

Soon, Lear spotted a thin line twisting across the landscape in the distance. "I think that's it." He nodded.

"Yep, probably. I wonder if anyone saw us up here?"

"I'm sure we'll hear about it if so!"

"I wonder what they'll say," she mused, then squeaked a little in surprise as he tucked his wings and dove back towards the ground.

"It's alright," Lear assured her as he leaned back, snapping his wings out in time to slow the descent.

"Well, now I can say I've flown," Winna said as he landed easily, then put her down. "I imagine my hair is crazy, though." She started brushing her fingers through the unruly curls.

"Just a little out of place." Lear reached out and helped her comb everything back into place. "There."

"Thanks!"

"You're welcome." He wove his fingers through hers, letting his eyes linger on her hair, then shook his head, and sighed. "Gods, your hair is lovely."

She wrinkled her nose. "It's messy."

"That doesn't mean it's not gorgeous."

"You really like it?"

"Winna, I love every square inch of you." He paused, grinning wickedly as he added. "Or I'm sure I will, once I see it all."

"Lear!" Her face burned bright red as she tried to cover it with her other hand.

He gave a low chuckle, and stole a very brief kiss, then changed the subject as he nodded in the direction they were walking. "That looks like a willow tree right there."

She peered through her fingers, then let her hand fall. "Yes, that's it."

They hurried along towards the old tree.

"Hello!" Winna called as they approached, then frowned. "I don't know what to call her."

"Let's see..." He paused, then addressed the tree in question, as they drew nearer. "Lady willow, we respectfully request a word!"

There was a pause, and then the leaves of the long, trailing arms fluttered as if some breeze was blowing, though the air was relatively still. The loose leaves and twigs swirled around, taking the vague shape of a woman.

"It's been many, many years since I've spoken with a human. Although, I can tell you're not human, young man, but I am unfamiliar with you," the hamadryad addressed them in a rustling voice that creaked with age. "But as you know I'm here, and are keeping company, I suppose there's no harm in it."

"I'm Lear. This is Winna."

"I am Sagebark."

"How do you do, Sagebark?" Winna bowed.

"Very well, little one," the willow replied, tone warming perceptibly. Clearly, she was pleased by the politeness.

"You...probably don't remember me, but I used to come fishing in the stream with my father when I was a kid." The mage's voice was full of fondness. It was obvious they'd been good times.

The leafy face shifted into a smile. "I have a good memory, for a tree! Of course, I remember. You and your father played hide-and-seek beneath my branches."

The young woman grimaced. "I hope that wasn't disrespectful in any way."

"Not at all, child, not at all." Sagebark assured her. "Now, I assume you didn't come to just reminisce with an old tree."

"Unfortunately not, though it is wonderful to know I can actually talk to you, now," Winna replied.

"We're after some information, and thought you might be able to help us, given how long your memory runs," Lear said tactfully.

"It is long indeed. What do you seek to know? I hear many things from the birds and the beasts of the wood." The hamadryad's tone was conversational as she drifted towards the overhanging branches. "But come into my branches, it'll keep the cold away a little better. I do not feel it, but I'm certain that you do, as a human, little one."

"Oh, thank you." Winna bowed a little, and they both followed the leaf-figure.

They ducked into the area beneath the willow tree's leaves, and settled down on roots there, at Sagebark's direction. Knowing that Winna was still likely a little chilled, Lear extended a wing, and used it to pull her closer before slipping an arm around her.

"Thank you." She smiled, shivering a little and leaning gratefully into his warmth.

"Now, what information do you seek? I'm happy to help as I can. It's rare indeed that I get to talk to anyone;so few humans I deem to be safe come by my stream anymore," Sagebark asked in a businesslike tone.

"That's sad," Winna murmured.

"It's just a part of life. And I do still have speech with plenty of fey folk and animals. They bring me the news of the world, and the gossip." She shrugged, smiling.

"We're after information about Winna's family. We're told they used to live in a manor house that was in this area, but it burned down a while ago and was never rebuilt."

"Oh! You're a Starling?" Sagebark clapped her leafy hands together in pleased excitement.

"Um, yes, that's my family name." Winna nodded, smiling a little.

"I recall your family very well, child.," Sagebark told her happily. "I had no idea you were a Starling! I'd have spoken to you and your father all those years before, if I had. They were great friends to us hamadryads, and long protected the forests and fields and rivers in these parts. Indeed, their protection still lingers over this land. That's why it remains so peaceful and safe here."

"Oh?" The young woman blinked. "Their protection?"

"It came with them when they came over the mountains and made this place their home." The hamadryad nodded, gesturing at the general area.

"I thought we lived in the manor?" Winna was clearly puzzled.

"Not always." Sagebark gave a rustling chuckle. "Your family came here when I was little more than a sapling. They were a family of great power and wisdom, and were welcomed with open arms in these parts. They were long revered, and spread their peace as far as they could. This area was dotted with small farms and homesteads before they came, but the towns that exist now were able to grow thanks to their influence, especially the one nearest to the manor, which is the town closest to where we are now. Many fey came into the area in the years after your family arrived. They were all mostly peaceful. They heard that this was a place to live where they could keep to themselves, so they came."

"O-oh my." Winna seemed a little taken aback. "First I learned we lived in a manor, now this! Where did we come from? We were healers even then, right?"

"Child, your family used to be far more than just healers.," Sagebark said gently. "The power has waned over the years as they married the locals, who lacked any magical abilities. Although there were never more than one or two children at a time, so your family never got very large. But yes, once upon a time, your kin had far more power than you do now. You come from a long, proud line of mages."

Winna stared at the hamadryad, stunned. "H-how...what?!"

"How do you know all this?" Lear asked. The tree was an absolute wealth of information.

Sagebark smiled. "Much like you and your father liked to come fish in the stream, your ancestors did as well. There was a young woman named Awenna, who I was particularly close to. She was the daughter of the lord who first came to these parts, and built the manor. You're named after her, if I'm not mistaken. The name has changed over the years, but Awenna to Winna, that's not a large stretch."

"Y-yes, Winna is a family name." The young woman looked stunned.

Sagebark nodded. "Languages themselves change over the course of so much time, as all things do. It's only natural."

"So when they came here, they could use other types of magic? They weren't just healers?" Lear asked. If they'd once been able to use more than just healing magic, there was far more to the story than he'd guessed.

"Yes. I was aware of it because I knew Awenna so well, but as far as most outsiders went, they kept it pretty well under wraps. I believe they worried that if the knowledge of their full abilities were known, it might put them in some kind of danger. I never did understand exactly what danger that was, but I don't doubt that they had their reasons, and I was happy to keep their secret. In the end, I think they only spread the knowledge of their healing abilities about. Though I understand that's now the only ability available to you at all, yes."

"Yes. My brothers don't have any magic at all, and I'm fairly weak," Winna murmured, looking disconcerted by all the new information.

"We know her family was blessed by a goddess, apparently before they ever came to these lands, going by what you've just told us. Do you know which goddess it was?" Lear asked. Truly, this tree spirit was a wealth of knowledge, and they'd been lucky the faun family had suggested they speak to her. They'd already learned far more than he'd hoped.

Sagebark frowned. "I'm afraid I don't. They never spoke of her often, to me anyway, and when they did, they only ever referred to her as 'the goddess'. Perhaps they didn't know her name; information does get lost over time. Or maybe they wished to keep who their patron deity was something of a secret. I don't blame them if the latter was the case. After all, they did seem to have some reason for it. But when they did speak of her, it was with the utmost reverence."

"Either way, it's a pity. Because all of that information would be very helpful right now." Lear sighed, shaking his head.

"We were told that there was a large bout of terrible sickness that hit the area. Is it possible that's when the information was forgotten?" Winna asked.

"It's possible. It was a truly terrible time; there was much death." Sagebark nodded. "But I have a feeling that they'd already lost a lot of their knowledge of the past already. I once asked Awenna where her family came from, and she said she didn't know, that this was the first real home they'd ever had."

"That's sad," Winna murmured.

"Very sad," Lear agreed quietly. If sickness had killed off most of Winna's ancestors while they'd lived here, it was entirely possible that, in the time before they'd settled within the ring of mountains, they'd been decimated by a similarly difficult-to-heal-illness. Magical illnesses were incredibly dangerous. Or maybe their enemies had picked them off one by one, and eventually the knowledge was lost that way. Whatever had happened, it was likely that they'd never know precisely how the information had been lost.

It was quiet for a few moments.

"What brought on this sudden interest in your family history?" Sagebark inquired curiously.

"We're looking to see if we can find the goddess' name so we can ask her to restore the power to the familiar she also gave to my family."

"I see." The hamadryad nodded. "That would be the cat, yes?"

Winna blinked, smiling in surprised delight that Sagebark knew about her kitty. "Yes! Diana. Do you know her?"

"No, but Awenna was very fond of her., and spoke of her often. I gather they were great friends." Sagebark laughed, then asked, "Does Diana not know the name of her goddess? Given she's a divinely-given familiar, she'd have served her goddess in the heavens before she ever came here."

"I...I never thought to ask!" Winna frowned.

"I think that's not the kind of thing she'd know," Lear interjected. "Diana is very wise, but she's still just a cat. I'm sure she knows your name, Winna, but...things like that are less important to cats. They're flighty and inherently a little silly, just by nature. She might not be as silly as Stroopwafel, but she has her moments." Lear thought of the times he'd seen the usually prim and proper Diana go bursting around the cottage in an attack of the zoomies.

"Well, we can still ask." She shrugged.

"Yes, we can."

"We'll have wasted a bunch of time doing this, if she does know..." Winna grimaced.

"It's not a waste. It's been interesting to learn all these new details about your family."

"Very interesting," the young woman muttered. "A little over-whelming."

It was quiet for a little while.

Lear broke the silence, "Sagebark?"

"Yes?"

"How long ago was it that Winna's family came to these lands? Right now, I just know it was more than three hundred years ago."

"Oh, let's see." Sagebark thought for a while. "It was…a very long time ago. Long enough for humans to forget that the Starlings didn't always live here."

"Five hundred years?" Lear guessed. That was a good, long chunk of time for humans, and not an insignificant amount of time for fey folk.

"I think…closer to seven hundred," the hamadryad replied.

Chapter 23

The Old Books

I had too much to think about as we made our way back to the cottage.

"Are you alright?" Lear asked softly as we soared through the sky once more.

"I'm just...baffled. I...I'd never really heard anything like what I found out today, which means my parents didn't know any of it, either."

"I'm not surprised, unfortunately. Information about the past is so easily lost, in some ways. It's very sad. Especially in this case, when it's important," he murmured. After a pause, the fey man continued, "I wonder if those books in the loft can shed any more light on the matter. Your family had to have kept them all these years for a purpose. They couldn't even read them, but they still kept them, you know? Surely that means they have some kind of significance."

"Maybe. I wouldn't know." I sighed. There was still so much I didn't know. There was so much my parents hadn't known. Although my father not knowing was less surprising, given he was a non-magical human. But my mother not knowing...that was troubling to me, somehow.

The cottage appeared, and Lear landed, but didn't put me down. Instead, he carried me inside, announcing, "We're back, ladies!" to Stroopwafel and Diana, who both looked up from the couch as the door opened. He carried me over to said couch, and put me gently down on a cushion. "There."

I rolled my eyes at him, but couldn't keep from smiling. "I still have to go take care of the animals."

"Nope, you stay right here and love on the cats. I'll be right back," he told me, then darted out the door.

I sat there, petting the cats as I turned over everything we'd learned that day in my head. It was...a lot.

My family had come from another place to live in these lands. They'd had more power than healing, but had hidden all but the healing power from everyone else for some reason. They'd lived in the manor house, and their power had dwindled over the long years as we'd intermarried with the locals. Any wealth and influence had slowly ebbed as well. Then the manor had burned, and they hadn't been able to rebuild it, so they'd moved to the cottage. The very one I still lived in.

Where had we come from? Why had we left wherever we'd come from? What was the reason we'd kept our full magical abilities a secret, and let everyone think we were just healers?

I sighed, petting my kitties still. "Oh my babies." Stroopwafel maowed, stretched luxuriously, then rolled onto her tummy for pets. I giggled, and pushed my fingers into her fur.

Diana maowed softly, as if amused.

"Diana, my love, are you feeling alright?"

Another, confirmatory maow.

"Good," I murmured, scratching the bridge of her nose the way she liked.

The door opened, and Lear came back in. "Done."

"Thank you."

"Of course." He nodded, coming to sit beside us on the couch.

It was quiet for a few moments.

"Diana, can I ask you something?" I asked my familiar quietly.

The diluted grey tabby maowed in reply.

"She said yes," Lear told me.

"I assumed as much." I smiled, then spoke to my cat familiar again. "Do you know the name of the goddess who gave you to my family?"

My sweet queen was quiet for a little while, then maowed and started to purr, her tail flicking slightly.

"She said it's been a really long time since she thought about it."

"Does that mean you don't remember?" I asked her, vaguely amused.

Diana maowed once more, and set her head down on her paws, her iridescent ocean eyes half-closed.

"She said she knows what she calls her, but it's not in any language we speak."

"Ah, I see. So I guess it wouldn't be very helpful, then."

"Probably not." Lear shrugged.

"Annie, do you know where my family came from?"

A soft maow.

"A long way away," Lear murmured.

My familiar followed that up with a few more maows.

"She said that your family travelled around for a long time before coming here. The goddess didn't ask her to start watching over them, and helping them, until just before they came here."

"I see. I guess you lived in the manor house before it burned?"

Diana continued, through Lear. "She said that she did, and that the fire was frightening, but that they all escaped with their lives, then came to live here. She likes it here; it's much warmer than the manor, which was drafty."

I smiled at my little cat. "I like it here too."

She purred contentedly.

"I don't think she knows much, powerful and wise though she is. She is still a cat, like I said."

Diana maowed happily, and the fey man chuckled at whatever she'd said.

"What'd she say?"

"She said she's certainly just a cat." Lear snorted. "Diana is surprisingly funny."

Annie's tail twitched annoyedly.

"Calm down, I didn't mean it in a bad way." Lear laughed. "You're a gem amongst cats and familiars, Diana."

My oldest friend gave a contented maow, clearly pacified.

"I love you, Annie." I bent and kissed her forehead, which made Stroopwafel jealous, and so, of course, I had to give her kisses as well. "You two are so silly!"

Diana maowed again a couple more times, stretching out and closing her eyes.

"She wonders why we're so curious all of a sudden. It's all ancient history."

"Because I love you, Miss Annie. And I want to get you some help, if I can, so we can keep helping other people. I know the villagers count on us." I sighed, stroking my sweet cat's soft fur.

She merely purred happily, likely half-asleep by now.

We sat there quietly for a little while.

"Let's have some tea," Lear said, getting up, and going to the kitchen.

"Do you need help?"

"No, stay there," he assured me.

I waited a little while, then got up anyway to help him. "I can make the snacks," I mumbled.

"No, it's alright, I would have done it after I'd gotten the sugar and stuff onto the tray," he said as he filled the sugar bowl.

"I don't mind. I want to help you, too," I told him, adding the treats I wanted to the tray he was preparing.

"Alright." I could hear his smile.

After a few moments, his arms slipped around me, and he pulled me back into his chest, planting a kiss into my hair. "Gotta wait for it to steep, now. This seems like a good way to pass the time."

"Oh...alright." I leaned back into him.

Lear kissed my neck for a moment, then broke away to ask, "Are you okay? I imagine that what we learned today was kind of unexpected."

"That's an understatement," I muttered.

"Fair. So it was...jaw-dropping? Befuddling? Astonishing."

"Something like that." I sighed.

He shifted, pulling away slightly and turning me around to face him. "How can I help?" His iridescent green eyes were gentle.

"I...I don't know, honestly." I shook my head, "I just need to be able to think it over."

"I understand." Lear nodded, leaning down to pull my mouth to his lips for a brief moment. When he pulled away, he plucked my curls gently with his long, deft fingers. "Your family was sort of royalty around here for a little while."

"Not really." I rolled my eyes "Sounds like they set themselves up as a power in the region. That's hardly royalty."

"I guess." He smiled. "I get the sense they did do their best to help people, even if they did keep the better part of their power under wraps...until it started to fade to just the healing powers."

"I...I don't know." I sighed, then leaned forward and into him.

"It's alright," the fey man murmured, planting a kiss in my hair.

"I wonder why they were traveling? Why they decided to hide their power? I even wondered how the manor burned down, if they had other powers!"

"Maybe their powers had waned quite a bit by then, enough so that they couldn't stop it."

"That would make sense... But none of that helps us get any closer to which goddess we need to look for," I muttered.

"We'll figure it out. Now I have some frame of reference for when your family came to these parts."

"I guess, if you can find a fey person who was closer to the family than Sagebark was. I don't know if you will, it seems like they kept to themselves, even if they did do what they could to help folks around here."

"While that's true, I was thinking about it being helpful for when I look in the books up in the loft. There's got to be a reason they were kept. Think about it, the house burned down, but the books were saved? How important must they be that they, among all things, were saved?"

"I...I hadn't thought about that." I lifted my head from his chest, chewing my lip. "I'll help you look, but I don't think that I'll be much help; I've looked through them before when I was a kid, and it all just looked like gibberish."

"That's okay. There's no guarantee that I'll understand them, either. Although I'm much, much older than you, and have known several languages since I was born, so there's a chance I might be able to decipher some of it. We'll see."

"I know I'm young compared to you, but how old are you, Lear?" I asked, frowning and leaning back to look at him better.

For the first time since we'd met, he flushed slightly, and looked away, muttering, "Far too old for you. Let's leave it at that."

I stared, open-mouthed at him, then burst into giggles. "You're blushing! I can't believe it, you're embarrassed!"

"I...can't...lie," he muttered haltingly, then admitted, "And I can't think of anything to suggest anything other than the truth at the moment."

I blinked, then had to laugh again. After a few moments, I wiped my eyes, telling him, "Lear, I love how honest you are with me. I do know you're older than me, likely a great deal older than me. I just never thought about how much until now, so it prompted me to ask."

Lear was quiet for a few moments, then mumbled, "Nine hundred and thirty-two."

"Years older than me, or altogether."

"Altogether." The fey man sighed.

"How does that fit into the fey ideas about age? I suspect it's not very young, but is that very old?"

The flush was slowly fading from his entirely too attractive face. "I'm neither here nor there in regard to age. Not old but not particularly young anymore. Some of us have been around practically since the beginning of everything."

"I see." I studied him for a little while.

He turned his gorgeous emerald eyes to me, and I found it was a little easier to meet them now, though doing so still made me blush. Lear smiled, apparently finally regaining his composure somewhat. "Well, at least I still make you blush too."

I rolled my eyes at him. "You're ridiculous, really."

"Ridiculously attractive." The fey man's brilliant smile flickered across his face.

"No, just ridiculous." I snorted, shaking my head, but then leaned forward into him again.

Lear leaned down and kissed my forehead. "The tea is probably done steeping." He pulled away, and picked up the now fairly heavily-laden tray of tea things in one hand without any difficulty. There was no way I could have managed it, but I wasn't fey-strong, like he was. It was more attractive than I wanted to admit, even in the little things, like easily carrying the tea tray. Lear took my hand and gently pulled me back over to the sitting area, setting the tray down carefully on the coffee table.

This time, instead of sitting with the cats between us, I sat down directly beside him. Though he slipped an arm immediately around me to pull me close, I leaned forward and poured us each some tea.

"Here."

"I could have done that."

"I know. But I also can, so...it's fine." I shrugged, leaning back into the couch and curling up with my own cup.

"Thank you." He kissed my temple.

I leaned into him. "You're welcome." I sighed contentedly.

Yes, we'd learned some admittedly kind of surprising things that day, and it was taking me a little while to adjust to it all, but nothing we'd learned had been anything bad. No, they were just things I hadn't known or expected, and really, that wasn't so bad.

I was curled up with the people I was closest to in the world, Lear and my kitties. And despite my worries about Diana, we were all alive and doing well enough. Things weren't so bad, really.

"Will it upset you if I get up to grab some of the books from the loft?" Lear asked after a few moments.

"Not at all." I shifted so he could get up more easily.

"You just were so cozy, and I hate to ruin that." He stood.

"Well, you'll be right back, I'm sure." I smiled at him.

The fey man grinned. "Yep." He darted away, and was back in the blink of an eye with several old tomes, which he sat on the table. "Let's make sure we're careful and don't spill any tea on them."

"Of course."

Lear settled back down beside me, and I curled up against him once more. He opened the book, and started to leaf slowly through the pages, studying them closely.

"I don't even recognize the language the words are in."

"They're familiar to me," he muttered, reaching out a long finger and tracing a line of writing.

"It's handwritten," I observed.

"Yeah, not printed. Maybe older than printing presses?" Lear arched a quizzical eyebrow.

"I don't know, we've had them since before I was born. It does make me think that it's not a book there are many copies of."

"Probably not. I think all of them are handwritten. At least, all the ones I grabbed are," he replied. "I think they're journals of some kind, if I'm being honest. Maybe personal journals." Lear fell silent, studying the book for a while. I drank my tea happily as he pored over the text. "It's not dissimilar to Faerie, when written."

"Oh? Is it fey?"

"No, but I think..." He frowned. "Faerie is a magical language, even when written. That's why we usually use the common speech, so we don't have to use our magic just to communicate."

"I didn't know that." I blinked.

Lear tore his eyes away from the book to smile at me. "That's alright. You don't know what you don't know. It's also why we can't lie. Faerie doesn't permit lying, given it's magical, and fairly binding in nature. So unless it's the truth, and as things are in reality, it simply can't be said."

"But you can't lie even in the common speech." I frowned.

"The gods decided when the common speech was slowly becoming more and more prevalent, that if fey folk were able to lie, we'd get up to far more mischief than we already did, so they made it so that we couldn't lie in any language. To be fair, all that did was make us apply all the fun ways to be deceitful that we'd already learned, as far as our own language went, to all other languages. Loopholes, half-truths, implications, just generally talking in a way so that we're not technically lying, stuff like that."

"Fair enough!" I laughed a little.

"But if this language is at least partly magical, I might be able to... hmm..." Lear put his hand flat against the book, and I felt his magic surging, which in turn drew a grimace of pain to his face.

"Don't hurt yourself," I murmured.

"I'm fine." He grunted, but then gritted his teeth and gasped in pain, "Ah!" The letters on the page suddenly glowed with a golden light, and he smiled triumphantly, then let the magic fade as he wiped his face. "That...was maybe too much," he admitted sheepishly. The book fell from his fingers, landing in his lap with a soft thump.

Chapter 24

Family History

"Please be careful!" I put my hand on his arm, "There's no need to hurt yourself just to figure out what these books say!"

"Winna, my love, some of the books up there are older than I am. That means that they were kept not just through the fire of the manor house, but also through your family's travels before that. They have to be important somehow."

"I...I guess."

"And if I have to deal with a little bit of pain in order to be able to figure out what they say, then so be it, I'll survive. Besides, the more I translate them, the easier it'll get."

"Fine, fine." I sighed, "I just...don't want you hurt."

He leaned down and kissed me briefly, murmuring, "I know."

When the fey man pulled away, he turned his attention back to the book, and smiled. "It did work, though." He pored over the book.

"I still don't recognize the language."

"It's the common speech, just from a long, long time ago. It was practically a different tongue back then," Lear explained. "This is... older than the oldest version I know, so it's not easy to read, but I can glean a little."

"Anything helpful?"

"Um...I think it's something of a recording of farm productivity for a specific season." He gave a wry smile. "So...no."

"For when my family still lived at the manor?"

"No. I'd be able to read that a lot more easily. I was alive for that. This is one of the books that's older than I am." Lear paused, and added quietly, "A lot older." He looked over the page a bit longer, then said haltingly, "It...speaks of a realm that I'm...not entirely familiar with."

"Oh."

"It rose and fell before my time. And likely that of my parents."

"How old are your parents?" I asked.

"Well, they're dead now."

I grimaced. "Oh, sorry."

"No, it's fine." He laughed.

I frowned, remembering something from a previous conversation. "I thought you said you didn't have a title, though."

"I don't. Grandad is still alive."

"Oh, I see. I guess you'll have it someday, then." That was an interesting thought. What would Lear be like as a duke?

"No, I won't, actually. My older sister will inherit the title and the lands."

"You have a sister?"

"Yes." He nodded. "We're not particularly close. She doesn't understand why I work when I don't have to. But I like to work."

"I'm glad you like to work," I muttered, "It's what brought you here."

"Yeah." Lear smiled at me.

We were quiet for a few moments.

Finally, he shook himself. "Well, as I was saying, this book is incredibly old. Both of my parents would be over three thousand if they were alive now, and this book predates that."

"This book is over three thousand years old?!" I squeaked, alarmed.

"Yes. I think these runes..." he flipped the book shut, but kept his finger inside the pages to mark his spot as he motioned at small marks that decorated the edges of the book's cover, "are runes of preservation and protection. I felt them when I translated it. I suspect many of the older books up there have similar runes on them, and it's probably what saved them from the fire. It's...unusual magic, and I've not seen the like of it before." He paused. "I'll have to study them some more; it could be incredibly useful, but only after we've figured out what we need to know. I might ask Dern about it, given he's a dwarf. He'll know more about runes than I do."

"Of course," I murmured.

It was quiet as he turned his attention back to the book.

Finally, the fey man sighed, shaking his head. "There are a lot of words I don't recognize. I think this one is the name of their homeland, because a few other words make me think they'd been working the land there for generations." He paused. "The name is...vaguely familiar, but...I can't place it."

"Would looking through one that's less old help?"

"Yes, but I don't want to go too young, or it might not be helpful, if the name of the goddess had already been lost." He set the book aside.

"Right." I nodded.

"I do think this one is not quite as old." He picked up another and traced the cover, explaining, "It's less worn."

"True." All I could do was offer one-word answers, and ask questions while he did the bulk of the investigating, at this point. It was frustrating, but there wasn't anything I could do.

Well, that wasn't true. I filled his teacup up again, and he took a long drink from it. "Thanks."

"That's all I can do right now." I grimaced.

"No, your company is helpful. Having someone to bounce all this off of is helpful." He smiled, "I appreciate and love you." Lear leaned across and kissed me for a moment. "I'm hopeful for this book."

"Well, open it up, then!"

Not needing to be told twice, he flipped through the book. "Still the same language, but let's see what happens." He closed his eyes, and grimaced again, but didn't grunt in pain as the letters glowed gold for a few moments, and shifted about on the page. "There," he murmured as the magic faded. "It's tiring, but doable."

"Well, stop when you get too tired."

"I will." He nodded, tracing the text with his fingers, then flashed a bright, excited smile and exclaimed, "I was right! I can read this much more easily!"

"Good." I giggled, pleased to see his excitement.

Lear fell silent as he read, while I sipped my tea, and petted the kitties as they slept.

"This..." He frowned, leaning back into the couch and staring out at nothing in particular. "This is familiar."

"What is?"

"The name of the place your family is from," the fey man muttered. His eyes were unfocused, and I sensed he was a thousand miles away, at the moment. "Magical humans from a place called Evarin."

"Are you saying that...more than just my family had magic?"

"Yes," he replied quietly. "It seems that all the people in Evarin had magic."

"Really?" I stared at him. "There was an entire kingdom of humans who could use magic?!"

"Yes, and that sounds so familiar to me." Lear sounded vaguely annoyed now, and muttered, "Evarin...why is that familiar?"

"Evarin," I said softly. My family's homeland. "That's a pretty name for a place."

Lear blinked, and his eyes focused. He smiled, reaching out to cup my face in his hand. "It is. I bet it was a beautiful place, too. You're beautiful, and so of course your family had to come from a beautiful place."

"That doesn't even make any sense!" I rolled my eyes at him, but leaned into the gentle touch. "Besides, you don't have to flirt anymore, you've already won me over."

"Of course I still have to flirt! It's now my job to make sure you don't forget that I want you, and think you're beautiful." He smirked, leaning forward to kiss me.

This time, I pulled away, asking him, "Will you...tell me more about what you read?"

Lear stroked my cheek gently, smiling. "Of course." He looked back down at the book. "The country was in something of a decline during this period," he muttered, turning the page. "Hmm..." He looked up. "Your...family was pretty religious, it seems."

"Oh?" As far as I knew, my immediate family hadn't been particularly religious. We'd thanked the goddess, and always used our powers to help people, which was the right thing to do with them, but we hadn't prayed to her, or gone to any temples, or offered sacrifices or offerings. Not that I knew of, anyway.

"Or maybe religious isn't the word. This book is much like the older one, full of farming records, but it also has a bit of political commentary, as well. The other one might have too, but it was too difficult to decipher."

"What kind of stuff does it say?"

"It talks about two groups of people that it refers to as the 'Untrue' versus the 'True'. Your family seemed to align itself with the 'True'. They're different factions. From what I can glean, the True had stayed true, for lack of a better term, to the goddess's charge and meaning for them, and the Untrue had abandoned that purpose."

"Okay." I nodded.

"The Untrue faction had gained a lot of power, according to this," he tapped the page he was on, "And they were beginning to mock and shun the families who belonged to the True faction and still practiced the old ways."

"The old ways."

"I'm not sure what that means, exactly, but typically it has some religious connotations," Lear admitted, shaking his head. "Which is why I think your family was religious. I'll figure it out. There are a lot more books up there. And I think that, if I can start with books from around this time period," he held up the book he had, "that it'll help me be able to work back through the older books by using the not-quite-so-old books as a language bridge, of sorts. They'll help me infer the meaning of words I don't understand, or need more context for, in the older books."

"I think I understand." I frowned.

"I'm basically treating the language in the older ones like a different language, or languages, entirely, but the newer ones are like languages that are far closer to the common speech, with enough words and roots in common (no pun intended), that I can translate easily enough. Taking what I've learned from translating the less-old language to the version we speak now, I can work backwards."

"Oh. That makes sense, yes." I nodded. "So, I guess you'll be spending a lot of time working on them for the next little bit."

"I actually don't think so." He shook his head.

"No?"

"I would be shocked to find that they don't mention the goddess's name in these texts somewhere. I highly doubt that they had any reason to hide her name back in Evarin, given that she's the one who'd blessed the entire populace with their powers. I'm kind of surprised I haven't run into her name sooner, honestly."

"Good point." I frowned.

Lear turned his gaze back to the book.

"Well, I'm going to weave a little, while you read," I told him.

"Sure." He nodded, but didn't look up as I stood, and went to my loom.

The clacking of the loom soon filled the air.

As I worked, my mind drifted over everything we'd learned so far.

An entire kingdom of humans who could use magic. How strange! Why hadn't I heard of it before? I thought humans with magic were rare. What had happened to them? Why had my family left, and come here? Especially if they'd be the only people with magic in these parts by coming here? Although, them being the only humans with magic in the area could have influenced them to keep the power a secret. Being able to heal was one thing, but if you could do a lot more than just healing, I had no doubt people would ask you to use those powers for them as well. If I were in my family's shoes, I would feel compelled to do as they asked, since I'd always been taught that the gift had been given to us specifically to help others, and that it was only right that we should help them, given that we could do something they couldn't. Maybe the fear of the pressure from others had kept them from sharing it? That's all I could think of at this point.

Suddenly, Lear murmured something.

"Hm?" I stopped weaving and looked over at him.

He repeated himself, "Marna."

Diana shifted, and maowed sleepily.

"It is?" Lear asked, blinking in surprise as he looked over at her.

Another maow, then she shut her eyes again.

"What'd she say?" I asked.

"She said that could be a loose sort of translation of her mother's name, though she's not heard it pronounced that way before." Lear turned his slightly startled green eyes to me. We stared at one another for a few moments, then he grinned. "Excellent! Now we just have to track down one of her temples! It shouldn't be hard.

"You think?

"Yes. Marna is still worshiped today. That's just my translation here of what they would have called her, but that's also what she's mostly known as now, from what I know."

"I've never heard that name before," I told him honestly, frowning.

"It's not so common in these parts," Lear told me, shrugging. "She's from an older human pantheon than is usually worshiped around here, so I'm not surprised."

220

"I see."

"Do you have a map of the world?"

"Yep! Let me get it." I went to the writing desk in the corner of the room, rummaged around, and returned with the map.

After clearing off the coffee table, we spread it out.

"Marna is more commonly worshiped along the coasts in the southwest." He traced his finger along one edge of the map.

"That's really, really far away from here."

"It is. But there'll likely be a temple somewhere that'll be close enough that, if we fly, it won't take too long to get to. It might be a super old, unused one, given her lack of popularity in more recent years, but it would still work."

We were quiet for a few moments.

"There's a story that I heard as a child, and that story is why some of this," he motioned at the ancient book, "seemed so familiar. Finally learning her name helped me figure out why everything felt so familiar."

"Please tell me," I murmured.

"It's something along the lines of, the children of Marna were strong, and did wonderful works. They had a big city, and were very wealthy." He paused, thinking for a moment. "They lived on the coast, and were revered. But eventually, what they had was no longer enough for them. They wanted more power and greatness, and started to take things they shouldn't, and do things they shouldn't. Their mother, Marna, saw what they were doing, and was sad. She took away their city and their things, and cast it into the sea."

I blinked, then frowned. "That's...grim."

"It's supposed to be. It's told as a cautionary tale."

"About greed?"

"For humans, it would be. For fey children, it's a parable about not getting too big for your britches. Though not being greedy is probably better." He smiled slightly. "The gods can always humble you, and often do."

"Do you...think that's what happened?" I asked him, looking

down at the book, now feeling a little scared of what we might find out. Had my ancestors taken things they shouldn't, and done things they shouldn't, either?"

"I don't know." He sighed. "I'd need to look more. I don't think the downfall of Evarin is in this one." He tapped the old tome that lay open in his lap. "The kingdom still seemed to be thriving well enough, though there was discord."

"I wonder if any of the books at all have the details." I stood and turned my gaze up to the loft. What other mysteries and answers did the old books up there hold? These two alone had led to even more revelations. I sighed, then shook my head. "Maybe that's...enough for today."

"Hm?" He looked up, having started reading again.

"I-I...I know we've learned a lot, and I want to be able to help Diana, but I need some time to process all of this," I murmured.

"That's fair enough." Lear smiled. He folded up the map, then stuck it into the book like a bookmark.

"You...don't mind?"

He stood, reaching out and pulling me close. "Of course not. I'm curious, but it can wait. If it's too much for you to continue right now, then that's fine. We've already learned so much. Hell, we've already discovered the goddess' name! I really didn't think we'd manage that in one day."

"We got lucky."

"I don't think we did," he told me. "Those books were preserved for a reason. Maybe that reason turns out to be you figuring out your family roots in your time of great need."

"I mean...it's...kind of just a selfish thing, not necessarily a great need, really," I mumbled.

"I don't think it is." He shook his head. "I know you want to do it to restore Diana's strength because you do love her, but your main motivation is so that you can continue to help people. Not to mention it's your main source of income, and it's understandable that you'd want to preserve that. And even if you did do it just to save Diana, that's really not entirely selfish. But if it somehow was...who cares?"

"Yeah?"

"Yeah," he assured me.

Chapter 25

Another Task

I shivered as I stepped in from the cold. "Brr!"

"Breakfast will be ready soon," Lear said, shooting a smile over his shoulder at me as he stood over the stove.

It wasn't the first time, nor would it be the last, that he'd made a meal for us, but at that moment, I felt a swell of pride that he'd come so far with his cooking skills.

Nowadays, we traded off who did what, as far as the chores and making the meals were concerned. Or rather, I tried to make sure that was the case, but often he beat me to it. It was a little frustrating, but I knew he only did it because he thought I worked too hard.

"What did you decide to make?" I asked him, nodding at the cooktop.

"I wanted to do crêpes, like you did that one time, but...that seemed a little beyond my abilities, at least by myself, anyway. So I decided to play it safe again, just sticking to things I know well." He flipped a fried egg onto the plate. "There are also biscuits in the oven."

"I think you could have done just fine with the crêpes, have a little confidence! You were better at making them than I was by the time we finished!" I patted him on the back, feeling really rather proud of him.

Lear shot me an easy smile. "Thanks, Winna."

"I'm...really proud of you for how quickly you've learned. I know you were really intimidated by it, but you've done really well, and I think you're a pretty good cook, now."

His smile widened into a beaming grin. "Thanks! I'm...glad you're proud of me. It's...it's nice to hear."

"Of course I'm proud of you." I giggled, adding, "Now whenever we do have that tea party, you'll be able to help me make the food!"

"At least the sandwiches. I can do that much. And I can chop the fruits and veggies."

"Nope, I'm going to make you do more than that. Besides, if I think you're up to crêpes, you can do just about anything!" I told him. "You did a pretty decent job on some of the recipes you made when I was sick, and you've had even more practice since then."

"Well, I'm happy to try whatever you want me to." He shrugged.

"I'll make a baker of you yet," I told him, then giggled. "I can just picture you in an apron!"

He paused, then shot me a slow, wicked smile. "I can make that happen, if you wish."

My face burned. "How is it that you can make anything and everything suggestive?! Even when it's not meant to be!"

The fey man's smile only broadened, "Lots of...practice."

"Lear!" I covered my face with my hands.

He cackled, "I'm just teasing you, Winna!"

"I knooooooow, but it's not faaaaair!"

Lear turned the burner on the stove down, and pulled my hands gently away from my face. "My love, would you like to know a secret?"

"Not if it's a dirty one." I pouted.

"While that is a perilously tempting thought, I meant it innocently." His iridescent green eyes were warm and gentle.

"Alright then. What's the secret?"

"The reason I'm so outrageous when I flirt with you is because I'm trying very, very hard. Harder than I've ever tried to get anyone's attention before."

"What do you mean? You already have my attention." I frowned.

"Fair. But I want to keep it. And I want you to know that I do want you, and for you to not forget it. That's why I won't stop, even now that I do know what I feel is reciprocated. I've never had to actively pursue someone so hard and so carefully before you. Normally, it hasn't taken that much."

Winna rolled her eyes. "Yes, yes, I know, you get around. Easily, apparently, I get it. Bragging about how easy your past conquests were isn't necessarily what a girl wants to hear from the man she loves."

"I don't mean it like that." He shook his head. "I mean...I want you more than anyone I've ever been with before, but I'm unused to having to flirt quite so hard at someone. You're far too sensible a person to just melt for me with just a half smile or a meaningful glance on my part."

"W-well, how could I just let myself fall for the first man who offered me a stupidly nice smile? That'd be silly," she muttered, red in the face.

"I'm sure I'm not the first to try it on with you. Paz definitely did, from what I gather."

"I mean, yeah, but he doesn't have a smile like yours. Nor is he as pretty."

"That's what I'm saying. You didn't just immediately cave. I still had to work for it."

"Lear, I caved pretty damn fast. How quickly are you used to having your way with people, if I've been the one who's taken the longest?!" She arched an eyebrow at him.

"Pretty quickly, to be fair. But again, the high fey courts are kind of like that, promiscuity and all."

"I see." The woman he loved frowned again, now squinting at

him a little suspiciously. "You keep saying that fey folk are promiscuous, but I've yet to really see any evidence of that beyond you flirting with me."

Lear snorted. "Well, maybe I'm just projecting. But there are a good number of pretty loose fey folk in the high courts, especially back in the feylands. They have fewer reservations overall regarding flirtations, relationships, and affairs. But you have a good deal more sense than most of them, it seems like. Definitely more than me." He bent and kissed her temple. "I like that about you. You're grounded and know yourself. It's a very attractive quality. Not that I don't find you physically attractive too."

"So you say," she murmured.

"Do you want me to go into detail? I'm happy to." He flashed another smile at her.

"No, that's quite alright." Winna narrowed her eyes again, knowing he'd only fluster her again, which was absolutely correct. He meant to describe, in great detail, how he dreamed of her wearing the red formal dress she'd tried on in Ama's shop, the one that had been too small, almost nightly since he'd seen her wearing it in the dressing room. Though, to be fair, she'd been beautiful in all the dresses she'd worn that day.

"You know me too well." He snickered.

"Yes, and yet somehow I still let you kiss me!" She rolled her pretty dark eyes at him.

"Which I'm very grateful for." Lear bent and did just that.

As they kissed, he heard the noise of someone approaching on the drive, and pulled away, muttering, "Another visitor? Really, why do they always have to come in the morning?"

"I guess they want to be able to get whatever it is dealt with before getting to the rest of their day." Winna extracted herself from his arms, much to his displeasure. "Are they human?"

He flicked his second set of eyes open for a brief moment. "Yes, yes. It's safe." He sighed. "I really wish they wouldn't interrupt, I wasn't done making you blush."

"There will be other times, I'm sure." Winna laughed as she drifted towards the door.

Lear darted over to her, putting his hands on her waist, and leaning down until his lips brushed against her neck to whisper, "Later, then."

He felt her shiver. "Lear!"

Lear chuckled, then stepped back as the visitor knocked on the door.

Winna stepped forward and shot him an annoyed look before opening the door. "Good morning! How can I help you?"

"Good morning, Winna." A woman stood on the doorstep. She was older than Winna, and seemed to be around the same age as Ama, which meant she was probably in her late fifties or early sixties. "I've come to consult you on a matter that I hope you can help me with."

"I'm happy to help. Please come in out of the cold." The young mage stepped aside, admitting the visitor. She motioned at Lear. "This is Lear, he's staying here until he's healed."

"Pleased to meet you." Lear bowed slightly.

"You're the fey boy, then?" Her tone was a little insolent.

"Well, I'm clearly not human, am I?" He arched an eyebrow at her.

"No, I suppose not," she muttered. "It's because of one of your lot that I'm having to come here at all!"

"Please don't be rude to Lear because you feel another fey person is causing you problems, Mrs. Tinna," Winna said coolly. "I will help, if I can, but I won't tolerate rudeness, especially when you're the one asking me for help. If it is indeed related to a fey person, I'll probably need Lear's help anyway."

"Fine," the woman huffed.

Lear smirked at her over Winna's head, then turned and went back to the kitchen.

"Now, how can I help you?" Winna asked, tone businesslike.

"Some tree spirit has enchanted my son!"

"Dryad or hamadryad?" Lear asked, pulling the biscuits from the oven.

"How should I know? You're all the same to me!" Mrs. Tinna scoffed. "You're all vile and dangerous, enchanting and endangering peoples' lives! Like my poor baby Wulf!"

"I assure you, fey folk are all very different." Lear straightened, giving her his most chilling smile. "And most aren't nearly as dangerous as I am."

Mrs. Tinna blanched, but riled, "Don't you go threatening me!"

"Unless you can be civil, get out of my cottage!" Winna snapped, going back to the door and throwing it open.

"All I said is that I'm dangerous. It's a statement of fact. Don't kick her out too quickly, Winna, I can handle racist assholes." Lear shook his head, keeping his tone mild.

"Such language!" Mrs. Tinna was suddenly full of righteous indignation.

"You brought it on yourself, lady," Winna replied coldly, but let the door swing shut. "You have one more chance. You better make it count."

Mrs. Tinna stewed for a moment, then finally spoke again. "Like I said, my son has been enchanted by a tree spirit. All he does is sit under the tree anymore, and talk to her. He won't eat, won't come in, won't sleep. It'll be the death of him!"

"Sounds like a dryad." Lear sighed. "Normally they're peaceful, but every so often, something like this will happen. They're very attractive."

"Well, I don't appreciate it!" Mrs. Tinna snapped.

"Frankly, I don't care how you feel, but I do worry for your son," Winna told her icily. "Lear and I will discuss the matter, and we'll be along shortly. Please leave."

"I don't want any other fey person setting foot on my property!" She stamped her foot, apparently doing her best impersonation of an angry toddler.

The young mage rolled her eyes. "Well, I can't break any

enchantment. As you well know, I'm just a healer. Lear is the one who'll be the most helpful, so if you don't let him on your property, you'll be sentencing your son to death."

Mrs. Tinna bristled. "Why, you little strumpet! How dare you-"

Lear's anger truly flared, and he abandoned setting the table. Daring over to the woman, he flicked his second set of eyes open, extended his claws, and set his wings free in a fraction of a second. He caught the rude visitor by the collar of her coat, and lifted her bodily from the ground, cutting her words off as he hissed, "Enough!"

The woman gave an awkward squawk as she dangled in the air.

"Lear!" Winna squeaked in surprise, her tone very worried.

"I can take any insult you throw at me, but I will not tolerate you speaking that way to Winna!" he hissed. Carrying Mrs. Tinna to the door, he threw it open. Lear stalked across the porch, down the steps, and then carried her quite a ways down the path before dropping her back on her feet. "Now go away! We'll be along to help your son, but not because you deserve our help! And don't you ever speak of Winna in such a way ever again. If you do, you'll have to deal with the wrath of the fey on your head!"

"Lear! That's quite enough!" Winna cried as she hurried towards them.

"Now leave!" Lear snarled, letting magic crackle menacingly across his shoulders, though it was really harmless.

The woman turned and fled.

The fey man watched in satisfaction.

"You're not really going to do that, are you?" Winna's expression and tone were deeply concerned as she came to stand next to him.

"What?" He turned to her, blinking in confusion and shutting his heat-sensitive eyes.

"Bring down whatever doom the wrath of the fey is on her!"

"By the wrath of the fey, I mean my wrath, specifically." He shrugged. "Cause I'd be furious. But I wouldn't hurt her, just so you know. I just wanted to scare her, anyway."

"Well, I think you managed it," she muttered.

"What an unpleasant person!" He laughed a little, shielding his eyes to watch the woman's hasty retreat.

There was racism in the feylands, but typically it was reserved for the half-fey, who were seen as less than, or impure, which was ridiculous, of course. Despite being a hodgepodge of various fey blood, Lear *was* fully fey, and he'd never faced it himself, so Mrs. Tinna's rage had been somewhat of a new experience for him. Asher, being a good man, did what he could do to put an end to such bigotry within his domain, but rooting out that kind of evil was difficult. Lear had never held with the idea that half-fey were inferior to fully fey folk. Indeed, several of his trusted squad members were half-fey, and were just as capable, intelligent, and strong as any of his fully fey soldiers.

Of course, any children he and Winna had together would be half-fey. That would be nothing short of wonderful. Half her, half him. They would likely be damn cute babies.

Winna shook her head, sighing. "I actually know her son, Wulf. He's a good man. Just a couple years younger than me. We were in school together."

"Oh?" Lear felt a flicker of jealousy, and reached out to take her hand.

They turned and walked back towards the house. "Yes."

"Is he handsome?"

"Mm." She frowned. "I guess he's handsome enough."

"I see," he muttered.

Winna arched an eyebrow at him as they went back inside. "Please don't tell me you plan to try and seduce him once the enchantment is broken just to get back at his mother."

"While I'm not above that in theory, no. I would never cheat on you."

"I was only joking...but that's good to know." She smiled at him.

They finally sat down to eat breakfast.

Finally, he couldn't keep from asking, "Do you really think he's handsome."

"Lear, you're not jealous, are you?" Winna smiled in vague amusement at him.

"Yes. I don't want you to like anyone other than me," he mumbled, pouting.

"You're the one that asked if I thought he was handsome! Besides, I didn't say I liked him like that, anyway. All I said is that he's handsome in response to your question. That's it. You're also far more handsome, you ridiculous idiot!" She threw her hands into the air in exasperation.

"How much more handsome?" Lear smirked, propping his chin up on his hand.

Winna rolled her eyes. "I'm not going to humor you. Just take my word for it."

"Did he ever try it on with you, like Paz did?"

"No, he's a good man, like I said." She shook her head, shrugging.

"Despite his irritating mother, apparently."

"Apparently," she echoed.

Chapter 26

Wulf and Rina

Breakfast had been very good, and I was sad to leave the warmth and comfort of my home at the behest of a woman who'd been so terrible to us. But Wulf needed our assistance, and that was that.

"So, you know how to break a dryad's enchantment?"

"Yes."

"How so?"

"I'm just going to talk to her. Normally, I could probably just use my own magic to break it, but not with this shitty poison still in me," he replied, shrugging as he kept pace with me. I was on Poppy, and riding at a steady, but fairly easy, pace.

"Think that'll work?"

"Dryads are pretty easily reasoned with, so there's really no reason not to try it first." He nodded. "And short of that, I do know other things we can try."

The Tinna family's large dairy farm wasn't far away, and we soon arrived.

Lear landed, raising an eyebrow at the small, manor-style house that sat at the end of the path. "Fancy themselves important, do they?"

"I can't talk, my family built their own manor without being actual gentry as well."

"We don't know they weren't gentry."

"Well, not gentry of this land, that's for sure." I snorted.

"Fair."

"Despite being apparently very racist towards fey folk, it's another reason why Mrs. Tinna was so rude, she thinks that just because they're the wealthiest family around, it means that she can do and say whatever she wants."

"Yes, because being a dairy farmer makes you all powerful." Lear snorted.

"I mean, there's no shame in being a dairy farmer, it's just her sense of entitlement that makes her awful. Besides, her husband doesn't act like that. Mr. Tinna worked hard to become as wealthy as he is, partly at his wife's insistence, because she was born into a wealthier family, and was used to the high life already."

"Ahh, makes sense."

"That's why their children are all decent, their father tempered their mother. And I don't think she was always so bad, if I'm being honest."

"You know, even though you live outside of town, you know a lot about the people in the area."

"Well, I do see other people fairly often, despite living outside of town, and fey folk aren't the only ones who like to gossip!" I laughed a little, then sighed. "Now, where do you think the dryad's tree is? I don't want to have to go to the house and deal with asking Mrs. Tinna how to find it."

"Hmm." Lear shaded his eyes and surveyed the property before us. "I think that's it over there."

I looked where he was pointing, and saw a lone tree in the distance. It was empty of leaves, given the time of year, and looked very sad. "Oh, yep. There's someone sitting beneath it. I bet that's Wulf."

"It *is* a man who looks about your age. Has golden hair."

"Yes, sounds like him."

"Do you like blonde hair?"

"What?"

"I can make my hair look blonde, if you prefer blonde hair." He shrugged innocently.

I frowned". "Lear, I don't like him like that."

He flashed a quick grin at me. "I know, but if you prefer blonde hair, I can-"

I cut him off, my face red as I admitted, "I like your hair exactly as it is. Don't you dare change it!"

His lovely green eyes blinked, and he reached out to brush his dark bangs out of his eyes. "You like my hair?"

"Lear, there's not much about you I don't like. Except maybe this sudden and very misplaced insecurity." I sighed, rolling my eyes, then turning to slide off Poppy.

As I swung my leg over the saddle, his hands came up around my waist, and he lifted me down, murmuring, "Easy does it." He pulled me back and into his chest, whispering, "I'll stop worrying then."

"Yes, please do," I muttered. We stood there like that for a moment. I felt his lips on my neck, and pulled away, smiling a little. "We should go before you turn this into an outdoor make-out session."

"I'd be one-hundred percent so up for that, in case you're ever interested," Lear said as he wove his fingers through mine.

We started walking towards the tree, leading Poppy along.

"I'm sure you would be!" I laughed, then sighed and said, "You know, I'm surprised you're the jealous sort."

"I was mostly joking. Mostly. And normally I'm not. But I also haven't had or wanted any serious relationship with anyone before you," he told me.

"No?"

"No. I was content to be single and just have flings. I don't want flings anymore."

"So I gather." I smiled.

"You believe me, right?"

"Lear, you can't lie, and your statements on the matter have left little to no wiggle room."

"I've tried to make that the case." The fey man nodded. "I'm glad you noticed."

"I didn't necessarily know it was intentional, but am also glad it was." I squeezed his hand. It meant he wanted me to know, in no uncertain terms, how he felt for me. That was...very nice, actually.

As we approached the tree, I took in the situation. Wulf was sitting on the ground, his back against the bark, and his head tilted up as he stared up into the barren leaves of the tree, a dazed, joyous sort of expression on his face.

Despite his rapt expression, Wulf looked rough. It had clearly been a couple of days since he'd shaved, and his clothes were dirty and rumpled. There was a blanket cast over his legs, and a plate of untouched food beside him, as well as a full water-skin. There were dark circles under his eyes, and a slightly gaunt look to his features.

Well, his mother *had* said he'd not been eating or sleeping or anything.

But what was most odd about the entire scene was that there was an ax sitting on the ground beside him.

"Oh yeah, he's got it real bad." Lear grimaced. "I'm surprised that such a young tree has a dryad attached to it already." He now addressed the tree, "We're not here to hurt you or anything. We just want to talk."

There was a surge of magic, and suddenly, a young woman poked her head out from behind the tree. She had pale green skin and burgundy hair, wore a short dress made of what looked like flower petals, and had large, purple eyes that reminded me a little of Lear's. Did he maybe have some dryad in him as well?

"Rina!" Wulf cried gladly.

"Just a moment, dear," she murmured, flashing him a sweet smile, which faltered as she turned a wary gaze towards us.

"You're Rina?" I asked, smiling reassuringly at her, going by the name Wulf had used.

"Y-yes."

"I'm Winna. It's nice to meet you." I bowed to her. "This is Lear."

Lear bowed slightly as well. "Pleased to meet you."

"What...what do you want?" The dryad watched us warily.

"We're just worried for Wulf. He's not eating or sleeping or anything, from what we understand," I told her.

"We know he's enchanted, Rina. It's okay, I see the ax, and can guess what happened," Lear said quietly.

"Would you...tell me what happened?" I asked him, surprised.

"I believe Wulf came to cut the tree down. She's young, and reacted in the only way she knew how, by enchanting him. It was self-defense."

I blinked. "Oh! Oh, how awful!"

"I-I didn't even mean to!" Tears came to Rina's eyes. "I-I just saw the ax and reacted!"

"It's alright," Lear said. "Can you undo the spell?:

"I-I think, b-but...I-I don't want to be cut down! I don't want to die!"

"Don't worry. We won't let that happen," Lear said firmly.

"I-I don't even bother anyone! The most I do is watch! I like watching the humans...they're so funny. Then the old lady, I think she's Wulf's mother, started watching me back, so I stopped."

"You think she saw you?" Lear asked, arching an eyebrow.

"I...I don't know. I was trying to be discreet." Rina grimaced. "I wasn't trying to pry, or anything. I was just curious. Humans are strange." Her eyes flickered to me, and hastily added, "I-I don't mean that in a bad way!"

"Oh, no worries! We're definitely odd!" I laughed.

The dryad seemed to relax a little. "Can you help me?"

"We'll certainly try to. But you have to release Wulf from the spell. He'll die if this keeps up. We're not nearly as sturdy as you are," I told her gently.

Tears came to her eyes again. "I-I know! I-I've been trying to get him to eat, to go inside to sleep, to stay warm, b-but he won't! H-he just laughs and says he loves me, and that he won't leave me, and isn't hungry! B-but I know that's just the spell talking! I-I know humans need to eat and sleep and be warm!"

"Well, I know Wulf from school. He's a reasonable man. I think that, if you release the spell, I can talk the whole thing out with him," I told her earnestly.

"You think?"

"Yes," I assured her.

"And I know how to propagate a tree so that the dryad that's bound to it can travel to the new tree. If we can't come to an agreement, that's what we'll do, alright?"

Rina sighed. "A-alright." There was a surge of energy, and a flash of green magic.

Wulf blinked, and shook his head. "What the...what happened?!"

"Welcome back, Wulf! Were you going to cut down this tree?" I asked, smiling slightly and putting my hands on my hips.

He turned his bleary grey eyes to me. "Winna?! What are you doing here? What...what day is it? And who's that with you? Is he fey?"

"This is Lear, and yes, he's fey." I snorted and continued, "Your mother came to me for help. You got yourself enchanted by a dryad when you went to cut her tree down," I told him, motioning at the tree.

Wulf staggered to his feet, rubbing his eyes. "Gods, I feel like death! There's a dryad in the tree, you said?"

"I wondered if you knew." I frowned a little.

"I-I'm Rina!" the dryad squeaked, hiding behind the tree. "I-I'm sorry! I-I didn't mean to cause trouble! I-I just don't want to die!"

Wulf blinked, looking at her as if for the first time. "I'm sorry. I had no idea this tree had a dryad in it. Ma just said she wanted this tree down, since it blocked her view of the pond." He motioned at the small pond a little ways away.

"Your mother asked you to cut it down?" Lear asked, arching an eyebrow at him.

Wulf studied Lear for a moment. If he was shocked to see another fey person, he kept it to himself. He finally sighed and told us, "She got a bee in her bonnet about it. You know how she gets." He cast a glance at me and shrugged. "Wouldn't leave me alone about it, so I finally caved, even though I actually really like this tree. It's the only red maple near the house." He looked at Rina. "I'm sorry, I never would have tried to cut your tree down, had I known you were here."

Rina flushed, but instead of red, she turned a darker green. "I-I'm sorry I enchanted you! I...guess I could have just shown myself and asked you not to."

"Well, you didn't know how I'd react, I'm sure." Wulf shook his head. "Not all humans are friendly towards fey folk."

"Your mother included?" I asked quietly.

Wulf smiled grimly. "Exactly. Dad has no problem with them. Ma does."

"I-I think your mother saw me," Rina murmured.

"So she contrived to murder her," Lear said, his tone was full of quiet fury.

"It would seem so." Wulf's expression hardened. "I expect she'll deny it, though. And we have no proof that she knew the tree had a dryad attached to it before I got enchanted."

"No, we don't." Lear sighed.

"I'll have a word with my father about this. He won't be pleased. This isn't the first time she's tried to cause trouble with fey folk. They've just as much a right to live as we do." He bowed to Rina. "I'm so, so sorry, miss."

Rina flushed deep green again. "I-I'm sorry too!"

"Please don't apologize. It's not your fault. You just reacted. I wouldn't want to die, either." Wulf smiled earnestly at her.

"Th-thank you," Rina murmured. "C-can we be friends? I-I didn't want you to stay out here all the time and not sleep or eat, or anything, but...it was nice to have someone to talk to."

Wulf seemed surprised. "Are you lonely?"

"Not many fey folk come around here. I...suspect they don't feel very welcome."

Wulf's expression hardened for a moment, but then he smiled gently. "Of course we can be friends, Rina."

The young dryad smiled shyly. "O-okay! Thank you!"

To my surprise, Wulf flushed slightly. "I don't mind sitting out here with you, since you get lonely. I can't all the time, but when I have some time to spare, I'm happy to keep you company."

"Oh, please don't go out of your way!" Rina shook her head. "Just when you have time!"

"It's no imposition," he assured her.

Raising my eyebrows, I looked to Lear, who smirked and winked at me.

"Well, we should...probably be on our way, huh?" I asked him.

Wulf turned to us, as if remembering we were there. "Thank you so much for your help. I'll be speaking to my father about this. He'll deal with my mother. She...didn't used to be so bad."

"She was awful to us earlier," I murmured, shaking my head.

"I'm sorry Winna, Lear." Wulf grimaced. "It's not right."

"No, it's not, but...well, we're alright." Lear shrugged. "Although to be fair, I did indirectly threaten her and provoke her."

"But only after she'd already been pretty rude." I pointed out. "She made me angry. Normally I'm more level-headed, but her attitude set off my temper."

"I know it takes a lot to make you angry, too. But even when we were kids, someone picking on one of your friends was always a sure-fire way to rile your anger, if I remember rightly." My old schoolmate gave a wry smile. "So I'm not surprised it upset you."

"Wulf! Oh my dear, you're well again!" Mrs. Tinna's voice cried.

I grimaced, seeing her approaching quickly. Intense anger flickered across Lear's expression. Rina gave a squeak of terror and immediately disappeared back into her tree. "We should go," Lear muttered.

"That's probably best." Wulf sighed, "I'll deal with her."

"Let me know if I can do anything to help," I told Wulf, hastily swinging back up into the saddle.

Lear launched himself into the air, and we left before Mrs. Tinna could reach her son.

As we retreated, I heard raised voices behind us.

"I think that went rather well, don't you?" I asked Lear, knowing his inhuman hearing would pick up my voice, even as he wheeled high above me in the sky.

Immediately, he plunged down to hover beside me as I rode along.

"Yes, it did. I expect Mrs. Tinna won't be best pleased with the situation, though." He grinned at me.

"I agree. I think he's inclined to be more than just friends with young Rina still. Although she's probably not all that young, is she?"

"No, just young for a dryad."

"Makes sense."

"Still an adult, though."

"Well, good." I nodded approvingly. "I hope they're happy together."

"Me too."

We soon arrived home, put Poppy up, and got back inside.

"Phew. Such a busy day and it's not even noon yet!" I sighed, holding my hands out over the heating stones as Stroopwafel wound her way around and through my feet. Diana purred loudly from her favorite spot on the couch.

Lear sat beside my little familiar, stroking her fur gently. "Indeed."

It was quiet for a few moments.

"I know you said you needed some time to process everything we learned, but do you mind if I try to get more information from the books today?"

I blinked. "I don't mind."

"I don't have to."

"No, I promise it's okay." I shook my head. "Just...if you find anything new, maybe...feed it to me slowly, in small bits. Is that okay?"

He smiled. "Of course."

Chapter 27

Diana Helps

L ear looked up from the ancient book he'd been reading. "Someone's coming." He flicked his second set of eyes open, then frowned. "They're fey. Well, that's a change of pace."

"And at least it's not another morning visit! Although we did already have a morning adventure today." I laughed, setting the loaves of bread I'd just pulled from the oven on the stove-top to cool.

I took off my apron as Lear flung the door open. He paused, then smiled, "Oh! Hi Pima!"

"I think we need to see Winna." Pima's voice was worried.

I quickly made my way over to the door as well, glad that my fey neighbor had finally stopped by. Indeed, Pima and Mira were both there on the porch. My eyes flicked immediately to the bandage on one of Mira's little hands, and I noticed that her eyes were reddened with tears, and she sniffled slightly. So this wasn't a social call, then!

"Please come in!" I told them. Hopefully, whatever was wrong with Mira's hand wasn't too serious. I'd still do what I could, but not having Diana's help would really put a damper on it. "All of your family is most welcome in my home," I told them, extending the welcome to Tip.

Lear stepped aside allowing our guests to enter.

"Thank you so much, Winna." Pima sighed. "Mira burned her hand. It's kind of bad. I know that Diana is without a lot of her power, but you're still a healer, and I'd appreciate your opinion on it, as well as any help you can give. Because any amount of healing magic is better than none, in my opinion."

Luckily, burns were manageable. Even if it was a really bad burn, I could at least do something, even without Diana. With repeated visits and magical treatments, I should be able to heal even the worst of burns, as long as it was a small area that was affected, like a hand. A burn over a larger area, as Biren's had been, would prove much more of a challenge now. I needed to tell everyone around here to be more careful when it came to fire, apparently, given this was now two burn patients in a row! Although, to be fair, the fire hadn't been Biren's fault, but still.

I nodded. "I'm happy to help however I can. How'd you get burned?"

"I-I got t-too close to the fire! I-it snapped and sent a spark out and caught my fur on fire!" Mira wailed, bursting into tears anew.

"Oh my!" I blinked, inwardly glad that I didn't have fur.

"Our fur is pretty flammable, unfortunately." Pima sighed, shaking her head.

"Well, accidents happen. And I'll do what I can."

"Thank you."

I led them to the couch, telling Lear, "Would you get a clean rag, the bar of soap from the sink, a bowl of cool water, and some bandages? You'll need to tear them up; they're in the closet over there." I motioned at the closet just beside the medicine cabinet. While the medicine cabinet held just that, medicine, the closet beside it held all of my other medical supplies like bandages, syringes, cotton, sutures, empty bottles, thermometers, and much more. It never hurt to have non-magical healing supplies on hand, just as a precaution, or in case I myself was the one hurt and someone else had to tend to me, much as Lear had when I'd been sick in the days after Veris' attack.

"Yes ma'am!" My handsome fey companion saluted at me, then darted around to gather the supplies I had requested.

-

Diana stretched, getting up. It was time for her to get involved. Helping magically was out of the question, of course, but she could definitely help in other ways.

She prodded Stroopwafel awake. Her sister opened a grumpy hazel eye, not pleased at being woken. Diana looked pointedly at the little faun who was crying on the couch.

Stroopwafel maowed, understanding her mission, then got up and stretched herself. She be-bopped over to Mira, then hopped up into the sobbing little faun's lap, immediately beginning to purr loudly.

Her silly cat sister had very little in the way of brains, but she was excellent at comforting people, and always happy to have the attention. Stroopwafel was also particularly good at purring, and purring was healing in its own right. As an added bonus, she even enjoyed belly-rubs, and only ever felt the need to bear-trap on Winna's face when the mood struck her. Stroopy also enjoyed biting Winna's ankles, or flinging herself at her human's legs when she didn't get the attention she desired quickly enough.

But Winna was Stroopwafel's person, which is why she behaved like that. Winna was also Diana's person, and Diana rumbled loudly as she made her way over to her person.

Her Winna.

She wove between the mage's legs, then hopped up beside where Winna was perched on the coffee table, examining Mira's hand. The tall, skinny fey man, Lear, hurried over with the rag, soap, bandages, and water that her mistress had asked for.

"It's not as bad a burn as you had me worried it was!" Winna smiled, tone reassuring. "Not that it's a...not bad one, but it's not as bad as I'd feared. I'll do what I can! It won't be fully healed, so you might need to bring her back in a little while for another healing session or two. I'll know more once I get it cleaned, but I can certainly help, even without Diana's magical assistance."

Diana maowed reassuringly. It was important for her Winna to have some confidence in herself again. She'd never had much before now, but now she had none. Sure, her magic wasn't as strong as her mother's, or any of her ancestors, now long gone, but it was still magic, and that was a lot more than what most people had around there. Well, save the fey folk, but it was still a stronger healing ability than most of them even had.

"Diana agrees!" Lear translated, smiling down at her.

It was a little strange, but not unwelcome, to have someone in the house who could actually understand her. It also meant he could understand Stroopwafel, too, but...well, that didn't really take too much, all things considered. Stroopwafel only ever had a few things on her mind: food, cuddles, or pets and scratchies. Sometimes kisses. Cause Stroopwafel did like kisses. Diana only really liked Winna's kisses, though she would tolerate them from others as needed. Stroopwafel welcomed the kissies from just about anyone, silly thing that she was.

Winna giggled, and reached down to scratch Diana between the ears, which felt very nice. She leaned her head up into the touch. Winna always gave the best scratches. Her short, neat fingernails always found the purrfect spots. "Good! I'll also send you home with some burn salve. That should help, too."

"Thank you, Winna!" Mira hiccuped, pausing from petting Stroopwafel to wipe at her tear-stained face with her other hand.

Stroopwafel maowed in annoyance at the interruption, but didn't move.

"Yes, thank you very much! I was very frightened when I saw her little hand all aflame!" Pima sighed, shaking her head. "And Tip is away today, visiting family. I panicked."

"Well, you were right to bring her here," Winna said firmly.

In all her long years, Diana hadn't been quite so fond of anyone.

Well, not since Awenna, anyway. Winna reminded her a lot of Awenna. They had the same hair, and similar personalities. Diana tried to call to mind any of her past masters and mistresses, but really couldn't remember any beyond Winna and Awenna, other than Winna's mother and aunt. Before her aunt had gone away, anyway. Even Winna's mother and aunt only stuck around in her memory because they hadn't been gone, or passed, for very long.

The years that had passed since Winna's parents had died had flickered by in the blink of an eye to her. But they had also been very peaceful, and she remembered much of them, at the same time. She suspected that Winna perceived time differently than she did, for now. As the mage got older, she'd see time more like Diana herself did. Neither fast nor slow, but ebbing on eternally, as Diana most likely would herself.

The diluted grey tabby cat remembered being little more than just a kitten. The family had finally settled into their new home. By that time, their powers had already waned considerably, but they could still do magic other than healing.

She padded through the big manor, in search of Awenna, whose lap was always open to her, much as Winna's was now. Awenna was most often in the library, poring over the very same books that Lear struggled to work his way through now. She'd been trying to read them as well, but never had any luck.

That had been so long ago. Diana had never bothered to learn how to read, either. It hadn't seemed particularly important, and no one had ever expected it of her, since she was a cat. But maybe if she had, she could have been more useful to her Winna.

It didn't matter. There was no sense in worrying about what might have been. Worrying wasn't very catlike, anyway.

She also remembered the day that Winna had been born. That Winna's mother had tried for a third child was unusual. The family had always kept themselves small, having usually only one child apiece, sometimes two. They hadn't wanted to draw attention to themselves, though they had wanted to continue the family line. It had become tradition within the family, eventually, even when they'd stopped living in fear of what lurked outside the protection the original family had brought with them. But when Winna's brothers had both been born without any magic at all, Winna's mother had wanted to try one more time, wanting to preserve the magical line, and Winna had finally been born.

"You know, you're my first fey patient," Winna said to Mira.

"Ahem." Lear cleared his throat, arching his eyebrow in amusement. "And what am I? Chopped liver?!"

Winna blinked, then laughed. "Sorry! I forgot! So you're my second fey patient, Mira!"

"That's still cool!" Mira sniffled, managing a smile.

"Let's get this cleaned," Winna said cheerfully, in her element.

Despite the crisis, Winna very rarely lost her head. She was a very practical woman. She might have a moment of distress, but she always pulled herself together quickly, and got to work, in Diana's experience.

Winna's weak magic surged into the little faun's burned hand, easing the pain. The mage then began to clean the wounded appendage very gently with soapy water.

Mira whimpered in pain, and her mother soothed her. Winna pushed more magic into the little girl's hand, trying to combat the pain from the soap, allowing Mira to turn her attention to Stroopwafel, who was still purring away in her lap. She distracted herself as best she could by petting the silly cat while Winna continued to work on her hand.

"Alright. The most unpleasant part is over," Winna told her. "I promise!" Diana's mistress inspected the wound again. "Yes, it's not terrible. You can come back, but I think the burn salve will actually work well enough on its own, if you use it every night with some new bandages."

"Okay. We'll probably come by anyway, just to say hi." Pima smiled.

"Of course! You two can come as often as you like!" Winna smiled, starting to push healing magic into Mira's hand.

"It feels nice!" Mira smiled.

"Yes, it does!" Lear grinned. "I'm often on the receiving end of it."

Winna frowned. "Speaking of which, it's been a while since I did a healing session for you."

"It's alright." He shook his head. "I'm slowly healing on my own. The progress is mostly thanks to you, though. Your help has let me heal faster than I would have otherwise."

The mage managed a smile. "Good. I'm glad to help."

They were all quiet for a few moments.

"It's really kind of nice to have company," Lear observed, settling himself down in the armchair.

"Yeah." Winna smiled. "I'm glad I have such good neighbors."

"I'm so glad Mira met you that day. We don't usually show ourselves to humans, but we've missed out on a good friend in doing so." Pima reached out and patted the young human woman's shoulder gently.

"Oh, don't worry, I understand! I know sometimes humans don't react well to fey folk." Winna sighed. Diana had a feeling her Winna was thinking about the unpleasant woman who'd visited earlier in the day, demanding their help, and treating the tall skinny fey man so badly, not to mention her Winna!

Diana should have walked right up and bitten the mean woman's ankles, or scratched her feet, but Winna wouldn't have wanted her to.

"I'm glad to count you as a friend, Winna." Pima smiled.

"And I you!" Winna beamed back.

It was good to see Winna happy. She'd been so scared after that strange bone creature had been hurting Lear, and Diana had intervened. Then Winna had been sick, then stressed, then overwhelmed and stressed...It was good to finally see her happy.

Lear, tall and skinny though he was, also made Winna happy, and that was good. Diana knew she'd judged him properly when they'd spoken for the first time.

Initially, that he'd hidden his actual identity and appearance from her Winna had angered and unsettled Diana. But once she'd learned he wasn't really hiding it, he was just injured, she'd forgiven him, though had still been a little wary for a time. But he'd now proved to be a good companion for her Winna, and he gave really good scratchies. Stroopwafel liked him a lot as well, as an added bonus.

Now her mistress was bandaging the little faun's hand carefully. Winna reached out blindly for another bandage as she focused on holding the first bandage in place, but she missed it, and groped across the table.

Diana padded forward and brushed against her errant hand, directing it to its intended target. See? No magic required to be helpful.

"Thanks, Annie!" Winna smiled, realizing what her familiar had done.

Diana maowed.

"She said it's her job to help you, even if she can't do it magically," Lear murmured.

Winna blinked, then paused and bent to kiss Diana on the forehead. "I love you so much, miss."

Diana purred.

"She knows. She loves you too," the fey man said.

Stroopwafel maowed loudly, annoyed at not getting attention, and they all burst into giggles.

"She says she loves you too!" Lear snorted.

"And I love you, silly Stroopy-lou! I'll give you kisses in a minute, alright?" Winna smiled down at her silliest cat.

Stroopwafel maowed in agreement.

Winna finished bandaging Mira's hand, and tied it carefully. "So yeah, keep it clean and dry, and put burn salve on it every night. Come back if you want to, and I'll gladly help again. I also suggest maybe investing in some of the same kind of heating stones I have here. Dern, the dwarf in the village, makes and sells them. They're a little expensive, but they work well, and it takes away the risk of a fire."

"Thank you, Winna, I'll have to talk to Tip about maybe getting some." Pima nodded. "Now, how much for this visit."

"Not a bit!" Winna shook her head firmly. "First visit is free!"

That wasn't true, Diana knew, but Winna had always hated charging for her services.

"Don't be ridiculous. Accept the money, Winna." Lear snorted.

"I insist." Pima pulled a coin purse from the pocket of her neat, teal blue pinafore. "We just have standard gold coinage, is that alright?"

Diana didn't understand the intricacies of money; indeed, it was an altogether silly concept, really, but the pretty gold coins reflected the light that streamed in from the window, sending it dancing across the coffee table. She batted eagerly at the flickering lights for a few moments.

"Yep, she can swap it in the village." Lear nodded.

"Oh, fine." Winna sighed.

Pima pressed some coins into Winna's hand, and she slipped them into her pocket without counting. "Thank you so much, dear." The mother faun's voice was warm and earnest.

"You're very welcome! Would you two like to stay and have some tea? I just got some bread out of the oven, and it's really delightful when it's hot like this!"

"That would be lovely, thank you! Tip won't be back until after dinner, and we were a bit bored at the house, I think," Pima said, then frowned a little. "Not that Mira getting burned is my ideal way of getting out of the house."

"No, of course not!" Winna laughed. "But it can be a silver lining, right? Her hand is going to be fine, and now we get to have tea together!"

"You all sit and chat. I'll make tea and cut up the bread," Lear said, going to the kitchen.

Pleased that Lear liked to help her Winna, Diana padded after him into the kitchen, brushing up against his legs.

"Oh, hello there, Queen Diana." He smiled, pausing to kneel and pet her gently.

She maowed quietly at him.

The tall, skinny fey man blinked, then smiled. "Well, you're welcome, but don't thank me. I help her because I love her. Just like you."

Diana blinked slowly at him, communicating her happiness that he'd stuck around.

He grinned. "I'm glad you're happy that I've stayed. I'm happy I stayed too, and I'll stay as long as I can. Then, when I do have to leave, I promise I'll come back. Even if I have to quit my job to do it. But I don't expect I will. I'm sure I can work things out with the higher-ups. Besides, the king, Asher, is a good friend, and a very reasonable person. He's the one who will have the final say in things."

She maowed again.

"No, I don't think I'll take Winna back. I don't think she'd like the fey capital. It's...too busy for her. And we can be a little cutthroat, which would upset her, I think. Besides, she doesn't want to leave here, anyway, which I understand."

Diana bobbed her head approvingly, and then wandered away, letting him get to making the tea as promised.

She hopped up onto the table and surveyed her cozy domain, feeling very content.

Chapter 28

Disaster

A crash of thunder startled Lear awake, and he blinked groggily, trying to figure out where he was, and what was going on. There had been another noise just after the thunder, and it took him a brief, sleepy moment to realize that it had been a scream.

Winna?!

Leaping to his feet, he abandoned the book he'd fallen asleep reading on the couch, and threw himself down the hallway at top speed. Practically blasting her door off its hinges as he barged in, he looked around wildly, demanding, "What's wrong?!"

Except there was no goblin with a knife. No ghostly Veris come back to haunt or kill them. No magic spell was affecting anything, either. His heat-sensitive eyes told him that only Winna and her cats were in the room.

Sniffles told him the young woman was crying. "S-sorry! I-I was startled awake. Th-that's all."

"Are you alright?" He drifted closer to the bed, concerned because she was clearly distraught. He'd sit, but wasn't sure if she wanted him to, given that it was her bed.

Lightning flashed again before Winna could reply, lighting up her frightened face as thunder crashed through the air once more. It was so loud that it sent the cottage trembling. The young human mage cowered, curling into herself.

Scared of storms? And it was a bad storm out there, too, the rain was lashing the roof in a torrential downpour.

Lear threw all caution into the wind, and took the liberty of going forward to sit beside her on the bed, then pulling her close. "It's alright. It's just a thunderstorm."

"I-I know!" Winna sobbed, pressing against him. "B-but th-the thunder k-keeps sh-shaking the h-house! L-like an earthquake!"

"I'm sorry," he murmured, hugging her tightly.

"M-my parents d-died because of an earthquake!" the young woman whimpered.

Oh, that's what it was. Not scared of storms, scared of earthquakes, and understandably so. The last two bursts of thunder had indeed made the house tremble.

Lear had never asked what had happened to her parents. She mentioned them often, and also that they were gone, but he hadn't wanted to upset her by asking, in case it upset her. He knew she'd tell him in her own time, and it seemed like that time was now.

"Ah." He sighed. "I'm so sorry, my love."

"W-we survived th-the big one! I-it destroyed a lot of the village, b-but our cottage is well-built, s-so i-it didn't fall! Th-the town w-wasn't so lucky. W-we went to help them, and th-things were much, much worse there. B-buildings had collapsed everywhere! S-so many people were trapped...Wh-while we were there, there was an after-shock a-and part of a building fell on them a-as they were t-trying to help the people who were trapped!"

"Oh, Winna," Lear murmured, shifting and pulling her onto his lap, and cradling her against his chest. Pulling for his magic, he released his wings, and brought them up around them like a fluffy cocoon. "I am so sorry."

The woman he loved slipped her arms around his neck, buried

her face into his shoulder and cried. Every time more thunder crashed, she flinched, and he squeezed her gently.

After a long while, the storm died down, and with it, her sobs slowed enough to sniffling, punctuated every so often by the jumpy staccato of hiccups as she tried to regulate her breathing.

Lear reached out and poured a cup of water from a carafe on the bedside table, then pushed it into her hands. "Drink."

Winna took the cup, and drank obediently, then leaned back into him. "Th-thank you."

He set the cup aside, and reached up to trail his fingers through her hair, telling her, "Now this is the part where I suggest I stay here to make sure you sleep, and accidentally-on-purpose fall asleep in the same bed, then we wake up later and make out or get up to more mischief. Or it would be, but I'm not going to take advantage of your sadness like that." He paused, then added, with a wink, "Not tonight, anyway." Not that he would ever actually do that.

Winna pulled away slightly, blinking, then burst into giggles, which was what he'd been after.

The fey man smiled, and leaned down to kiss her cheek. "Maybe some other time." He paused, then asked softly, "Are you alright?"

"Y-yeah." She rubbed her eyes with her fists, and looked very young for a moment. "Thank you, Lear. N-normally, I have to just sit here and cry and be scared."

"Instead you can sit on me and cry and be scared." He grinned wryly.

But she shook her head. "I-I wasn't really scared once you were here, so it was much better."

"Oh, well good." Lear leaned down and kissed her gently and briefly. "I was serious about leaving, though. If I stay much longer, I won't have the willpower to leave at all. Will you be okay once I go back to my room?"

"Uh-huh." She nodded, leaning forward for another smooch. "Thank you."

The fey man smiled, reaching up to stroke her face, then stood. "Anytime, Winna. I love you. Goodnight."

"I-I love you, too," she murmured.

Lear turned and forced his feet to take him from the room, pausing a moment to sigh once he was in the hallway. Every bit of him wanted to charge back into her room and draw her into his arms, kiss her with every ounce of passion in his fey body and -

He shook himself then. Thinking about it wouldn't make things any easier. It would, in fact, make it worse, and make it that much harder to not go back into Winna's room. But she didn't want that. She wasn't there yet, and that was okay.

The fey man was dragging himself down the hallway, back to his own bedroom, when a noise outside caught his attention.

A horse was galloping at top speed towards the cottage.

Frowning, Lear went to the living room area, flicked his second set of eyes open, and peered out into the rain, which had started to let up as the storm began to pass. Indeed, a horse was approaching, though it was starting to slow.

The fey man watched as the figure leapt off, and staggered up the front steps. Recognizing the visitor as Jedda with his heat-vision, Lear flung open the door before the man could knock.

"What's wrong?" he asked, readying himself to hear the worst. Jedda wouldn't have ridden so quickly to the cottage in the middle of the night, on the tail-end of a terrible storm, if something very bad hadn't happened.

Jedda stumbled into the house, muddy and wet. "Get Winna and Diana!" he cried.

"Jedda, what's wrong?" Lear helped steady him.

"There was a mudslide in the village! I was sent to get them so they could help! Lots of houses were destroyed! They must come quickly!" Jedda gasped.

There was a soft noise of a door opening, and Lear's heart sank as Winna appeared in the opening of the hallway, wearing a robe and fluffy slippers. "Jedda?!" she murmured, frowning. "What's wrong?!" Diana and Stroopwafel were on her heels.

"A mudslide in the village. They need help," Lear told her, watching her closely, not sure how she'd take the news, given that her ability to heal others had been so significantly reduced very recently.

Winna's face paled, and her balance wavered.

Diana maowed softly.

"Oh gods!" the young woman whispered, sinking to the ground, hugging herself tightly.

Jedda was shaking his head, going over to the young woman, reaching out to help her up. "We don't have time to wait, Winna. Please get Diana's basket and let's go!"

Lear darted forward, using his fey speed to make it to Winna before Jedda did. He knelt by her side, drawing her close. Thinking it would only upset Winna more to have to explain on her own, he said, "Diana has lost most of her power. She did so to protect us when we were attacked at the cottage. It's...my fault, but...well, most of her power was used up, and won't come back any time soon."

Diana maowed softly; it sounded sad.

"I-I...I-I can't do much to help!" Winna burst into new tears. "B-but I-I'll still go! I-I have to!"

"I know. I'll go too, but...they can't expect too much. They rely so heavily on you, and you relied so heavily on Diana, I'm concerned they'll be angry when you can't live up to their expectations," Lear said, looking up and frowning at Jedda. "It's not fair if they blame her for not being able to help as well as she wishes she could."

Jedda swiped his hand over his haggard face. "Ah, lass...I'm sorry to hear it. But the villagers know you. They know you're not as strong as you wish. I don't think they'll be angry."

"I-I hope so! I-I'm so sorry!"

"It's alright, sweetie. But why didn't you say anything to anyone sooner?"

"I-I...I...I don't like being useless. It's...embarrassing. I-I'd hoped to figure out a solution before it became a problem! B-but now it is a-and I-I'm sorry!" she wept.

"You're not useless, and it's not your fault," Lear assured her, helping her stand. "You go with Jedda. Diana will stay here and watch the cottage and Stroopwafel." At least it would give the proud, old familiar something to do in their absence. "And I'll go into the forest and see if any fey folk with healing abilities are around, even weak ones, and will ask them to come help as well. Hell, I'll ask any without healing abilities to come, we're all pretty strong and fast, and that'll help with rescue efforts."

"Tark heard when they came to tell me. He was gathering some of his folk to head into town while I rode out here." Jedda nodded.

"Alright. We have a plan." Lear stepped back, but kept his hands on Winna's shoulders. "Take a deep breath."

She did so, and Jedda got her a glass of water, which she drank, murmuring, "Thank you."

"Will you be okay without me?"

Winna smiled weakly. "I'll be with Jedda. It'll be fine. But I should get going. Even a weak healing ability is better than nothing, right now."

"You're right," Jedda agreed.

Lear bent and kissed her gently. "Then go. I'll be along as quickly as I manage, and will send along as many fey folk as I can.

"I love you," she whispered.

"I love you too." He grinned, then darted out the door.

-

I paused to take a moment's comfort from Diana and Stroop-wafel, then stood and took a deep breath. "Alright, Jedda. Let's go."

We left hurriedly, and climbed onto Jedda's horse. I rode behind him, clutching him tightly around the middle, and hoping my coat would be warm enough to last the long hours we'd be spending in town.

The rain was falling much more slowly now, but as the horse

raced along, it hit my face like tiny, stinging pebbles, and I lowered my head so his shoulder shielded me a little.

The ride was silent, except for the noise of the horse's galloping hooves and the nightly noises.

Soon, Greenwood came into view, and I choked back a sob, already able to see some of the damage. What seemed like a good portion of the face of the large, steep hill behind the village had slid away, crushing and destroying buildings in its path.

"It'll be alright, lass," Jedda told me quietly.

"I-I can only do so much!" I whimpered. "Th-this is terrible!" Because, of course, a tragedy would happen so shortly after I'd lost the largest part of my ability to help them.

We rode past buildings. The village was dark except for whatever lanterns and lights people had scrounged up in the madness. That said, the town square was fairly well-lit, thankfully. There were lamp-posts placed evenly along the perimeter of the square, and I could tell that's where Jedda was headed. Given that it was the most well-lit area, at the moment, it was probably being used as a headquarters of sorts for the burgeoning relief efforts.

As we rode into the square, Jedda checked his horse to a canter, then a walk. Finally, we stopped, and both swung down. Many villagers were already gathered there.

"Winna!" someone shouted, and I heard several other folks crying my name, their voices relieved.

"She's here!" someone called.

Full of devastation, I turned to face them, barely able to contain my tears. They'd started to gather around Jedda and me, all talking at once.

I motioned for them to quiet down. "P-please! I-I'll do what I can," I told them, then felt my face crumple as I continued, telling the full truth, "But I-I...Diana recently chose to sacrifice a-a good deal of her power to save my life recently. Sh-she...only has enough to keep herself alive anymore. I-I...I-I'll do everything I can, but...I-I...." Tears coursed down my face, but I managed to choke out, "Y-you all know I'm not very strong! I-I'm s-so, so sorry!"

Silence fell.

"So you're useless now, huh?" a voice snapped.

It cut like a knife, and I cringed. Lear was right. They were going to be angry, and I was going to have to deal with it.

"Now see here-" Jedda bristled.

I cut him off, "N-no, it's true. I'm not nearly as helpful." Taking a deep breath, I wiped my face, and looked out at them again. "But I'll still do whatever I can to help. Because I can still do more than nothing, even without Diana's help."

This still didn't pacify them. "Some healer you are!"

"Can't do anything without that cat! Why did she even bother saving you?!" another shouted.

Someone else began to berate me as well, "You just hide in your cottage and-"

But Bekka's voice sliced through the angry tirade, "Enough!" My former schoolmate stomped forward to stand in front of me, whirling to face them all. "How dare you!" she snarled, dark eyes blazing with fury.

Her brown skin was smeared with mud, which also clung to her usually fluffy curls, though they were currently deflated. Given that she seemed unhurt, except for a few scratches, I had a feeling she'd been helping already, probably since the mudslide had actually happened.

Bekka continued to berate the villagers around us. "Winna was *born* here! She's one of us! I went to school with her! Many of you, or your children, went to school with her too! Her family has only ever done what they could to help us! Can't you see she's hurting right now, too?!" My friend glared at them, feet planted wide, hands on her hips as she raked them over the coals, standing up for me in my moment of great shame. "She lost people she's known her whole life today as well! And despite knowing that she'd lost a good deal of her ability to help people, she still came instead of hiding in her cottage, like you accuse her of! Don't you remember how her parents died?! They were in this village, helping us then, too! And Winna was with them! She healed Mrs. Parsin, even after her parents had died in that aftershock while they were trying to save her! Yes, she had Diana's help then, but she was just a kid; she didn't have to be here at all! But she *was* here. And she's here again now! Even when she knows she can't do much more than us, she *still* came! We are in *no* way entitled to her help or her gift, but Winna and her family have always shared it with us selflessly! Every single one of you should be f*cking ashamed of yourselves!" she snapped.

Finally, looks of shame crossed their faces, and there were sheepish murmurs here and there.

I took another deep breath, gratefulness welling in my chest for Bekka. Up until now, I had considered her to be a casual friend, someone I wasn't particularly close to. I was wrong. Bekka was a good friend. A wonderful friend. I'd have to work hard to be half as good a friend to her as she had just been to me.

My voice wobbled again, but this time from deep-seated gratitude, which pulled more tears to my eyes. "It's okay, Bekka. They're just scared and worried, and hoped I could help. I'll be okay." Reaching out, I took her hand and squeezed it. "Thank you so, so much. And you're right, I'm going to do what I can." I looked out at the now more subdued group of villagers, and took a deep breath to calm myself. "Some of you have met, or have heard of Lear, the fey man who is currently my patient. He went to go search for fey folk who might be willing to help us, and then he'll come to help as well. They're strong, far stronger than us, and there may even be some with healing abilities as well, but I don't know, as I've always heard the ability is somewhat rare. That said, I'm sure at least a few will come, and those hands will be worth ten of our human ones, just by the nature of their strength. Some can even fly."

"Tark and some of his firebug folk are already on their way," Jedda interjected. "They can fly, and will be able to provide good lighting in the rest of the village, thanks to their flames."

"Oh, that's good, I never considered they could do that. But that's very good. That'll be extremely helpful." I blinked.

It was quiet for a few moments.

I broke the silence, in control of my emotions once more, clapping my hands briskly and announcing, "Well, we don't have any time to waste! Let's get going!"

At this, the group broke up, and we began to move quickly around the village, helping where we could.

I found the area where the survivors had been putting the most grievously injured folk, those who'd already been pulled free from the wreckage, anyway, and got to work.

Just as I was starting to get my first patient stable, I heard a buzzing noise, and looked back. A large group of lights soared through the sky in our direction.

"Tark!" Jedda, who was busy trying to lift a fallen piece of wall, called, sounding relieved. "Can we borrow some light over here? Wings would be helpful too!"

The firebugs had come, and in force. There were cries of surprise and alarm, and some in delight, as the flying fey began to dissipate throughout the town, each one cranking up the flames that leapt up from their backs in order to provide better lighting.

"Sorry it took so long, but we're here now!" Tark cried as he flew up, immediately throwing himself into helping Jedda.

Despite the devastating circumstances, seeing the villagers of Greenwood accepting help from the fey folk brought a little hope to my devastated heart. Maybe some kind of good would come of this terrible disaster after all.

Chapter 29

Lear's Return

Even from above, Lear could see that the town was well-lit, which kind of surprised him. Then he recalled that Jedda had said the firebugs had been alerted, and were going to help as well. Their light alone would be a tremendous help, though they'd be able to do more than just act as sentient lamps. They might be able to get into small places, and reassure anyone trapped that help was on the way. Not to mention that their usually cheerful demeanors would help boost morale. They'd also be able to help everyone stay warm, whether that was those being rescued, or the rescuers themselves.

The fey man wheeled above the village, searching for Winna.

As he looked, he saw the fey folk he'd sent ahead of him. They were all doing whatever they could to help.

Pima and Tip had come, of course, and they'd brought as many of their kin as they could gather in a short amount of time. There were only five or six other fauns in total, but that was more than none. One of their number even had a slight healing ability as well. It was actually even weaker than Winna's, from what he understood, but would still be helpful.

A few nymphs and dryads had come along as well. He'd stopped by the Tinna's farm very briefly to talk to Rina, and she'd said she'd try to gather the few of her kind that she knew. Clearly, she'd kept her word. Indeed, she was there herself, working alongside a very grim-looking Wulf, and a much older man who Lear judged to be Wulf's father, given their likeness. Of course, the mother was nowhere to be seen, but that was really no surprise.

The nymphs and dryads weren't particularly strong or clever, but they were doing what they could by using their plant powers to control the trees and vegetation to lift or shift areas of mud and debris, under the careful direction of Wulf and his father. As Lear watched, Rina caused a tree to sprout quickly beneath a piece of fallen wall. Wulf kept a hand on the wall so it wouldn't shift off the growing tree, and it rose just enough for a small girl to scramble out from where she'd been trapped.

Several brownies raced back and forth, their appropriately brown ears flapping as they hurried along, carrying supplies to the larger, stronger helpers. There were a few pixies fluttering around the healing area, doing their best to help. Given their small size and delicate nature, they could do little more than help bandage the injured, dispense medicine, or carry messages. But there was no job too small during a disaster. Some pixies were very courageously slipping into very small cracks and crevices, smaller than even the firebugs could fit into, in order to see if anyone was trapped anywhere beneath rubble or mud.

There was even an intelligent, mid-sized dragon, Windscale, who usually stayed deep within the forest. She was moving large boulders away from destroyed houses so smaller searchers could carefully creep inside to see if there was anyone who could still be helped. Dern's little friend, Silver, prowled around near to his larger relative, seemingly eating anything and everything he could that he thought might lend aid in some way.

Dern himself was doing what dwarves did best, moving earth. Though he was a smith and a craftsman, dwarves, as a people-group, were primarily miners, and Dern was, therefore, by long-held custom, good at digging. He was busy coordinating excavation efforts, and between giving orders, he was wielding a shovel to great effect.

If he told anyone back in the feylands about this, fey folk and humans working in tandem, and willingly, they'd never have believed it. Asher would be proud to see his people choosing to take an active role in their community. Lear himself was proud.

Finally, the fey man's sharp eyes caught a flash of gold, and he did a double-take, focusing in on Winna's familiar curls. He tucked his wings and plunged through the air, snapping them out to catch himself and land lightly, then immediately stowing them away with a brief burst of magic.

Someone gave a cry of dismay, but he ignored it, darting forward to Winna's side.

"I'm here," he murmured, reaching out to put a comforting hand on her back.

"Thank goodness." The woman he loved shot a small, tired smile at him over her shoulder.

"I'm going to go help."

"Okay." She nodded. Not only did she look exhausted, but she also seemed emotionally drained. Having to do what she was doing would surely do a number on a person's emotional and mental health. He'd have to check in with her about how she was holding up later, right now, he needed to get to helping.

Not giving two shits if anyone saw, he bent and gently kissed her forehead, then strode off to see what he could do to help.

Something told him that Jedda would have a good idea of what he could do to help, so he searched for Winna's surrogate uncle.

The sun began to peek up around the mountains that encircled the entire area for miles as Lear finally spotted his quarry, and called, "Jedda!"

"Ah, you're finally here!" Jedda tossed a large branch onto a pile of debris, and turned to smile tiredly at him. Despite the exhaustion that lined his face, he seemed genuinely pleased that the fey man had finally arrived. Understandably so; Lear knew he could do things no one else could, even amongst his own kin.

"I'm sorry it took so long; I flew pretty far afield. But I believe we'll have even more help beyond the fey folk that are already here, before too long."

"Oh!"

"Yes. After I'd stopped to send the fey folk who I knew would help this way, I flew to the next town over to ask for their help as well. Scared the hell out of them, I'm afraid, but after some pleading, and invoking Winna's name, I was able to convince them that we really did need help here. They were going to gather supplies and then make their way here, but it will likely be a good while before they actually arrive, I think. It wasn't a short distance if you can't fly."

"That'll be Meadowton. It's where Winna's brothers live, and it is a decent distance away." Jedda nodded. "They'll probably come with the other villagers."

"Good. Oh, I also found a group of dwarven merchants as I was flying back. They were on their way here anyway, and said they'd pick up their pace once I'd told them what happened. I think they had some kobolds with them as well, so more diggers." Kobolds and dwarves were often found together, since dwarves worked in mines, and kobolds lived underground, often in said mines.

"That's good news." Jedda wiped his face with an already filthy handkerchief. "We could use more diggers. And the dwarves will be able to help us get some temporary housing put up. Enough houses were destroyed that we'll struggle to get everyone into the homes that are left."

"Yes." Lear nodded. "There's some space at the cottage. There are two empty bedrooms, but lots of space otherwise, between the loft and the living area. We could probably take a few on for a bit. I doubt Winna would mind me offering it."

"She wouldn't. We'll be putting some of the dislocated folks up as well." Jedda nodded.

There was a slight pause.

"Well, what can I do? I'm strong and I'm fast and I can fly. I can see heat with my second set of eyes, and hear very well. I can also do a good variety of magic, but I'm currently limited in how much of that magic I can use at once, since I'm still healing."

"Don't worry, lad, we'll put you to work." Jedda slapped his shoulder. "I think you'd best be a one-man retrieval squad."

"How so?"

"We've not been able to get to that area at all, yet," Jedda pointed at the largest part of the mudslide, "Because, of course, we're having to start at the outside and work in. The firebugs and pixies flew over it, of course, but they couldn't see anything, and I don't want them just going into the dirt blind."

"Got it." Lear pulled his wings out, then leapt into the air, opening his second set of eyes. "I'll see if there are any survivors, and do what I can to get them out on my own. Please have Dern send Silver my way; he'll probably be incredibly useful in getting people out, now that I can direct him."

"Will do." Jedda nodded, then hurried away as Lear turned midair, and flew towards the worst of the mudslide.

-

"Winna? Are you alright?" Bekka's voice cut through my doze.

"Oh!" I gasped, straightening. "I-I fell asleep! Goodness!" I blinked, rubbing my eyes. "I'm so sorry!"

"No, it's fine, honey." She smiled reassuringly at me. My old schoolmate looked as tired as I felt.

"You look exhausted too." I yawned.

"I am."

I started to stand, but she put a staying hand on my shoulder. "Go ahead and rest. I just wanted to make sure you were okay. You look awfully pale."

"I'll be alright. But I should get back to it. I just meant to take a quick breather, but I guess I dozed off." I grimaced. I'd been using a lamppost in the square as a chair. It hadn't been particularly comfortable, but it hadn't mattered, and I'd still dozed off. The low, rhythmic chanting of the dwarves as they worked must have lulled me right off the sleep.

It had only been a few hours, really, but I was exhausted from using my magic nearly constantly since I'd started.

Suddenly, Lear bolted down from the sky, landing beside us.

Bekka jumped in surprise, sending her soft curls bouncing wildly about her head. "Oh goodness!"

"Sorry." Lear grimaced.

"No, no, it's fine! I guess I'm awake now!" She laughed.

"I just wanted to bring you some good news. Villagers from Meadowton just rode in." He motioned at the far side of the square.

Several carts were driving up, loaded with supplies and people armed with shovels.

"Oh!" I staggered to my feet, and Lear reached out to steady me. "My brothers will probably be with them."

"Jedda said they'd probably come." The fey man nodded.

Right on cue, two voices I knew very well called, "Winna!" in unison.

I looked in their direction, and waved tiredly, calling, "Hey, hey!"

There was a flurry of blonde hair, and Pava threw himself on me in a hug, practically knocking me over.

"Careful!" Lear protested from beside me.

"Winnaaaaa!" Pava sang as he pulled away, then frowned. "You look awful, child!"

My eldest brother didn't really look his forty years, and seemed to be only a little older than me, and I probably only looked just twenty or so. His luxuriously wavy, golden hair gleamed in the morning sun, and I'd have felt jealous, since his hair was always so effortlessly nice, but now was not the time for that. Normally, his blue eyes sparkled with laughter at all times, but they were far more serious than usual, despite his lighthearted greeting.

"Hey Pava. I feel awful," I admitted, rubbing my eyes.

"I'm so sorry, honey." My brother swept a sad gaze over my

shoulder at the half-destroyed down, murmuring, "This can't have been easy for you."

"It...wasn't."

He squeezed me again gently. "I love you, sweetie. I'm so glad you weren't hurt. In the mudslide or while cleaning up."

I knew his mind dwelt on how our parents had died. "Me too. But the goddess protected me."

Pava shot me a slightly curious look, but smiled. "Indeed she did. It's good to see you. Other than the obvious," he motioned at the devastation around us, "you look well. You're eating enough? Diana taking care of you?"

I chuckled. "That's a silly question, you know she is."

Pava smiled. "Of course! That cat is an angel."

"She really is."

"Winna, you need to rest," Lear cut in, tone concerned, drawing Pava's attention.

My brother's crystal blue eyes widened almost imperceptibly as he took in my fey...companion? Boyfriend? Significant other? I still hadn't decided quite what I wanted to call him. I'd go with a significant other, I guess.

"I actually just woke up from an unintended nap." I grimaced, shaking my head. "I was taking a break and just nodded off. I need to get back to helping."

"You can't help anyone if you're too exhausted. You'll only hurt yourself if you push too far." Lear shook his head, tone stern. "Take a little while and rest more. And make sure you eat, someone took it upon themselves to make food."

"If you don't mind waiting, Vim was going to set up and start cooking as well." Pava motioned at my other brother.

Where Pava was flamboyant and talkative, Vim was quiet and reserved.

"I might do that, then. I haven't eaten your food in a long time, Vim." I smiled at my other brother.

Vim nodded, coming forward for a hug now as well. "It's been a while." He had auburn hair and brown eyes, and was a little shorter and stockier than Pava, who was of a tall, slim sort of build, a little more like me. Vim favored our father, while Pava and I looked more like Mom.

"So, who's this tall fey drink of water?" Pava asked, grinning mischievously at me, despite the grim circumstances.

I was too tired to protest him teasing me. "This is Lear. Yes, we're dating. He's technically a patient too."

Pava blinked, surprised at my bluntness. "You really are tired. No protesting, no squeaking in annoyance! Your boyfriend is right, sit down, and I'll get you some food."

"See?" Lear smiled gently, then sat down. "Sit with me."

"But I can-"

"No buts! Sit." Pava shook his head sternly, crossing his arms as his big brother persona came to the surface. Although, he was a father now, too, so it was probably just as much that.

"Fine." I sighed, resuming my seat.

"I'll go find you some food, and Lear, I'm sure he's hungry too."

"Thank you." Lear gratefully lowered his head in a slight bow.

"Be right back!" Pava bustled off.

"He's very efficient." Vim snorted, smiling a little. "I should go unpack my things and get started."

"Alright, don't let us keep you." I nodded, leaning into Lear, which prompted him to put an arm around me, and pull me close.

"Are you hanging in there?"

"I'm just...tired." I sighed.

"I know this is all very distressing." He motioned at our grim surroundings. The injured and dead were laid out in the square, the living on one side, the recently departed on the other, waiting until arrangements could be made for their proper care when things were less urgent.

I sighed. "I'm managing."

"But will you be okay?"

I took a deep breath, then smiled weakly. "Yes. This is my job.

This is what I do. I have to handle it, no matter how I feel inside." I'd managed to keep the worst of my grief, guilt, and sadness at bay so far by saying that mantra over and over.

There was a pause.

"I know...that you're probably having to deal with people you know, and I...know some of them have already passed." He motioned vaguely at where the dead townsfolk were. "Are you managing in spite of that?"

At his question, the emotions threatened to break through, and I closed my eyes, taking a deep breath before answering. "I've...I've done what I can, even though it's not enough. People died before I could get to them. After I got to them, too. It's hard, Lear. I-I...I can't do enough. I can never do enough!"

"It's not your fault, Winna."

My voice broke, and tears leaked down my face. "B-but-"

"No, not your fault," he cut me off, shaking his head. The fey man reached up and carefully wiped the tears off my face with his handkerchief. "None of this is your fault. This is a terrible, horrible situation that nothing could have stopped. Even if I were up to my full power, and knew this was about to happen, I couldn't have stopped it. Natural disasters are stronger than anyone's magic. You are not to blame. You're doing your best in a bad situation, and your best is enough. But please don't be afraid to cry. Don't hold it in, it's not healthy, alright?"

I forced myself to take a deep breath. He was right, of course. "A-alright."

Lear squeezed me gently, planting a kiss on my temple.

There was a slight pause.

Finally, he spoke again. "Jedda told me what happened when you first got here. I was worried they'd let their anger and fear get to them, but it sounds like Bekka set them straight."

"Yes, bless her!" I sighed.

Lear took one of my hands, weaving his fingers through mine. "Has anyone else been rude to you since then?"

"No, they've been grateful that I've done what I could since then. You're right, they were just scared, and thought I'd be able to make everything better, and then when I couldn't, it only made them even more scared, so they lashed out, even if only briefly, until Bekka said her piece."

"It's not fair of them."

"No, but I do understand." I shook my head.

"Well, as long as you're not upset." He switched topics. "So, tell me about your brothers."

"Pava and his husband make clothes. Very, very nice clothes, actually. Vim runs a tavern. You'll hear Pava fuss over my clothes while he's here. Vim will do all the cooking, because even though his business is a tavern, he's really more of a cook than anything. He's good at it."

"I see. They seem nice."

"They are. Good big brothers, too, even though I don't get to see them very often."

"Do they have kids?"

"Yes. Pava and Jiven have four, and Vim and Mina have two."

Just then, Pava bustled up, carrying a platter with two steaming bowls of soup, a rustic loaf of bread, and some cheese. "It's not much, but it's warm! Smells good, too!"

"Thanks, Pav." I smiled as Pava set the tray down in front of us.

"Thank you," Lear murmured, gratefully lowering his head again.

"Now, we can catch up more later, but I should go help. Take a little while to rest. Vim and I might not have the gift, but we're still fully-trained healers otherwise, and I think they've busted out your salves from the shop."

"I told them to." I nodded, "It'll at least help a little."

"Good." Pava smiled, then took up what I'd been doing, bandaging and helping, which made me feel a little less bad for taking a break.

"They're trained as healers too?"

"Yes. It is the family trade, even if they don't have the magic to go with it." I nodded. "Pava thought about going away to train as a proper doctor, but decided he wanted to make clothes instead. He's good at it." I shrugged.

It was quiet for a little while as we ate.

"What do they have you doing?"

"Retrieval in the biggest part of the mudslide," Lear said quietly. "It's...quite sad, really. Most of the people I've pulled out are already gone. Or have soon died."

"I'm sorry, Lear," I murmured, reaching out to squeeze his hand gently.

"It's alright. I'm a soldier. I've seen plenty of death before now." He sighed.

"That doesn't make it any easier." I shook my head. "I'm glad you're taking a break."

"Silver needed it. I've been having him eat dirt as a way to help me clear it away whenever I find someone. I think he was starting to get a little sick. His preference is metal or ore, of course, but dirt will do in a pinch, though it's not quite as tasty for him."

I smiled. "Poor pumpkin. But I'm glad he's helping."

"He was happy to be able to have a set job." Lear nodded. "Even if it was kind of a grim one. But someone has to do it, and I don't really know the people I'm digging out, which makes it a little easier."

"Thank you, Lear," I said softly. "You took on a sad, thankless job."

"Not thankless. Every time I've gotten someone out, a family member or friend has thanked me for retrieving the body." Lear shook his head. "They've shown me more gratitude than they've shown you."

"Well, that's alright. I think it's more important that they show gratitude to the fey helpers than me. You and your kin have no compunction to be here, and only came out of the kindness of your hearts."

"No, you deserve their thanks too." He frowned.

"That's not why I do it." I shook my head. "Not that it's why all you fey folk are, but...well, of course I'm going to help, that's my job. You lot don't have to be here at all, but you are, just the same. I doubt anything quite like this has happened before, fey folk and humans working side-by-side."

"I'll agree that it is...unusual." He smiled a little. "It's good, though. Proof that our races can get along, and quite well, when needed. No one back in the feylands would believe this if I told them. Not without seeing it with their own eyes."

"I just hope we don't do anything to ruin it. Humans are good at that," I muttered.

"We're not bad at it either." Lear snorted, amused.

"Lear?"

"Hm?"

"I love you," I whispered.

"I love you too." He grinned at me, then pulled his wings up around us, blocking out the world, and kissed me. It was a long kiss, and deeper than usual as well, but he finally broke away, muttering, "Fangs. Venomous fangs."

I smiled, telling him. "It's okay, I think. You're always careful. I-I don't mind a bit more intensity...just...keep your head."

"I'm afraid I'll lose my head and forget. That's why I don't," he told me, grimacing a little.

"Well, that was fine, just now. So if you want to kiss like that, it's alright."

The dark-haired fey man smiled a little, reaching out to stroke my face with his finger, then let it fall, and lowered his wings. "I'm glad you like kissing me," he murmured.

"I think it would be impossible not to," I mumbled, my face heating.

Lear laughed, then sighed. "I should get back to it."

"Me too. That food really helped."

"Uh huh, sure, just the food helped." His emerald eyes sparkled mischievously at me. "Nothing else?" He leaned down once more and ran his lips along my neck.

"Lear!" I protested, unable to keep from shivering as my face flushed bright red.

The ridiculous fey man gave a low chuckle, brushed his lips gently against my forehead, then launched himself into the air, and headed back to work.

"What a mess." I shook my head, watching Lear soar through the air.

Chapter 30

Making Plans

"A re you Kirk?" Lear asked a brownie hurrying down the path near where he was sitting, resting for a few moments.

The little creature paused and turned, blinking its large brown eyes at him. "Yes, I am. Can I help you?" The brownie was carrying a shovel and had some rope looped over his shoulder.

"I think so. I'm trying to find the location of a specific temple, and have been talking to all the other fey here whenever Silver and I have needed breaks." He motioned at the little dragon who was curled up, dozing beside him. "I was told you might be able to at least point me in the right direction?"

"I see." Kirk nodded seriously. "Yes, I'm familiar with a lot of temples in the area. I like going to see them all. They're all very lovely buildings."

"Windscale said you enjoyed their architecture." Lear nodded.

"What temple are you looking for, specifically?"

"One to Marna. Do you know if there's one in the area? Or even remotely nearby."

"Hmm..." Kirk thought for a moment, more wrinkles forming on his already wrinkled face. "I've heard of Marna, though she's a slightly odd one to be after. A pretty old deity, if I'm not mistaken, and not very popular in these parts. I do think there's a temple somewhere west of here, but I've never been, so I can't say where it is." If the brownie thought it was odd that Lear was trying to find the location of a temple despite the destruction around them, he kept it to himself.

"Honestly, just knowing that there's one somewhere in the area is helpful, thank you." Lear bowed his head gratefully.

"One of the pixies, Willowdown, originally came from west of here, over the mountains. There's a pixie grove in the forest out that way. She might be able to help you. Want me to send her your way?"

"Yes, I'd really appreciate that." Lear nodded, then motioned up at the main part of the mudslide. "I've been working up there, so if I'm not down here, tell her to call for me, and I'll come down."

"Alright!" Kirk nodded, then hurried off.

Silver needed some more rest, so Lear sat there a good while longer.

He turned his mind to Winna. Was she holding up alright?

Hopefully, she wouldn't tire herself out too much, either. Magical exhaustion was dangerous. But given that she'd been resting when he'd last seen her, he suspected she was doing her best to make sure that didn't happen, because if it did, she wouldn't be able to help anyone. No one had said a word to them as they'd rested and eaten, probably because they all had needed to take breaks as they'd worked too. Or he hoped they had, anyway. As urgent as the situation was, being too exhausted to lift a finger wasn't going to help anyone. That held true for non-magic users as well.

On top of being worried that she would exhaust herself, he was worried about the toll seeing such terrible sights would have on the woman he loved. From injured friends, dead former schoolmates, to places from fond memories that were totally destroyed, it had to be distressing.

As a soldier, he was a little more used to seeing the dead, but knew it had to be hard on Winna. Although, that said, Lear knew she said she'd helped her parents and Diana when that earthquake had hit so many years before, the one that had led to her parents' death. This mudslide probably brought back a lot of painful memories for her.

He hoped she wouldn't blame herself too much for anyone who passed; there was only one of her, and only so much she could do. Of course, he fully expected her to treat each death like a personal failure on her fault, so great was her sense of duty to her community. They really didn't deserve her.

With thoughts of concern for Winna still flickering through his head, he sighed, then shifted, kneeling next to his little dragon helper. "Hey, little one, it's time to get back at it."

The little dragon opened its eyes, then yawned and stretched the same way Diana and Stroopwafel did, then stood.

"Thank you. You've been a great help and comfort to me." He smiled, patting Silver's little head, then scratching beneath his chin.

The dragon gave a happy sort of yip, and wagged his tail.

"I wonder if Winna would let me have a dragon like you in the house." He grinned. "I bet she would."

Another cute yip.

"Are you holding up okay? I know it's not exactly happy work."

Silver gave a soft whimper, but nodded.

"I know, I know. It's sad for me too." Lear sighed. "But I am extremely grateful to you."

His small friend gave a sort of rumbling purr, and then started to hop back up to the top of the mound of dirt.

Lear crouched, meaning to launch himself back up into the air so he could land on top of the enormous mound of dirt, but heard a pretty, tinkling voice call, "Wait! Wait!"

He straightened, turning. Silver paused as well, looking back curiously.

One of the pixies flitted up, and stopped, hovering midair, panting from flying so quickly. "Just a minute!"

"You must be Willowdown." Lear smiled a little tiredly.

"Yes! Kirk told me that you were looking for a temple to Marna!" She said brightly. The little pixie woman had short, bright purple hair, and silver skin, with large pink eyes. Her wings were the traditional butterfly-like wings of her kind in a creamy, butter shade of yellow.

"I am." The fey man nodded. "Can you help me?"

"Yes, I can!" Willowdown beamed. "I heard Winna telling someone that you two were trying to find a temple so she could maybe get her familiar's power restored so she could help more people, but I didn't realize I'd be able to help! There's a very old temple to Marna in the forest, east of the mountains. It's about three days' worth of travel, I think, if a human decides to walk it, but you're big and strong, and could probably make it a lot more quickly. Especially if you can fly some of the distance." Her eyes flickered to Lear's wings, which were impressively large and strong. "Could you fly with another person and a cat?"

"Yes. Not the entire way, but enough to make the trip faster. Can you give me directions? Even vague ones will help."

"I can do better than that." Willowdown smiled. "I've flown over it before, and I can show you where it is on a map."

"Excellent! Thank you!" Lear bowed low to her.

"Oh, stop it, you!" She giggled, then smiled sadly. "We'll benefit too if Winna's familiar gets her power back because then we can go to her in times of need as well, now that we know she'd welcome us."

"Her name is Diana."

"That's a pretty name." The pixie nodded her head. "We would never go to Winna before you came, but now that we know she'll accept fey folk as patients, we will, and she'll be able to help us most effectively if Diana has her power back."

"I know. It'll help everyone who lives in the area. That's why she wants to do it. And it'll save lives in the immediate future." He motioned at the destruction that surrounded them.

"Yes, of course," the pixie murmured sadly, surveying the scene around them.

There was a pause.

Willowdown clapped her hands, getting back to business. "So, as to where the temple is." She flicked her wrist, and a magical map in tones of glittering blue appeared before her, hovering in the air as she did. "You'll want to cross over that mountain," she pointed at the map, then over at the mountain in particular, on the pass to the left, "Then you'll have to travel south-west in the forest until about here." She touched a spot on the map with her tiny, delicate finger. The spot where she touched glowed golden for a moment, then enlarged so it was much easier to see. "There aren't any distinguishing landmarks once you're past the mountains, I'm afraid. It's all forest, but the temple itself is in a clearing, and since it's hallowed ground, you'll be able to feel it as you get closer."

Lear studied the map closely, committing it to memory. "Thank you very much, Willowdown. That was more than I'd hoped to learn today."

"I'm so glad I could help!" She beamed at him, letting the map disappear. "Now, I should get back to helping."

"Me too." Lear sighed.

"Good luck on your journey, when you do go on it!" The little pixie waved, then darted off at high speed.

"Well, Silver, let's get back to work." The fey man turned to face the enormous remnant of the mudslide.

-

What a day.

Vim's cart rattled along the path, back towards my cottage.

Lear and I were stretched out in the back of the cart, and Pava was sitting on the bench by Vim.

"Gods, I'm tired." I groaned.

"Me too," Lear muttered, rolling over and pulling me closer.

"Why don't you two sleep until we get to the cottage"

"Cause if I do, I probably won't wake up until tomorrow morning." I yawned, but was indeed already half asleep. "And I have to help the folks in the cart behind us find places to sleep, and make dinner and make sure the animals are fed.,

"We'll do that, Winna," Vim told me firmly. "We're not as tired as you two. I was only cooking all day."

"Vim, that's tiring work too." I shook my head.

"Not as tiring as what you and Lear were doing." Vim's tone was stern.

"I was helping with the hurt folks too, but I can't use magic, so I literally can't tire myself out the same way you can. And we were at it some five or so hours less than you."

"Those poor firebugs must be tired," I murmured sleepily. One was flying ahead of us, lighting the way.

"Tiv, go home," Lear called to the little fey bug. "We know the way, and the other cart won't lose us, even though it's dark."

"Are you sure? I don't mind!" the firebug buzzed earnestly.

"Yes, go home." Vim nodded. "I grew up driving this road."

"Alright. Safe travels!" The bug floated off.

As the light from the bug faded, I let my eyes drift fully shut, and sleep finally overwhelmed me.

I woke as the cart pulled to a stop outside the cottage, and felt oddly refreshed.

Stretching, I shook Lear awake. "Come on, handsome. I'd carry you in if I could, but there's no way I'd ever manage it. I don't think my brothers could either; all that muscle is heavy."

The fey man's gorgeous green eyes flickered open. He studied me for a moment, then asked, "Are you flirting with me?"

I giggled. "Only a little."

"That's a dangerous thing to do, just so you know." He sat, tilting his head side to side and popping his neck.

"Oh?" I hopped out of the cart.

He followed suit, but slipped his arms around my waist, and surrounded us with his wings for a moment as he whispered, "I can't be held responsible for what I do if you get me too worked up." He trailed his lips down my neck.

A shiver ran through me, but I leaned into him, snorting. "Lear, you won't even kiss me too hard because you're afraid of poisoning me. I don't buy it." Maybe it was silly to be flirting at such a serious time, but if I didn't at least try to keep some levity in my life, I wouldn't be able to keep going.

"Well, that's no fun!" he protested, and let his wings fall, but I saw he was smiling. "Although you're not wrong."

I popped up on my tiptoes and kissed him briefly as the other cart pulled up. "We should get inside and start getting things ready. Pava, can you take the horses to the barn, and take care of the animals? Vim will need to go ahead and start on some food. It's long past dinnertime, but we all still need to eat, I think."

"Of course!" Pava nodded, going and starting to unhitch the horses.

"I'll get into the kitchen," Vim said, going inside. I heard him greeting the cats as Lear and I lowered the tailgate of the other cart, and started to help people get out.

Lear hopped up into the conveyance and started to carefully lift one of its occupants out. I'd brought several of the worst of the injured with me. Only ones that were stable enough to be moved, anyway. There had been more injured folks who had been hurt worse than the ones I'd brought, but they just weren't safe to be moved, and I could only pray that they'd last through the night, in the temporary housing that the dwarves had so kindly built. Dern had even given over his entire stock of magical ovens and heating stones to help heat the structures so that no one who had to stay in one would have to try to keep a fire going.

I helped a little girl jump down, and then her mother. Her father was one of the injured in the cart that Lear would need to help get out.

After getting everyone indoors, we made sure they all had enough space, and anything else they might need, before settling down for a brief rest while we waited for Vim to finish making a late dinner.

"I'll have to go back into town tomorrow to help again. As much as I can, anyway. I can't do as much as I wish I could." We were sitting at the table, sipping cups of hot, herbal tea.

"I was able to talk to some of the fey folk whenever I was taking breaks, and one of the pixies knew of a temple of Marna that's not too far away from here," he told me. "I'm not saying you shouldn't go back and check on your patients in the morning, but I think we should go ahead and make for the temple immediately after that."

"Oh?" I blinked, surprised.

"Yes. It's about three days' worth of travel to get there, on foot, but if I can fly us for some of it, we'd get there more quickly."

"Could you fly the whole way?"

"On my own, yes, but flying someone else takes a lot more energy." He shook his head. "As much as I wish I could."

"That's okay. Even just some flying would help." I shrugged, then frowned. "And we'll need to take Diana with us. But what will everyone think of me if I leave?"

Pava, also sitting at the table, spoke up, "I'll be around; I know I can't use magic, but I'm a competent healer otherwise. Vim is, too, but he's an even better cook. If anyone raises a stink, we'll tell them where they can shove it."

"Besides, you'd be leaving to do something that will only help them in the long run," Lear reminded me.

"Why are you needing to leave?" A woman sitting nearby, called Ona, asked. She was a cousin of Ama's, and sometimes helped in the clothing store. I'd gone to school with one of her sons.

"We thought we might try to ask the goddess who gave Winna's family their powers to restore Diana's magic fully, so she and Winna could heal you all properly. There's a temple not super far that we could get to easily enough," Lear told her.

"Oh. That'd be okay. I don't think anyone would be upset if that's why you left." Ona shrugged.

"The problem would be if she doesn't grant the request," I muttered.

"You have to try, don't you?" Ona's husband, Biv, said, shrugging a little. He had a badly broken leg, but had been stable enough to move.

"I think it's a risk worth taking. My Biv will heal, regardless of if you get Diana's power restored or not." Ona patted Diana, who was sitting by her on the floor, fondly. "But there are some folks who won't. The ones that had to stay in town."

"They might die while I'm gone though, and if I'm here, I could stop that!" I sighed, shaking my head.

"For how long, Winna?" Pava murmured. "Sweetie, you're doing your best, I know, but..." his voice trailed off.

Tears stung my eyes. "I-I know. I-it's not enough. I-I just...I-I can give them a little more time, and-"

"It'd be better to go, and at least try." Pava shook his head, reaching out and patting my hand. "I'll do what I can to keep them stable. And the faun with a little bit of healing magic can at least ease their pain."

I took a deep breath. "Well...alright. But I don't want to upset anyone by leaving."

"They won't. They'll understand," Biv said, "They can blame us if they get angry, but how could they blame you? You're doing the most you can for us."

"I-I'm certainly trying to."

"Then we'll go tomorrow. We'll get up, go into the village, tend to the folks that need it the most, then we'll go," Lear told me. "We'll travel as quickly as we can. I'll fly us as far as I can manage, and then we'll walk. Once I'm revived, we'll fly again."

"It'll really be okay?" I murmured.

"Yes." The dark-haired fey man nodded, tone firm.

"Diana, are you up for a little flying? You can stay in your basket," I asked my oldest and dearest little friend.

She gave a chirpy, encouraging maow that Lear didn't have to translate.

"Alright then." I smiled.

"I think we could get there in a day and a half pretty easily. Of course, then we'll have to get back, so it'll take us around three days. Maybe faster, depending on how quickly we can walk, and how much I can manage to fly."

"Will you all manage without us for three days?" I asked, looking at Pava, and then Ona and Biv. "That's quite a while."

"I think we'll be able to do it in less," Lear reminded me.

"We'll manage," Pava assured me. "We'll stay here and take care of the cottage and the barn animals and Stroopwafel while you're gone, too."

I took a deep breath. "It's kind of a long time, especially for the people who are really badly hurt. They might pass while I'm gone, and...that...will stay on my consciousness forever."

"I hate to say it, dear, but those people are going to die anyway, unless you can get Diana's magic restored," Ona said grimly.

"Winna, it's going to be okay." Lear assured me. "I don't want them to die either, but right now, this is the one thing that we can do that, if it works, will save all or most of them."

"You're right, you're right." I sighed.

There was a pause.

Lear reached out to squeeze my hand gently. "Once we eat, we'll pack and then go straight to our beds."

Chapter 31

Protection

"Y ou know, this will be the farthest I've ever been from home,"
Winna told him as they set out from town.

She'd been loath to leave her other cat, Stroopwafel, behind, but
knew it was necessary. Many tears had been shed at their parting, but
Lear reminded her that she'd have one of her cats with her, and that
was better than none, which had cheered her up a little.

After going into Greenwood and tending to the wounded there as
best they could, Winna had explained her plans. The villagers had
understood, and even urged her to go, as he suspected they might,
given that if Diana could get her powers restored, it would save lives
and improve outcomes.

Jedda had lent them a horse to use for the first leg of the journey,
which would be over when they reached the tall mountains that
encircled the area, encompassing it all in a basin of sorts.

Once they reached the mountains, their steed would struggle to
make it up the mountain paths, and Tark, who was traveling with
them for the first part as well, would get the horse back to town. This
way, Lear could save his strength for later, but they'd be able to make
better time than they would if they'd been on foot.

"Yeah?"

"I've not traveled much. My world is pretty small, I guess. That's probably pretty sad, huh?"

"Not really. It's very common."

"You've traveled a lot though, haven't you? I'm sure that mer-village wasn't the only interesting place you've been."

"Yes, but I'm in the military, right? There are fey folk who have never left the feylands, and never will," he told her.

"Oh."

"Yep. So don't feel bad, okay."

"That does make me feel better," Winna murmured.

"My children haven't been out of this area either," Tark chimed in. "Though my wife and I did move to the area before they were born, we haven't left it since. There's been no need to. It's a lovely, peaceful place. Although the winters are very cold!"

"They are that! This one has been mighty cold, too! Although normally we have more snow."

"True, true." Tark nodded. He was buzzing along easily beside them, carrying Diana in her basket. She was sitting upright, with her sweet face poking just out of the basket so she could see.

"Are you sure you're not tired?" Winna asked.

"I'm fine, Winna!" the firebug assured her. "My people have high endurance when it comes to flying."

"Probably more than me, even. Firebugs are made to fly, whereas I'm a strange amalgam of fey blood that just happens to have wings." Lear laughed.

"Well, it worked out to a very nice amalgam." The young woman giggled.

"I'm glad you like it." He snorted, "You've been a little flirtatious lately."

"I'm settling into the idea of dating you, and have gotten a little more comfortable," she murmured.

"We've really only been on one date. Once things have calmed, we'll go on more."

"I mean, we do live together."

"That doesn't mean we shouldn't still set time aside for proper dates," Lear told her firmly.

"Alright then." He could hear her smile.

Time wore on, and the mountains grew nearer.

Soon, they were riding past large, rocky outcroppings that sprang up from nowhere as the path sloped gently upwards.

Finally, they stopped and dismounted, as the terrain had grown steep, the path climbing the mountain in earnest.

They rested for a little while as they ate an early lunch, letting Diana out of her basket to stretch out in the sun, which was surprisingly warm.

"Well, I should probably head back," Tark said, standing, then taking the horse's reins and flying up onto its back.

"You'll be able to control it alright?" Winna asked, standing, full of concern. The firebug did look awfully small up in the saddle.

"Yes! I've ridden horses before!"

"Alright then." Winna nodded. "Have a safe trip back! Tell everyone we made it off okay!"

"I will!"

"It's about time we head out, too," Lear told her.

"Of course."

They began to gather their things, and Diana maowed a sleepy farewell as Tark rode off, back the way they'd come.

Soon, everything was stowed away into their packs, and Diana was curled up in her basket, now fast asleep, thanks to all that warm sunshine. Lear had the idea to tie the basket to Winna's waist, so she didn't have to hold it the entire time.

They faced the mountain. It rose before them, tall and cold and proud.

"So, you're gonna fly us over this?"

"Yep." He stepped forward and scooped her up. She was light as a feather, even with Diana's basket tied to her. "I expect I'll need a rest at some point. We're not going over the entire mountain, I'll take us up and around, but going up is a lot more work than going across, because I can glide when I'm moving across, but going up involves a lot more wing-work."

"Makes sense." She nodded.

"Ready?"

"Yep."

"Diana, are you ready? You know not to look out or anything until we say so, right?"

A sleepy, slightly annoyed maow was the response.

"Alright, alright. Keep your hat on!" He snorted, "I just don't want you to get hurt."

A low purring from the basket.

"Silly goose," Winna murmured.

"Alright, let's go." Lear held the woman he loved close, and launched them into the air with a powerful leap.

Winna screamed until he unfurled his wings and began to pump, shooting them higher into the sky.

"It's alright!" He laughed. "I won't let you fall!"

"I'm still just not used to that takeoff!" she cried.

-

"Phew." Lear sighed as he landed lightly, putting me down. "That's tiring."

"Thank you, though."

"You're welcome." He nodded. "Although I'm not sure if you should thank me, I know you spent a while trying to calm down after takeoff, but that's the easiest way to do it."

"It's okay. It's just a little disconcerting, but I know you won't drop me."

"You're right, I won't." He smiled at me.

"Alright, Diana, you can come out, now," I told her, kneeling for a moment to untie the basket from around my waist.

My fluffy little familiar leapt easily from the basket, and then stretched luxuriously.

"Oh, to be a cat who just had a nice nap." I smiled, reaching out to scratch her chin just the way she liked it. "Were you warm enough, dear?"

A confirmatory maow.

"I don't think I need to translate that." Lear laughed quietly.

"Nope!" I smiled, now stroking her silken fur, murmuring, "Oh my pretty little queen." I bent and peppered her face with kisses, then stood, asking her, "Are you good to walk for a while? Or do you want to ride in the basket again?"

Another maow.

"She said she'll walk, and will let you know when she wants to ride again," Lear translated.

"Alright." I nodded.

"Let's see." Lear looked around, getting his bearings. "That's the way we should go." He pointed, and we started walking. Or rather, picking our way along through the rocky, still snowy, terrain.

"It's so high up that it's much colder! There's even still snow around." I shivered a little, drawing the cloak closed around me.

Diana maowed.

"She said she's fairly comfortable, temperature-wise, but then again, she has a fur coat," Lear translated again.

"Of course!" I giggled.

It was somewhat rough going, and every so often, Lear had to hold Diana and me, and jump down from a high point that we couldn't see any other way down from.

"Ugh, I hate that! Falling is so scary," I muttered, shaking my head as he put me and Diana back down.

"We're not really falling. I'm jumping down." Lear snorted, then turned to look back up at where we'd come down from. It was a particularly high cliff-face, and possibly the tallest one we'd come down.

"Still, very scary." I shook my head, trying to rid myself of the anxiety that had filled me. It had been particularly bad during that last leap down.

"Hey, what do you think that is?" Lear asked suddenly, frowning and pointing at the cliff.

"Huh?" I turned to look. "I don't see anything."

"I...I think it's a carving, or something. Look!" He leapt up onto a slight outcropping of rock, pointing at the stony wall. There was indeed a deep line in the rock.

"It's just a fissure or something." I frowned, then saw he was tracing along the line with his hand, and noticed that there was another line it met with. "Hold on." I turned and picked my way about ten feet back. "Actually...I think you're right." I blinked, now staring and stunned.

Lear hopped down from the cliff, bent and scooped up Diana, then darted over to where I stood so he could get a better look. He put Diana back down, and she licked her paw primly, then languidly groomed her face as we stared in confusion at the strange carving on the cliff face.

"What does it look like?" I asked, unable to make any sense out of what I was seeing. There was certainly some purpose to the carving; I just couldn't figure it out.

"A letter of some kind. Or - I know!- it's a rune! Not one I recognize, but more like the ones on the old books at the cottage!" My fey companion's voice and expression were full of excitement from our discovery.

A strange sense of unease filled me. "How'd it get here?" I asked him.

"It is like one of the book-runes..." Lear muttered thoughtfully. "A lot like them, actually. That makes me think it's probably some kind of protective rune."

"If you say so." I frowned at it.

"Stay here for a bit, I have a theory, and if I go alone, it won't take me long to see if I'm right," he told me.

"Alright. We'll stay here, Miss Annie." I shrugged, sitting on the ground, and opening my cloak for Diana to join me. She did, and soon we were toasty warm together as Lear darted away at inhuman speeds.

True to his word, he wasn't gone for more than ten minutes. "I was right!" He flashed a bright grin at me. "There's another on down that way on another rock facing, and yet another I could see on a large boulder just on the next mountain over."

"What does that mean?"

"Remember how Sagebark mentioned that your family had brought some kind of protection here with them?"

"Yes. Are the runes that protection?"

"I think so." He nodded. "They've got to be carved into all of the mountains surrounding the area, creating a sort of shield of protection that covers the place they settled in. Honestly, it's perfect for it, I'm sure that's why they decided to settle here. There was plenty of room for them to move about, but it wasn't so big that it couldn't be protected with runes." Lear gestured at the rune before us.

"Oh wow." I blinked, then frowned. "Which means we're outside of that protection now, aren't we?"

"Yes, we are. But we'll be okay. I'm here, and there's no reason to be afraid. These parts are generally pretty safe as well." He motioned in our general vicinity.

"If you say so." But some sense of urgency and worry gnawed at me. "Let's get going, all the same," I told him, standing. "Annie, why don't you ride again?"

My sweet kitty hopped back into the basket without protest, and we continued to make our way down the mountain.

As we descended, the sense of unease that had risen in me grew ever stronger.

Finally, I couldn't bear it anymore. "Lear."

"Yes, love?" He smiled over at me.

"I...I...don't feel well."

"Like, sick?" He frowned, immediately reaching out to take my hand.

"No, like...something's wrong. Ever since we saw that rune, i-it's felt like...something's just...wrong."

"Hmm." He stroked my hand gently with his thumb. "It could be that you're reacting poorly to the lack of the protection that the runes surrounding your homeland protect. You were born within its borders, and have never left it. It's understandable that your body might react with fear to being away from it."

I chewed on my lip for a bit. "You think?"

"Yes, I do." He nodded.

"Alright." I sighed. "I just...I'm frightened. I-I don't even know what the protection actually feels like, a-and I'm frightened!"

"It's okay, Winna." He reached out, taking my other hand. "I won't let anything happen to you."

"I-I know. I trust you." I really, really hoped he was right because his words comforted me, but didn't actually make the worry and fear that had settled on me fade.

Lear flashed a wicked grin at me. "A terrible decision, really!"

I rolled my eyes at him, but had to smile, which I knew had been what he was after. "You're a mess."

He bent and kissed me briefly. "I know." When we broke apart, he said, "Let's fly again for a bit."

"Are you up to it?"

"Yes, going down will be easier, since I can glide more. Once I'm tired, we can walk until the sun starts to set, then just stop for the night."

"We don't have a tent though, right? I just thought about it, but surely we're not just going to sleep outside? It's awfully cold."

"Give me a little more credit than that!" He laughed. "I'll make us a shelter, don't worry. I've slept outside enough that I know how to make a little shelter quickly enough."

"If you say so," I muttered, doubtful. What would we do, dig a little divot in the ground? He'd probably try to convince me to snuggle close for body heat. I guess that...wouldn't be too bad, really, snuggling up close to him. Lear was very warm.

Then I remembered that we had brought along one of the heating stones from the cottage, turning it off while it was stowed away in the pack. Well, there went my thoughts of cuddling close with him, but... well, he probably wouldn't mind anyways.

"Alright, let's go," he said, stretching out his enormous wings.

We tied Diana's basket, with Diana inside, back to my waist, and Lear scooped me up again.

"Ready?"

"As ready as I ever am for this part." I sighed, steeling my nerves.

Lear kissed my forehead, then easily launched us into the air.

I actually managed not to scream this time.

Chapter 32

Camping

L ear peered around at the little grove of trees we'd stopped in. Fragrant needles covered the ground in a soft carpet, and a stream bubbled happily nearby. We were tucked just behind a small hillock, which provided even more protection from the wind. "Yes, this will do nicely." He nodded approvingly.

"So I guess I'll get to see you build that shelter now, huh?" I asked him, smiling a little.

"You certainly will! Can you start a fire?" There was no point in using the heating stone outside; the heat would dissipate immediately, and we wouldn't really benefit from it. It was better used in an enclosed space, and a fire would do until we had that. It would also help to keep away any curious or unfriendly animals.

"Sure." I nodded. "I'd say I'd start on dinner, but it's just bread and cheese and dried stuff." We'd brought enough food with us to last the entire trip, so we didn't wind up having to forage for anything, which would be a waste of time.

"That's alright. It's better than nothing. Oh, we can bake a few of those potatoes in the coals, too."

"Good point. So at least one hot thing. And I can start on that, once the fire has been going for a little while." I nodded.

"Now, our shelter." He grinned at me, then bustled about as I started to gather wood for the fire.

I saw he was also gathering wood, but in the form of large, fresh boughs from the pine trees, whereas I was collecting older, long-dead, dry branches with brown needles.

Diana was loafing on top of her basket, watching our antics in vague, catlike amusement.

I arranged the wood, and soon had a little fire crackling away merrily. Once there were a few coals, I'd push some potatoes into them to bake.

Lear had finished gathering branches, and had a large pile accumulated, and had moved on to gathering rocks about as big as my fist.

Soon, he had a good number of stones. The fey soldier then took a few moments before selecting three large branches; two had large forks at the end, and the third was nearly straight. Once he had the ones he wanted, he broke all the little twigs and branches off of them.

Using his immense strength, he easily shoved the two forked branches securely into the ground, forked ends up, and laid the straight one across. Lear then quickly peeled some bark off some smaller branches, and used it as a string of sorts to secure the joints of the makeshift structure.

From the shape of his in progress construction, I had a general idea of where he was going with the temporary structure.

I felt his magic surge, and he grimaced a little, but continued on. The rest of the branches, still bearing their smaller limbs and all the needles, floated into the air, then leaned up against the straight cross-branch one by one. The fluffy parts with the needles were pointed upwards, and the flatter part where they'd been cut off the tree, with his claws I suspected, were against the ground, as they were less likely to slide around.

"There!" He smiled. "And now..." Another surge of magic, and the stones he had collected soared into the air, settling against the base of the sticks to help keep them in place. "They won't be as likely to slide with the rocks there," he told me.

"Ah." I nodded.

"One more thing, then we'll be done," he told me. After one more surge of magic, large quantities of leaves from the trees that weren't pines floated, as if on a breeze, to the shelter, and settled down like a blanket on the branch-walls. "There!"

"Very nice." I smiled at him.

"It goes a lot faster with magic."

"I'm sure! I imagine most things do!"

"They certainly do."

The fire had now burned long enough that there were some coals, and I was able to push the potatoes in. We wouldn't really be able to eat the jackets, thanks to the ashes, but the insides would still be good and hot!

Lear pulled our things into our little shelter, leaving the foodstuff out, and laid out blankets over the ground. "The ground is cold, but having the heating stone will help." He pulled the stone out, and placed it in the back of the shelter, then left and put a few branches over. "That can be the door. It'll help keep the heat in."

"Good idea." I nodded.

He came and sat by me, stretching out one of his wings, so I was shielded a little more from the cold. "There."

"Thank you."

"I just realized that I can't use my line about snuggling and body heat because we brought the heating stone, so this will have to do." He sighed regretfully. "What a shame! It's such a good one, too!"

I laughed, though I'd thought the very same thing earlier. "You're a mess! Besides, it's probably over-used!" If I'd thought of it, it almost certainly was.

"I try." Lear grinned. "And yeah, probably."

Diana hopped up from her basket, and stretched, then joined me under Lear's wing, maowing sweetly as she did.

"No, of course I don't mind, Annie. You only saved our lives."

Lear rolled his eyes amusedly. "You don't even have to ask. I'm fairly fond of you, too."

I reached out and scratched her ears gently, then pulled apart some pieces of dried meat we'd brought with us for her, breaking it up into pieces for her. "There, will that work for your dinner, sweetie?"

A confirmatory maow was her reply before she started to eat.

"Good."

We sat there for a while in the cold night air as the sun set. Soon, stars twinkled above us.

It should have been a nice, cozy, albeit chilly, romantic sort of scene, but the fear that I'd felt consistently since we'd left the protection of the runes on the mountains still gnawed away at me, not to mention the guilt about all the injured people that I'd left behind.

I took a deep breath and pushed the unpleasant thoughts away.

"You okay?"

"I'm...alright."

He studied me for a moment, then shook himself. "Well, let's eat. The potatoes will probably be done soon." He handed me bread, cheese, dried meat, and an apple. "I even had the liberty of getting this while you were checking on your patients this morning." He produced a small wax-paper packet from his bag with a flourish.

"I wondered where you'd gone off to." I peered curiously at the bag in his long fingers.

"Here, open it." He pushed it eagerly into my hands, gorgeous green eyes sparkling like a child's. "It took some work to make sure it didn't get squished as we traveled, but I managed it!"

I opened the package, and stared down at its contents. A wave of unexpected emotion crashed over me.

Inside were nestled a bunch of the tea cakes that I so dearly loved, as well as some candy.

"O-oh!" I squeaked, trying to hold back tears.

"Are you upset? I'm sorry, I thought you'd be happy!" Panic rose in his voice.

"I'm not upset!" I assured him wiping my eyes.

Diana climbed into my lap and started to purr.

"Then why are you crying?!"

"Happy tears, Lear. Th-this was...very nice of you." I sniffled.

"Oh. Well, you like them. They're your favorite, I know that. I thought it might cheer you up a little after you've had such a rough time of things lately," he said softly, his green eyes full of concern.

It struck me that he was anxious to please me, which brought a watery smile to my lips. "Well, it worked! I-I just...no one has ever done anything that nice for me out of the blue for no reason."

"Firstly, that makes me sad to hear. Secondly, I didn't do it for no reason. I did it because I love you, and wanted to cheer you up, like I said." The fey man shook his head.

"What must they have thought when you went to the tea shop and the candy shop during that crisis?" I laughed a little.

"Actually, I think I managed to endear myself to them," he told me thoughtfully. "I had to find the tea-shop owner, which Bekka helped me do. I asked after the cakes, and told her that it was to cheer you up because of how horrible you felt at not being able to help more, even though you were doing what you could, and she practically melted. Told me to just take what I wanted, but I did insist on paying her. Then she asked if I wouldn't want some candy for you too, and of course that seemed like a pretty good idea as well, so she helped me with that too."

"Her sister owns the candy shop." I nodded, smiling. "They probably saw this ridiculous face of yours, all sparkling and excited to do something nice and of course she melted!"

"How is my face ridiculous?" he asked, sounding taken aback.

"Ridiculously attractive, I meant."

"Oh, that. That's nothing." He waved his hand jokingly, then leaned down and kissed me. When he broke away, he asked softly, "They really cheered you up?"

"Yeah." I giggled, leaning into him. "I haven't had candy very much. Mom and Dad would never buy it for us! Cakes every now and again were one thing, but candies were usually a no. Rots your teeth, apparently."

"It does." Lear nodded. "But every so often is fine."

"I kind of forgot it exists." I laughed.

"Eat some."

"And spoil my dinner?"

"You're thirty years old, Winna, I think it'll be okay."

"Oh, yeah. I'm an adult!" she giggled.

Lear burst into laughter, and squeezed me close. "Gods, woman, I love you."

"I love you too, Lear." I sighed happily, then popped one of the candies into my mouth, wincing because it was shockingly sour. "Oh goodness!"

"What?"

"It's sour! Taste it!" I grinned, shoving one into his mouth before he could stop me.

"Oh god!" He grimaced. "That's awful!"

He made to spit it out, but I put my hand over his mouth, feeling mischievous. "Nope! You gotta eat it! You're the one who picked it out!"

The fey man rolled his iridescent eyes at me. "I didn't, actually. They just gave me some of the most popular stuff."

"Oh fine." I dropped my hand so he could spit it out.

"It's not so bad, now." Lear shook his head.

"Yeah, the sourness goes away pretty quickly."

Soon we turned our attention to the actual food, and had ourselves a merry little meal. I was even able to forget my strange sense of foreboding for a little while. The warm potatoes were a delicious main course, and then we finished with our cheese. We ate some of the sweet treats Lear had bought, but saved enough so we could enjoy them throughout the course of the journey.

Diana eventually stretched and yawned.

"Tired?" Lear asked her.

A sleepy maow.

"Alright." He nodded, opening the branches so she could go in, then he told me, "You go get cozy. I'll stoke up the fire and bring everything else in." He motioned at the food bag.

"Okay." I slipped into the makeshift shelter. "Ohh, it's really warm and cozy in here!"

"Good!" Lear said from outside.

Diana settled down on the blanket-floor, as near to the heating stone as she could get, and I started to get out the rest of the blankets we'd packed.

Lear's bag was enormous and heavy, but thanks to his fey strength, he'd carried it without any trouble. I'd packed what I could into my own bag, but I was comparatively weak, being only human. Not that I was all that much of a weakling. I was used to managing a small farm on my own, after all. That meant I was somewhat stronger than most people expected of me, and I was glad to say that I had never needed a man to open a jar. Not that I'd be displeased to ask Lear to do so, in the future, if I were being honest.

My fey companion soon entered as well, bringing the foodstuff in, as promised.

We got the blankets spread out into two sleeping areas.

"I know it feels toasty in here, but...you know, it'll probably get colder still. I bet it won't be as warm as the cottage," I told him innocently. "Cuddling up really would be the warmest option, because then we can both be beneath all of the blankets that we're not lying on top of, instead of each having half of them. And you know, body heat and all."

"Hmm." He pretended to think seriously, then shot a grin at me. "Well, if you insist!"

We rearranged the blankets into one big pallet.

"There." I nodded, then felt the need to add, with my face very red, "No funny business though, alright?"

"No, no funny business." He laughed, leaning down to kiss me briefly.

I took off the cloak and my coat, and we got ourselves under the blankets.

Lear drew me close and planted a kiss in my hair, sighing contentedly. "This is nice."

"Uh-huh."

"As much as I'd like to get up to mischief, I already agreed to no funny business, and you need rest, because we have another long day ahead of us tomorrow."

"Goodnight, Lear."

"Goodnight, Winna."

"Goodnight, Queen Diana."

"Maow," said Diana sleepily.

Chapter 33

Shades

Diana's maow woke me.

"Mm?" I rolled over, blinking in the dark.

Lear was still asleep, likely desensitized to hearing cats maow at night, thanks to Stroopwafel's fairly frequent nighttime serenades.

But Diana rarely bothered me at night, so I made myself stir.

"What's up, miss?" I yawned. "Do you need to go potty?"

Another, more insistent maow.

I went and held a branch away from the door so she could leave to do her business.

But she didn't, and instead hissed at the open entryway.

Blinking, I let the branch fall back into place. "Diana, what's wrong?"

She maowed again, now urgently.

The unease and tension that I'd been able to forget suddenly filled me again.

Hurrying to Lear's sleeping form, I shook him. "Lear, I need you to translate!"

"Mmm...what's up?" He was very cute when he was sleepy, but I didn't let myself focus on that.

"What's Diana saying?"

She maowed again, the fur along the ridge of her back raised, and her tail fluffy.

Lear was sitting up in an instant, his second set of eyes flicking open immediately. "What?!"

Another maow as he looked around wildly. Diana raced across the tent and hopped into her basket.

"Lear, what's wrong?!"

He motioned for me to be quiet, and began to gather our things, looking around constantly as he did.

So it was some kind of emergency. I threw what I could into my own pack, and grabbed the water skins.

"Out of time!" he cried suddenly, tossing the pack onto his back, grabbing Diana's basket, scooping me up, and launching us all through the roof of the shelter, his arm over me to protect me from the heavier branches.

A squeak of surprise escaped me as we flew high into the air, then his wings caught the air, and we surged further upwards.

Much to my terror, I saw shapes around our campsite as I looked down, illuminated by the embers of our dying fire.

Except there was nothing to illuminate, really.

They appeared to be made of pure darkness. But instead of being flat on the ground, like the shadow demon had been, these were standing upright, and each had glowing red eyes.

Some reached up towards us, shadowy arms stretching and growing as they did. I heard the hiss of terrible voices crying something about...starlight? It was hard to tell between my yelp of fear and the wind as it rushed by.

Lear shot us forward with a great flap of his large wings, leaving the terrifying creatures behind.

"What were those?!" I cried.

"Shades!"

"What?!"

"They're a type of demon!"

"Oh gods!" I gasped.

There was a maow from the basket.

"She said that they used to hunt your family, and it's why they had to move around so much."

"Oh goodness!"

My little familiar maowed a few more times. "She said she didn't know about the protective runes, and thought that the shades had given up chasing your family, since it had been so long since she'd seen any, and they were able to settle down like they did."

"So it's not magic or something like that they're after? Is it specifically my family?"

A sad, but confirmatory maow was the response.

"Yes," Lear translated.

Panic filled me. "What are we going to do?!"

"We're going to continue on. We were able to get some food and good rest, and it'll have to do. I'll fly us for as far as I can manage. Hopefully, we'll be pretty close by then, and can hurry to the temple. Once we're there, we'll regroup and make more plans," Lear told me, his tone firm and reassuring.

"O-okay."

We flew along in silence for a long time. Dawn began to break across the sky. The sunrise was magnificent, but did little to ease my fear and concern.

"Diana, why do the shades hunt my family?"

A set of maows. "She doesn't know. She said she doesn't understand violence, and just wishes it would stop."

"Me too, Annie, me too." I sighed.

I could hear Diana's purrs from the basket, and managed a smile, knowing she was doing what she could to comfort me, even from there.

I still had more questions, though, so I continued, "My aunt left, she wanted to travel...I think she's the only one of us Starlings that ever really left the area within the mountains, at least that I know of, anyway. Do you...think the Shades got her? She did seem to just vanish."

There was a pause before the familiar replied. "She says it's possible, but Shades weren't the only ones who hunted your family, from what she knows about it. It could have been any number of foes that made her disappear."

"What?! Why didn't you tell us this?"

"Again, she thought that the family's foes had finally given up. It could just as easily be that your aunt got lost at sea, or some other unrelated tragedy occurred. But now she thinks that, if the shades haven't given up their long-held grudge against your family, then the others haven't forgotten either. She says she really had thought, given all the time that's passed, even just since she'd started taking care of your family, that they'd all given up or forgotten."

"That's...really not good." Bless Diana, but she was just a cat. Just like she didn't understand violence, she didn't really understand hate or grudges.

"No, it's not," Lear said. This was his own opinion, not a translation for Diana.

"Maybe we should go back, Lear," I murmured.

"At this point, we're closer to the temple than to the mountains and their runes. It makes more sense for us to regroup there than to try to make it back."

"But then we'll be that much further away from safety!"

"It's going to be okay, Winna. We'll get Diana all healed up, get some rest, and then we'll make our way home."

"How, though?"

"Well, Shades aren't known for being particularly bright. So we'll play it safe and take turns on watch so they can't sneak up on us again."

"I...I guess. What if they find us when we're in the temple? Before I can pray and ask the goddess to heal Annie?"

"A demon couldn't go into the temple. It's hallowed ground."

"Good."

"Besides, they really only prefer to come out at night, given their nature. I doubt they'll show their faces or bother us during the day; they're usually too sleepy and sluggish, so we'll be able to slip out of the temple easily enough, provided the sun is up. Although it might put us a little later getting home than we'd hoped, but that's okay. Better than getting killed by Shades."

"I'll say," I muttered.

"Just so you know, I've been in worse scrapes than this before, and I'm still around," he told me, smiling grimly.

"I don't really see how anything could be worse than what we're dealing with right now." I frowned.

"What happened with Veris was a worse situation than this. That I survived was down to pure dumb luck, if I'm being honest." He shook his head. "I sensed his presence just a moment before his poisoned barb hit me, and changed into a cat. He assumed the poison would have just as much effect on me. He's not able to change shape, so he didn't know that it wouldn't affect me nearly as much in cat form, and thought I'd be trapped in that form, and die. So he just went on his way, and I escaped and wandered long and far before I found my way to you."

"That was a lucky break," I told him, shaking my head in near disbelief.

"Yeah, and I managed to survive," he told me lightly.

I frowned, confused for a moment, then rolled my eyes. "Only you could flirt at a time like this!"

"It's my job!" He laughed.

Lear flew for hours, forcing himself on when even I could see he was exhausted. He'd started to waver a little in the air, which was concerning, as I didn't want to fall from the sky, whether from him losing his grip on me due to sheer exhaustion, or all of us falling from the sky for the same reason.

"Lear, just land. We can take a little bit of time and eat, and then walk the rest of the way as fast as we can manage. I'm hungry, and you've got to be starving. I'm sure Diana is hungry too."

A soft maow from the basket confirmed it.

"Alright." He sighed, and slowly began to descend.

Soon, we were standing amongst the trees of the forest again. It stretched for miles and miles around us.

"Do you know what sort of place the temple is in? Like, is there a town somewhere? I feel like we'll see it soon, if we're getting as close as I think we are."

"The pixie said it's in the forest. There aren't any towns around here for miles and miles."

"I wonder why it's here, then." I frowned.

"Who knows? There's a chance your family built it. Although why build it outside the runes of protection?" he mused.

"I doubt we'll ever find out." I sighed, shaking my head. "Unless you know, Diana?"

She shook her head.

"I didn't think so." I shrugged, setting my pack down and pulling out the food.

"Let's walk and eat," Lear told me.

"That's fine. Unless you're too tired? You flew for a very long time."

"It's my wings that are tired, my legs are fine." He shrugged. "You should ride in your basket still though, Diana. We'll make better time. Is that okay?"

She hopped obligingly back into her basket in response.

"Thank you." He nodded.

After making sure Diana had food, Lear and I took some bread and cheese, and began to walk. I had Diana's basket in the crook of my arm, leaving my hands free to hold my food.

"So, since we've never been to this temple before, and Willow-down only told you where it was, how are we going to find it in this enormous forest? I know we're probably getting close."

Lear grinned. "Give me a little more credit than that! The pixie did show me where it was on the map, and I took some time to find its general location on the map, after you'd gone to sleep back at the cottage."

"Well, good." I sighed. "You haven't looked at it at all during the trip, I didn't realize you had it."

"I memorized where it was easily enough. It'll still be tricky in the forest, given there aren't really any landmarks here, but given that we are pretty close just by how much we've traveled, I'll probably be able to feel it soon. I know we're going in the right direction."

"You'll be able to feel it?"

"Hallowed ground is magical in its own right, so I'll be able to feel it." He nodded.

"Huh. That's interesting. Have you been to many temples before?" I'd never been to a single one.

"No, I've never really been inside one. Temples aren't really my thing. I always waited outside while whoever I was with took care of their business."

"So I take it you didn't go for worshiping purposes?" I smiled a little.

"No, I'm not particularly religious." He shook his head. "Never found any specific god or goddess who wanted to claim me, or me them."

"I see." I nodded.

"Besides, the fey gods are not nearly so kind or peaceful as a goddess like Marna. She's primarily a goddess of humans, from what I understand. It's hard to want to worship a god or a goddess that isn't particularly benevolent, but I could see myself wanting to deal with her."

"You don't have to say that just to be nice!" I laughed.

Lear smiled. "I am actually serious. She seems alright, as far as they go. Although I'm interested to know why the power waned."

"I do think it had to do with the family starting to marry people without the gift. Which makes sense, given the gift was hereditary."

"Fair enough."

"In some ways, the gift is also a bit of a curse," I mused. "We can't die of old age, but certain illnesses and injuries certainly can kill us. All of my ancestors died really unpleasant deaths, if I'm being honest. My brothers are lucky, in some ways. They'll probably have very long lives, yes, but they will eventually die of old age...if nothing else gets them first, and they're sensible, so I expect nothing else will."

"One can only hope," Lear murmured. I knew that fey most often died from illness or injury as well, given they had the same immortal lifespan.

"I do hope. I wish peaceful deaths for them, surrounded by loved ones. I'll live to see it, too. Unless something happens to me in the meantime."

"Don't talk like that," he said quickly, now upset. "You'll live a long, fruitful, and happy life. And I'll be with you for it, for as long as you can stand me, alright?"

I blinked, then smiled at him. "Alright."

"Maybe someday we'll get married, and have kids. Wait, if you want kids. Do you want kids? We don't have to have them if you don't want them."

"I'm not opposed to kids, no." I shook my head. "I just figured it would be better for me to stay single, and let the bloodline die, since any kids I have would likely not have the gift, either."

"The good news is that, if we were to have kids, they'd be half-fey, and that means not only would they be ridiculously cute, with my eyes and your hair, or my wings and your fingers and toes, or my scales and your freckles, but," he grinned broadly now, "they'd also have magic of their own. It'd be different from yours of course, and more like mine, but they'll have just as long a life as any fey person."

I blinked, then smiled. "You know, I hadn't thought of that."

"I knew you hadn't. That's why I brought it up."

"Then maybe that wouldn't be so bad," I murmured.

"I think it'd be kinda cool," he agreed.

Chapter 34

Decisions

We walked on for a while longer, then Lear paused, closing his eyes for a moment.

"What's up?" Fear rose in me for a brief second.

"Nothing. I can just feel the hallowed ground of the temple. Took me a minute to realize it, but that's definitely what it is," he replied. "It's not far, now."

"Oh, good!" I sighed in relief.

Though we were already walking fairly fast, we quickened our pace until I was moving at a decent jog. "Phew, I need to exercise more!" I laughed, already breathing a little heavily.

"Hmm, I like that idea, it's very...moving." He let his eyes drift suggestively down to my chest, which was, unfortunately, bouncing as I jogged along.

"Lear!" I reached out to whack him.

"And to hear you panting like that..." Lear's voice trailed off, also suggestively.

"Oh gods! You're going to give me a coronary!" I fanned my face, which was hot, but not just from the effort of our quick pace anymore.

He, of course, kept up easily, not breaking a sweat. I knew he could move a lot faster, and likely would have just scooped me up and ran, but I suspected he was still tired from flying as much as he had.

"It's just ahead," Lear said as my pace began to slow.

I could see the trees beginning to part, and caught flashes of white marble in the clearing that was our destination.

Suddenly, Diana gave a shrill growl of warning, and before I could react, a dark splotch appeared on the ground before me, growing suddenly into a shade before my eyes.

Lear's power crackled, and I heard him scream in pain, thanks to the lingering poison in his veins, as a sword made entirely of magic materialized in his hand. The fey man surged forward, slicing through the shade like butter.

Then he caught me around the waist, and darted forward, pausing every couple of seconds to ward off another shade as they appeared. He was breathing fairly heavily now as well, likely from the effort of using the magic, which had to have hurt terribly, and from having to carry me while running, even though he was already exhausted.

"Can you kill them all before we get there?!" I cried, terrified they'd manage to kill us before we made it.

"I'm not killing them! It just makes them have to reform. I'm just buying us time to get to the safety of the temple!" he grunted.

"Why are they out; I thought you said they preferred the night?!"

"I don't know! Maybe you were, he grimaced and sliced through another shade, "too much of a draw for them to wait for night!"

"Gods, that's the worst prize in the world!" I lamented. There was nothing I could do, either.

But we made headway. Or rather, Lear made headway. Diana and I were little more than useless baggage in his arms.

Then the ivy covered, white marble temple was before us, and safety was in our grasp.

"Get inside!" he shouted, letting go of me and pushing me

towards the door, turning to fend off yet another shade as the onslaught continued.

Suddenly, I could hear hissing speech from the Shades as they clashed with Lear. "No, little child of starlight, come and play!" They laughed. "We've looked long and hard for you! You filth! You traitors!"

With the terrible voices chilling me to the very core, I staggered forward, caught my balance, and then raced towards the door to the temple. I clutched Diana's basket tightly with both of my hands as Lear followed, still moving backward as he protected us, practically on my heels.

Then my foot was on the marble threshold, and I stepped inside the temple.

Immediately, a sense of safety I hadn't felt since we'd left the land surrounded by the protection runes filled me. We would be safe here, it seemed.

"Finally!" I gasped, setting Diana's basket down. "Well, you were right, Lear." I turned, meaning to say something about hallowed ground feeling obviously safe to me, now that I was standing on it, but saw he was still outside. "What are you doing?!" I cried.

"I-I...I miscalculated!" he cried, blocking the blow of a shade, then slicing the appendage off.

"What?! What do you mean?!"

"I-I've never been into a temple before, so I didn't think about how I'd be granted entry! Temples must be considered their deity's dwelling place! I guess there's usually a priest or a priestess who could grant me entry, but obviously this place doesn't have any of those! There's no one here to invite me in, so I can't enter!"

"Yes, you can, just step inside!" I cried.

"It's not a matter of me not wanting to because of some stupid rules, I can't! Physically can't!" He fell back a step, which should have carried him into the doorway, but instead it was like he was leaning against an invisible wall. "See?!"

"Oh gods! A-and this isn't my home! I-I can't invite you in!"

"I know! Just make your wish, Winna! Then we'll get out of here!"

But there was no way that would be possible. Not with him as tired as he was. He'd barely been able to run with me, there was no way we'd be able to escape from that many Shades.

Diana had left her basket, and was now standing beside me as I sank to my knees, wracking my mind desperately for a solution.

"L-Lear, there're too many of them!" I sobbed.

"Pray, Winna! We'll manage, just pray!" he shouted back, still managing to hold his own against the Shades' attacks.

I lifted my hands, trying to gather my thoughts to cobble together some meaningful kind of prayer, but my thoughts were terrified, scattered, and Lear's grunts and gasps as he fought kept breaking through what little concentration I could gather.

As I continued to try to get my act together enough to pray something that made any sense, I suddenly felt magic well beside me. Before I realized what it was, the power darted forward.

Horror filled me as it struck me what was going on, and as my eyes opened, I saw Diana stepping out of the doorway, glowing feebly with what little magic she had left.

It was the only thing keeping her alive.

"DIANA, NO!" I screamed, staggering to my feet and reaching for her, but it was too late; she'd already passed through Lear's legs.

Instead, a six fingered hand reached out, and scooped up her small form. "No, Annie! Winna would be so sad without you!" Lear said as he clutched the little cat to his chest.

But the damage had already been done. It had taken too much of her magic to even try to do what she was going to do, and some had ebbed away with the effort. It was magic she couldn't afford to lose, and she slumped in Lear's arms.

"DIANA!" I screamed.

At that moment, one of the shade's shadow-limbs broke through Lear's defenses, which were hobbled as he clutched my little familiar close.

It pierced his flesh with a sickening crunching noise, slamming into his chest from a terrible, odd angle beneath his left arm. A strangled cry of pain and rage tore itself from Lear's throat. Immediately, he severed the limb, and staggered back, once more hitting the barrier that kept him stranded outside.

Terror filled me.

I was going to lose both of them, and die here in this temple, alone, trapped by the Shades that prowled outside!

"Marna, I don't know if you can hear me, but I am a descendant of those of your children who stayed true—" whatever that meant, but the words were coming to me as if divinely inspired, "—and by the mark on my hand, surely I have the right to grant a fey man entry to this abode!" I cried, paused for the briefest second to let the words sink in, then shouted, "Lear! Please come inside!"

As if a pane of glass had broken, Lear immediately fell backwards, carrying Diana's limp form over the threshold of the temple with him, and scrambling until they were both entirely inside the temple. Finally safe.

I bolted to his side, and pulled him, and, therefore, Diana, away from the door, as if the Shades could get in.

But Lear had been right about them not being able to enter the hallowed ground of the temple, thankfully. The evil creatures were throwing themselves against the opening, only to bounce off the same kind of barrier that had blocked Lear's entry just moments before.

"I...I thought the priests near the door were just there to be hospitable..." Lear groaned, clutching his side with his free hand. "I never...never thought about it. Gods, how stupid!"

"I-it's okay!" I sobbed. "You're inside now! You're safe!"

"Diana," he said softly, holding the little cat out to me.

I caught up my oldest and dearest friend, and held her close, immediately starting to pour my magic into her small body, but also reaching out a hand to push it into the fey man who I loved as well. But split like that, it wasn't enough to help either of them.

"Focus on Diana, Winna. I've got more time than she does." But he grimaced as he spoke, "I...I think the shade's magic from where it got me is reacting in a bad way with the poison already in me, but I...I still have more time."

"D-don't say that!" I whimpered, but did as he said, concentrating on pushing all of my magic into Diana, whose breathing was shaky and shallow, though I kept hold of Lear's hand for comfort. "Wh-what am I going to do?!" I sobbed.

"Ask the goddess to heal Diana, Winna." Despite our fraught situation, his tone was now calm and subdued.

"O-oh, right! Th-then, i-if she does it, we can just heal you togeth-er!" I gasped, having not thought of that.

But my small familiar stirred, maowing weakly.

"What? Don't say anything, and don't move, Diana, just...just rest! I-I'll get you help! You'll be healed!" Gods, I hoped that was true. Surely the fact that I'd been recognized as having the right to give Lear entry to the temple, meant that I did actually have some sort of claim on the goddess, and she might at least deign to hear my request.

"She said that an injury dealt by a shade can't be healed by normal magic, given it's a demon." Lear sighed, shaking his head. I could see pain written in his expression, and knew he was suffering. "I...wondered. It does feel different."

"What?!"

Another quiet maow.

"She said...hang on, I'm not telling her that!" he protested weakly. "She needs to choose you, not me! I don't matter! Not like you do! I'm little more than a murderer, Diana, whereas you're the familiar of a goddess, sent to help Winna help others!"

"I-I don't want either of you to die!" Tears coursed down my face. But in my heart, I knew I could only pick one, if I was going to be able to get a prayer answered. Unless allowing Lear in had counted as my prayer? Oh goddess, please don't let that be the case!

"Winna, don't listen to Diana. She's selfless, but not thinking clearly. I know she just wants you to be happy, with me, but...if she

316

lives, you two will go on to save many more lives. Even just when you make it back to the village. My life is filled with violence and bloodshed. It's not worth much. You save her, and go save more people, and live a long, wonderful life!"

Diana gave a very faint snort, and I took its meaning. My dear, sweet cat was telling me to pick Lear, to choose happiness for myself.

"B-but you won't be there!" I shouted. "I-I don't want to live that life without either of you! I-I love you, Lear! I-I wanted to have kids and live a ridiculous amount of time! Y-you said we'd be together! Y-you lied!"

Lear pulled himself close, the pain in his expression not a physical one, this time. "I didn't. You know I can't. I wanted to be there. I'll watch from the other side, and wait as long as it takes, alright? That's the truth now." He put a gentle hand on my leg. "I love you so much. But it's okay to let me go."

"I-I can't let either of you go!" My words were barely coherent.

"Winna, my love, you have to." His tone was gentle.

I was choosing between my past and my future. My dearest friend, and last link to my parents, and the man that I loved, who had so suddenly come into my life, and changed it forever.

Diana was purring very weakly, ultimately reassuring me that whatever decision I made, it was okay, but that it was my decision to make.

I took a very ragged, deep breath, trying to center myself. "I-I love you both very much!"

"Winna, you have to make a decision. Diana is fading, and I don't think Marna holds with necromancy, as much as you love your sweet cat," Lear murmured.

"I-I know." One last deep breath, and I closed my eyes.

I could see a long life stretched out before me. Lear and I getting married, having children; those kids growing up, and eventually having families of their own. A long, happy family line stretched out before me, and I wanted it with every ounce of my being.

But there were people in the village who also had a shot at happy lives, but only if Diana lived. What I wanted didn't matter. My gift was for helping people, and the decision to save Diana was ultimately the one that would lead to that.

Lear was my heart, but Diana was my soul. And if I didn't choose Diana, the deaths of every villager that died from here on out would be my fault entirely, were it something I could have otherwise prevented by having Diana's help. But in doing so, I was staining my hands with the blood of the man I loved.

"Winna, love, it's okay. Let me go." Lear's voice was soft.

Diana gave a whimpering sort of maow, and her breathing caught for a moment.

Then my mind was made up.

Chapter 35

The Goddess's Gift

Winna began to pray, her words barely a whisper. But there was more pleading earnestness in that hushed, desperate voice than most could summon at a normal volume.

Tears flowed freely down her beautiful face, over her freckles, down her cheeks, and slid off her chin, dropping down onto poor Diana's pitiful, limp form.

As Lear heard her words, relief and melancholy filled him.

The prayer ended, and she was quiet for a moment, then opened her dark brown eyes. They were full of devastation at the choice she'd just had to make.

"I'm proud of you, Winna." Lear reached out to put his hand over one of hers on Diana's fur. "You had the choice between yourself and others, and you chose others. It's alright. It was a choice well made."

But her tears didn't fade. "D-Diana i-isn't healed, though!" she cried. "I-it hardly matters wh-what I chose i-if the goddess didn't hear it!"

"Winna, love, sometimes...sometimes the answer is just no," he told her quietly. "And not because you don't deserve it, or because of anything you did wrong. Just because it's no." He squeezed her hand gently, and grimaced as the pain from the injury spread further.

"Y-you're both d-dying!" she screamed, shuddering violently from her tears.

Lear hauled himself totally up, and sat beside her, weakly extending a wing out around her, and drawing her close. "It's okay. Everything has to end at some point, even fey and familiars."

"I-I'll go too, soon, though! Not all that long after you two. For as long as I can last after the water runs out! I-I can't leave here. Th-those Shades aren't going to leave, now that they know I'm trapped in here, alone and trapped!" Winna choked on the words.

"Give me some more credit than that. I might be dying, but I'm still a wily bastard."

She gave a hysterical snort. "What do you mean?"

"I'm stubborn, and don't want the shade's injury to get the best of me. If I take a page from Diana's book," he stroked Diana's fur gently and fondly, "I should be able to do something similar to what she did when she banished Veris, and what she intended to do earlier. But... between magical exhaustion and the poison reacting to my magic, I will die." He paused. "The good news is that I'm dying anyway, so I might as well give it a damn good purpose. It should be a massive blast, and will destroy the Shades. I don't doubt more will come if they sense you, but it'll buy you some time. You'll have to run, and try to make it to the mountains. There is a path up it, we just didn't take it because what we did was faster. Take the path, and get to safety. I know it'll be hard, given the situation, but you can't stop to sleep. You have to push through until you make it past the runes."

"I-I don't know if I can do it! N-not alone!"

"Winna, you can do anything you set your mind to," he told her firmly. "And I need you to live for me, alright? Live the life that we won't get together. Please fall in love again, with some entirely unsuitable rake like me. Just be happy, okay?"

The woman he loved took a deep, shuddery breath. "O-okay."

Diana's breathing paused, then resumed, and they both looked down at her.

"It's time. Say goodbye, my love." He nodded at the little cat.

Winna burst into tears anew, and lifted her small friend up with one arm, keeping hold of Lear's hand with the other, and burying her face into Annie's fur for the last time.

"I-I love you, my miss! My queen! My Diana! I-I'll miss you more than you'll ever know!" she gasped, struggling to breathe in her grief.

The sweet familiar gave the faintest of maows.

"She loves you, too. So, so much."

Lear began to well his magic. It would take a moment to get it all together, and he didn't want to make Winna linger there for too long after Diana went on. It would only cause her more pain. Instead, he'd take the sweet cat, have Winna stand by the door, and release what would arguably be the largest bomb of magical energy to ever have existed, all with one purpose - to kill Shades. The temple would be quite the tomb for Diana and him.

Or that's what he'd planned to do.

But, as Diana was taking a rattling last breath, a warm glow filled the room, and time seemed to stand still.

Winna's head jerked up, and they both shifted, looking towards the altar that stood on a raised dais, not far from where they were sitting.

A golden figure formed, blurry and incorporeal at first, but then fully materializing.

It was a lovely woman. She had curly, honey-blonde hair, large, azure-blue eyes, and features very similar to Winna's.

"M-mama?!" Winna gasped, staring in astonishment.

"In a way, honey," the woman spoke. Only it was less a voice, and more like her words hummed through them like a glorious melody.

Lear felt his heart leap, and the intense pain growing in him faded a little as he murmured, "It's Marna, Winna."

"O-oh!" the young woman stammered, jaw dropping.

"I thought this appearance might not be so alarming as a great, glowing figure." The goddess smiled somewhat sheepishly.

Suddenly, Diana stirred in Winna's arms, and maowed softly. Her fur was glowing softly, and she leapt lightly down.

"Diana?!" The little mage was still stunned.

"Hello, my girl!" Marna giggled, bending to scoop up the gray tabby and hugging her close. "I've missed you! The heavens aren't the same without my sweet kitty around! But you've done so, so well!"

"Sh-she has!" Winna choked out. "B-but i-it's her time to go, now, isn't it? Th-the answer was no...A-and you're going to take her home, right?"

"Oh, child." Marna's face creased with worry, and she reached out to wipe away the young woman's tears. "Of course not. The answer wasn't no! It just took me longer than it should have to get here. The bureaucracy in the heavens is more ridiculous than you'd believe!"

"Y-you're going to heal her?!" Winna squeaked, a look of pure wonder filling her expression.

"My dear, you didn't travel through mudslides, Shades, and sheer terror just for me to not heal Lear as well as Diana!" Marna laughed.

"What?" It was Lear's turn to be gobsmacked. A human goddess healing a fey person was...unheard of.

"But there are some...jurisdictional issues surrounding that point, which is what caused my delay. I was arguing it out with my fey counterparts, and was almost too late. For that, I must apologize." She bowed her head slightly, then continued, "That said, I'm fully prepared to heal you, Lear, but given my final agreement with the fey gods, I'll need to mark you as my child as well."

"I-I'm...I'm fey, though," Lear mumbled, totally mystified.

"Yes, I am aware." Marna giggled, reaching out to pat his head. Suddenly, he felt like a very small child.

"What...what will it do?" he asked a little warily.

"Your purpose will be to help people, but I think you've rather come to like that about Winna, which is why you urged her to pick

Diana, as she did. The only thing that will happen is the mark will appear on your hand."

"So...no more...fighting?" Lear was only a little embarrassed by how disappointed he sounded at that.

"That's not what I said now, is it?" She flashed a brief smile at him. "Not that I approve of bloodshed, but you must do what you have to in order to protect those who are innocent, and in need of help. But mostly, I want you to keep Winna safe, and keep her company."

"Uh...right."

"But also, don't feel like you have to care for the world and neglect to care for yourself." She turned, now speaking really to Winna. "Which is something you should work on, my dear."

"B-but I'm supposed to help other people!"

"You can do that and still take care of yourself," Marna said gently. "The gift wasn't given for you to run yourself ragged. Which you do. And sometimes you let yourself get run over like a doormat. That's not what it means either."

"Like when the villagers got mad at you," Lear muttered.

"Yes. Precisely that. Luckily, your friend Bekka intervened. Give her my thanks, it was a kind deed well-done."

"I-I will." Winna nodded.

"Now." Marna reached out and took Lear's hand. "Do you assent to be my child?"

The fey man arched an eyebrow at her, and asked the most important question, "Can I still marry Winna, if I do?"

"It won't make you related in any way, so yes." The goddess nodded.

"Then gods, yes." He grabbed her hand quickly.

"Lovely." Marna smiled.

A strange feeling filled him. It was unlike anything he'd ever felt before, and totally indescribable.

Every single bit of pain fled his body. "That's...an odd feeling," he muttered.

"It must be!" Marna laughed. "And there we are! All healed!"

Diana purred loudly, rubbing briefly against Lear, who held up his hand to examine the new mark that had appeared on the back of it. It was identical to Winna's in shape and size, but his was a dark black.

"Was Winna's family's mark originally this dark?" he asked. "Or rather, her people's marks, I should say."

"Yes. It faded significantly over time as the bloodline got thinned out by other people." Marna nodded. "That's just the nature of how it works, I'm afraid."

Winna was now brimming with curiosity, and eagerly asked, "Why was my family on the run? What brought us to the area behind the protective runes?"

"Your ancestors were on the run because they were being hunted," the goddess explained.

"By the Shades and other foes, right? Why were they hunting us?"

Marna sighed. "It's a long story, but...you read about the Untrue and the True, yes?"

"Yes, I was able to decipher enough to read a bit about them." Lear nodded.

"The Untrue eventually seized control of Evarin. They'd stopped using any of their powers to help others, and sought only to increase their own power and will and greatness. The True resisted, but their numbers were so few that they couldn't do much, and were forced into hiding within their own kingdom, unable to flee because it was difficult to move in any large numbers. The remnants of those who remained true were hunted down one by one, and killed." Marna paused, expression deeply sad. "Some of the Untrue did truly despicable acts in my name, claiming that it was my will. Some even sold their souls to dark powers to get what they wanted. When I finally got the approval from the appropriate heavenly committees," she rolled her eyes at this, "which took absolutely forever and came with a cost on my part, I withdrew my gift, and cast the capital city, which was in a lovely spot on the coast, into the waters so it could never be rebuilt."

"You killed them all?" Lear blinked.

"No, no! The city was mostly abandoned by the time that happened. Sorry, I didn't mean to make it seem like it happened all at once. The people fled, realizing that their powers were gone. I guess it did lead to many deaths though, in that their immortality was stripped from them as well." Marna sighed. "It was an unfortunate side effect. Most of them went on to live very normal human lives, just blending into societies all over the place, and trying very hard to forget what they once had been, everything that had happened."

"You said there was a cost for you as well?" Lear asked.

"Yes. I was banned from appearing to or speaking to my remaining children for a very, very long time," Marna explained sadly. "As time passed, I feared that my children, those who had remained true, would dwindle away to nothing. But after much pleading with the heavenly courts, I was able to secure permission to save your family. I was allowed to speak to them, and provide them with some aid. That's when I sent Diana to help your family, and I told them of a place I'd found and prepared for them, somewhere they'd be safe."

"So they carved the runes into the mountains after you told them about the spot?" Lear asked.

"No, I put the runes in place myself, then came to lend my Diana to them. I didn't have much more time than that before I had to return to the heavens. I was able to assure them that I'd not forsaken them, and that Diana was there to help them, but that was about it."

There was a pause.

"So...my family remained True?" Winna asked hesitantly. "We kept at least some of our powers, and it was only just starting to fade in totality by the time my brothers and I were born."

"Yes. The only reason it dwindled was because there were no more of my children for them to marry and have kids with." Marna nodded.

A thought occurred to Lear. "But if the Untrue had lost their power, what could they really do that would make her ancestors have to stay in hiding? I mean, I know you said they had other enemies..."

"Well, the ones that sold their souls for more power had really quite terrible ends." Marna grimaced. "The evil beings immediately called in the debt and thus enslaved them for all eternity." She motioned at the entrance to the temple, where the shade still threw themselves against the barrier. "They became Shades. They hate anyone with the power of my gift still running through their veins."

"Oh gods! That's terrible!" I gasped. "That's why they said that!"

"Said what? I didn't think Shades could talk." Lear frowned.

"Winna can hear the remnants of their voices. You'll be able to now, as well." the goddess nodded.

"They said something about starlight the first time they attacked us, then just now called me a child of starlight, and said we were traitors," Winna said thoughtfully.

"Your last name used to be Starlight, but in an attempt to help hide your identities, it was changed to Starling. And the Shades weren't the only evil beings to hate my children, like you mentioned, Lear. Before the evil crept in, my children fought long and hard against many evil beings, and became the focus of their hatred. So, similarly to Awenna becoming Winna, Starlight became Starling. Close enough for comfort, but not the same."

"They were running from a lot," Winna said slowly.

"Yes. Life on the run like that wasn't much of a life, I'm afraid. It broke my heart to see them struggle, so once I was finally able to come down to help, I did. Unfortunately, the runes I made could only truly shield them from Shades, since making areas inaccessible via magic isn't allowed for deities except where demons are concerned. Otherwise, I would have given them a true haven." Marna sighed.

"So any other enemies could still have found them?" Lear asked.

The goddess nodded. "That's why they stopped using their magic in public, other than healing magic, even before they went to their new home. Then, once they were there, they continued that practice, only using their powers in public to heal, since they couldn't bear to not help their neighbors. They *were* still my children, after all."

"How was it that they forgot your name?" Winna wanted to know. "Surely *that* would have been too important to forget!"

"Much like they stopped using their magic, they stopped saying my name, lest someone overheard, and carry word to their enemies. I don't blame them." Marna shrugged. "Eventually, it was only told to their children once they came of age, alongside other information about who they were, and why they lived life on the run."

"So if their parents died before they came of age, then they wouldn't know your name, or their heritage?" Lear tilted his head to the side.

"Yes, and that's what happened, unfortunately. It was actually Awenna's grandparents, her father's parents, who passed on before he came of age. Shades caught them unawares."

"That's sad! He must have been so lonely!"

"It was," Marna murmured. "I was truly scared the line would end with him." She was quiet for a few moments, then smiled. "But it didn't. He was strong. Even though he didn't know about his past, nor could he read the many books that the family had carried around for centuries in order to remedy that, he still stayed true."

Chapter 36

Home Again

M y brain whirled. She'd connected all the dots, and I now could see the history of my family laid out before me.

I was proud to be a Starling. Or a Starlight. Whatever. Starling was what I knew, and I think I wanted to continue using the name that I was familiar with.

"Thank you, Marna." I bowed low to her, now. Or as low as I could, since Diana was sitting in my lap, purring loudly.

"No, thank you, child, for staying true, even when you didn't know my name, or any of your history." Marna beamed at me.

"My question is why is there a temple all the way out here?" Lear muttered.

"There used to be a city! It was long ago." Marna laughed. "It was part of a civilization that rose and fell before your family ever came to these parts."

"That's a long, long time," I murmured.

"It is." the goddess agreed, then clapped her hands lightly, as if getting down to business once more, and announcing, "Now, I have one last gift to give."

I smiled. "I have my best friend and the man I love, what more could I want?"

"Goodness, I do really like you!" Marna giggled, as merry as a schoolgirl. "It's because of those answers that I want to reaffirm the full gift for you. And, when you get back home, ask your brothers, them and their families as well, if they want it. That they didn't receive the same weak version of it as you did was, again, just because the bloodline was diluted. There's no shame in it, but that's just what happens when there's no one else with the gift that you're not related to who you can marry." She sighed, then shook her head regretfully.

"O-oh!" I stammered. "I...well, thank you, but...I..." I chewed my lip nervously.

"What troubles you, child?"

"I...don't want to...be tempted like the others were," I admitted in a whisper, looking down at my hands, which rested on Diana's fur. "I-I'm only human."

"Good gods, Winna!" Lear snorted. "That's why you should accept! That fear will keep it in check!"

"Lear is right." Marna nodded. "Your concern betrays your heart. It's true. As true as those who remained True all those years in the past."

"Had I...not chosen Diana, would...you still have come?" I asked haltingly.

"Yes, sweetie. My coming wasn't contingent on you choosing Diana over Lear. Choosing happiness and love is understandable. I'd have healed them both and offered to restore the gift all the same."

"Yeah?" I murmured, looking up.

"Yeah. Wanting love isn't a crime. Nor is wanting happiness. That's only natural. Wanting happiness to the detriment of others, that's where you get in trouble."

"I see." I nodded.

"Now, will you let me restore the gift?"

I took a deep breath. "Lear, will you help me learn how to use it?"

"Absolutely." He flashed a bright grin at me.

"Then yes, ma'am. And...thank you. Thank you for everything. I...I thought I was losing two of the people I love most in the world."

"You'd still have had Stroopwafel, your brothers, and their families," Lear reminded me gently.

"I-I know, but...I'd have still taken the loss very hard," I whispered.

"I know. That's why I came. You've been so strong for so long. Sometimes a girl deserves a break." Marna smiled.

Joy now filled me, and I giggled, "Yes! Yes we do!"

"Now, give me your hand." The goddess held out her own hand to me, and I took it.

A strange feeling filled me for a moment, and the mark on my hand darkened to the same black as Lear's.

"There." She smiled.

"Oh!" I gasped as I felt more magic than I'd ever had flooding my veins. It surged through me, sparking out of my fingertips.

"Whoops, let's be careful, now." Lear reached out and caught my hands, and I felt his magic surround me, and help tamp my own back down.

"Thank you." I scooped Diana off my lap and into my arms, and leaned into him.

The man I loved, and my oldest friend.

They were both alive.

"Now, my time with you is running out, and I have to leave. Goddess, I don't want to. It still feels like there's so much I haven't gotten to tell you! But I'll already be getting a talking-to for staying as long as I have, but...well, it's fine. They can just get over it!" Our patron goddess grinned mischievously, and stood.

Lear helped me to my feet, and I kept Diana in my arms.

"Will I ever get to see you again?" I asked softly.

"Of course! I'll have to come to give the gift to any of your family members who want it," she assured me. "Although your nieces and nephews might need to wait until they're older before they make that decision for themselves. And I do suggest you build a temple or some kind of shrine, it makes it easier."

"And this time we know for sure she can invite me in." Lear laughed a little.

"That didn't actually have to do with my rules, or it being hallowed ground. That was the fey rules not quite understanding the situation fully, but once Winna said what she did, they understood and relented, recognizing our claims to one another."

"I gathered as much." Lear nodded.

"It won't matter with my temples or shrines anymore, because as my child, you are welcome at all of them."

Lear smiled. "Of course."

"Well, I must go." Marna sighed. "You can take care of the Shades now, right, Lear?"

A most wicked smile stretched over the fey man's face, and his response was practically a purr of satisfaction, "Absolutely."

"Then goodbye, but not forever!" Marna waved to us.

"Goodbye!" I nodded, leaning into Lear, who waved his own farewell.

Diana maowed sweetly.

There was a bright flash, and then Marna was gone.

It was quiet for a few moments, then Lear caught me and Diana, and spun us both around, cackling somewhat maniacally.

"Goddess, it's good to be alive!" he cried. "And now I get to kick some shade ass. Then we can go home and I can teach you more magic and we can get married and-"

"I'm getting dizzy!" I interrupted, and Diana hissed in protest.

Lear stopped. "Oh, sorry." He put me down and steadied me, grinning rather stupidly. It was entirely adorable.

"But you're right, we should start making our way home. The injured townsfolk still need help, and as quickly as we can manage."

"Yes, of course. Let me go take out the garbage first." The fey man grinned wickedly once more, then turned on his heel, and headed towards the door.

"Please be careful," I called, following anxiously behind him.

"Don't worry, Winna! And make sure you watch, I'm back up to my full strength, so I can put on quite a show for you!" He stepped out the door, and began shooting enormous blasts of pure magical energy.

The Shades gave ear-splitting shrieks, and tried to flee, but Lear was entirely too fast for them, now. He was apparently full of energy, too, after being healed, which had probably replenished his normal energy as well as his magic. He darted back and forth at full speed until they were all gone.

"There. See?" The fey man smirked, turning back to us.

"That was impressive." I blinked, and Diana purred loudly.

"And kind of attractive?" He walked with a rolling, almost lazy gait back to the temple. Putting his arm up on the doorway, he leaned over me in a very ridiculously attractive sort of way.

My face heated, but I held his gorgeous gaze. "Maybe a little," I teased him, reaching out and walking my fingers up the buttons of his shirt, holding Diana in my other arm.

"Gods, and the fey are the ones who are supposed to be enchanting!" He groaned, then leaned down, and kissed me firmly and deeply before breaking away. "Faaangs, ughhh..."

"That's going to get old. We'll have to figure something out." I pouted a little.

"Gods, I know!" He sighed, then smiled. "But I bet that if we work together, we could come up with some kind of antidote in case an accident happens, now, cause you can do a lot more things than you could before. You just have to learn how."

"I bet you're right." I smiled. "I'm...excited to learn more."

"I'm excited to teach you," he murmured, now gentle. I loved how he went from ridiculously flirtatious to gentle and earnest so quickly. I knew the earnest side was really more what he was actually like, but the flirtatiousness was all good fun.

We kissed again for a moment, but I pulled away and said, "Let's go home. I need to heal some people."

"Winna, this is incredible!" Pava breathed, awestruck at the new-found power his little sister now wielded.

"It really is!" Vim agreed, looking fairly impressed as well, but he was a little harder to read, Lear found.

"I'm just grateful she agreed to answer my prayers," Winna murmured. "She didn't have to help me at all. And then to restore the gift to its full power for me..." Her voice trailed off, and she shook her head, still not fully adjusted to the idea yet.

"That would be poor repayment for someone who's apparently stuck to what she was supposed to be doing with her powers." Pava snorted, shaking his head.

The woman Lear loved sat up, finished healing her patient, and wiped her face. They'd been back in the village for just a little while, and she'd already healed the three of the most badly injured people, thanks to the restored gift, and Diana was on stand-by in case she got tired or needed help, but was, at the moment, busy providing some much-needed stress relief to the traumatized villagers by providing pets and purrs, as well as permitting ear scratches and even a few kisses.

Winna was quiet for a few moments, then finally spoke as she stood, going to the next patient. "There's...there's more, and it concerns you two."

"Oh?" Pava raised an eyebrow at her.

"She said she'd give you the gift too, if you want it," their younger sister murmured.

Lear watched her brothers closely. Pava looked startled, and Vim only blinked, which he assumed meant he was surprised as well.

"What?" Pava finally asked. "Like...give us magic too?"

Winna looked up at them as she worked, smiling. "Yes. It does come with the caveat of having a magical lifespan, too. I know that sounds great, but...well, it has downsides as well. Please think long and hard about whether you want to accept. And if you do turn it down, she won't be offended; she was very nice."

"I won't do it," Vim said immediately. "Not if it means I have to watch my family grow old and die, and not be able to go with them."

"The offer wasn't just for you," she told them, "It includes your families as well. But she said to let the kids wait until they're older before they decide if they want it or not, and that makes sense."

Pava and Vim stared at her, then one another, in silence for a few moments.

"I'll have to talk to Jiven," Pava murmured.

"And I'll have to talk to Mina," Vim nodded.

"Of course. I don't expect you to make the decision now. Like I said, take some time and think it over. I think we'll need to build a temple before we can really talk to her again anyway, if any of you want to accept the offer."

"Thank you, Winna." Pava smiled a little.

The young woman stood, finished with that patient as well.

"You're making quick work of this, now." Lear smiled at her.

"Yeah." She smiled back, then looked down at her patient. "I have a lot more to do, though. You said the dwarves already got the temporary housing up?"

"Yep! They worked incredibly quickly! But that's no surprise, really, they're very hard workers," Pava replied.

"On that note, the villagers staying at the cottage returned here, to the housing. We told them they could stay, but they wanted a bit more space for themselves," Vim told his sister.

"I'd have been fine if they'd wanted to stay, but I don't blame them for wanting more space." Winna shrugged.

The pretty healer slowly made her way through the townsfolk who were the most badly injured.

"Phew, I'm getting tired! I think I'm finally coming to the end of my magic, but I'm shocked how many people I got through before getting this far!"

"You got through all the people who were very badly hurt," Lear observed.

"Yeah, I did! I did my best to push through at the end." Winna smiled, putting her hands on her hips as she surveyed her patients. "Now I can move on to people who weren't as badly hurt, with Diana's help. I bet we'll be able to get through them by the end of the day!"

"A break first, though. Then you can get back to it."

"Alright. I should probably eat, I'm pretty hungry."

"It's about lunchtime." Lear nodded as Vim walked up. "And here's your brother with a tray of food."

"You angel!" Winna smiled at her brother.

"Well, I try." He winked cheerfully at her.

They gratefully accepted the fragrant bowls of soup that he handed them, as well as some soft white bread, a smoky cheese, and some salad of winter greens he'd managed to pull together with an oil and vinegar dressing. It was altogether very nice, and they sat in relative silence, scarfing it down.

"Ohh, that was so good." Winna sighed.

"I need another bowl."

"I'm not surprised, you eat a lot."

"Takes a lot to power these muscles." He winked at her.

The woman he loved rolled her eyes, but smiled. "Oh hush."

Lear grinned at her, then went and got his bowl refilled. As he settled back down on the ground, he could see Winna's eyes now roving the workers who were carefully beginning to move the bodies of the dead away to finally be buried, her expression full of sadness.

"Three people died while we were gone," she murmured.

"Winna, it's not your fault," Lear told her in a calm, even tone.

The young woman was quiet for a few moments, then took a deep breath. "I-I know."

"Please don't blame yourself. Given how weak your magic was before that, I suspect they'd have died anyway."

"I just...I feel so guilty. And their families must be so upset to know I could heal them now. I can't imagine how much it hurts, especially to see me healing everyone else."

"Has anyone said anything to you?"

"No."

"And I don't expect they will. They knew what the situation was, and how it might play out."

"I know, I just-"

"No, Winna. No." He shook his head. "It's not your fault. You're not guilty. Sometimes bad things happen, and you're not answerable for that. You didn't cause the landslide, but you did everything you possibly could."

Winna took a deep breath. "You're right."

"Say it."

"What?"

"That it's not your fault."

"It's not my fault."

"Again."

"Lear..."

"Come on."

Winna huffed. "Fine. It's not my fault."

"Good. And please believe that." Lear bent and kissed her forehead. "I love you very much."

"I love you too."

He grinned at her. "We're going to get married!"

She smiled back, a little tiredly. "Yeah."

"We could...get married very soon. Or wait, if you'd prefer."

"You'd rather it be soon though, wouldn't you?"

"Yes, but if you need to wait, I'm content to wait as long as you need."

Her dark eyes searched his face. "It...it could be sooner. I'd... planned on waiting, but...after all the madness at the temple, I...I'm okay with getting married soon. I came far too close to losing you."

"Then let's start planning the ceremony. We can wait until the town is more stable, of course."

"Yes. We could...maybe build that temple and have the ceremony there."

Lear smiled. "I think that's an excellent plan." He felt his smile falter.

"What's wrong?"

"Do you...want me to bind myself to you, too? Magically, I mean."

"What? No, you convinced me that it wasn't necessarily a good idea, and I respect that you don't like the idea."

He was quiet for a few moments, reaching out to brush some of the blonde curls from her face. "I would bind myself to you."

Winna's face heated, but she shook her head. "I think we should try out being married for a while. If it seems like we're working out well enough, we could revisit the idea."

Lear nodded. "A fair suggestion." He dropped his iridescent, green gaze. "Just say the word, and I'll do it though, alright?"

Recognizing the magnitude of what he was saying, she squeezed his hand. "Thank you, Lear."

"I love you."

"I love you, too."

Chapter 37

A Wedding

I studied my reflection in the mirror, and nervously smoothed out my skirts.

The fabric was fine and soft, a sage green that complemented my skin tone and hair perfectly. Pava had outdone himself, really. The dress was excellently cut and sewn, and he'd even let me embroider little pink flowers all over his handiwork. Altogether, the effect was very nice.

"You're a vision, Winna! Like a flower fairy, and there may be some of those in attendance, so we'll have to ask what they think!" Ena smiled at me. She'd done my hair, taking her time to lovingly weave some of it into a gorgeous coronet, leaving the rest to spill over my shoulder. She'd used some special hair product she had to make my typically wild curls complacent, and they looked a little like a golden waterfall.

"I don't know about that, but I do feel very beautiful!" I smiled at her.

"That's because you are, darling!" Pava laughed.

"Oh, let me fix this really quick." Bekka bent and straightened my skirt in the back, her bouncy curls bobbing sweetly as she smoothed the fabric out. "There!" As Ena had dealt with my hair, Bekka had done my makeup. I wasn't wearing a lot, but the look she'd gone with was very fresh and delicate and springy, which was appropriate for the dress, and the weather, which had turned fine and warm with the onset of spring. Flowers lifted their heads from the ground as sleepy animals made their way out of hibernation.

Soon, I would be planting my garden, spending my days alternating between working the ground, and making regular trips to town to sell my balms in person. Only this time, I'd have Lear's help for as long as he could stay.

Lear would have to return to the feylands before too long, of course, but we were to be married first, so our claims on one another would be official. Once he was there, he planned to ask for permission to set up a mushroom ring, which would let him travel to and from the feylands to our home here via magic. I desperately hoped the king would allow it. Lear assured me it wouldn't be a problem, that the fey king, Asher, was his childhood friend, but I still couldn't keep the anxiety that it wouldn't happen totally at bay.

But today wasn't a day for worrying about stuff like that. Today was a day to be happy, and to look forward to the rest of my long life with the fey man I loved.

There was a knock at the door. "Are you ready?" Vim asked. "Remember, the music is your cue!"

"Yes, of course!" I smiled at him through the mirror.

"You look lovely!" He beamed at me.

I turned slowly and smiled. "Thank you! And thank you all for helping me!"

"Of course!" Bekka smiled.

"Now go to your seats, you'll see me again soon!" I laughed, ushering them from the room.

They all filed out, the door swinging lightly shut behind them, leaving me alone for a few moments in the empty side chamber.

I took a deep breath, and spoke aloud to the room. "Well, mama, I...don't think this is what you imagined for me, but...I'm okay. We're all okay." I knew she wouldn't, couldn't reply, but I continued anyway. "I wish you were here." Tears came to my eyes, but I breathed deeply and blinked rapidly, needing to finish saying what I wanted to say. "You and Daddy would like Lear. He's a good man. He built this temple all by himself. Of course, it didn't take him that long, thanks to his magic and ridiculous strength, but still." I snorted, then sighed. "I know I've been through a lot, especially lately, but Lear, Diana, and the goddess have taken good care of me." Suddenly, lovely harp music began to play from the main part of the temple. "I have to go. I love you." I didn't need my parents to be there for me to know they loved me and were proud of me.

As I left the side chamber, I went to the entrance to the temple proper, and stood for a brief moment at the end.

The temple was packed, so much so that people were lined up around the walls, standing in the antechamber, and even out on the lawn.

Diana padded up, sitting down beside me as I paused. Looking over at her, I took a deep breath, then asked, "Are you ready?"

My oldest and dearest friend blinked her gorgeous blue-green eyes slowly in reassurance at me. We began to walk down the aisle together, keeping our steps to the sedate pace of the harp's lovely melody.

Friends, both old and new, beamed as Diana and I made our way down the aisle. Dern and Silver were there, but Windscale was too big to fit into the temple. Instead, the large dragon waited outside for the reception, which was to be held on the lawn of the temple. Rina, Wulf, and Wulf's father, but not his mother, were there. Several pixies flickered around above everyone's heads, and I caught sight of Willowdown, who waved cheerfully at me. Bekka and her mother, Mrs. Amani, were there, as were Mira, Pima, and Tip. Ama was there too, seated with a brownie named Berry, whom the seamstress had hired to run the shop so she could focus on sewing. The tea shop owner, Moira, and her sister, Siobhan, the woman who owned the candy shop, were both there. Indeed, they were the ones who'd made the wedding cake that everyone would soon get to enjoy.

My family, of course, was sitting at the front of the temple. With them sat Sagebark; she was able to attend because, with permission from the landowner, we'd built the temple quite near to her tree and the stream. It was only fitting that she should be there at the ceremony, given that she'd known our ancestors for hundreds and hundreds of years.

Most of Jedda's family was sitting with my own, except for Jedda, who was standing at the front of the temple, by the altar, beaming down at me as he waited for me to approach so he could perform the wedding ceremony.

With him stood Lear.

My soon-to-be-husband was devastatingly attractive in the simple black fitted suit that he wore. He had on a crisp white shirt, but no tie, and if any other person had tried to pull off such a casual outfit, they'd have come off as under-dressed as they really were. But thanks to Lear's fey good looks, what he wore was irrelevant because he made it all look impossibly good.

My face heated as his green eyes stayed riveted on me with a burning intensity.

As I stopped and turned to face him, he groaned. "Gods, you look divine." But it was said so quietly that only I could hear him.

Diana walked away, but instead of going over to my family, my familiar decided to hop up onto the altar, where she settled into a magnificent loaf, purring loudly and blinking slowly at me. Powerful familiar though she was, she was also still just a cat...and I loved her for it!

"Lear!" I whispered. "Not now!...You look wonderful. Please never take that suit off."

"My love, that's the idea behind getting married, taking this suit off." He smiled wickedly at me.

I could only roll my eyes, and hope he didn't notice the shiver he'd made dance up my spine.

"Are you ready?" Jedda asked, turning to us with a set of ornate, ceremonial shears, as well as a similarly decorated ceremonial bowl.

"Yes." I nodded.

Lear had walked Jedda through the steps of a fey marriage ceremony. It was fairly quick, but that meant there would be more time for partying. And oh how fey folk love to party. So Jedda would perform the ceremony, but Lear would do some of the magic required, though we wouldn't actually be magically bound, as we'd previously discussed. That could always come later, if we decided it was what we wanted.

"Welcome all! We're here today to join these two, very much beloved, people in matrimony!" Jedda began.

The crowd gave a cheer that brought a smile to my face. They were all quieted by a vaguely annoyed maow from Diana.

Stroopwafel, who I couldn't stand to leave home while Diana got to attend, maowed in response to Diana. She was prowling irritably around the large, spacious cage we had her in, over in a corner of the temple. One of my nieces was keeping her company, and murmured, "Shh, silly Stroopy!" I had to repress my giggle at my mess of a cat.

"Now, if there aren't any protests or reasons why these two should be married, we'll begin!"

Lear stared daggers at the room, as if daring anyone to speak up and protest.

"Lear, no one is going to protest." I snorted.

"I'd like to see them try," he muttered.

Unfortunately, Stroopwafel decided to maow again right at that moment, and the entire room burst into raucous laughter.

It took several minutes before we could all calm down, and only really subsided when Diana arched her back and hissed at everyone.

"Sorry, miss!" I giggled, having been just as guilty of mirthful laughter as everyone else.

Jedda finally handed my soon-to-be husband the shears. Lear reached out to take one of my loose curls. "Ready?"

"Of course."

He snipped about an inch of hair off, and placed the lock into the bowl as Jedda held it forward. Handing the shears to me, he bent down so I could reach easily, tilting his head to the side so I could cut off a piece of hair from the back of his head, on the bottom layer, so it wouldn't be as noticeable.

I carefully selected a lock from the bottom part of the back, and snipped about an inch off as well, also placing it in the bowl.

Lear then took the bowl in his hands, and held it out for me to put my hands on as well. There was a surge of magic, and the bowl glowed briefly, sending up a brief puff of white steam, and drawing a gasp of awe from the audience, and me, if I'm being honest.

When the light cleared, there were two golden bands lying at the bottom of the bowl.

Reaching in, Lear pulled the rings out, and handed me one, letting me slide it onto his left ring finger. He took my hand to do the same, and as he did, murmured, "With this ring, I thee wed."

"I now pronounce you man and wife! Or, fey and wife, in this case!" Jedda announced, then added, "You may now kiss the bride!"

"Not too hard though because fangs." I sighed in mock-dejection.

There was another surge of magic as Lear reached for me, slipping his arms around my waist and flashing his smile. "The jokes on you! I had Dern add a rune to my necklace so I can hide my fangs at will, too!" And indeed, as he leaned down, I noticed gaps in his teeth where the venomous fangs usually were.

His lips connected with mine.

Oh what a kiss it was.

-

Lear watched the party-goers, smiling in amusement at their antics as the sun began to set. Bonfires flared to life, more barrels of booze were brought forth, and folks hustled to pile the banquet tables with more food.

The preparation for the wedding had taken weeks, between building the temple, sewing the clothing for the ceremony, and preparing all the food. But everyone had been glad to take part, and no one had complained. He and Winna had worked just as hard as everyone else to prepare as well

After the terrible destruction and grief caused by the landslide, people were happy to finally have something to celebrate.

The fey man looked around to where he'd last seen Winna. She'd been enjoying another piece of the delicious wedding cake with Bekka. He found her old school friend, but didn't see his new wife.

Frowning slightly, he stood, and flicked his second set of eyes open, knowing he'd be able to spot her more quickly that way.

When he finally found the mage, he was a little surprised at where she was. Though, really, he shouldn't have been.

Lear went to join his wife in the temple he'd built for her.

In the fading light of sunset, he could see Winna sitting on the stairs at the front of the temple, leaning against the altar with her cats on either side of her. Both were purring loudly as she petted them in unison. Once the ceremony was over, she'd immediately freed Stroopwafel from her cage, whereupon the silly cat had been watched by her nieces and nephews, providing them with endless amusement, as well as getting lots of pets, scratches, and kisses. But his gentle wife must have gone and retrieved her silly cat so she could sneak away and have time with them both.

"Are you alright?" he asked quietly.

Winna looked up, startled, then smiled. "Yes. I needed a break from all the people. Kitty time sounded like a good idea."

"Doesn't surprise me." Lear joined her, reaching out and picking up Diana to place on his lap so Winna could scoop up Stroopwafel and smother her with kisses.

Both cats continued to purr loudly.

"You should be out there, partying! I assume you really like a good party!" Winna told him, rubbing her face against Stroopwafel's tummy.

The cat promptly bear-trapped her head, forcing Lear to help his new wife extract herself from the kitty claws. Despite the fact that she'd been scratched, they both giggled the entire time, since it was too happy a day to be frustrated or annoyed.

Lear sighed. "I do like to party, you're right, but I'd rather be here with you, at peace with the cats."

"Yeah?"

"Yeah."

They were quiet for a few moments.

"I love you, Lear," Winna murmured.

"I love you too, Winna." Lear beamed at her. His *wife*. Finally.

Never had he imagined that failing a mission would end in him finding his way to true happiness for the first time in his life. He'd also never thought he'd fall in love properly, or if he was even capable of doing so. It was quite a relief to know he was. Or maybe it was just Winna he was capable of loving? Whatever the reason, it didn't matter. The gorgeous healer had captivated his very heart and soul, and he was hers forever. For better or worse, in sickness and in health, richer or poorer. All hers.

Winna reached out and caught his sleeve, her face flushed slightly. "Would you kiss me again? Like with your fangs put away?"

Lear immediately used his magic to hide the fangs, and told her, "I'm going to kiss every single freckle you have."

"That's gonna take a while." She smiled a little.

"I hope it does. I presume you have them on more than just your face."

"You're...not wrong," his wife mumbled, her face now bright red.

"Well, we'll go back to the cottage and then have all night," Lear murmured in her ear, which made her shiver.

Giving a low chuckle, he pulled her mouth to his.

The end (for now).

Acknowledgments

There are SO many people I need to thank! I know I won't get to them all, but I'll do my best.

JaCey Titus

Mary Cummings

Shantya Runkle George

Alexandra Corrsin

Innate Ink Publishing

Meagan DeCoster

Lisa J Hogan

Phoebe Ravencraft

Scott

Angel webster

Heather Evans

Mangamolly 1991

Ricardo Andrés Acevedo

malphades

Christine E. Schulze

Em Rowene

Mary Caite

Sandy and David Alton

Ashley Mockbee

Christine Jaeger

Kristi Mills

Cheryl Mills

Amy Shertzer

Rebecca Alder

Jolene McKinley

Kristin Harris

M.A. Remy

Kane Drake

Thank you all so much, words cannot express how much your help and support means to me. You all are the absolute best!

🩶 Sarah, Diana, and Stroopwafel

P.S. Please, please, please leave a review on Amazon, Goodreads, ALL the places you can think of for my book, and if it's not available on that platform, reach out to me and I'll see what I can do! It would be MUCH appreciated!

About the Author

Sarah Uzzle is a writer and artist from Kentucky. She's the humble servant of two kitties, Diana, a Queen among cats and benevolent ruler of her peasants, and Stroopwafel, a goblin menace to society who is trouble incarnate. Sarah enjoys reading cozy murder mysteries, daydreaming about new stories, pestering her fluffy overlords for kisses, drawing her characters and silly sticker designs, and watching anime.

Follow Sarah on her social media for a lot of shenanigans!

instagram.com/sarah.u.cozy.romantasy.author

tiktok.com/@sarah.uzzle